T0354461

SURPASSING

THE

CRUCIBLE

SURPASSING
THE
CRUCIBLE

A Story of Inspiring Leadership and Teamwork

R.W. Riley

SURPASSING THE CRUCIBLE
A STORY OF INSPIRING LEADERSHIP AND TEAMWORK

iUniverse books may be ordered through booksellers or by contacting:

iUniverse
1663 Liberty Drive
Bloomington, IN 47403
www.iuniverse.com
1-800-Authors (1-800-288-4677)

Because of the dynamic nature of the Internet, any web addresses or links contained in this book may have changed since publication and may no longer be valid. The views expressed in this work are solely those of the author and do not necessarily reflect the views of the publisher, and the publisher hereby disclaims any responsibility for them.

Any people depicted in stock imagery provided by Getty Images are models, and such images are being used for illustrative purposes only.
Certain stock imagery © Getty Images.

ISBN: 978-1-5320-6089-2 (sc)
ISBN: 978-1-5320-6090-8 (e)

Library of Congress Control Number: 2018912534

Print information available on the last page.

iUniverse rev. date: 10/02/2018

INTRODUCTION

The 1980s were fascinating times for the US Army. It was right after the tragic Vietnam War and the evolution the Army made was remarkable. I was both a witness and a product of that war period and the transition that followed.

I consider myself a serious student of U.S. Military history. In all of my readings I haven't seen much written on the monumental changes made to the reserve components (RC) during this time. Especially down at the company level units in all the "hometown" armories and reserve centers throughout the country. It's important to understand that vital part of our Army's recent past.

The Vietnam War era was distressing and close to ruinous for the Army. Equipment and weapon systems were either worn out or obsolete. Heavy mobile warfare planned for employment in Europe and the counterinsurgency operations implemented in Southeast Asia left the Army without a cognizant and enduring military doctrine which to focus on. Making matters worse, undisciplined soldiers, drug abuse, racism, and mediocre to poor training were widespread within most Army units. Being a soldier at this time sure wasn't fun, rewarding or meaningful.

The good news was that Army leadership post Vietnam understood the enormous problems and struck out to fix them. With the ending of the draft, the Army rebuilt itself around the concept of an all-volunteer force and the "One Army Concept". It was explicitly designed to integrate the Army National Guard and Reserves into its wartime missions.

Army leaders evolved the new "AirLand Battle" doctrine, focused on the acquisition of new weapons and equipment to support that doctrine, tied both together with rigorous training programs, and concentrated on leader development initiatives that increased both officer and noncommissioned officer professionalism.

The 1982 edition of Field Manual 100-5: Army Operations, stressed that the Army had to "fight outnumbered and win" the first battle of the next war. To meet that requirement, the Army needed to better employ the nation's superior advantage in technology. To achieve that, the Army began work on the "big five" equipment systems: the M-1 Abrams Tank, the Bradley Fighting Vehicle, the AH-64 Apache Attack helicopter, the Blackhawk helicopter, and the new Patriot air defense missile system.

Under the One Army principle, the Army transferred many essential technical services and combat units to the Army Reserve and Army National Guard. Considered as both a unity and economy measure, some Active Army divisions were reconfigured with only two active-duty brigades instead of three. Upon mobilization, they were to be assigned their National Guard "roundout" brigade that trained with the division in peacetime. These One Army plans ensured that equipment modernization would extend to the reserve components.

By the late 80s the newly conceived Training and Doctrine Command (TRADOC) had created a sound set of schools that trained officers in their principal duties at each major turning point in their careers. The noncommissioned officer (NCO) corps also required a new formal school structure. This ultimately paralleled that of the officer corps.

All heavy armor units underwent a regular cycle of evaluations, known as the new Army Training and Evaluation Program (ARTEP). Periodically, both active Army and reserve-component units went to the National Training Center at Fort Irwin, California, where brigade-size forces fought realistic, unscripted maneuver battles against specially trained and equipped Opposing Forces that emulated Warsaw Pact armies.

Light infantry forces exercised at the Joint Readiness Training Center at Fort Chaffee, Arkansas. Using the same training principles and meeting the same tough standards, they also were evaluated using the ARTEP.

By 1989 the claim could realistically be made that the nation's One Army had arrived at a sound doctrine, the proper weapons, an appropriate organization, and a superiorly trained, high-quality force able to fight any prevailing war for which the nation needed them.

That was the big picture. The more detailed picture was down at the company, battery, troop level, a place that perfectly suits the term "where the rubber meets the road". This is where the young officers and the NCO Corps were truly tested and challenged. As the freshly written manuals, new weapons and pieces of equipment arrived at the armories the soldiers were entrusted to put it all together. It wasn't easy making these massive changes without a lot of friction. Change is hard.

After serving four active duty enlisted years, I was commissioned a 2nd lieutenant in the Army National Guard in 1983 from ROTC. I took command of my first Army National Guard infantry company as a captain in 1988. I experienced all these changes first hand from the perspective of an RC soldier and unit leader. The challenges were many and stressful with the additional factor of having to deal with the uniqueness of RC requirements which made for serious testing of the officer and NCO Corps.

I wrote this book in order to tell a story about those changes and the way the RC soldiers had to deal with them, not at the major command level, but at the local armory. During this most demanding period, company commanders and the cadre had their leadership abilities challenged to incorporate these immense changes and to more importantly, make them a standard function of company operations. My observations were that the RC soldiers met all the challenges head on. Some we quickly overcame but some provided headaches that took time, patience and much ingenuity to complete.

This novel is about an RC infantry battalion required to step up and perform at the U. S. Army's highest training level. They are sent to fight the world class OPFOR at the JRTC. This is the battalion's story of their determination to prove they are equal to their active duty brothers.

In particular the story drills down on how the battalion's lone Combat Support Company with ingenuity and wildly aggressive leaders used brain and fortitude to make a fresh name for the "Guard Guys" killing all those OPFOR. By their outstanding performance they generate a reputation of assertively fighting and to become more than average. They became an exceptional unit in our "One Army". Because of their bright success, they are asked to do even more.

R.W. Riley

PROLOGUE

Rourke is standing in the commander's hatch with his tank down in a hole and scanning the valley to his front with binoculars. The gunner is traversing the turret using his magnified tank sights looking for the enemy. Along the whole front of the security force the engineers have constructed a series of obstacles. First are triple strand concertina wire then a mine field and then a tank ditch finished up by another row of triple strand concertina wire. A pretty impressive set of obstacles that would make any unit hard pressed to get through.

All six of the security force vehicles sit in their dug-in fighting positions approximately two thousand meters from the front of the obstacle. Enough range for the tank's main guns to reach anything in the obstacle. Rourke's tank sits at the last position on the left flank of the security force. He feels really uneasy about having no friendlies protecting his left. He keeps involuntarily glancing to his left hoping he doesn't see the enemy sneaking up on him.

And here they come! Both Rourke and the gunner see the huge cloud of brown dust coming up the valley. They are headed directly for the middle of the security force.

Rourke makes out that enemy tanks are leading with some engineer vehicles right behind them. It looks like they are going to force a breach of the obstacle right in the middle and have the tanks provide cover fire. Artillery rounds start impacting near him and off to his right. He sees smoke starting to build on his side of the obstacle. The enemy is using artillery smoke to conceal their attempt to breach the middle.

Just when it is really going to start getting busy, the whole enemy force makes a sharp right turn heading north, kicks it into high gear and goes racing to the far end of the obstacle. Rourke is a little taken aback.

His heart is beating even faster. Under his breath he mumbles, '*Oh Shit... something's up*'. The whole enemy armor battalion is flying from right to left across his front.

He realizes they are making for the far-left end of the obstacle. He can barely cover that end of the obstacle because of the extreme range, two kilometers or more, and the roll of the terrain puts that side of the obstacle slightly uphill from his tank. Meaning, the enemy tanks will have a range advantage of about 500 meters and they will be shooting down hill on his exposed position.

Before he knows it, there are tanks making their way through the obstacle. The enemy combat engineers had been working all night, without being detected, to clear a path over at that end of the obstacle.

Rourke tells his crew over the intercom, "We've got to fight from behind the out-cropping of black rocks behind us. Otherwise we're dead. Driver, I want you to gun this thing up and when I say go I want us to shoot out of the back of this hole like a rocket. We've got to get about thirty meters back and turn left and get behind the rocks."

The driver confidently confirms, "You got it!"

Rourke pulls up his binoculars and takes another look. The tanks are almost through.

"Driver, hit the gas!"

Rourke hears and feels the engine rapidly start to roar. He commands, "GO!"

The driver yells, "Here we go!"

Everyone braces for the sudden lurch backward and upward out of the fighting position. It is a hell of a lurch. Even though he thinks he is ready, he still gets slammed to the front of the commander's hatch. It takes his breath away. He reaches forward to steady himself and catch his breath. The tank stops just at the right place. The driver kicks it into forward gear, spins the tank to the left and races to the rocks.

Rourke commands, "Take us to the left side... Gunner, direct the driver to get us a shot."

Rourke looks up to see the first tank getting through the obstacle, turning to his left and coming fast to Rourke's position. If the enemy destroys the two closest tanks, they will have a clear path to the main defense further up the valley.

He reaches up to the push to talk switch on his CVC helmet. Pushes it forward to enter the security force radio network and implores for someone, anyone to promptly call in artillery on the enemy breach. He is way too busy at the moment to do it himself.

The gunner quickly directs the driver to the best covered position on the left side of the rocks. The enemy tank is at 800 meters and closing fast. Exposing the tank turret just enough to clear the main gun tube from the rocks and lining up the sights, the gunner announces. "Identified!"

Rourke immediately yells, "Fire." Four hundred meters away the enemy tank is eliminated.

This is just the beginning. Two more tanks are racing toward Rourke after clearing the breach. The enemy secures the way into the flank of the security force and they are determined to ram the whole armor battalion through this opening as fast as they can.

Dedicated to:

Robert E. Acton
SFC USAR (Ret)
Citizen-Soldier
The Perfect Role Model

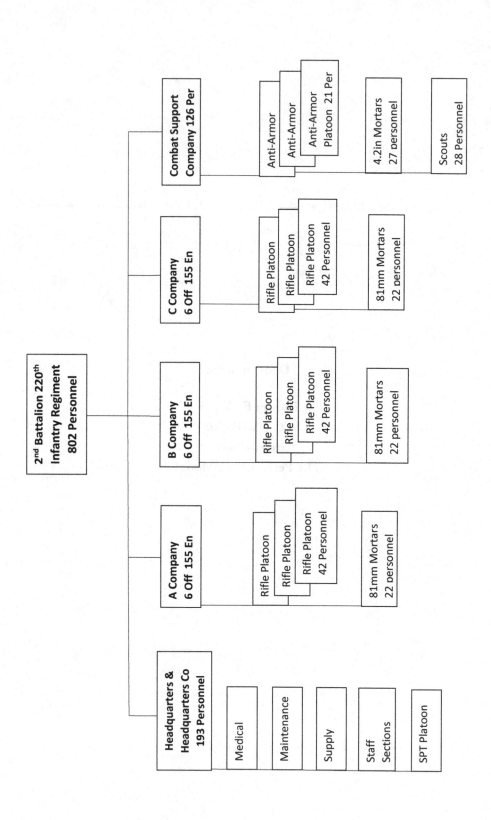

CHAPTER 1

"I'm glad I'm in the Army, not only for the people who are in it and for the breadth of experience which it offers, but because of the feeling I have of belonging to an outfit which really matters, one which has a mission of tremendous significance." - General Maxwell D. Taylor

Country View Apartments
Bluffton, PA.
Friday, 17 March 1989
07:50 Hours

Army National Guard Captain, Devlin Rourke, dressed in jeans, work boots and a flannel shirt, is patiently sitting by the phone, slowly drinking a cup of coffee in his apartment watching the clock. He is waiting for 08:00 hours. He should have been on his way to work at a residential construction site but he knows his business partner will understand his tardiness. After all they have been best friends since seventh grade. He found some errors in the latest set of blue prints and needs to get them to the job site before the crews get to the second floor. At 08:00 Rourke is going to make an important call to his infantry battalion headquarters. Specifically, to the Operations Sergeant, Gary McCallister.

This is in response to a phone message that Sergeant McCallister left on his phone the night before, "Captain Rourke, please call me tomorrow morning, first thing, it's very important, first thing, Sir."

But he has ten more minutes to wait. While sipping his coffee he looks around his living room and decides that this is definitely a man's apartment. His last "girlfriend" or really more like the woman who tried to develop a more compelling relationship for eight months, described his furniture as belonging to the "early construction period". His two large bookcases, the entertainment center which holds his TV, stereo system, VHS player, his coffee table, and the two end tables were all made by Rourke. They are constructed with 2 X 12 pine planks that had been stained as oak, had one coat of polyurethane and held together using six-inch lag bolts. He admits the furniture isn't pretty, if anything, it is strong and sturdy.

Rourke smiles. Funny how it seems that every guy who enters his apartment always comments on how impressed he is with Rourke's furniture-making ability. Most even inquire how to make their own. On the other hand, most women who enter his apartment seem to almost bite their tongues to avoid saying anything about his furniture. Usually with the comment of, "My, what a nice living room… everything seems so… solid."

Sitting there, Rourke realizes that by simply looking at the contents of the two floor-to-ceiling bookcases, you can tell he is definitely preoccupied with the military. He had joined a military book club four years earlier. This means he orders at least one new book a month. There are also other military books that Rourke had picked up at the PX bookstore during his times on active duty. Naturally, there are several shelves with stacks of field manuals and a couple of Army regulation binders thrown in.

Rourke stops smiling and begins a little self-reflection of his life. He remembers what one of his female companions told him right before she walked out the door for the last time, "Devlin, I don't think you'll ever get serious about a new relationship. You already have one… you're married to the Army!" For right now in his life Rourke knows she is right. Unless there's a special woman out there that understands his commitment to military service and his relishing the military culture he is resigned to being a bachelor.

Two minutes till eight. Time enough for a quick coffee refill before the call. As he starts to refill his cup he laughs. He looks down and realizes even his coffee cups are military. He picked up the whole set from his head company cook when they got new replacements for the mess hall. Rourke smiles and shakes his head, *'Man, I got to get a life'*, knowing full well he is happy with the one he has.

He knows that McCallister will be sitting down at his desk with his first morning cup of coffee at precisely 08:00 hours.

At 08:00, Rourke makes the call to the battalion operations number. On the second ring he hears, "Second battalion two twentieth Infantry, Sergeant McCallister, can I help you, Sir or Ma'am?"

Rourke replies, "Sergeant McCallister, this is Captain Rourke, what's up?"

"Hey, Sir, thanks for the quick response. Are you at work? I know you usually start early."

"No, I'm at home. I should be at work but you said on the machine it's important and I got the impression it is kind of urgent. Soooo, what's up?"

McCallister eagerly replies, "You're going to love this. We're going to the JRTC! That's right… The Joint Readiness Training Center… Fort Chaffee."

Rourke jumps up off the arm of his couch with a quick adrenaline rush, "No Shit! This is Great!"

"Yes, Sir, I knew you'd love it. We got the word yesterday morning."

Rourke stands there considering the significance of this news, "When do we go?"

"We go in December, Sir."

Rourke realizing the short preparation time becomes concerned then asks, "Man, that's only what…. ten weekend drills or twenty National Guard days away. Man, this is going to be tough… active duty guys prepare for months."

McCallister replies, "Yes, Sir, that's why we're getting more days to prepare. Extended weekend training days."

Rourke pacing around the coffee table, cheerfully declares, "Man, this is one hell of an excuse to drink massive amounts of green beer tonight. It is Saint Patty's night tonight... I was planning on just having a few, but now... Katy bar the door!"

McCallister responds, "Yep... After we got the word yesterday morning, we spent the rest of the day on the phone trying to get all the details on what to do for this. Well, this is not going to be our Annual Training requirement. There is no AT this year. They're calling this a training deployment." McCallister stops to emphasize, "Which means more days and... way more money! We spent all day yesterday on the phone with the state headquarters, the division headquarters in Harrisburg, and of course our brigade."

"Well... are they going to support us?" Rourke asks.

"Oh yeah. Especially the division. The Division Commander, General Holland, wants this to happen in the worst way. He's offered us anything and everything in the division to help our battalion be successful. We're getting any piece of equipment we want and a shit load of man-days for training."

Rourke asks, "What about our state headquarters? They'll be the ones getting the money from National Guard Bureau for this."

McCallister emphasizes the point, "They consider this pretty damn important and prestigious for Pennsylvania. No one is going to say it out loud, but both the National Guard... and the active duty guys are going to use this to try and make their arguments. If we fail, the active guys will go to congress and make the case that money spent on the Guard is... maybe, let's say... excessive. If on the other hand we do well, the Guard will go to congress and ask for more money, 'cause obviously we're worth it!"

Rourke interjects, "That's nothing new. They do that all the time. There's always a fight over money. Though I don't understand it... these Reagan years have been very good to everybody in uniform."

McCallister continues, "The Division Commander already assigned an action officer to coordinate all the assets and resources for this mission. The action officer will ensure we get what's needed from any unit in the division."

"Sergeant McCallister... This is... no shit... really great news for our battalion! OK, back to business. You called. What do you need from me?"

"Hey, the Colonel is pretty excited too. He wants to have a meeting tomorrow with all the company commanders, first sergeants and training

NCOs. He wants to get a quick jump on this. You'll need to bring your personnel, vehicle, and equipment status."

Rourke is surprised, "Get a quick jump!... Boy, I'll say. Tomorrow is Saturday. Does the battalion commander really think he can get everyone for tomorrow? At what time?"

McCallister understanding the challenge of the extremely short notice pauses for a second, "Well, he's hoping. He'll take whoever comes... even if it's one guy. He just wants to get on top of this. Meeting starts at 13:00 hours. That should give you time to throw up all the green beer from tonight. We should finish up by 17:00 hours. Oh... and... you're getting paid for it! We've already been authorized the additional day's pay from finance. The colonel down at the finance department says he'll ensure we get paid out of our regular funds... and just reimburse it with the monies coming from the Guard Bureau later on."

Rourke is again surprised and exclaims, "No Shit! We're getting paid for it. This won't be the typical "gratis" meeting? Alright then... Well, you know I'd be there regardless. I'll call my First Sergeant and Rob right after I hang up to give them the news and the requirement. I'll have Rob call you back by 10:00 and let you know our status. Man, I still have to go to work."

"Thanks, Sir. Looking forward to seeing you tomorrow at 13:00 hours."

Captain Devlin J. Rourke, Commander, Combat Support Company (CSC), better known as the Dragon Slayers, 2nd Battalion 220th Infantry, 28th Infantry Division, Pennsylvania Army National Guard, sits back down on the couch, puts both hands behind his head, and lets the news sink in. A smile crosses over his face, a great big smile. This *really* is Big! Either this opportunity at the Joint Readiness Training Center (JRTC) at Fort Chaffee, Arkansas or a rotation at the National Training Center (NTC) at Fort Irwin, California would really test him and his men, all 126 of them. After serving Uncle Sam for over twelve years with active duty and reserve time he knows down to his core he is ready.

Rourke was prior enlisted and was commissioned a reserve officer in the Army National Guard as a 2nd Lieutenant in an Armored Cavalry Squadron six years earlier. His extensive schooling and training throughout the eighties sets him apart from his peers. He is not your typical National Guard Captain. On top of that, Rourke's outlook and attitude makes him a maverick. He encourages new ideas and concepts from his soldiers. He is not a *"go along to get along"* kind of leader.

Captain Rourke is unique in that he is a highly trained cavalry officer in an infantry battalion. He commands the single CSC which is one of the five companies in a standard infantry battalion. With his battalion commander's approval and encouragement, Rourke transformed his infantry company into an operational light cavalry troop.

<hr />

For many years now, the Army has been pushing the "One Army Concept". That the active and both the Army Reserve and Army National Guard are one big team. The policy's origins are seeded in the "lessons learned" after the Vietnam War. Notably, the policy sought to redress the reasons why the American people failed to maintain support for US Military participation in the war. This fact was not lost on General Creighton Abrams, Chief of Staff of the Army. Never again would America go to war without support from the American people. War's success is grounded on the total commitment from its society. Abrams knew that having all your military, including right down to the citizens in "Hometown USA", was imperative to gaining support for a war commitment. Consequently, he initiated unparalleled force structure changes to put enough direct combat, combat support and service support elements in the Army National Guard and Army Reserve to ensure that no future war could be fought without including them.

That's the official policy, but not everyone is buying in, especially some in the active side of the "One Army". Many active duty soldiers believe that giving the Guard and Reserve some of the newest equipment is taking it from the active units that really need it. Some even have feelings of resentment toward the reserve components.

Rourke has personal experience with active duty guys verbally expressing their misgivings about the abilities of "weekend warriors". Most times it was masked within the spirit of good ribbing or humor, but it was always a dig at the professionalism of Guard soldiers. A few times Rourke felt it went far enough for him to respond with a "Fuck You" followed by a mock smile and a look that challenged the joke teller to say something else negative about the Guard. They never did.

The times Rourke is on active duty, whether at a school or on an active duty assignment, he believes he is personally responsible for putting the Guard in a positive light. He knows he is always being judged. During his last school at the Infantry Officer Advance Course at Fort Benning, Rourke had excelled within his 15-man small group class.

Very early on during one particular tactical exercise Rourke went to the rescue of a fellow classmate who was failing in his briefing of his assigned operations order. It was a battalion level operation that had 1st Lt. Zack Pillow, portraying an infantry battalion commander, giving his classmates and the instructor, who portrayed his company commanders and staff, how they would conduct an attack on an enemy battle position. It was going terribly wrong.

It was obvious that 1st Lt. Pillow hadn't spent much time preparing or possibly he didn't understand some basic maneuver principles. Rourke, who had been assigned as Pillow's XO, stepped in at a point he felt he could intercede to explain the logistic support for Pillow's plan. By using terms like, *"the commander wanted battalion maintenance to establish a vehicle collection point right here in order to get vehicles back in the fight to conduct an envelopment of the enemy's right flank during the second phase of the battle"*. As Rourke went through his portion of supporting Pillow's weak plan, he was adding muscle and meat to it through the logistics side. Rourke's hope was that Pillow could pick up on the improvements and incorporate them when he continued his own maneuver portion. Pillow fortunately did pick up on Rourke's efforts. He finished his operations order with a satisfactory ending.

As Pillow was finishing up, Rourke looked around to his classmates. Every one of them was looking back at him with a small discernable smile. Some gave a little nod to convey they understood what Rourke had done. All soon developed tremendous respect for their National Guardsman in their small group. At the end of the day, as everyone was leaving, the instructor called on Rourke to stay behind so he could talk with him. The conversation was short, "Lieutenant, you saved Pillow's ass. Well done. I now expect more from you."

Fort Benning is the home of the Army Basic Infantry School, the Army Airborne School and the Army Ranger School. You can almost feel testosterone dripping from the walls of building 4, Infantry Hall, the big school house on post. Physical prowess is worshipped there. Rourke knows that Physical Training (PT) is important to the professional infantrymen at the Infantry School. Any weakness by a student especially by a reserve component soldier is looked upon with disfavor. Rourke was never big on being a PT expert. Scoring high was important but maxing the PT test was never a personal goal for him.

When it comes to physical activity Rourke has an advantage. He is considered by many to be a natural athlete. Rourke does have an impressive record on the athletic field especially in team sports. Much of his time as an enlisted soldier was spent as the "company jock". In basketball, he played both guard and forward, in football he was the quarterback, in fast pitch softball he played second base, he was asked to play on the post volleyball team even though he had never played traditional volleyball before. He left active service the owner of thirteen individual trophies for his exploits on the athletic field. His best gifts are his quickness and his eye-hand coordination.

At Fort Benning, Rourke is introduced to the game of universal Frisbee during their early morning PT sessions. It is like soccer only throwing a Frisbee from player to player down the field to score. Rourke loves it. He is an excellent Frisbee thrower and he can also catch any Frisbee thrown in his direction. With his size of 6'1" and 210 lbs. and his quickness and coordination, he plays universal Frisbee like an exceptional football linebacker playing pass defense.

Rourke is able to angle his approach, use his body to catch the thrown Frisbee every time. A lot of the opposing team challengers going up to catch an oncoming Frisbee against Rourke end up on their asses. It isn't always intentional but it does happen more times than not. Soon he doesn't have many opposing players going after or competing for close thrown Frisbees. During games against other small group classes most wins go to Rourke's small group. He soon has a reputation as an aggressive and complete athlete. Once again, the National Guardsman in their small group earns respect from his active duty classmates.

Rourke knows this JRTC opportunity will highlight his time in command and indeed his career in the Army National Guard. Opportunities for Army Guard units to attend either one of the national training centers are very few and far between. Having a Guard battalion come out of a national training center with a recognized endorsement of success would be one hell of an achievement.

Rourke feels that if given an honest chance, as compared equally to active duty units, he could take his National Guard Company and do exceedingly well against the best proven "enemy" in the world. That would be either of the national training center's professional Opposing Forces.

At both training centers, units experience force-on-force and live-fire training. At both places it is a practical seminar in battlefield life, death, and combat power, taught in the most vivid way possible. They are considered and really are the institutions of higher military learning. Going to one of the national training centers is the equivalent of a professional football team going to the Super Bowl or a baseball team going to the World Series. That's why Rourke desires in the worst way to attend one of these training centers.

Soon after joining the cavalry squadron he is introduced to the Squadron's Operations Officer, Maj. John Patterson. Patterson had just left active duty and had come to the squadron one year prior. Patterson's last two-year assignment on active duty was as an Observer Controller at the National Training Center in California.

One evening, after the day's training was finished, Patterson sat down with Rourke and a couple of lieutenants on the back steps of the officer quarters with some cold beers to provide some in-depth insight of the NTC. This lively conversation was the genesis of Rourke's compelling desire to participate in one of the national training center's rotations. Rourke wants tested by the best.

Patterson began, "Gentlemen, let me start by saying that the NTC is solely designed for the mission of training soldiers for war in a setting as close as possible to the reality of combat. The training is based on three pillars; a trained and experienced opposing force, a group of knowledgeable professional trainers serving as exercise Observer Controllers known as OCs, and finally, a sophisticated instrumentation system to gather data and provide the raw data for assessing unit performance. All the

OPFOR vehicles are US equipment visually modified by fiberglass panels to resemble Soviet tanks, personnel carriers, air defense systems, light reconnaissance vehicles, and even helicopters."

One of the lieutenants asked, "Who gets to be an OC?"

Patterson grinned and replied, "Why the Army picks only the very best soldiers. The rumor is only the top 10% in each branch get to be OCs. Now that is only a rumor, but personally I believe it to be true." This brought a smile to everyone's face.

Patterson explained that the OCs are teams of U. S. Army officers and non-commissioned officers on regular assignment to the training centers. Teams of OCs are assigned to each battalion task force rotation and accompany the visiting units to be trained throughout that rotation. For simplicity, these units are designated as the "Blue Force". The OC teams' functions are to control the battle, assess results, and provide an After-Action Review (AAR) at the conclusion of each engagement. Other OCs act as training analysts in a central Operations Center located on the main post at Fort Irwin, California and Fort Chaffee, Arkansas.

In order to achieve realism and adjudicate "kills", "hits", and "near misses", both training centers feature a complex system of computers, laser engagement devices, and communications networks to collect data from encounters between the forces.

Patterson went on to state, "There are no "I shot you first" arguments. Everything is recorded. It's right there on the playback screen at the AAR. Many a unit commander has embarrassed himself by declaring that his instructions to his subordinates were clear and concise. Only to have the Chief OC turn on the battlefield computer playback for everyone to hear and see the commander giving confusing and baffling directions to his unit."

Patterson then jokingly referred to both training centers as the world's biggest laser tag games.

Rourke asked, "Just how good is the US Army's laser system?"

Patterson explained, "The laser-based engagement simulation is done with the Multiple Integrated Laser Engagement System, known as MILES. MILES provides a degree of realism in casualty assessment eclipsed only by actual combat. Everything and everybody carries a laser transmitter commensurate with their weapon and wears a laser receptor harness. The system will tell you if you're being near-missed or hit. It can tell who is doing the shooting and whether or not you deserve to die."

Patterson finished his beer. Made a gesture to the lieutenant sitting beside the cooler to pass him another. He pulled the top and took a big swig.

"The third part of the world class training is that all this data is sent by radio and microwave back to the operations computer, which displays the information on several kinds of screens, each showing different data. This is a complete data recording system for every shot fired, every radio transmission, every movement of every tank and unit on the ground."

Another swig of beer, "Operations Center analysts can then observe everyone's actions on the battlefield and communicate with the OCs back in the field. Between the two of them they prepare the AARs and lessons learned material. The OCs depend heavily on the data processed by the operations center computer and instrumentation systems. Simply put, sophisticated instrumentation helps training analysts and the Blue Force units determine what happened, why it happened, and how revealed deficiencies could be corrected before leaving the training centers and being ready for the next "real" battle."

There was a long pause as Patterson looked at every lieutenant. "Because we have the national training centers, we have the best trained Army in the world... period!"

Rourke knows he has to get to one of or preferably both of the national training centers. He has to!

CHAPTER 2

"There is only one tactical principle which is not subject to change. It is to use the means at hand to inflict the maximum amount of wound, death, and destruction on the enemy in the minimum amount of time." – General George S. Patton Jr.

US Army National Training Center
Fort Irwin, CA.

The NTC battlefield is a remote desert landscape. It's a thousand square mile section of the high Mojave Desert in the remote eastern part of California. It reminds you of Hollywood's colorful western cowboy movies. Picture John Wayne in the movie "She Wore a Yellow Ribbon", large expanses of open brown desert along with brush and cactus covered hills and a few barren mountain ranges.

If Rourke has his choice of training centers, he prefers the NTC. Rourke considers himself a Cavalry Officer assigned to an infantry battalion. He started his officer career as a 2nd Lieutenant in an Armored Cavalry Squadron in the Indiana National Guard. He is both a Cav scout and Cav tanker by trade.

He spent three years in the squadron as an armored cavalry platoon leader, and a year as a fire support officer, before moving to western Pennsylvania and having to hook up with the 2nd Battalion 220 Infantry. The cavalry squadron for the Pennsylvania Army Guard is in Philadelphia. It is at least a five-hour drive. Way too far to drive for weekend drills. If he wants to stay in the combat arms branch, it means transferring to the infantry. Such is the way of moving around the country while a guardsman.

He has already been to the NTC four times. All four times using the training funds from the Key Personnel Unit Program (KPUP) (pronounced: Keep Up). His first time out at Fort Irwin he was stuck in the Operations Center watching all the rotation's battles on the video and computer screens. A good and valuable learning experience but just not enough. His next rotation, one month later, he asked the National Guard Liaison Officer at Fort Irwin to get him assigned to an OPFOR unit as an augmentee with a ground unit.

Success. He is assigned to Alpha Company 3rd Bn. 63rd Armor which during force on force rotations is the OPFOR's 1st Motorized Rifle Battalion. At first the company commander, Captain James (Jim) Stanton, didn't know what to make of Captain Rourke. This is the first captain he gets as an augmentee. Most augmentees are enlisted soldiers and once in a while a few lieutenants.

After an hour or so of Jim trying to find out just who this National Guard Captain is and how professional and proficient he is, they actually hit it off. Over the course of the rotation, they become friends. So, he has Rourke ride with him as his ammo loader on his tank for the whole rotation. MILES tanks don't fire real tank rounds. They fire simulations from a small holder mounted on top of the main gun tube. Therefore, there is no need for a loader. The loader position is an empty position during the rotations. Standing in the loader's hatch next to Jim in the commander's hatch is a perfect position for Rourke to watch and learn.

Jim takes Rourke under his wing and provides him a world class experience on how the OPFOR fights. And they do know how to fight. The opposing Blue Forces have never actually won their battles with the OPFOR. At best they "do well" according to the NTC training staff. When the NTC staff characterizes your Blue Force unit as needing "more work", that really means you got your ass handed to you by the OPFOR.

Rourke fills a spiral notebook he carries all the time with OPFOR methods, techniques and the standard operations that the OPFOR successfully use every rotation. It forms the basis for his After Action Review and Lessons Learned report that he will provide to his battalion when he gets back to Pennsylvania.

Thanks to Jim, Rourke is able to see and participate in how OPFOR and Blue Force brigade and battalion level operations work or... don't work during battle. Reading books and manuals are one way of learning, sitting in classrooms, going over a sand table exercise, are all typical ways of learning Army operations, but commanding your own tank and having your heart invested in a real-world battle in the desert of Fort Irwin is truly the best way to learn.

Jim and Rourke spend hours and hours standing next to each other in Jim's tank turret. Rourke standing up in the loader's hatch and Jim leaning over his tank commander's hatch providing Rourke with explanations and answers to what events are going to take place and what is happening at that moment.

After finishing this rotation, Rourke sits out the next rotation and then goes back to Fort Irwin on his 3rd KPUP funded rotation. This time, once again assigned to Alpha Company 3/63, Rourke asks Jim for his own tank and crew in order to experience the fight down at the crew level. And what an experience. Half the tank battles Rourke gets into, he loses.

The reason he is able to get out of the other half alive is because of his Alpha Company driver and gunner. Leaning on their years of OPFOR experience prevents him from feeling totally embarrassed at the end of battle OPFOR After Action Reviews.

Once again after finishing this rotation he sits out the next rotation and then goes back for his 4th KPUP funded rotation. Jim again gives him a tank and crew. Experience counts. Rourke spends this time out in the maneuver box being a killing machine. The culmination of his learning is the last battle of the rotation.

The night before this last battle Rourke is assigned to the OPFOR recon and counter recon mission to be followed by a repositioning at first light to the forward security mission in front of the OPFOR main body. The Blue Force is going to conduct a deliberate attack on the OPFOR as their last mission of the rotation.

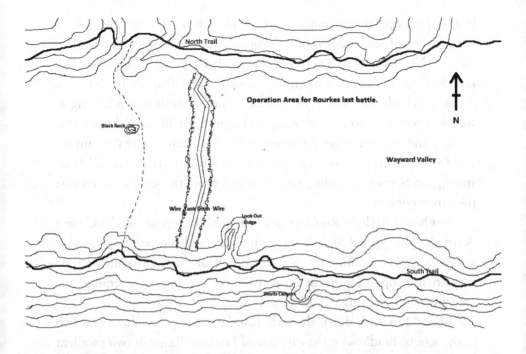

Just before night Rourke moves with the OPFOR recon, counter-recon platoon to preplanned positions along the expected routes the Blue Force scouts will take. This is based on years of experience of fighting previous Blue Force battalions who seem to be using the same old battle plans. Rourke's position is in the low-lying hills off to the front and right of the OPFOR defensive zone. The expected route of the Blue Force is the fast avenue of approach, down the middle of the valley. They will come directly out of the east and race directly west down Wayward Valley into the OPFOR. But the night before, they will have their scouts work both sides of the valley along the hills on either side. They're hoping to use the high ground for observation of the OPFOR defense.

Rourke backs his tank into the small 100-yard long Devils Canyon and positions his tank behind a large pile of rocks alongside the right of the canyon wall. His tank is completely hidden from anyone looking down the canyon. Standing in the tank commander's hatch, the only thing that will be visible is his head. The tank is pointed north toward the South Trail. His main gun tube is traversed 25 degrees to the right to clear the pile of rocks and ready to fire at anybody that moves 30 yards into the canyon.

That night there are three Blue Force Bradley scout vehicles that drive by the opening of the canyon. All stop and use their thermal sights to do a quick scan and search down the canyon. Each time he holds his breath -- waiting. None decide they need to move further into the canyon. Rourke's tank is completely concealed behind the rocks. Even if one of the Bradley's' decide to check out the canyon, going against a tank isn't a fair fight. Rourke's plan is to kill the Bradley and then move in behind the killed Bradley and use him as cover before making his escape out of the canyon.

To fulfill his mission Rourke sends radio reports to the OPFOR Intelligence section regarding the route and times the scouts moved past the canyon opening.

Just before daylight Rourke moves out of his hide position, drives back down the canyon making a left turning west, and proceeds down to his assigned fighting position on the valley floor for the security mission. As they are moving out from the canyon Rourke's tank gunner reminds the crew that there are three Bradleys out there.

About 200 yards down the trail, Rourke turns a corner and sees two of the scouts' Bradleys on the east side of Lookout Ridge in two excellent overwatch positions about 100 yards directly to his front. Both Bradleys have their back ramps down. The soldiers are sitting on the ramps enjoying some MREs for breakfast. Weapons, helmets and web gear are either scattered around or hanging from the back of the Bradleys.

The shocked looks on the faces of the scouts caught off guard by the surprise, sudden approach of an OPFOR tank from their rear makes Rourke laugh out load. Their focus is completely to their front which is the direction of the OPFOR main defense. It becomes a mad dash to find weapons and gear.

Rourke calls into the intercom, "Two Bradleys, front, caliber 50." This cryptic voice command lets the gunner know that he has responsibility for killing the two vehicles with the main gun and that he would dispose of the troops with his fifty caliber machine gun. Two quick main gun shots from the gunner kill both the scout vehicles. Rourke rakes the dismounts with his commander's machine gun --- Twenty seconds later - it is, "Splash Two!"

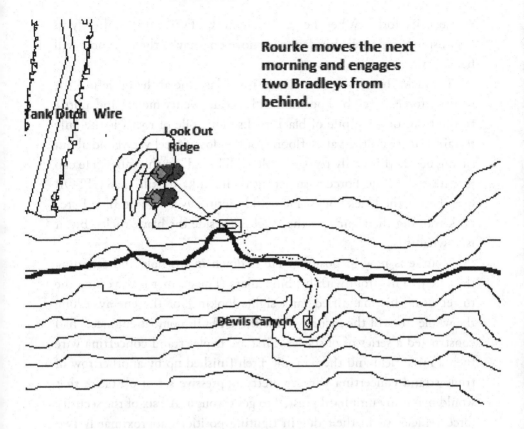

He finds out later that one of his brother OPFOR platoon tanks killed the 3rd scout Bradley further down the trail. So, ends the Blue Force Scouts' abilities to provide their commander with an intelligence picture of what he is to face during the planned attack later that morning.

Rourke rapidly moves down the trail, breaks out of the hills, and makes a right turn heading north in order to descend to the desert floor to his assigned dug-in fighting position.

The OPFOR combat engineers did their job well that night. There are six pre-dug fighting positions about 100 meters apart, running north to south across the center of the valley. This is where the OPFOR security force is going to fight. Each position is perfectly dug in facing east toward the expected oncoming Blue Force. Rourke's tank is assigned the third dug in position which puts him in the middle of the security force. When he gets there an OPFOR tank is already in his position so he tells his driver to move on, maybe the next hole will be empty.

No luck, the only open position is the last one at the far left of the security force. Not a bad position. It is about twenty meters and a little to the front of a big pile of black rocks. This pile of rocks is the only terrain feature on the valley floor. Rourke doesn't feel very good about sitting beside this easily recognizable "bill board" in the valley. He can just hear the Blue Force instructing their tanks to kill that OPFOR tank beside the black rocks. He could picture every single Blue Force tank training their guns on the "sucker" beside the black rocks. But it is… what it is.

Rourke is now in position. He is down in his hole and scanning the valley to his front with his binoculars. The gunner is traversing the turret using his magnified tank sights looking for the enemy. Along the whole front of the security force the OPFOR combat engineers had constructed a series of obstacles. First are triple strand concertina wire then a mine field and then a tank ditch finished up by another row of triple strand concertina wire. A pretty impressive set of obstacles that would make any unit hard pressed to get through. All six of the security force vehicles sit in their dug-in fighting positions approximately two thousand meters from the front of the obstacle. Just enough range for the OPFOR tank's main guns to reach the expected Blue Force vehicles entering the obstacle.

And here they come! Both Rourke and the gunner see the huge cloud of brown dust coming up the valley. They are headed directly for the middle of the security force.

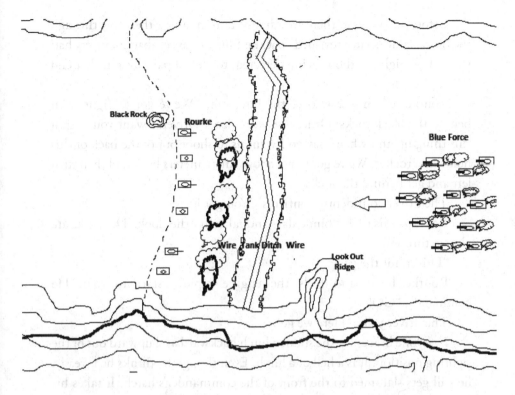

Rourke makes out that Abrams tanks are leading with some engineer vehicles right behind them. It looks like they are going to force a breach of the obstacle right in the middle and have the Abrams provide cover fire. Rourke sees smoke starting to build on his side of the obstacle. Blue Force called for an artillery smoke screen to try and blind the OPFOR and conceal their attempt to breach the middle.

Just when it is really going to start getting busy, the whole Blue Force makes a sharp right turn heading north, kicks it into high gear and goes racing to the far end of the obstacle. Rourke is a little taken aback. The whole Blue Force armor battalion is flying from right to left across his front.

He realizes they are making for the far-left end of the obstacle. He can barely cover that end of the obstacle because of the extreme range, two kilometers or more, and the roll of the terrain puts that side of the obstacle a little uphill from Rourke's tank. Meaning, the Abrams tanks have a range advantage of about 500 meters and they will be shooting down hill on Rourke's exposed position.

Before he knows it, there are Abrams tanks making their way through the obstacle. It is later revealed that the Blue Force combat engineers had worked all night, without being detected, to clear a path over at that end of the obstacle.

Rourke tells his crew over the intercom. "We've got to fight from behind the black rocks. Otherwise we're dead. Driver, I want you to gun this thing up and when I say go I want us to shoot out of the back of this hole like a rocket. We've got to get about thirty meters back and then turn left and get behind the rocks."

The driver confidently confirms, "You got it!"

Rourke pulls up his binoculars and takes another look. The tanks are almost through.

"Driver, hit the gas!"

Rourke hears and feels the engine rapidly start to roar. He commands, "GO!"

The driver yells, "Here we go!"

Everyone braces for the sudden lurch backward and upward out of the fighting position. It is a hell of a lurch. Even though he thinks he is ready, he still gets slammed to the front of the commander's hatch. It takes his breath away. He reaches forward to steady himself and catch his breath. The tank stops just at the right place. The driver kicks it into forward gear, spins the tank to the left and races to the rocks.

Rourke commands. "Take us to the left side... Gunner, direct the driver to get us a shot."

Rourke looks up to see the first tank getting through the obstacle, turning to his left and coming fast to Rourke's position. If the enemy destroys the two closest tanks, they will have a clear path to the main defense further up the valley.

He reaches up to the push to talk switch on his CVC helmet. Pushes it forward to enter the security force radio network and implores for someone, anyone to promptly call in artillery on the enemy breach. He is way too busy at the moment to do it himself.

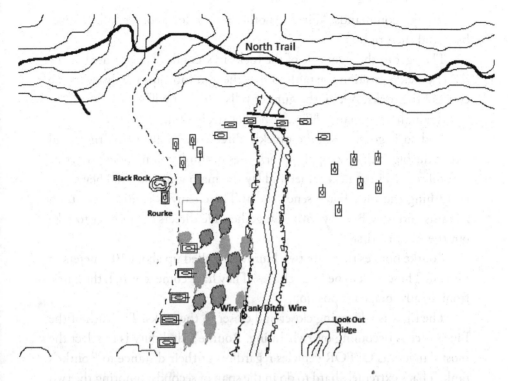

The gunner quickly directs the driver to the best covered position on the left side of the rocks. The Abrams is at 800 meters and closing fast. Exposing the tank turret just enough to clear the main gun tube from the rocks and lining up the sights, the gunner announces, "Identified!"

Rourke, trying to control his excitement and the adrenaline surging through him, immediately yells, "Fire." The Abrams yellow strobe light blinks on. A Kill! Four hundred meters away.

This is just the beginning. Two more Abrams are on their way after clearing the breach. The Blue Force finds their way into the flank of the OPFOR security positions and they are determined to ram everybody through this hole as fast as they can.

The adrenalin is surging through Rourke and his crew. They all know this is going to be a fight of who is the quickest to react and to fire! In a controlled and steady voice he says. "Gunner, get us another kill then we're moving to the right side."

The gunner who has been tracking the next tank in line immediately replies, "Identified!"

Rourke commands, "Fire!" Another strobe for another kill. "Driver back and then right."

They get to the right side of the rocks in seconds. The gunner has the driver quickly position the tank so that the gun tube just barely clears the cover of the rocks. Again, the gunner yells, "Identified!"

Again, he commands "Fire." Another strobe-kill.

And so it goes… Rourke quickly directs the tank to the right and left of the big rock outcropping, then uses his tank commander's override control to select the next target and lay the main gun onto it. They shoot everything the Blue Force sends them. The enemy is coming fast, both Abrams and now Bradleys mixed together. He directs the gunner to take out the Abrams first.

Rourke notices there are two Humvees pulled up about 100 meters to his rear. These look to be OC vehicles. They have come to watch the battle from an advantageous position.

The fight is advancing closer and closer to the rocks. The rush of the Blue Force is becoming overwhelming. Rourke's vital duty is to select the most dangerous OPFOR vehicles regardless of their distance to Rourke's tank. That's extremely hard to do in the span of seconds. Ignoring the two Bradleys tearing across the desert 700 meters away, in order to take on the Abrams that is setting up to fire on you at 900 meters away, challenges your instincts. The attack is so fast that some Blue Force vehicles are killed only 50 meters away.

The final Abrams kill is just to the right of the rocks. This Abrams has raced down from the obstacle weaving his way through the "dead" tanks and Bradleys and gets to the front of the rock right when Rourke has just told his crew, "Move right, Gunner! Abrams to the right!"

Just then the Abrams slams on his brakes sliding around the right corner of the rocks while trying to traverse his turret onto Rourke's tank. Rourke with his main gun tube pointing at the Abrams, stands straight up in the commander's hatch, and instantly crosses his arms over his head. This is the safety signal used to signify the intended target is too close to fire on with the tank's main gun explosive simulators. The OC standing outside his vehicle and watching 100 meters from the rear of Rourke's tank anticipated this and shot the Abrams with his "MILES God Gun". Another Kill!

Rourke looks back up the "path of death" for any more targets. The attack has stopped. He scans from right to left looking for any more targets. He sees one. It is a lone Abrams out by the obstacle breach. Just sitting there. "OK crew, we've got one more Abrams just sitting out by the obstacle. Let's get one more. Driver, move over to the left of the rocks... I think we can get a better shot."

The driver pulls in and stops at what he thinks is a good covered position. The gunner reports, he has the Abrams, but just barely in the right side of his main gun sight. "We need to move further forward to get the best sight picture." The gunner explains.

Rourke agrees, "Driver, just creep us forward. Gunner, as soon as you get a good sight picture, take the shot... Don't wait for me."

Rourke's tank starts slowly edging forward. Each inch forward is another inch of exposed tank facing the stationary Abrams. Suddenly Rourke sees a puff of smoke from the Abrams. Instantly Rourke's strobe light goes off. "Shit!... God damn it!... Shit!... I can't believe I got us killed!" Rourke is really pissed at himself. It is his fault. He got greedy. The Abrams commander is smart. He knew he had the better sight system and the better standoff range with an uphill advantage. All he had to do was wait for Rourke's tank to expose itself just a little.

Rourke has the driver back their tank, with the strobe brightly flashing, away from the rocks. The driver and gunner both get out of the tank and are sitting on the back of the turret drinking cold water retrieved from the cooler. Rourke jumps off the back of the tank, places his hands on top of his head, takes a couple of deep breaths and walks around in little circles attempting to burn off adrenalin and walk off the frustration.

He can't believe he committed a rookie mistake. What he should have done was hunker down behind the rock and let the Abrams eventually come to him. Patience. He has never been a patient guy. And this time he paid for it.

One of the Humvees pulls up next to Rourke. The passenger door opens and he sees the Commanding General of the NTC, Major General Wesley Clark, get out and go directly over to Rourke. "Hey, that was quite a battle." Looking up to the crew he continues, "Do you know who finally got you men?"

Rourke unhappily replies and points to the north, "Yes, Sir, that Abrams way out there."

"Well that Abrams is the Blue Force Task Force Commander. You stopped his task force. It would be only fitting for him to kill you, don't you think?"

Rourke looks at General Clark, still with the look of disappointment and laments, "I guess so, Sir."

"Don't be so down on yourself. We had to call off the Blue Force attack. You pretty much annihilated them. We're going to have them reset and try this again with the lessons learned." With that the General smiled, reached out, and shook Rourke's hand. "That really was a great job by you and your crew, Captain. I'll see you at the end of rotation OPFOR get together." The General's Humvee takes off toward the Blue Force's Task Force Commander's tank.

Rourke's gunner yells down from the back of the turret. "Not bad, Captain, you keep this up and you'll make Major real soon."

Rourke looks up at the two crewmen. "Yea, but if I do, I'm taking you two with me." He pauses to consider what to say next. "It was a good fight, we fought as a crew and we fought well... I think your commander should know you guys did most of the work."

The gunner looks up and points back to the OPFOR main defensive line and responds, "All right, sounds good, Sir... you can tell him right now... Here he comes." Rourke looks back toward the west and sees a lone OPFOR tank speeding directly to his position.

The OPFOR tank stops right behind Rourke's. Jim looks down from his commander's hatch with a big smile across his face. "Sorry I can't stop and swap war stories with you. I've been told to report to the Blue Force after action review."

Rourke smiles back. "Surprisingly you seem pretty happy about that. You told me before going to the Blue Force AAR is kind of a pain in the ass. What gives?"

Jim's smile gets even bigger. "This time I get to tell them their whole task force was stopped by *A single National Guard Captain*! I'm going to love this! See you back at the company tonight." Jim speaks into the intercom and the tank takes off with Jim offering a thumbs-up salute as he drives by.

After twenty minutes every OPFOR vehicle gets the radio call for change of mission. That there is a Blue Force reset for the next day and that everyone is to move to their company assembly areas. Within twenty minutes Rourke and his crew get to check out the exact damage they inflicted on the Blue Force. The count is: seven Bradleys and nine Abrams, plus one M-113 APC smoke generator and one M-113 APC Medic Track that got caught in the brawl.

Rourke's latest successes on the NTC battlefield are pretty impressive. But what makes this last rotation and this final battle distinctive is that he has his own CSC Executive Officer, First Lieutenant Bob Kiser, accompany him on this rotation. This is Bob's first NTC rotation. With Rourke's knowledge of how the augmentee program works. He talked with the National Guard Liaison to have both Bob and himself assigned to Alpha Company.

Rourke asked Jim to have Bob assigned to one of the company's tanks. Bob is an infantry officer, not an armor officer, so Bob rode in the loader's hatch of a platoon leader's tank with the terrific opportunity to observe all the action.

Bob observed his company commander's achievements from his own tank sitting three fighting positions down the security force defensive line and would later describe it as, "The Fight at the Big Black Rock". When they got back home, Bob let both the battalion staff and especially the Dragon Slayers know that their commander was one "Kick Ass" fighter at the NTC.

Rourke knows he has performed well on the MILES battlefield. As a professional soldier he feels pretty good about what he learned on those four trips to the NTC. He knows it certainly makes him a better battlefield tactician. He better understands what the stresses of a real battle will generate. So far, it is the decisive test of his leadership ability.

As he explains to Bob while travelling back home to Pennsylvania, "Now we have to transfer all this newly gained knowledge to our men. Training for the Dragon Slayers is going to be harder and a whole lot more meaningful."

CHAPTER 3

"Commanders are responsible for everything that their command does or fails to do." - US Army Officers Guide.

"Don't be buffaloed by experts and elites. Experts often possess more data than judgment. - General Colin Powell.

Rourke knew his battalion was selected because of the outstanding annual training they completed this past year. The active duty evaluators were impressed. They noted the excellent performance on all the required evaluation reports. All the battalion's companies received excellent 1-R Readiness reports. The evaluators also conveyed those impressive results to the leadership of the 28th Division and the State Headquarters during the "End of AT Briefing".

It was no bullshit. The battalion conducted its company level and battalion level Army Training and Evaluation Program (ARTEP) missions flawlessly and to standard. Not an easy thing to do for an active duty battalion let alone a Guard unit with limited training time.

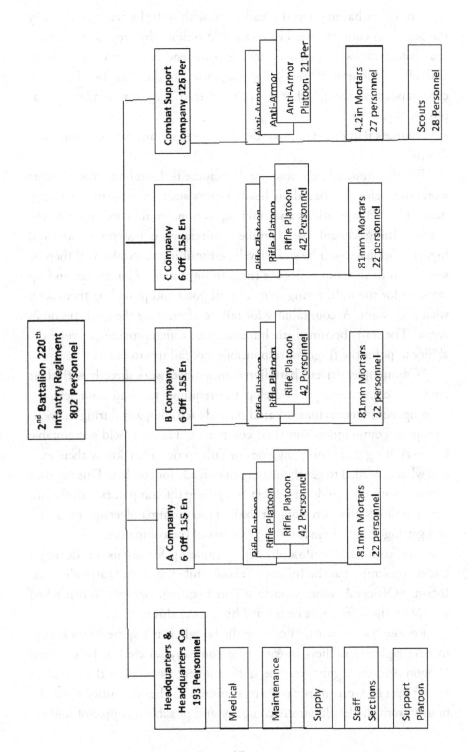

The credit has to go to the leadership within the battalion. Especially the battalion commander. His command philosophy creates the culture that fosters teamwork and constant improvement. Based on his experience and observations over the years, Captain Rourke classifies battalion commanders as using either a "staff centered" or "commander driven" philosophy.

Rourke's Battalion Commander, LTC James Francone, is commander driven.

Rourke understands that "staff centered" battalion commanders work through their battalion headquarters staff sections to get things done. The S-3, operations and training section, would come up with the yearly training schedule based on the requirements of the commander and higher headquarters. The staff developed training schedules will then be sent down to the companies for them to implement. Companies end up working for the staff, trying to meet staff goals and providing them with what they want. Accountability for failure of meeting the goals becomes vague. The staffs become little bureaucracies which provide everyone the ability to point the finger of responsibility of failures to others.

"Commander driven" battalion commanders work directly with their company commanders to develop the required tasks to complete the training requirements for the battalion and each company during the year. Company commanders run their companies. They are held accountable for everything their company does or fails to do. They know their men and what is needed to get their companies ready for combat. This requires strong leaders that guide and direct everything the companies accomplish. The battalion staffs then work for the battalion commanders by supporting and getting things done from the requests of the companies.

The "command philosophy topic" came up for discussion during a leadership seminar at the Infantry School while Rourke was attending the Infantry Officer Advance Course at Fort Benning, Georgia. When asked to explain the differences he framed his answer this way.

Rourke started with, "Let's say the battalion is required by division to have eighteen soldiers in each rifle company selected to be certified Dragon Anti-tank gunners. The staff centered concept has the battalion S-3 set up a Dragon gunner training committee. The committee would be mostly from the headquarters company and possibly a couple of soldiers from the line companies. The Dragon committee would be scheduled by the S-3 section to rotate to each company to train and then test for certification. The committee needs to travel to all five company locations in order to complete the training for the battalion. This concept is efficient and is great if all you are worried about is getting the numbers correct for reporting to division HQ's.

Rourke went on, "Two major concerns with this are the companies now have to adjust and change their training schedules at the last minute to accommodate the committees new scheduled arrival time and training location. Training schedules are usually pretty tight on times and the tasks that are needed done. Having battalion interject a new requirement into company training for the convenience of the new committee is disruptive to the companies' scheduled training time. Some other required training is going to suffer. It always pisses off the company commanders and the companies' leadership.

The real problem is that committees aren't going to be on the battlefield to make any corrections or fixes if there are problems or Dragons aren't working. Calling up the battalion S-3 section in the middle of a fire fight to ask to re-constitute the Dragon Committee for immediate problem solving isn't going to work."

Rourke ended with, "Operating and overseeing the repair of the company's weapons is the job of experienced squad leaders or section sergeants. With new systems coming on line, sergeants need trained first. They then train their soldiers to be weapon operators and gunners. It's how the Army has been successfully operating since its beginning."

Rourke believes in his heart that commanders and the chain of command is the only way to develop combat ready units. The responsibility of a well-trained unit lies with that unit's own leadership, starting with the commander.

* * *

Francone's standing as a "command driven" commander is happily recognized by Rourke soon after Francone takes command of the battalion. The very next month he announces his first 'Commander's Call'. Rourke is looking forward to the meeting with his four other fellow company commanders to see what the new battalion commander is like.

At his first meeting with his company commanders, along with putting out goals and the objectives for meeting them, Francone tells his five commanders that he wants them to challenge his staff. Not to question how they do their jobs, he will handle any short comings in his staff, but if the commanders need something, not to be bashful about asking for it. He expects his staff to work to fulfill the obligations put on them by the company commanders.

Rourke experienced this commitment to the company commanders first hand. Several months after taking command of CSC, the company had a Battalion Command Inspection. This is an in-house inspection done by the battalion staff to help the companies stay up to date and on track with Army and National Guard requirements and regulations. This was Rourke's first inspection as a commander. The staff typically spends the morning going through all the company's files and records and physically inspecting some equipment. Then around 14:00 hours they would call the company leadership together and provide a briefing on their findings.

Rourke's attitude about inspections is it is a tool to be used to help identify problem areas so they can be fixed. Many in the Army feel an inspection is a reflection on the performance of those in charge; therefore, failing an inspection is to be avoided by all means. Many superiors use results of inspections as a club to beat up their subordinates. On a few occasions units will sometimes cheat or falsely pencil in paperwork in order to pass an inspection to avoid the unpleasant consequences.

Two months prior to the inspection Rourke announced to his leaders that they would work to make sure the inspection deficiencies from the previous year were corrected but there would be no concealing or pencil whipping to cover any deficiency. "We need to find out what's broken so we can get it fixed. I'll take the beating for failures in any areas."

The inspection day came and the staff spent all morning going through the company's records and equipment. The S-3 section examined the training files, The S-2 checked all the physical security files and checked the dates to see if they squared with the weapon issue and arms room security. The S-4 went through the kitchen and mess records. Maintenance scrutinized the motor pool records. The battalion commander observed the soldiers in formation and their performance and military bearing around the armory.

At 14:00 hours the staff convened a debriefing to announce the results of the inspection. The presentation started with the S-3 section. They didn't have a lot of good things to say. Next was the S-2 section. They didn't have a lot of good things to say either. The S-4 followed suit and the battalion maintenance team also put a bad light on the results of the inspection.

As the last briefer from maintenance finished, he said, "This concludes this year's inspection." Then every one of the staffs got up to leave. Rourke who had been sitting attentively in the back row diligently taking notes, jumped up and in a slightly loud voice asked, "Could I say a few things?"

Francone who has also been sitting in the back row off to the right corner, in a louder voice says, "Of course, we all would like to hear what the commander would like to say." Looking around the room to ensure that everyone got the message to sit back down, he looked over at Rourke and states, "By all means, Commander, we all would love to hear what you have to say. You have our attention!"

Rourke made his way to the front of the room. He opened his note book on the podium, slowly looked around the room and started his comments, "First I would like to thank the battalion staff for coming here to visit the Dragon Slayers and providing us with some great information on what we need to work on to improve."

The staff, who up to this time had never received comments from the companies or the commanders on their inspection results, was stunned. They had always basically trashed the companies, got up and left. Starting at 14:00 hours had been the perfect time to give the briefing, head to their cars, get back to the headquarters armory in Bluffton to file the inspection results, have final formation, and then head home. They didn't know what to make of Rourke asking to speak. But he started off thanking them so possibly this would be quick and they could still get out of here in a decent time.

Rourke continued, "You all did a very thorough job. I just want to take a look at a couple of items." Rourke went on to explain that a lot of the items selected as a deficiency were actually beyond the scope of the company personnel. Many of the deficiencies are to be worked on by both the staff and the company. He noted that the depth required in finding these deficiencies obviously showed how expert the staff was in their respective areas.

Looking down and running his pencil along the pages of notes, he then cited those problem areas that required the staff to come back down to the company within the next couple of months to help get them fixed. Rourke remarked that looking in the company visitor log, there weren't any visits by any of the staff during the whole of last year. He stated that the company failed the same inspection the previous year. He looked at each staff section, reset his pencil in his hand and asked, "When can I put you down for coming back to do your job and help my guys get this right. We're all going to get this right… this time." Rourke gave them the smile that said, "Don't come to my house and beat me up in front of my boss, when half this is on you!"

At that point, half the staff turned to see what the battalion commander was doing and if he was going to let his staff get run over by this company commander. Francone crossed his arms and said, "I believe everyone needs to give Captain Rourke," Francone breaks into a small grin, "the commander of the Dragon Slayers, the exact time you and your folks will be supporting his company."

Everyone got the message. The commanders will run the battalion.

CHAPTER 4

"I may not have been the best combat commander, but I always strove to be. My men depended on me to carefully analyze every tactical situation, to maximize the resources that I had at my disposal, to think under pressure, and then to lead them by personal example." - Dick Winters (1/506 Airborne Infantry Regiment, WWII)

Headquarters, 2/220 Infantry
Army National Guard Armory
Bluffton, PA.
Saturday, 18 March 1989
12:10 Hours

Captain Rourke parks his truck outside the old red brick armory building located, like many old armories in small towns throughout Pennsylvania, just off Main Street. Parking is always a pain in the ass in Bluffton. Fortunately, He finds a spot in the alley next to the armory. Just before he opens the door to go in he takes a couple of steps back to look at the old armory. This is a typical old armory that was built back in the 30's. Constructed near the center of town with red bricks. Every old armory he has ever seen is built with red bricks. Each one is built differently. The architecture is basically the same but the buildings are all uniquely designed for the type of Guard unit that is housed there. Inside each has a hardwood full size basketball court as the drill floor. After all these years just about every floor board squeaks when you walk across the room.

Back in the day, most armories were the focal point of the community's social interaction. You couldn't talk to the town's "old timers" about the National Guard Armory without them telling you how they went to the armory Saturday night dances with their favorite gal. Or went to pick up a gal. The armory is used for community blood drives, polling places for voting and a myriad of other events for the community. Armories were part of the community fabric in the 30's, 40's, and 50's. There is history there. During WW II the hometown guard unit typically mobilized in the armory and marched directly through town, passed waving neighbors, friends and family on the way to the train station on to war. During natural disasters, the governor calls out the guard from those same armories to meet the call of help from other local communities.

Rourke walks through the battalion conference room doorway 45 minutes early. He sees LTC Francone sitting and working at the end of the table, smiles and asks, "You think we're ready for this, Sir?"

The colonel looks up, smiles… "Devlin, very good to see you… and you're early. As usual."

"I've never missed a Line of Departure time, Sir. LD times are sacred for the Cav."

Francone confides, "I was hoping you would be early. I want to talk to you in my office."

"Sure, Sir. Am I in trouble or is there a much more pleasant reason?"

The colonel sits back, crosses his arms, and inquiries, "May I tap into your knowledge of JRTC? You just recently came back from there. October, right? I read your after-action review. It is a good paper on the tactics and techniques you observed. I want to ask you your opinion on the fight… the actual battles. Grab a cup of coffee and follow me in."

Rourke passes on the coffee and follows the colonel across the hall into his office. The colonel sits down behind his desk. He picks the closer of two chairs in front of the colonel's desk.

Both Rourke and LTC Francone arrived at the 2/220 Infantry Battalion two years ago, just two months apart. Rourke arrived first, took command of CSC as a first lieutenant. Then the Colonel arrived two months later to take command of the battalion. Neither one knew the other prior to their meeting the day before the Colonel's first drill. Rourke moved from an Indiana National Guard Cavalry Squadron. Francone was promoted and transferred up from their sister battalion, the 1st Battalion 220th Infantry located south of Pittsburgh.

Francone liked the aggressive CSC Commander. Rourke requested a meeting because he lived in Bluffton which would be easy and convenient for Francone to talk with one of his commanders on an off-drill day in Francone's office.

Rourke had his own agenda. He wanted to attend the active duty resident six month Infantry Officer Advance Course at Fort Benning. He needed the colonel's permission and pull with the brigade and division to get him a seat at the Fort Benning Infantry School.

He also wanted to talk to the Colonel about turning his Combat Support Company into a "light cavalry troop" for the battalion. This would be a drastic change for an infantry battalion commander to accept. Infantry battalions are notoriously known for not knowing what to do with their anti-armor TOW platoons. Invariably commanders set them up in some far-off overwatch position in the training area waiting for the "bad guy tanks" to show up. All the CSC commanders he knows are infantry officers without any knowledge or experience in utilizing their platoons in a Cavalry role.

Rourke knew the structure of his company, the three TOW (Tube-launched, Optically tracked, Wire-command link guided missile) mounted Humvee platoons, the scout platoon and the heavy mortar platoon. With his pedigree as a Cav Officer he could have them conducting reconnaissance and security missions that would really give the battalion an advantage on the battlefield. He made the pitch to Francone. Low and behold, Francone liked it and… fully embraced the whole concept. Wow, a forward-thinking battalion commander! Rourke was going to love this!

Rourke sitting back and comfortably in his chair, "Well, what actually do you want to know, Sir?"

The Colonel leans forward clasps his hands together on the desk, looks at Rourke and asks, "Do you think we could… in any possible way beat the OPFOR?"

Rourke takes a deep breath, sits up straight, looks directly at the colonel and explains, "I have never heard of anyone EVER… beating the OPFOR at either the JRTC or the NTC. The OPFOR advantages are just too big to overcome." Rourke pauses. The colonel gives Rourke a "go ahead and continue" wave of his hand.

"OPFOR knows the terrain. When they brief their guys before battle, they talk like they're fighting in their own back yard… and they are! They know exactly where every nook and cranny of the terrain is, where every fighting position is, and the exact fields of fire for every one of those positions. When they brief the Operation Order they reference and use the local names for all the terrain features they'll be operating in. They don't say: go to Check Point 23 orient to the west and be prepared to engage the enemy. They say: go down to "old rocky" over by the "whale" and shoot anything coming up the "broken trail". Every OPFOR soldier knows exactly what that means."

He stops for a second, composes his thoughts and continues. "They've been working together for so long. They fight a new battle every month. That's twelve times a year for three years. Doing it together! On the other hand, the Blue Force at best has the whole battalion together for maybe one year. That provides minimum time only for whatever training they get at home station to prepare for the NTC or JRTC."

Rourke continues. "The OPFOR knows their enemy. They know the Blue Force front and back. It's experience again. Blue Force uses the same tactics almost every rotation. We all read the same field manuals. OPFOR leaders know the Blue Force tactics that they'll be going against during each selected mission. There are no surprises."

"OPFOR crews are expert one-on-one fighters. Blue Force crews always hesitate when they run into an OPFOR vehicle. And when they hesitate… they die. They just don't have the experience. Like any job that requires a particular dexterity and skill, the most experienced always win."

Rourke sits back for a second, pauses to reflect on what he is going to reveal next, "Sir, OPFOR attitude is geared to not just winning… but crushing the Blue Force on every single battle. My first OPFOR AAR was an eye opener. The regimental commander, the colonel… got up first and went on a ten-minute tirade about how we just beat the Blue Force, so now... we have to kick them while they're down, jump up and down on them, crush them, gut them, and annihilate them. It blew me away! This is the regimental commander! Every OPFOR soldier's attitude is: "We are here to kill... this is war... and we will win."

He leans forward and confides, "Our best chance is the first battle. That's the only time we'll have all our assets, both people and equipment that work. After that, you start down a death spiral of losing assets... and never being able to catch back up. Our logistics and support guys have never been tested like this. They'll try and do the right things and they'll try and do them faster... but they'll never catch up and they don't know any short cuts to use. Many a rotation has ended with the Blue Force at only 50% of men and equipment operational. That's considered "combat ineffective".

Picking his next words carefully, "Sir, I believe, you have an advantage over the active duty battalion commanders. They have their active duty careers they're worried about. The Army says your performance at the Training Centers will have no effect on your career, you're there to learn... but that's bullshit. Those who "do well" seem to get more opportunities to attend career enhancing schools or assignments. Consequently, they would never "go off the reservation" and try anything radical. They may tweak a tactic or two but it won't be radical. That's partly why they're so predictable to the OPFOR."

I also think we can have an advantage as a National Guard battalion. They hardly ever face a National Guard unit. Frankly their opinion about us is pretty low. You know active duty attitudes toward the Guard. They will underestimate us. We need to take advantage of that... at least for the first battle."

Rourke sits back and waits for the colonel's reaction.

The colonel looks at Rourke, takes a couple of deep breaths, is obviously considering everything Rourke spelled out. He then stands up and announces, "Devlin, I want you to give that same briefing to the companies."

"Even about the Blue Force Commanders?"

The colonel smiles, "Yes. I think we're going to be... Radical!"

Rourke and the Commander walk across the hall to the conference room. Sergeant McCallister is standing just inside the door. "Sir, everyone except First Sergeant Anderson from Bravo Company and Sergeant Roman the training NCO from Charlie Company is here. The S-3 and S-4 both made it also."

CHAPTER 5

"The only place success comes before work is in the dictionary." - Vince Lombardi.

Confrence Room
2nd 220th Infantry Headquarters

Colonel Francone takes a look around the room and is pleased. This is the heart of his battalion. And he feels very good about this. They all came on the shortest notice he has ever given, and he truly appreciates it. His commanders are all there. He is pretty proud of his five company commanders. They are all solid leaders. He also feels they are the best commanders in the brigade. He knows they are the reason his battalion was selected for this prestigious opportunity to represent the National Guard. All have their own unique personalities and all lead their companies differently. A little over a year ago he described them to his boss, the new brigade commander, Colonel Roger Collins, this way.

Alpha Company is led by Captain Carson Young. Carson had some active duty time as a young infantry lieutenant. He is a solid tactician. He knows the strength and weaknesses of his NCO's. He seems to always put the right guy in the right position. He takes care of his soldiers and cuts them a break when needed. Carson is always dependable and well respected.

Bravo Company is led by Captain Andrew (Andy) Daugherty. Andy is a strong commander. His challenge is that his company is located in one of the most sparsely populated counties. His company is never above 85% in required personnel. Bravo Company is always given the smallest area to defend. They never let this get them down. They just hustle and work harder to successfully complete their missions.

Charlie Company is led by Captain John Bynum. John is the quiet one. He is soft spoken, never raises his voice, never seems to get excited, and takes everything in a calm and controlled manner. He takes care of his soldiers and they always look out for him. There is never a bad word said about John. He is well respected by everyone. There is never any fanfare with Charlie Company. They just always get the job done.

Headquarters Company is commanded by Captain Dale Walker. Dale has a great sense of humor. He enjoys a good laugh and is quick to see the funny side of things. This works well as a Headquarters Company commander. His men are scattered among every staff section and support element in the battalion. He works with all ranks and the most varied Military Occupational Specialties (MOS's). Versatility and flexibility has to be Dale's mantra. Dale is the perfect Headquarters Company commander.

Combat Support Company is commanded by Captain Devlin Rourke. If there is such a thing as a natural leader it would be Rourke. His guys in CSC love him. Mostly because he fights for them. He is able to get them more fuel, more ammo, more training areas and stretch their available training time. He encourages and rewards initiative from all his soldiers. He is not an infantry officer, but a cavalry officer. He trains his platoons to operate independently. Infantry officers are taught how to set up fixed impregnable defenses, how to use inter-locking fires, how to mass fires to totally destroy the target. Rourke teaches his men to move quickly, to never stay in one place too long. To shoot, then move, and then communicate and coordinate with everyone in the battle, to find the enemy before they find you and then to punish them before they can recover.

Colonel Francone starts the meeting. "Before you guys give me your stuff, and before I give my stuff, I want Captain Rourke to give us some of his stuff about JRTC. He just returned this past November." Francone gives Rourke the signal, you have the floor, with a sweep of his arm.

Rourke stands and provides the staff and fellow company commanders with the full briefing he has just given Francone. As he finishes he looks around the room at the intense faces of everyone and asks if there are any questions. There are none.

Francone stands. "Alright everyone let me give you some of my stuff… consider this command guidance for everyone." He clears his throat and walks over to a white paper flip chart at the front of the room. It is obvious he has been working on this since the battalion received word of the selection two days ago.

"Just like the rest of you professional infantry soldiers, I've been studying everything I could about the JRTC since they started the JRTC a couple of years ago. This is infantry fighting in the woods of Fort Chaffee, Arkansas. Those woods are just like our woods here in Pennsylvania." Francone looks around the room. "So, I'm thinking this is going to be a little like us being in our neighbor's backyard. It's not ours, but it's not new to us either."

The colonel flips over to the first briefing sheet entitled: Admin.

"We have no Annual Training (AT) this summer. Training will be at company level at your armories. We will try to get together for at least two long weekends at one of the company's areas." Francone looks to see that everybody understands the impact of no AT prior to JRTC.

He continues from the chart, "The Division Commander will insure we get whatever we need for equipment. Get me a list after this next drill."

"Personnel… we will be able to pick up some volunteer soldiers from both the first battalion and from the 1st of the 221. We'll get a list after this next drill. Hopefully you get them and start incorporating them into your company within the next several months. Work with the S-1 for this."

"All your drills after this March drill will be Multiple Unit Training Assemblies (MUTA's). All will be MUTA Sixes. That's all-day Friday, Saturday, and Sunday."

"November's drill will be a "load out" drill. Don't plan on any training then. Have your company ready to *"fight"* on Sunday's October drill."

He flips to the next sheet entitled: Local Training.

"You all have local training areas. I expect all your companies loading up and moving out from your armories *"No Later Than"* (NLT) 10:00 on Friday mornings. I don't expect you to return to the Armory till Sunday afternoon. When you get back to the armory, don't worry about a complete cleaning of everything... wipe it down, put it away. You'll be pulling it out on the next Friday drill. Don't worry about scrubbing down the armories. Don't worry about any inspections. We've got bigger fish to fry. I'll take care of anyone from higher up that might stop by during the week to cause any trouble."

Francone surveys the room looking for any questions on this. Everyone understands and agrees. He flips to the next sheet entitled: Getting Ready and Getting Smart.

"Everyone needs to dig out their Field Manual (FM) 7-8, *The Infantry Rifle Platoon and Squad,* and Field Manual 7-10, *The Infantry Rifle Company.* Dale, and Devlin... you two will also read those FMs and you also have your own FMs to read. Devlin, I'll be talking to you later about your Dragon Slayers and what I have planned." Dale and Rourke both nod their understanding of the colonel's request.

Francone continues, "Everyone's got their Standard Operating Procedures (SOP's). You've worked hard on getting them together and workable. And I know most of them are made up of parts stolen from the 82nd Airborne, 24th Mechanized Infantry Division, and the 7th Light Fighter Infantry Division. You've exchanged Platoon and Company SOPs with one another. I've looked over each one of them and they're good." Francone pauses, "The hard part is getting our soldiers to read and follow them... and that goes for some of the soldiers sitting in here!" This brings a little bit of laughter from everyone.

He reaches down on the table and picks up a small 7 x 5 black note book. "In addition to the SOPs every leader has a "smart book". I know we got these from the Infantry School at Fort Benning. It's full of tasks, and mission checklists. They are great to use when you're tired and having a hard time getting your thoughts together. Have your leaders practice using them before, during and after every mission. We all need to go to the smart book as second nature."

Dropping the note book on the table and picking up another manual, "Rourke told us the Blue Force always hesitates and they always lose because of it. We need to practice our *"standard battle drills"*. Start your training Friday morning and end your training Sunday with your battle drills. Set up squad contact lanes with MILES…Yes, we will be getting MILES for every company for every drill. We may win or lose just because of our battle drills."

He finishes for now and then invites each company to brief the staff and the commander on the status of their personnel. How many they have, how many are MOS qualified, how many can't pass the physical training test, how well they did on the weapons ranges, how many have medical issues, and any other miscellaneous problems they might have. Next each company reports equipment status, then weapons, then vehicles.

By the time they are done, everyone has a pretty good idea of how the battalion stands and what is needed for the JRTC. Francone is feeling pretty good about the status. It seems all his companies are staying on top of the basics. Now if they can only put up a good fight.

Dale from Headquarters Company is the last to brief. Asks if there are any questions. There are none. He sits down.

Francone gets back up and heads to the front of the room. "I have some final words for you before you take off for home and finish your weekend with your families. Once again, I want to thank you for being here. It means a lot to me and the battalion."

Gentlemen, this is a Big Deal! Our battalion getting selected for the JRTC is huge. We will be looked at by many, many people. Important people. So, we will be getting a lot of attention this whole year. There will be folks that want to come out and congratulate you and some who want to give you good advice on how they would do it."

Francone surveys the room to make sure everyone understands the importance. "You will have visitors. Expect everybody from your local congressman to the Chief of the National Guard Bureau and everyone in between. I've asked the Brigade to set up a kind of… visitors clearing house. The hope is that they can head off all the visitors before they get to you. But don't be surprised that in the middle of a fire fight you have a couple of civilians walking around shaking your guys' hands. Suffice to say we'll be working on this all year. Be patient and be nice. Call the battalion when your surprise visitors arrive. Enough said."

He scrutinizes the room. "Rourke says nobody wins at the training centers. I want to win. I want to beat the shit out of the OPFOR. I want to Win!"

Francone is smiling and pointing at the room, "From now on this battalion's motto is: B… S… O… Three. That stands for: Beat the Shit Out of the OPFOR. You got it? Every soldier when saluting calls out. B… S… O… Three." Francone's expression changes to a man on a serious mission. "I want to Win."

CHAPTER 6

"It is a proud privilege to be a soldier – a good soldier [with]discipline, self-respect, pride in his unit and his country, a high sense of duty and obligation to comrades and to his superiors, and a self-confidence born of demonstrated ability." - General George S. Patton Jr.

Army National Guard Armory
Combat Support Company 2/220 Infantry
Manchester, PA.
Tuesday, 21 March 1989
10:00 Hours.

It takes him awhile to find a parking space. He drives around the building twice. Gives up and parks down the street in front of a row of houses. Actually, the whole area is residential houses, old houses right in the middle of town. And right in the middle of the houses is the town's old armory. Back in the day, all armories were built in the middle of town so the National Guardsmen could just walk to their drill. So, there he stands on the sidewalk looking at the old building. The front door is on the end of the building. You can tell it is built that way to accommodate the houses

45

and streets that were already there prior to the building of the armory in the early 1930s.

Staff Sergeant Ben Eikenberry trots up the steps of the red brick armory, opens the big door and enters the building. He stands in a small alcove. Right in front of him is a stairway leading up to what he assumes are some storage rooms. To the right of the stairs is a hallway that leads to the drill floor. Off to the right along the hallway are entrances to two offices. Eikenberry steps into the larger office. This is obviously the orderly room. A large counter runs the length of the room. On a portion of the walls are various 6' X 3' status boards. Military pictures and posters cover most of the room. The company guidon is in the corner. Three desks are behind the counter. Only one of the desks is occupied right now.

Sitting at the occupied desk is Sergeant First Class Robert (Rob) Donnelly, the full-time training NCO and during drill, the Platoon Sergeant for 2nd TOW Platoon.

Sergeant Donnelly looks up and remarks in a surprised voice, "You must be our new transfer from active duty." Donnelly gets up and walks around his desk to shake hands over the counter. "You know you didn't have to show up in uniform, but I'm glad you did. It shows your professionalism. I appreciate that."

Eikenberry smiles, shakes hands, and explains, "Well, I try to be professional, but to tell the truth, I didn't really know how to report to a Guard unit."

"You don't really need to actually report till this weekend for our drill. That's when you'll meet your Platoon Sergeant, the First Sergeant and the Commander. Well, anyway, welcome aboard," Donnelly confirms with a smile.

Eikenberry is starting to feel pretty good about his decision to join the Guard. He did have the option of just getting out of active duty and starting his civilian life without any thought of continuing his military career in the Guard. But he likes the military and wants to stay in at least a little part of it, and hopes the Guard will do that for him. Eikenberry asks, "Just what is a Combat Support Company? We didn't have any in my battalion or even the brigade. It's like a Delta company, right?"

Donnelly walks around the counter and offers, "Let me walk you around and give you the nickel tour... the low down on who we are."

Donnelly looks right at him and says with all sincerity, "You're going to like it."

They go from top to bottom in the armory and then the motor pool. All along the way Donnelly answers Eikenberry's questions and, in the process, explains what the Dragon Slayers are all about. A couple of times Eikenberry sees what he assumes to be unit members in a few of the rooms and asks about it. Donnelly confirms they are members that have come in on their own time in order to get things ready for the upcoming drill. He assured him this is routine. Most of the unit members stop by the armory to square away something for their section, platoon or get something taken care of with supply, admin or training or meet up with members of their platoon to go over training requirements or anticipate needs for drill. Donnelly assures him there is always somebody in the armory every day.

Donnelly explains that CSC is made up of three TOW Anti-Armor platoons, each platoon with six Humvees, the scout platoon with twelve-gun jeeps with trailers, and the Heavy 4.2 mortar platoon with five old M88 commercial Dodge pick-ups. The company support elements consist of two supply guys, one personnel sergeant and four cooks. The maintenance sergeant belongs to Headquarters Company but is assigned to CSC during all the drills.

Delta Anti-Armor platoons in active duty units are simply five TOW platoons with four TOWs per platoon – twenty TOW Humvees.

Donnelly declares that the Dragon Slayers aren't your typical infantry CSC. They are actually a light cavalry troop, made that way by their Cav company commander. That everyone in the company loves it. He believes they are good at and getting better at conducting cavalry operations. It makes for a lot of movement during drill. The soldiers feel they are actually learning and executing essential operations.

Every soldier leaves the armory on Sunday afternoons both tired and feeling a great sense of accomplishment. As proof, Donnelly points to the fact that CSC has just received the 28th Division's highest award for soldier retention. This past year only one soldier left the company and got out of the Guard. That is because his civilian job shipped him overseas. Donnelly sums it up by assuring the "Command Climate" at CSC is excellent.

CHAPTER 7

The truth of the matter is that you always know the right thing to do. The hard part is doing it. - General Norman Schwarzkopf

Army National Guard Armory
Combat Support Company 2/220 Infantry
Manchester, PA
Saturday, 24 March 1989
06:30 Hours

After parking his truck just down the street, Rourke walks up the sidewalk to the armory front door. "Hey who called this meeting?" Rourke calls out to First Sergeant Donald (Don) Johnson, Sergeant Donnelly and Staff Sergeant Matthew Sutherland, the personnel sergeant, all standing at the door while Donnelly works the key in the lock.

Matthew jests, "We heard that they give away free coffee here on Saturdays, but only at the crack of dawn."

Rourke replies, "Matthew, that is the only reason I would be here this early. And it's only because I know you make the coffee."

As they all enter the armory hallway, the First Sergeant groans to Rourke, "I've got some bad news about Sergeant Conner."

"Hey, Top, let me dump all this stuff on the table upstairs and I'll be right down to your office." Rourke carries a big green canvas shoulder satchel that he bought at some army surplus store. Rourke's satchel is always filled with books, manuals, magazines and other research or reference material.

Most infantry officers are issued a canvas map case that is a throwback to one of the world wars. It is only large enough to hold a single manual and one folded map along with slots to hold a bunch of pens or pencils. The map case is affectionately known to everyone in the infantry as a "fag bag". Rourke feels he could never carry one around because they are carried mostly by staff officers and besides all the stuff he needs to carry would never fit. After dumping out his satchel on the upstairs conference room table, Rourke heads back down to the First Sergeant's office.

First Sergeant has his office right across from the orderly room. A key location to keep an eye on anyone going into the company's business and information center, better known throughout the Army as the orderly room. First Sergeant likes to know what is going on at all times. Rourke leans against the door frame. "What have you got for me, Top?"

Johnson looks up with a depressed expression, tilts his head. "You've lost your Scout Platoon Sergeant for JRTC and… maybe forever."

Showing amazement and disbelief, Rourke asks, "What the fuck happened?"

"Well you know Sergeant Connor works at a metal fabrication and engineering shop." Rourke nods his head in acknowledgement. First Sgt. continues, "Wednesday afternoon he somehow got his hand caught in a machine, and it tore the shit out of his left hand. They rushed him to the hospital. I'm told by Sergeant Lewis, who works with Jim at the shop, that as of yesterday he'll be lucky if the doctors don't amputate his hand."

Rourke can feel his chest tighten, lets this sink in for a minute. "Has anyone from the company gone over to the hospital?"

Johnson nods, "Yeah, both Rob and Matthew went over last night. And there have been a couple of guys that stopped by yesterday. You know how word spreads in the company. I'm sure 90% of the company knows by now. We were going to call you but figured telling you now would be just as good."

"How's his family taking it? How about his wife Darlene?"

"Well everyone is pretty shaken up, as you can imagine. Matthew contacted Chief Halberstat over at the battalion personnel office yesterday. The Chief will be working with Darlene on everything the Guard can do." Johnson lifted his shoulders in a shrug, "In the meantime all our prayers are with him and his family."

Rourke is processing the information. He looks down for a few seconds, remains leaning against the door frame with his arms crossed, just thinking.

"Sir, as much as we don't like to think about it, we have to put in a replacement, and it should be today."

Rourke nodded his head, put his hands on his hips and asks, "What are you thinking?"

"Well, last night I stopped by the armory here and pulled the two files for Sergeants' Davis and Callahan, both scout section sergeants."

Rourke states, "Both very good men. In your humble opinion who should get the job?"

Johnson thinks for a minute. "After looking at both files and giving it some tough thinking... I'd be happy with either one. They both have excellent records. The scouts' think highly of both... The only difference is that Davis has a little more time in service and time in grade as a staff sergeant. Davis started out here in the company and of course Callahan transferred in a couple of years ago from active duty. They're both solid NCOs."

"I agree. But you do know that the active duty experience Callahan brought to the scouts has made them one of the best scout platoons, at least in the brigade and probably in the division. His tactical knowledge and individual soldier skills are the best I've seen. He's a great teacher and mentor to some of the younger soldiers, and the whole company thinks the world of him. He *will be* a great Sergeant Major someday."

With a quizzical look, Johnson asks, "Yes, Sir. All true. But have you ever wondered why with his skills and talent he left the active duty?"

Rourke breaks out in a smile. "Yes, I have! And when he first got here, I was very curious after about the third drill. Anyone could see he is very,

very, good at soldiering." Rourke raises his eye brows and points to the First Sergeant, "That's why I called his old unit and asked to speak to the company commander. The commander wasn't in so the first sergeant took my call... I asked him why Sergeant Callahan is no longer in the active Army." Rourke hesitates. First Sergeant Johnson begins to smile and signals the "give me what you've got" with both hands for Rourke to give him the "low down" on Callahan.

"OK, Top.... Well it seems that our super soldier, Staff Sergeant Douglas Callahan, got himself in a little trouble with the Battalion Sergeant Major's daughter. That's right...I said Battalion Sergeant Major's daughter. The First Sergeant would *NOT* tell me what the problem was, but he did say that Callahan's future and his career in the Army was probably never going to go anywhere after that."

Johnson showing a mischievous smile then asks, "Do you think that after a couple of beers I should ask him about...Battalion Sergeant Major's daughters?"

"Nah...I'd let it go. That's water over the dam... or under the bridge... or whatever they say. Besides... I want my imagination to run with this. Whatever he did isn't going to match what I come up with!" Rourke finished with a big grin.

"So, you're picking Callahan for platoon sergeant?"

"No... I'm going with Davis. I think he kind of earned it a little more. He's been loyal to the company all these years, and I think it's important for the soldiers to know we rate loyalty as highly important. We'll give Callahan the next slot that comes open in the TOW platoons. I'm thinking the 1st TOW after JRTC. It'll be time for Sergeant Winters to move on."

"OK, when are you going to tell Davis?"

"I think, "we" should both tell him right after formation... which is in ten minutes." Rourke looks at his watch. "I also want to meet with the company leadership... E-6 and above, upstairs in the conference room. A little guidance about JRTC. I'll tell everyone at formation. Everyone else can load up for the move to the training area this morning."

After the company formation is told to fall out and moves on to training, the leadership is walking across the drill floor. On the way upstairs, Rourke and the First Sergeant catch Davis's attention. "Hey, Sergeant Davis, before you head up to the conference room for the meeting, Top and I want to talk with you."

Davis looks at both of them and says, "Yes, Sir."

Rourke starts, "I know you heard about your platoon sergeant, Sergeant Connor. So, let me get to the point. Top and I think you'd make a great Scout Platoon Sergeant. We want you to take the job."

Both Rourke and Johnson stand there smiling anticipating Davis to say, alright! Or you bet! Or this is great! But Davis looks down, taking a long pause, looking back up at Rourke and stammers, "I'm really glad that both you and Top asked me to take the position. That means that you both believe in me. Like I said, that means a lot to me. But... I'm not going to accept it."

Rourke is a little stunned, straightens his back and puts his hands on his hips, "Why, what's up?"

"If we weren't going to the JRTC I would take it. But since we are, and this means a lot to the company, the battalion and the Pennsylvania Guard I know that Doug will be a better Platoon Sergeant for JRTC. He is a better field soldier than me and he's already been to JRTC on active duty. Let's just say, right now he's the right guy for the job. I'll get another shot later."

Both Rourke and Johnson are speechless. Rourke puts out his hand and assures, "Davis is a hell of a man. That's quite a decision. Thanks for putting unit before self. We know that with you backing up Callahan your platoon is going to do well."

First Sergeant puts out his hand and says, "We're pretty sure that after JRTC there are probably going to be some changes and another opportunity for you."

Before the meeting gets started Rourke and Johnson grab Callahan and pull him aside to give him the news.

Staff Sergeant Douglas Callahan is not your typical Army National Guard soldier. His first active duty assignment was with the 7th Infantry Division. They made a name for themselves as the Army's new "Light Fighters". Which really means everything they take into battle is not hauled by trucks or jeeps but is carried on the backs of each Light Fighter. Most of those ruck sacks weigh on average 70 pounds. Therefore the

"Light" in light infantry means, they can deploy anywhere, anytime, quickly because they don't require a lot of logistics support.

Being accepted as a member of the 7th means you have to graduate from the Light Fighter course. A course designed by the 7th to weed out the weak and faint of heart. Probably the hardest two-week course in the Army. Just coming out of the 7th is impressive enough, but Callahan has even more to recommend him on his resume.

After infantry school and being awarded the Military Occupation Specialty (MOS) of 11 Bravo, he graduated from airborne school, jungle school, military mountaineering school, anti-armor school, and the 82nd's own Recondo School. And just last year while in CSC, he was the honor graduate of air assault school. Schools are a considerable addition to everyone's knowledge but it's just as important to have that "on the ground learning" you get from being assigned to some distinguished units.

His last assignment was in the 82nd Airborne Division. Callahan started out assigned to the 1st of the 507th airborne battalion. They have a storied history and maintain a level of excellence that remains one of the best in the 82nd. He was also with 1st squadron 17th Air Cavalry of the 82nd. This is where Callahan picked up the secondary MOS as a 19 Delta, Cav Scout.

During Callahan's second drill, Rourke spotted Callahan wearing the highly regarded 9th Infantry Regiment "Manchu" belt buckle. At the beginning of the century the U.S. Army dispatched the 9th Infantry Regiment to Qing China during the Boxer Rebellion and the China Relief Expedition where the regiment earned the nickname, "Manchus". That buckle is only awarded to those assigned to the 9th that complete the Manchu 100. It's a ball-busting 100 mile road march that's hard to endure. Many a soldier has never made it. The Manchu's are one of the brigades assigned to the 7th Infantry Division. That made Callahan a Manchu from the 7th Light Fighters. Rourke thinks this is *Pretty damn impressive*.

First Sergeant and Rourke intercept Callahan on the way upstairs after he has given instructions to his scout squad for them to load up. Rourke puts up his hand and tells Callahan, "Hold up a minute, Sergeant Callahan."

"Yes, Sir. What's up?"

"Congratulations… you're the new Scout Platoon Sergeant."

"Thank you, Sir, and thanks, Top. You know I'll do my best."

Rourke and First Sergeant both offer their hands. Callahan shakes both and announces with a pretty wide grin, "Let's have a good meeting upstairs, gentleman." Then he heads for the stairway.

Top looks at Rourke and quips, "I think our new Scout Platoon Sergeant is pretty confident in his abilities to lead the platoon."

"Oh yes he is… and I know we're both confident he'll be one of our best." Rourke says with a smile.

———————————⬥ ⬩ ⬩ ⬥———————————

Rourke bounds up the stairs to the conference room. He enters the room and then moves to the front. "Guys, I don't have any audio or visual material," Everyone smiles because there is never any audio or visual material, "so this is coming from my notes that I've been writing the past couple of days. Get out your note books. I also have a few articles copied from Infantry magazine to pass out."

Rourke had Rob print two articles about TOW Humvees at JRTC. "I want you to read them both and pass them off to your troops. These are two articles on some innovative ways to use TOW platoons. We will adopt a couple of the points from these articles. You all know I don't believe in reinventing the wheel."

Just then Sergeant Hyde from 3rd TOW pipes up with, "Yes, we know, Sir…there isn't an original line in any of our SOPs." The room bursts out in laughter followed by several people offering a few more remarks about how it is good we didn't have to pay for the use of the bootlegged material.

Rourke puts up his hands and jests, "Bring it down… Sergeant Hyde, I'm surprised you even know that. The way you and your guys don't seem to be able to follow it!" Laughter again by everyone. Finally, Rourke gets control of the room and starts into his briefing.

"Gentlemen, JRTC, as you know, is going to be the biggest test of our company and your abilities. This will probably be the biggest test ever in our Guard careers. So, let's not fuck it up! We're a solid company. We know our shit. We have very good soldiers. And we have very good leaders." He looks around the room. "I'm talking about you. Yes, occasionally I get on your asses for a couple of hic-ups here and there…but on the whole, you're pretty squared away NCOs." Rourke with a shrewd grin says, "I'll be talking to the lieutenants later about their performance." The lieutenants throw up their hands and shake their heads in disbelief. The room flares up with the NCOs offering some good ribbing to the lieutenants.

"Alright let's get into some business." Rourke begins again. "As I talked about in formation try to get over to the hospital and let Sergeant Connor know that we want him to get well and get back on his feet. Sunday after drill would be a good time to take your guys and do an assault on the hospital waiting room. I don't know the visiting hours, but I'm sure that a whole bunch of soldiers showing up would convince them that Sergeant Connor's "fan club" should be able to see him."

Rourke lets the laughter die down. "Back to mission... We are, according to the battalion commander, going to approach JRTC with a bit of a different angle. First our "enemy" is not going to be the regular Warsaw Pact variety we normally play to. Our JRTC enemy is a guerrilla type force with some captured armor vehicles operating in a small third world country. There won't be any battalion level operations as we've done in the past. The companies will be operating in company AOs (Area of Operations) looking for and fighting the bad guys." Rourke let that sink in. "So how does that affect us?"

He proceeds to go through what his plan is for the next three drills. "Gentlemen, your reference manual for our operations is ARTEP 17-57-10 MTP, Mission Training Plan for the Scout Platoon. This will be the bible for all of us from now until we complete JRTC. Specifically, I want you working on," he begins thumbing through the manual to select the missions and tasks for everyone, "of course, everything in chapter 5."

Someone from the back groans, "You know that's over half the manual."

Rourke looks up and scoffs, "So... what's your Point?" He looks back down and continues, "Study Command, Control and Communications. I would give us a T, for trained up for those tasks, but we need to stay on top of them. You screw those up and the rest goes down the drain."

Rourke looks up to confirm everyone has got that and then continues, "Under Maneuver... We want to... Occupy an Assembly Area, Conduct Tactical Movement, Perform an Area Reconnaissance, Execute Actions on Contact, Support a Hasty Attack, Conduct a Screen, and Execute a Dismounted Patrol." Rourke scans the room. "Under Combat Service Support... Perform Resupply Operations, Prepare to Evacuate Casualties, and Perform Platoon Maintenance Operations."

He drops the book on the table, puts his hands on his hips. "It's a long list I know but if we can execute these to standard, and… we will execute them to standard, we'll do well." Rourke holds up the manual. "This is the bible. Study it. Rob's got plenty of copies for us." Pointing at Sergeant Donnelly and grinning like a used car salesman Rourke states, "See Rob and get your new and updated ARTEP… Today!"

Sergeant Donnelly points to a small stack of manuals on a chair behind him, smiles and jokes, "Come and get 'um!"

"We'll be adding one more mission to our rucksack of knowledge. We'll be heavily involved with… Counter Recon. We'll be setting up Hunter Teams and Killer Teams. The battalion commander believes, along with everybody else, that if we kill their scouts before they kill our scouts… meaning all of us." Rourke points around the room to emphasize CSC is now the battalion cavalry scouts. "We will defeat the OPFOR. I will get you the Mission Training Plan for that at a later date. In the meantime, work on what we have."

Rourke points to a calendar on the wall, "Next month's drill is a MUTA 6. That means Friday, Saturday and Sunday. That means Friday morning at Zero Seven Hundred. If you or any of your guys think you're going to have a problem with your employer let me, and I mean ME… let me know. I'll try to fix it here. If not, I'll take it up the chain." He scans the room for any remarks. "OK, let me know if you get anything."

Rourke takes a second to gather himself, "I'm trying to impress upon you a sense of urgency… that this is real important to everybody. I want you to do the same with your guys. A lot of people are going to be looking at us. Keep that in mind. Any questions?" There are none, just a lot of solemn and earnest looks coming from everyone in the room. "Alright… Move Out and Draw Fire!" Rourke thunders at them, with the effect of everyone jumping up beaming and with a little more motivation in their step.

CHAPTER 8

"If you as a leader allow people to halfway do their jobs and don't demand excellence as a prerequisite to keeping their job, you will create a culture of mediocrity. If you allow people to misbehave, underachieve, have a bad attitude, gossip, and generally avoid excellence, please don't expect to attract and keep good talent. Please don't expect to have an incredible culture." – Dave Ramsey

CSC Platoon Sergeant's Room
Sunday, 25 March 1989
After Final Formation
17:20 Hours.

"Hey Sergeant Eikenberry come on in here." Sergeant First Class Carl Winters, 1st TOW Platoon Sergeant, calls out from the doorway of the basement Platoon Sergeants' room. He's waving Eikenberry into the room. "It's Ben, right?"

Eikenberry steps into the room and says, "Yes, it is, Sergeant".

Winters smiles and explains, "Ben inside this room... the NCO den of malicious plotting and here-to-fore doers of fantastic deeds... in here we use first names. There are no secrets kept here, and the walls are sound proof. So those young studs that are in charge can never get a jump on us old soldiers."

Eikenberry takes a quick look around. At one time this was a large storage room. It has been recently painted a bright blue and trimmed in orange. Gives off a positive atmosphere. It has an assortment of pipes, wires and duct-work running along the walls and ceiling. There is a large heavy-duty plywood table in the center with eight odd assorted chairs around it. There are four other old, overstuffed chairs located randomly around the room. A bookcase is full of Army manuals and magazines. There are seven double door wall lockers along the walls. An old beat up Army mess hall cooler is sitting in the far-left corner. Two overhead fluorescent sets of lights provide plenty of bright light.

"I know we are busy this drill and you might not have met everybody. Let me start and go around the room." Winters points to the first soldier on his left. "This is Gordon Hamilton, Mortar Platoon Sergeant. The next guy with the cold beer is Michael Stewart, 3rd TOW, then Rob Donnelly, 2nd TOW, the new Scout Platoon Sergeant, Doug Callahan, his scout sidekick, Jim Davis, and that's Matthew Sutherland, our admin guru drinking the cheap beer." Winters turns to Eikenberry and exclaims, "Everybody, this is Ben, my 1st Section Sergeant."

Everybody flips up a hand and answers either, "Hey, Ben… Welcome, Ben… Yo, Ben."

"Nice digs!" Eikenberry exclaims looking around.

Sergeant Hamilton speaks up. "Yeah they are. And relatively new. We never had a Platoon Sergeants' room till Captain Rourke came on board. He went through the whole building and rearranged most of the rooms after about a century of nothing ever changing."

"Is this where you do soldier counseling?" Eikenberry asks.

"Nope not in here." Donnelly explains, "This is senior NCO territory. E-6 and above. Rourke told us that this is our domain and he didn't even want to see a lieutenant in here. He says he is going to take care of the lieutenants… And he does! And that's another story. We do our counseling up in the recruiter's office during drill. He's not recruiting during drill."

Stewart takes a drink of beer, smiles and asks, "Well how do you feel after your first… *Army National Guard Drill*… Guardsman?"

This pleases Eikenberry. Yes, he is now an Army National Guardsman! "Well to tell you the truth, it feels kind of good, like I actually did some useful training. And… I am tired. I had no idea you guys go all drill like this. Does every guard unit go like this?"

Winters answers. "Nope, maybe some of the other companies in the battalion… but most other units do two eight-hour days and go home." Winters continues. "If you want to stay a Dragon Slayer you've got to be… *Committed!*" Everyone in the room is now grinning and nodding their heads. "It wasn't always like this. We can look at this in two parts, before Rourke and after Rourke. Everything changed after the *Cavalry* arrived!"

Sergeant Matthew Sutherland laughs out loud. "Let me tell you how the Cav arrived here at CSC." A couple of the guys get up and go over to the cooler, reach in and pick up a can of beer. Donnelly offers Eikenberry one. Eikenberry does a "toss me one" signal. This is going to take a while so everybody gets comfortable.

Matthew leans forward, looks around to make sure he's got everyone's attention.

"Captain Rourke arrived here a little over two years ago. It was a Sunday afternoon on drill weekend. I'm in the orderly room at my desk. In comes this guy in civilian clothes, walks up to the counter and says he's Lieutenant Rourke, at the time he was a first lieutenant, and would it be possible to see the commander. Well, we knew he was coming. Battalion called us and said the next company commander is stopping by on Sunday.

"I guess Rourke showed up at battalion the week before and said he has to transfer from Indiana and asks about Cav units in Pennsylvania. They told him the closest is in Philadelphia. The battalion commander is there, so they talked in his office. Rourke asks what positions are open in the battalion, expecting to be told he would be given a staff position so the battalion leadership could check him out. You know, see what kind of officer he is.

"The Battalion Commander, it was Colonel Anderson at the time." Matthew pauses to think for a second. "Francone came a couple of months later." then continued, "He asked Rourke what he wanted to do. Rourke, being the young trained up first lieutenant he was, said he wanted to command as soon as possible. Anderson said he has a company that needs a commander right now. Captain Garvin the CSC commander had moved to Allentown six months before and wanted in the worst way to transfer to another battalion out east. The drive was killing him.

"Garvin really wasn't much of a commander anyway. We were basically just following the battalion training schedule for two eight-hour days. Just really putting in time. We also had the highest number of excused absent and... unexcused absent soldiers in the Brigade!

"So anyhow, I take Lieutenant Rourke into Garvin's office and introduce Rourke. Garvin jumps up from his desk, thrusts out his hand and offers, "Oh yeah, the new commander! Let me show you around."

Matthew grins. "The look on Rourke's face is of shock! He told me later, he was wondering why a new first lieutenant would be offered a prestigious commander's position as a transfer, not just from a sister battalion down the road, but from two states away. Something wasn't right. That's why he came down to look at the company the Sunday before he would say yes."

Looking around and seeing that everyone is intensely listening, Matthew goes on. "So, Garvin walks Rourke all around the armory. The place is pretty much a mess. Soldiers are either sweeping the floors or looking around for places to hide till final formation. They walked around the outside of the armory talking; I could see them from the window in the orderly room. They walk over to Garvin's car which is parked right outside in the alley. I see them shake hands, Garvin gets in his car and drives away...and to this day, no one in this company has seen him since. Lieutenant Rourke comes into the orderly room, asks me to call the battalion. He gets on the phone with Anderson and says... 'Sir, I'll take the company.' Things around here haven't been the same since."

Donnelly jumps up, looks around holding up a beer can, gesturing to see if anyone wants a new one. Goes over to the cooler, picks out another, walks back to the table, "Now Ben, let me tell you about Captain Rourke's first drill. Or rather, our first drill together.

"Back then first formation was at eight o'clock, not seven, like it is now. Rourke shows up early at 07:15 hours. Both Matthew and I were already here. We say welcome and offer him some coffee. He says sure. Top walks in at about that time. Rourke who positions himself at the entrance of the drill floor says he'll take the company after Top gets the formation together and does his first sergeant stuff.

"Oh, I forgot to tell you. Rourke is wearing his black cavalry Stetson with gold crossed sabers on the front and wearing tanker boots. You know the ones with straps and buckles. That is the only time he has worn either since. The message then was things around here are going to be different!

"Rourke is prior enlisted. I know he spent three years in Germany. He got out as a Spec 4. Got his commission from ROTC while going to school on the GI Bill. He's what Marines call a Mustang Officer." Donnelly takes a second to regroup his thoughts. "Rourke is 6'1", 210 lbs., he's pretty fit. I understand he was a hell of an athlete back in Germany. Played football, basketball, and fast pitch softball for some Army all-star teams back then. So, anyhow he really looks sharp. At the time he is 28 so not some fresh newbie officer. Everyone coming on to the drill floor has to walk by Rourke. And looking at Rourke... you now know... there's a new sheriff in town!"

Donnelly takes a deep breath, takes a chug of beer, and starts again. "So, Top gets the formation together, the five platoons lined up across the drill floor, calls, 'At ease.' And then starts to call roll from the 1379 roster on his clip board. That's the form number for our payroll roster. Everybody assigned to our company is on the 1379.

"Rourke is off to the side of the formation where he is supposed to be. Rourke walks across the drill floor and right up to Top at about the fifth name that Top called out. Top stops, looks at Rourke with a confused, what's up, look on his face. Rourke leans in toward Top and says in a calm and like an... instructional voice. 'Top, from now on we don't call roll. That's what they do in grade schools. We in the United States Army have a procedure called "Receive the Report". So, if you will, please receive the report from our platoon sergeants.' Then he turns and walks back to his position.

Donnelly gets animated and exclaims, "No shit! Within two minutes of his first company formation, *Commander* Rourke is setting a new course for the company. Well, Top takes a couple of seconds to compose himself, he calls out, 'Receive the Report.' And of course, we all fuck it up! We haven't conducted a proper formation since... Hell, I don't know when. Finally, Top's had enough of us and does an about face and waits for Rourke to present himself.

"Rourke walks back out in front of the formation. Top salutes and says, 'All present or accounted for.' Which is a lie and everybody knows it.

Back then we didn't know who showed up till Top called their name. That practice changed that day. Rourke smiled, 'Thank you, First Sergeant. I'll take the company.' Top salutes again, does a quick about face and moves the fuck out. Rourke takes a couple of seconds and commands, 'Post.' And then our lieutenants move like their asses are on fire out to the front of their platoons. Then he gives the company, 'Stand At Ease.'

"Captain Rourke's got a strong and clear voice...it's loud. He doesn't ever really need a microphone, he can... Project! So, Rourke looked up and down the formation and said, 'Good morning, Gentlemen. My name is Lieutenant Devlin Rourke... I am your new commander.'

"Then he moves forward toward the formation and starts walking left and right in front of the company. Everybody is waiting for him to talk. He stops, looks at the company and says in a slow and deliberate voice, 'From this point on. This company will meet... or exceed... every US Army standard... always. Let me say that again... from this point forward this company, our company, will meet or exceed every US Army standard... Always! Got that?'

"Everybody is nodding their heads up and down, but inside we're like... what the hell does that mean. I don't think this guy is going to be cutting anybody any breaks.

"Rourke goes on. And I'll never forget this, 'You are all soldiers in the US Army. Look down at the tag over your left pocket. It says US Army. Not the National Guard. Not the Reserves. Everyone with a US Army tag over their left pocket is a US Army soldier. We all get paid by the same federal payroll system. That's right... we are paid by the federal government for our time in uniform. You are part of the U.S. Army. It's called the reserve component. We are a component of the Army. So, when you walk through that door into this armory in that uniform... you are a US Army Soldier. Therefore, you will comply with all the rules and regulations of the US Army. As your commander... I will ensure that you do.'"

Donnelly takes another drink. "Yep... we just got us a new sheriff!"

Matthew clears his throat ensuring everyone has his attention. "That's just the first formation. I'm the full-time personnel sergeant. So, let me tell you what happened next." He looks up like he's contemplating the next event in the story. "So Top and the Platoon Sergeants get together and figure out who's here and who's not. Finally, Top hands me a list of the AWOLs. Captain Rourke anticipated this and steps into the orderly room and says, 'Let me see that list.' I hand him the list with four AWOLs and five excused absent soldiers. He looks at both of us and points to Top's office.

"We're all standing in the office and he asks, 'How does a soldier get permission to miss drill here at CSC?'

"I explain that a soldier usually calls the week of drill and either gets hold of the supply sergeant, Sergeant Donnelly or me. We're the full timers. We listen to the reason and then give them permission to miss drill.' Captain Rourke shakes his head and says, 'OK, we'll fix that later.'

"He looked back at us and asks about the AWOLs. 'What's the procedure to follow up on the soldiers that just decided to take the day off?' I said we try and call them at their home to see if they just forgot or some other excuse. Rourke then asks how successful we are in getting the AWOLs to get into drill before lunch.

"I explained not very, mostly they are just blowing us off. They know it's us calling, they just don't answer. They know that after six AWOLs we put in the paperwork to get them discharged.

"Rourke gets this determined look on his face, then grins and says, 'Not anymore. Matthew, type up four warrants and then call the county sheriff's office to get a couple of deputies to track down our AWOLs.'

"I have to explain we don't do that here in Pennsylvania. We're required to use constables to enforce warrants. He says, 'OK, call the constables but I want to talk with them before they go.' I then have to explain that I've never typed up a warrant. That we really hadn't done that before. Rourke says, 'That now changes too.' He tells me to call the Chief over at battalion personnel and have them fax over a copy of a warrant. That he wanted to sign the warrants and have them in the hands of the constables by 11:00.

"So, the constables, two of them, show up. I give them the warrants and Rourke talks to them. He tells them that he wants the AWOLs in hand cuffs and to park out back and slow walk the perpetrators across the drill floor. Have them wait in the hallway outside Top's office. And to stand beside them to encourage people not to talk with them.

"About an hour later the constables bring in the first AWOL. They walk him across the drill floor in cuffs and park him outside of Top's office. I let Captain Rourke know we got one and what does he want to do. He tells me to get the soldier's personnel file, come into his office and set up two chairs against the wall that will be behind the soldier who will be standing at the captain's desk. He calls for First Sergeant to come in and talk to him about what kind of soldier Specialist Webb is.

"Top says he's not bad but needs to see the light and grow up a little bit more. Rourke says he's got it and tells Top to have a seat. He wants to have Top and me sitting behind the soldier in the two chairs against the wall while he addresses the guilty party standing in front of his desk.

"Rourke then tells me to have the constables' un-cuff Webb and send them back out for another AWOL and to tell the soldier to report to him.

"Well, I tell Spec Webb to report to the commander. Webb is a little shook up having to walk hand cuffed past the company and then having him wait that extra fifteen minutes so that everyone could make an excuse to walk by Top's office to give Webb that 'boy you fucked up' look.

"Webb walks into the commander's office, comes to attention, salutes and just says, 'Sir.' Now you know and I know that's not how you "Report" to an officer. Webb just wanted to get this over with. But it just got way worse!

"Captain Rourke takes this long pause, looks up at Webb with the most disgusting look on his face. Then he slowly stands, puts his hands on his hips and asks in a rather forceful voice… 'Who the Fuck are you… and what the Fuck are you doing in my office!' I thought Webb is going to piss himself. He says that he was told to report to the commander. Rourke roars out, 'That is not how you "REPORT" to an officer! Get your ass out of my office… have Sergeant Sutherland instruct you on the proper way to report to an officer! Move Out!'

"I meet him outside of the office. I tell him that he needs to move to within one foot of the front of the commander's desk. Come to attention. Properly salute. And say, 'Specialist Webb reports as instructed, Sir.' Man… Webb is shook up, but I get him calmed down so he can focus and get this done. I asked him if he's ready. He takes a deep breath, says yes. I say, 'Whenever you're ready, go.' He turns around walks into the commander's office, stops one foot from the desk, gives a pretty sharp salute and says, 'Specialist Webb reports as instructed, Sir.'

"Once again Captain Rourke takes a long pause, slowly stands, looks at Webb and asks him, 'Does this look like your fucking living room, or is this my office?' I swear Webb's forehead is starting to sweat bullets. He says, 'It's your office, Sir.' Rourke looks right at Webb and explains that Webb shouldn't just go walking around and getting into other people's offices. That the proper and polite thing to do is to knock on the door and "Request" permission to enter. Then he says, 'Now get out... and try this again.'

"Webb goes back out and is really sweating bullets now. Webb tries it again. Eventually gets it right. So, Captain Rourke starts asking him questions like, 'Why are you absent from drill.' Webb of course gives some lame excuse. Rourke looks right at him with the "don't bullshit me look" and says, 'Don't even try to bullshit me! You didn't come in because you just didn't fucking feel like it.... Right?' Webb timidly admits, 'Yes, Sir.'

"Captain Rourke starts in on him about his obligation as both a man and a soldier. And that he isn't putting up with a soldier acting like some irresponsible teenage kid. Rourke is really good at chewing ass. And I've got to tell you he's perfect at making these guys feel like shit for being AWOL. Sometimes he'll give them Article 15's and sometimes he just withholds a day's pay from the 1379. Depending on the situation. But he always ends it the same way. He says, 'The First Sergeant and your Platoon Sergeant say you're a pretty good soldier when you're here. How about you grow up and realize your responsibility to yourself and your fellow soldiers... And get your ass here... and on time. I need good soldiers... so get here! You're dismissed.'

"We then get a phone call from the constables. They think the next guy is with his girlfriend in the movie theater downtown. Captain Rourke tells them to get a hold of the manager, have him stop the movie, turn on the house lights, walk down the aisle, hand cuff that little bastard and bring him to me. And they do. We go through the same process for each of the next two soldiers. This actually becomes our SOP in handling soldiers needing a little discipline.

"He always talks to Top and sometimes the Platoon Sergeant to gauge the soldier's attitude and talks with me to review the info in his records. He always has Top and me sitting behind the soldier so he can look at either one of us to check and verify the soldier is telling the truth. There have been times where both of us are shaking our heads no while the soldier tries to blow smoke up the commander's ass. At that point Captain Rourke says, 'Hey First Sergeant, I think he's trying to blow smoke up my ass. What do you think?' And then Top attacks him from the rear... so to speak. They haven't got a chance!

"After delivering the "movie AWOL", the constables go back out for the next one. We go through the process, and this guy gets an article 15, took away a bunch of money with reduction in rank. All because he got kind of smart with Top. This really pissed off Captain Rourke. I think Top really appreciated the support.

"So, the constables call again. This next kid, and he is a kid, he's nineteen. I informed Captain Rourke that he just joined the unit six months ago coming from basic and AIT. The kid is with his family at a restaurant having a family meal. Captain Rourke takes this long pause and you know he's thinking about whether to let this one go. He tells the constables not to cuff this one. To politely as possible go up to the kid and ask him to accompany them to the National Guard Armory because obviously he forgot he has a drill. Then, before they enter the armory, put the cuffs on him.

"The constables bring him in and have him in cuffs waiting out in the hallway. Guess who shows up? Mom and Dad from the restaurant! Mom sees junior in cuffs standing in the hallway and starts to cry. Top and Captain Rourke ask the parents to please come in the commander's office. Captain Rourke does a great job of explaining that the weekend drill is important. That all 126 men in the company now have an obligation. They took an oath. That their son is now part of the Army and would be required to act and behave accordingly.

"His mother has stopped crying by then and asks what is going to happen to junior? Captain Rourke says he would take into consideration his youth and first-time mistake and just give junior a stern talking to. But the next time he would pay a steep penalty. Dad spoke up and says that this would never happen again. Captain Rourke thanked them both and reassured them junior's future in the Guard would be a positive experience. They left the armory feeling better about their son and the Guard.

"Captain Rourke next called in the "dejected" Private Combs. Has him report, which Combs did correctly. He then looked at Combs with the '*get your head out of your ass look*', leaned forward and asks, 'Private Combs did you learn anything the past 60 minutes?' Combs has this sincere, serious look and says, 'Yes, Sir. Never miss a drill!'

"Captain Rourke says, 'Very Good. Now get out of here and go report to your Platoon Sergeant.' Combs is a Spec 4 today and is a pretty solid troop... in your platoon, Ben!" Matthew exclaims with a big grin.

Matthew continues, "At the end of that day, both Top and I told Captain Rourke we felt pretty good about the way CSC now handles soldiers needing discipline. We ask him if that's the way they did it in the Cav. Rourke laughs out loud. He looks at both of us, 'Gentlemen, I spent four years active duty... and got out as a Specialist... Barely! Most of my friends made E-5 before they got out. Believe me I know how a commander can deal with a "wayward" soldier. I spent a little time in the "old man's" office... standing at attention... and hoping for mercy.'"

Matthew points his index finger up and finishes with, "That's why you've got to love a Mustang!"

CHAPTER 9

"The first responsibility of a leader is to define reality." –
Max Depree

Army National Guard Armory
HQ 2/220 Infantry Battalion
Bluffton, PA
Monday, 27 March 1989
09:00 Hours.

Rourke walks into the battalion operations and training office with a
smile and whistling a rock tune he just heard on his truck radio. Sergeant
McCallister leaning back in his chair at his desk, smiles and says, "Bad
Company, right?"

Rourke sings out, *"Feel Like... Maakiiing Love!"*

McCallister shakes his head, grits his teeth, looks like he just heard
finger nails on a chalkboard and says, "Captain Rourke, please... please...
give it a break!"

"OK... but I still feel like it!"

Rourke is stopping by battalion headquarters to drop off his "wish
list" of vehicles. He needs to get this in as soon as possible. The vehicles

are crucial for his company to operate down at JRTC. He wants ten Humvees for the Scouts, six Humvees for the mortars, and four Humvees for the company headquarters folks; XO, first sergeant, supply and one for himself. All this is to replace the old gasoline jeeps and pickup trucks. He hands the list to McCallister.

What's important about making all his vehicles Humvees is that his maintenance problems would be greatly simplified. Instead of trying to find repair parts for three different types of vehicles he would now only have one type. He is requesting two different body styles of Humvees, one as a weapons carrier, just like his TOW Humvees, and the rest as utility vehicles able to carry small amounts of cargo. But still basic repair parts for one vehicle type.

With everyone in Humvees only diesel fuel would be required. Making it a lot simpler for the fuel guys to keep CSC topped off. Rourke knows as a cavalry trooper that keeping your "mount" fueled up at all times is a cardinal rule to maintaining mobility on the battlefield. He learned long ago that whenever you come across a fuel point, even if it isn't yours, to pull in and top off.

Occasionally this would upset the real owners of the fuel point. Fuel is expensive and is carefully budgeted into training requirements. Having some other unit steal your fuel ticks you off. So, this is where, at the time newly commissioned, 2nd Lieutenant Rourke put into practice the old axiom, it is better to ask for forgiveness than seek permission. "Gee! I'm sorry, I didn't know." That did work most of the time. But there was that one time the Mechanized Infantry Battalion wanted their fuel back. Later, the Cav Squadron had to send over one of their fuel trucks to replace Rourke's "Mistake". All the Cav thought the Mech Infantry were a bunch of assholes anyway. So, nothing ever came of it.

Next, Rourke wants to talk with the battalion full time training officer, Captain Henry Swoon, about getting his share of MILES gear. He knows the three rifle companies would be making sure they get everything they need. It is vital for them to practice full up with MILES gear. He didn't want to be short changed on receiving everything he requests. The Dragon Slayers are going to play a critical part in fighting the OPFOR. They also have to be experts on using MILES as individual soldiers.

When Rourke first came to CSC he was quite experienced with vehicle

MILES sets because all of the CAV tanks and armored personnel carriers (APCs) are set up as MILES compatible. He requested the Training Aids Department down at Fort Indiantown Gap to provide MILES vehicle sets for his eighteen TOW Humvees. They were thrilled that someone wanted the sets. Apparently, they had a bunch sitting around the warehouse for a while not being used. But... the sets are for APCs only. Not a problem for Rourke. He would adapt them.

Sergeant Donnelly and a couple of other soldiers drove down to the Gap and picked up all eighteen sets. Matching them to the Humvees was difficult. There was a problem with the electronic hook-up with the Humvees electrical systems which Rourke had anticipated. With all the civilian electronic professionals in the company a solution was quickly found. To make it work, a homemade wiring harness was designed. The harness and how it works was shown to Rourke before the first 'force on force' MILES battle between the platoons out in the training area took place. This is not the only time Rourke feels really proud of his men's initiative and ingenuity. It would happen again and again.

Rourke talks with the training officer about extra ammunition for his mortar live fire down at the Gap in August. He wants double what is currently forecast for the training. Rourke knows that Captain Swoon has used the DA PAM 350-38, Standards in Training Commission (STRAC), to forecast the usual required amount of ammo.

Rourke doesn't like Swoon. They got off to a bad start when Rourke first came to the battalion and it just got worse as time went by. He just assumed, based on his experience in the Cav, that the training officer worked for the battalion commander and all the company commanders. That, if you needed something for training, the training officer would bust his ass to try and get it for you. Apparently Swoon never got the memo.

After a while, Rourke got tired of pounding his head against the wall and arguing about what the written training requirements were, so he just went around Swoon to get his stuff. This obviously pissed off Swoon. So, every time he got the chance he would try and screw Rourke. This mortar ammo forecast is going to be Swoon's newest attempt.

He has two things going for him that Swoon can't overcome. First, Rourke knows more about army training regulations than Swoon. Rourke's experience and background provide him the knowledge of how the regulations are to be implemented for good use. Swoon's limited experience is only with the infantry and only with this battalion.

Rourke's lessons in training management started when he first got commissioned in the Cav. In addition to being assigned to Charlie Troop as the 3rd platoon leader he was given the additional duty of running the Troop Cavalry Scout Certification program. This is a program designed to ensure that all C Troop soldiers in MOS 19D know their jobs. This requires sending the Scouts through a training lane that compells them to demonstrate both individual and collective or squad tasks to Army standards. The lanes need all sorts of pyrotechnics, smoke, artillery simulators, machine gun and rifle blank ammunition. This means digging into all the required regulations and manuals to create the most realistic training possible. Rourke had to figure out the amounts and types required to be ordered eight months in advance.

After that first year Rourke was assigned the new additional duty as Tank Gunnery Officer for the Squadron. All the Cav tankers in each of the three troops had to complete and qualify as tank crewmen on the practice and qualification ranges. A big job that meant ordering the right types and right amounts of ammo.

Along with each of these additional duties Rourke still had to run the standard weapons qualification ranges for his platoon and the troop. This included the .45 caliber pistol, M16 Rifle, M203 Grenade Launcher, M60 machine gun, M2 .50 caliber machine gun, M72 Light Anti-Tank Weapon (LAW) and the M202 Flash Incendiary Rockets.

During Rourke's fourth year in the Cav he was assigned the new position as a Fire Support Officer. He was put in charge of running the heavy 4.2 inch mortars through their ARTEP Mortar Qualification and firing night time illumination for night tank gunnery.

All of these tasks and duties meant he had to get intimate with all the regulations of ordering, receiving, picking up, storing, distributing and firing just about every type of training ammo and live fire ammo, range training devices, and sub-caliber simulators.

Being a lieutenant in the Cav means understanding training for combat with everything in the Army training inventory. What all this means is Rourke has seen, applied and utilized many more training resources and systems than Swoon.

The second reason Rourke can get around Swoon is that Rourke believes that Colonel Francone really doesn't care for Swoon either. It was never said but there are indicators Francone would like a new training officer. But because Swoon is full time and it is extremely difficult to get rid of full time staff he would just put up with Swoon for the time being.

As he goes into the training officer's office he shuts the door behind him. No one needs to hear their predictable heated conversation. "Henry, we need to add more ammo to the mortar live fire in July."

Swoon sitting straight up in his chair with his arms crossed looks agitated. "No... we... don't. That ammo request is put in on time and meets all our yearly requirements."

Rourke stands squared up with his hands on his hips and leaning against the front of Swoon's desk and fumes, "Yeah, for a normal year... I'm pretty sure even you realize this isn't a normal year."

"Look, my hands are tied. Directives from our state training officer say we will use the requirement in STRAC to forecast and order all our ammunition for the year. He has a budget he has to follow."

"That's bullshit. There are exceptions to everything based on the situation."

Before Rourke can continue, Swoon points his finger at Rourke. "Rourke, that's part of your problem. You think you're so exceptional. That the rules don't apply to you."

"This isn't about me! This is about getting my soldiers ready for one of the biggest events this battalion will EVER do! And this is about you doing your job!"

Swoon feels contempt for Rourke. "Rourke, you always ask or demand more than any of the other companies."

Rourke knew this was going to happen. He knew Swoon was going to end up pissing him off. And that the rest of the conversation was going to be a couple of octaves louder. "That's because I'm NOT like any of the other companies. I own all the mobility assets... eighteen Humvees and twelve Scout jeeps... and have most of the firepower!" Rourke is really trying to control his temper. He wants to finish by screaming, "You Fuckin' Dumb Ass!" But doesn't.

Swoon, still sitting with his arms crossed, shakes his head in disgust. "There are guidance and directives that must be followed."

"Yes, there are… you just don't know how to either find them or use them. As far as money… the National Guard Bureau has already authorized more money for our state to be used to support us. If you look a little more in the STRAC and use NGR 350-1… in Chapter 7, you can use them to justify more ammo. It just takes writing a couple of letters!" Once again Rourke holds his tongue from ending with "Fuckin' Dumb Ass!" Rourke goes on, "Don't you think that the division commander will approve it anyhow?" He leans in toward Swoon to make his point, "If we asked for Nike Hercules missiles… the division commander would ensure we got them!"

"I'll write the letters… but I'm not promising anything." Swoon declares.

Rourke changes the subject to MILES. "You know everyone in the maneuver area or the maneuver box at JRTC needs to be in MILES."

Swoon nods his head, "I know everyone has to have MILES on. I will ensure that you have 126 individual sets for training. Thanks for stopping in." Swoon slides his chair forward to move closer to his desk so he can get on with the work sitting on top and to signal Rourke to leave.

Rourke doesn't move. He demands, "You also know that you need to get all those additional Humvees I requested to be prepared at least with Velcro strips to accept MILES receptors? And I'm pretty sure most of them don't currently have any ready since our CSC has been the only company in the state that has Humvees that are MILES equipped."

Swoon glowers up at Rourke with a little surprise. He didn't even think of that. Now he's got to accept defeat and tell Rourke that he'll insure they come ready for MILES. "Yeah, I'll make sure."

Rourke takes a minute just to stare at Swoon with a little contempt, turns to his right, opens the door, walks out and closes the door behind him. He looks right at Sergeant McCallister who is grinning from ear to ear. McCallister crosses his arms letting it be known he really enjoys watching and in this case listening to Rourke and Swoon go at it.

McCallister points to the door, "You know, Sir, that the door is not sound proof."

"Yeah, I know… I know you also get some perverse pleasure out of it too."

McCallister jokes, "I chalk it up to professional development. Why, just hearing two squared away Captains working together to solve a common military problem… you can't get that from reading a book, Sir."

Rourke leans over the desk, "Hey, smart guy, you know you'll be the one getting those Humvees… my Humvees ready for MILES."

McCallister looks at him with an air of confidence and explains, "Sir, I've already called down to the Gap to make preliminary arrangements for your Humvees. As soon as the logistics guys get us the Humvees, they'll be sending them over to the Gap to Training Aids and properly get them equipped… Done!"

Rourke answers, "Gary, once again… I'm in awe of the quick and efficient operations, of Operations… Now, is the commander in?"

"Yep, in his office."

"Thanks."

Rourke walks across the office into the hallway and then down past several doors to the end of the hall across from the conference room to the battalion commander's office. The door is half open. He knocks on the door jam.

Colonel Francone calls out, "Come on in."

Rourke steps into the office, "Sir, I just dropped off my vehicle list and talked with Captain Swoon about a couple of things. Thought I'd stop by." Rourke usually didn't have anything for the colonel but always thought it best to just stop by in case the commander has something for him. This time however, Rourke did have one request… a big request!

Francone is now smiling and puts down a field manual he has been studying. "I'm sure, Devlin… that… that went pleasantly." Knowing full well that the Rourke vs. Swoon "meetings" meant friction or even occasionally something a little hotter. "I'm glad you stopped by. Have a seat."

"Yes, Sir, what can I do for you?"

"I wanted you to know that I'll be spending most of my time with the rifle companies. And most of my staff will be circulating around the rifle companies." Rourke is nodding his head in acknowledgement. "You know I have confidence in your abilities to conduct the right training."

"Yes, Sir, I've got it."

"Alright, focus on recon, security and counter recon. Keep in mind I'll have the rifle companies operating in the woods and you'll be working along the dirt roads and trails. It's going to be key that you keep track of the company's locations all the time. If we get in trouble in the woods… I'll be calling you to come in from the closest trail to help."

"Yes Sir, we've got it… we'll be there and we'll be ready."

Francone leans back, pauses for a second and fixes his eyes intently at Rourke. "Devlin, I believe that your efforts in counter recon may be the key to our success. If you're able to take out their eyes and ears, their scouts… we'll have a fair chance of fighting them even up. Making it harder for them to locate us in the box… takes away their big advantage."

"I understand, Sir, and I'm working on a couple of techniques or methods on how to do that. I'm going to need the scout platoon under my command to accomplish the counter recon mission. And I'm probably going to need them the whole time. You're really going to have to totally buy into the Dragon Slayers, all of them, being your Cav Troop. I'll be prepared to support the rifle companies with all my guys and provide you with security, recon and counter recon missions."

Asking an infantry battalion commander to give up his scout platoon is like asking him if you can take his eighteen-year-old daughter to the premier of an X rated movie and by the way, can she "sleep over" at your house for the next two weeks.

There is only one scout platoon in an infantry battalion. They are assigned to the CSC for support and to be taken care of logistically, but battalion commanders control all their tactical assignments. Traditionally they are the only "eyes and ears" of a battalion. They are the asset that is supposed to find the bad guys before they find you. Rourke wants to take that asset away from the colonel and put it in with his TOW platoons and make one unit that would fill the scout role and a lot more as a Cavalry troop. Rourke has integrated the scouts into his Cav operations at home station and a little during the two-week annual training when the opportunity presented itself. They had molded together as one unit. But he has never asked to take over the command and control of the scouts… until now.

Francone examines Rourke's face and rolls this very significant request over in his mind, going through different scenarios and courses of action. Finally, he responds to Rourke, "I hope you're as good as I believe you are." A long pause. "The scouts are yours."

CHAPTER 10

"Increased responsibility means dealing with more intangibles and therefore more complex uncertainty. Leaders can afford to be uncertain, but we cannot afford to be unclear. People will not follow fuzzy leadership." – John Maxwell

Army National Guard Armory
Bluffton, PA.
HQ 2nd Battalion 220 Infantry
Saturday, 8 April 1989
08:30 Hours.

This is going to be a big meeting. Whenever you walk into the Bluffton armory drill floor and there are 24 tables set up in the middle in a huge square you know this is a battalion meeting. All the companies, the staff and support elements will be there. There is a company or element placard taped to the front of each table so everyone knows where they are supposed to set up and therefore you can tell who is missing.

There are four large, green thermos containers, stacks of white Styrofoam cups on two tables at the back of the drill floor. Coffee and orange drink. Stacks of additional folding chairs are available for any element that brings extra bodies. They will be set up behind the assigned unit tables so everyone can maintain unit integrity. There will be a lot of filled folding chairs today behind every table. In front of the battalion commander's table is an additional table with an overhead projector on it. The screen is already up and set off to the side ready to be pulled into place for the presentation.

The meeting is scheduled to start at 09:00 but there are already a lot of soldiers standing around, drinking coffee, mingling and connecting with others trying to take advantage of the time before the start of the meeting. A lot of laughter and hand shaking going on.

At one minute before nine, the Battalion Sergeant Major Daniel Morando walks to the middle of the floor and in a typical booming Sergeant Major's voice announces that the meeting is starting, waits a few seconds and then introduces the battalion commander. "Gentlemen, the Battalion Commander." Everyone jumps to their feet at attention.

Colonel Francone walks to the center of the floor, looks around and says, "It's going to be a long day, so please take your seats." Francone starts with a welcome to everyone while walking in front of every table all the way around the circle. "Once again I would like to thank you for getting here and on time." Pointing to the guys on the folding chairs behind their company leadership, "And I would like to thank all the additional devoted soldiers that also showed up. I appreciate your dedication to our battalion." With a little smile, "Let's hope we can get everyone paid for their time. I'm assured by the S-1 that everyone will be paid!"

Someone sitting with Bravo Company calls out. "It'll make the wife happy, Sir!" Everyone chuckles, glances around at each other and happily agrees.

Francone smiling in appreciative understanding, "Well that's no shit." Pausing long enough to get everybody's attention again, "Here's today's agenda, our S-3, Major Dye will start off with the operations we're planning. This is not the operations order. The JRTC Staff will be coming up here in June to collaborate on developing the training goals and what our missions are going to be. We'll produce the Op order sometime after our meeting with JRTC when everything has been finalized. But there are some ARTEP missions, battle drills, operational techniques we want you guys to start using. Just a heads up... we're going to be moving and moving and moving in the box. I don't want the OPFOR to lock us in a position. Practice moving."

Francone looks around the floor to ensure everyone understands so far. "Next the S-2, Captain Easton, will give you a briefing on what our enemy will be like. It will not be the traditional Soviet Warsaw Pact enemy we've been working against these past ten years. This is a different enemy. Consequently, we have to fight them differently. That's why we have the changes in our battalion mission and how we're going to fight. Don't worry… it will all become clear to you after the S-2s briefing."

Francone continues to talk and walk around the tables. "The S-4 will be talking to all you logistic guys about the challenges we'll all be facing. There is no mercy or looking the other way in logistics at the JRTC. We don't order it right… we DON'T get it. Anticipate your needs, be proactive, ask for more. We don't run the Logpac correctly we will run out of water, food and ammo. The lesson will be learned the hard way. We will starve! So please pay attention. I hate losing… but I really hate losing on an empty stomach!" Everyone appreciates the humor, so everyone is smiling and chuckling around the tables.

"Captain Wright, our S-1, will go over the requirement for getting replacements on the battlefield. If you've read anything out of the lessons learned publications, not getting your replacements is just as devastating as getting wiped out in a battle. This is where you start down that death spiral of not getting enough soldiers to keep up the fight. Everyone trying to do more with fewer men. It doesn't work… EVER!

"Captain Ronconi, our Motor Officer, will go over the requirements for keeping everything rolling. Captain Rourke and Captain Walker need to particularly pay attention.

"Sergeant McCallister will go over MILES. We fuck up on MILES, and it's over. He's got updates on MILES claymores and AT-4s." Francone holds up his index finger to emphasize the point, "Zero, Zero, Zero your weapons! Pay attention!

"Sergeant Major will finish up with… "Taking care of our soldiers", and not just for JRTC, but NOW! Our success will be determined right here… right here at home station! Get your soldier problems squared away now. Sergeant's business… IS… Army business. We don't accomplish anything without soldiers. And we want the best soldiers."

It is a long day. Information just keeps coming. All of it good. Lunch is even tasty. The whole day gives the battalion an opportunity to get together and share in some all-important camaraderie. All five companies are spread around western Pennsylvania. The only time this many of the battalion soldiers get together is at annual training. It is good to break bread together.

CHAPTER 11

Never tell people how to do things. Tell them what to do and they will surprise you with their ingenuity. - General George S. Patton Jr.

Combat Support Company
Local Training Area: R&P Coal Company
Manchester, PA.
Friday, 21 April drill
10:45 Hours.

The Dragon Slayer's 3rd TOW Platoon Leader, 2nd Lt. James (Jim) Petrone, is comparing his map with the terrain where he is standing. No doubt about it, this is a tough field problem Captain Rourke gave the young lieutenant. Establish a screen line 500 meters long over hilly, wooded and broken ground. He knows Rourke has picked the worst part in CSCs local training area to have a screen line established. Ideally, he would have set up his six Humvees so that they could spread out and cover the 500 meters and be able to at least see the TOW section to their left and right.

Petrone is standing about where he thought the midpoint in the screen line is. He has already sent out two of his sections. One went to the left the other to the right. This is to find the left and right ends of the screen and to quickly put up a hasty screen line while he figures out how to displace the whole platoon for complete coverage. He was given a pretty thorough operation's order at his platoon's assembly area. He felt sure everyone has the concept down. They would operate as a well-oiled machine.

He knows one of the other platoons is conducting their assigned platoon mission against his screen. Probably the 1st TOW, led by 1st Lt. Trevor Foley. Petrone and Foley have a fun, little rivalry going on. Nothing like competition to add a challenge to any event. This is going to be force on force MILES action that everyone loves. And Petrone would love to kick Foley's ass. The 1st TOW platoon most likely will be conducting an area reconnaissance and should pick up Petrone's platoon on a screen. But, not before Petrone's men spot them first. The 1st TOW will be moving slowly to complete the recon in their area. 3rd TOW will hopefully be in covered and concealed positions by then. Everyone is eager for a fight!

The one thing that Pennsylvania has is plenty of hills. And Rourke is now on top of one so that he can overlook the actions of the 3rd TOW and the 1st TOW. Along with his driver, Specialist 4 Josh Tibbs, they are using binoculars to put some eyes on the two platoons. Josh is indispensable to Rourke. He is a very bright college student majoring in Engineering.

Rourke has been gently pushing Josh to apply for Officer Candidate School. But Josh wants nothing to do with it. His plan is to use the National Guard college money to finish school and then move on to better things in the world. After two years as Rourke's driver he is trusted to do many things that most Specialists would never be entrusted to do. Rourke really likes him and enjoys his company.

Rourke asks Josh to focus on and try to pick out the 1st TOW conducting their recon while he is checking out Lt. Petrone's plan to establish the screen. Rourke is convinced that the secret to good platoon leadership is the ability of the lieutenant to quickly run through his multiple courses of action, be decisive and pick one, develop a simple plan then convey the plan so that his entire platoon understands and then moves like the wind to put it into action.

Josh picks out two of the 1st TOWs Humvees slowly moving through their assigned area approximately 800 meters away. They are moving slowly with some dismounts clearing heavy underbrush. Josh lets Rourke know their location. This gives Rourke an idea of when they should be seeing each other. He guesses 30 minutes till the radio is alive with reports of "enemy sightings". Who would get the upper hand and have the advantage?

So far Rourke is impressed with Lt. Petrone. As soon as he gets to his assigned screen location he starts his platoon moving to deploy on a FRAGO. A FRAGO is a fragmentary order, used to quickly provide guidance for movement and to get things going before or after the issuance of the full operations order.

Petrone is personally moving along the screen line placing his TOW systems to complete the screen. There are holes in the screen line but Rourke can tell that Petrone will be filling in those holes by moving his six Humvees and possibly dismounting some of the TOW systems to cover the hilly broken ground in between. Petrone's screen line does have a little bit of an advantage in altitude. They are on the high ground. Rourke guesses they are about twenty feet higher than the 1st TOW that is moving up hill on its recon.

Rourke's estimate on time is right on. Petrone reports in on his assigned company radio frequency, "Black 6, this is Blue 1, over."

"This is 6, Go."

"Two enemy vehicles at grid 356529 moving north." The grid location puts them on the very left side of the screen line. The 1st TOW is spotted by 3rd TOW platoon's 2nd section right in front of them.

"Roger, contact Catapult for assistance break." Long pause. "Engage at your discretion out."

Now it is going to get very interesting rather quickly. 3rd TOW spots and reports to the company commander two of 1st TOWs Humvees. Rourke tells him to call the Dragon Slayer's mortars for a fire mission and that he can engage with his own TOWs.

Rourke is listening for the request for fire on the mortar freq and listening for Petrone to give a direct fire mission to one of his TOWs on his platoon freq. There is no call from the 1st TOW so they haven't yet realized they have been spotted.

Josh is monitoring the mortar freq. He turns to Rourke, "3rd TOW just called in a correct formatted call for fire… Sounded like his driver."

Rourke nods his head and orders, "Call 1st TOW in two minutes, give them the grid and tell them they're receiving indirect fire."

Josh has this. He has worked the indirect fire side of all of Rourke's field problems for the last two years. Rourke has trained Josh well. Josh will have no problem getting a 13F MOS, Fire Support Specialist, as a secondary MOS, if it is possible.

3rd TOW, Section 1, Sergeant Hyde, calls into the platoon network with the six-digit grid of the "enemy" vehicles when he sees them. Everyone in the platoon checks their maps to find the location on the ground.

Rourke is monitoring the platoon freq. He hears Lt. Petrone utter just one word… "Anybody?" It is a question to all in the platoon asking who can identify the enemy and who has a shot? Rourke is again impressed. Instead of having the guys' right in front of the enemy shoot, he is asking to see if anyone else can get a shot.

And lo and behold Sergeant Hicks from way over on the right side of the screen says he can. "Blue 1, Blue 4, I can tag one from my location." The shot will be from about 1400 meters away, but it is an angle from across the screen line. Most people expect to be shot at from the front. Therefore, they watch for the enemy smoke and flash directly to their front. Rourke can see Hicks's hide position through his binoculars. To make it an even better shot, Hicks is backing his Humvee behind a small mound of trees and bushes. This will provide even more concealment for the TOW smoke and flash simulator back blast. No one from 1st TOW would be able to see the shot.

Petrone announces, "Take it."

Rourke can see the ATWESS simulator on the back of the TOW missile launcher flash. A couple of seconds later a flashing strobe on the front of a 1st TOW Humvee goes off. The radio monitoring the 1st TOW platoon internal freq starts broadcasting, "Contact! Contact! Contact front. We're taking direct." A few seconds later, "We're taking indirect fire!"

Rourke receives a radio call from Lt Foley. "Black 6, we're in contact with both direct and indirect. Vicinity 3552, over."

"Roger, can you determine who or what you've got?"

"Negative 6, we lost one, we're going to work the problem to see what we've got, break." Pause "This may take a while; we'll be working Catapult on this, over."

"Roger, good copy. Develop the situation. Keep me informed."

Lt Foley and his platoon just got punched and take a vehicle hit on the recon mission. Foley has some good experience and is a solid platoon leader that easily controls his men in tough situations. He knows the area recon mission is over and he knows that Rourke knows it's over. If Rourke had wanted him to withdraw he would have told him. Foley now wants 1st TOW to discover what's out there.

Foley knows he's got somebody in a defensive position to his front. It could be just a two TOW section or it could be a platoon. He wouldn't put it past Rourke to put two platoons against him.

Right now, his platoon goes to ground and is pulling security all around. Sergeant Winters, his Platoon Sergeant, is working the radio and getting a location and status report from the rest of the platoon. Rourke knows Foley will be studying his map, talking with his leaders and formulating a plan to find out who is out there and try like hell to get some big-time pay back… especially if it's Lt. Petrone.

After a long twenty minutes Rourke receives a call from Foley, "Black 6, this is Red 1, over."

Rourke replies, "This is 6, send it."

Black 6, we've been working the problem… we have an enemy platoon set in defensive positions from grid 325523 to grid 320526, over"

"Roger, what's your next COA, over?" Rourke wants to know what Foley is going to do next. As far as Rourke is concerned he has completed his mission. He found and identified an enemy platoon in his sector. Is Foley going to try to maneuver and fight through the enemy?

Foley sends his next message, Black 6, we're going to drop HE and WP and move to… from A83 right 2… up 5… Will notify and wait, over."

This makes Rourke smile. Foley knows he is in a bad position. Trying to maneuver on a well-hidden enemy without an overwhelming advantage is foolish. Foley is going to drop artillery high explosive and white phosphorus smoke on them, using that as a screen, he will fall back to a safe area and await further instructions. This mission is over.

This is going to take a while so Rourke tells Josh to load up, that he wants to look in on the other two platoons further to the north. He hasn't heard anything significant on the radio since they started their missions. They are given the same missions against each other.

Rourke sits back in his jeep, takes a big swig of water and reflects on how the Dragon Slayers are so lucky to have such a great local training area. It is 23,000 acres of partially wooded, partially open, hilly and remote land, and an ideal training area. Damn, they are lucky. Most National Guard units have just a couple of acres to practice some dismounted training.

When he initially took command, that first week he got his copy of the CSC yearly training schedule. He sat down with Rob, the First Sergeant and a couple of the senior NCO's and went over the schedule. He was shocked.

CSC made three trips to Fort Indiantown Gap each year for their "field" training and of course, their two weeks annual training. Rourke couldn't believe they only had three weekends to train out in the field and to make it worse, they had to drive five hours one way to the Gap just to get that. They spent half their time on the road in convoy. He asked his leadership why they didn't have a local training area. The consensus was by everyone, it is, what it is.

Rourke then asked what they did for training at the armory during the rest of the time. He got all kinds of answers. But mostly it was classroom individual soldier tasks. Rourke thought, no wonder he's got the highest AWOL and excused absent rate in the brigade. Rourke had to occasionally sit through some of that in his time. It was always terrible.

He joined the Army to be a soldier. That meant going out and fighting the bad guys and all the challenges that offers. He knew his young soldiers in the company wanted the same thing. Based on the conversation with the NCOs regarding their current poor training opportunities, he knew he'd be one of the AWOLs himself. This situation sucked! Rourke was not going to command a unit that sucks.

He is going to create a unit where all its members actually want and look forward to drill weekend. But to do that he has to get them out to the field. Hell, this is supposed to be a combat ready infantry company. Right now, they are infantry in name only. Getting a local training area was now the biggest priority for Rourke.

This actually is one of the reasons that Rourke and Swoon don't get along. After that meeting with his NCOs about the lack of training, Rourke went to the Battalion Training Officer, Captain Swoon, and asked him to help CSC find a local training area. The request was for training support, so Rourke thought the full-time training officer could take the lead in what Rourke believes is his most important obligation to his soldiers. Swoon, who has already solidified his dislike of Rourke, glowered at Rourke and said in a most unpleasant tone, "I don't do that sort of thing… you're the commander… that's your job."

Rourke just smiled and replied in the most sarcastic voice he could muster, "I'm so sorry, Henry, I didn't mean to put you out. Silly me, I thought being involved with providing the battalion soldiers… with the best possible training is sort of… you know… YOUR JOB!… Don't worry; I'll take care of it." He quickly made a right turn and marched out of Swoon's office.

Sergeant McCallister was sitting there in the outer office with the "smile of the cat that ate the canary". Rourke, shook his head, rolled his eyes and put them square on McCallister, smiled and said, "Gary, quit enjoying this."

McCallister's smile got bigger and he said. "Sir… It's hard not to."

Combat Support Company is in the town of Manchester which is in the center of Manchester County. Manchester County is a rural county with a lot of farms, coal mines, state game lands, a large state park with a beautiful lake, and small towns and villages.

The next day during lunch Rourke called Rob at the armory. "Rob, what kind of aviation assets does the Pennsylvania Guard have?"

Rob replied, "We have an Air Cav troop in Jefferson, that's south of Pittsburgh. Why, what's up, Sir?"

"I would like to see if I could get a bird to do an aerial recon of the county to find us a training area."

Rob, sounded a little confused. "Can you do that? I never heard of anyone asking for a chopper for something like that."

Rourke explained. "We had an Air Cav troop in my squadron. We used them all the time for all kinds of stuff. Hell, for a while we used a chopper to deliver chow from one armory to another during drill. Pilots need flight time in order to stay current. Having one fly me around the county on a recon should easily fit into one of their required missions."

"Well you need to talk with Top."

Rourke replied with a confused, "Top?"

Rob explained, "Just so happens Top is good friends and went to school with the State Aviation Officer, Colonel Jacobson... Yeah, he's from Manchester. He stops by once in a while to shoot the shit with Top. He's a good guy. Down to earth."

"All righty then! Call Top and see if he can arrange a flight with his good buddy the *State Aviation Officer!* No Shit... Don't worry about the day or the time... I'll make sure I can make it. Thanks Rob... This is going to work!"

About two weeks later Rourke met up with an inbound OH-6 Air Cav scout chopper at the Manchester Municipal Airport. After a full brief with the pilot, explaining the mission and then showing him on the topographic map, the flight pattern he wanted to fly, they took off.

What a great day to fly. No wind, sunny with blue sky as far as one could see. They spent all afternoon at about 1,200 ft looking down at all the large tracts of land that would meet the requirement of supporting CSC with land area and terrain features.

The pilot did a great job of assisting Rourke by going higher, lower or hovering so Rourke could identify on the map the exact piece of property. At the end of the day's flight, Rourke had identified four areas he believed would work. A trip to the county building to the Recorder of Deeds Office revealed the owners' names. He then stopped by the armory and gave the list to Rob and asked him to make some phone calls to try and make appointments with the land owners for him.

Three days later Rob called Rourke at home. "Hey, Sir, we're in luck. Three of the choices were a No Go right off the bat. They didn't even want to consider helping us. But the one that does is the R&P Coal Company. Sergeant Peters from 2nd TOW runs heavy equipment for them. I called Tony and he went up to the main office just to get a feeling on a request to use their land."

"It turns out the Project Manager for all of Western Pennsylvania was in the 2nd Infantry Division in Korea. He's a proud vet. He wants to talk to you next week. Could you make it Tuesday at 10:00?"

"Hell yes, I'll make it! I'll be in Class Bs."

"Sir, do you mind if Matthew and I both go along. If they give us a go… either me or Matthew will be dealing with them for all the times we'll be using it for drill."

"Roger that… make sure you're both in "B" also."

It was a go. A big time Go! Four weeks after the initial meeting there was a signing ceremony of the local land use agreement. It was held at a nearby restaurant between the Pennsylvania Army National Guard and the R&P Coal Company. The agreement was for the use of 23,000 acres of land located ten miles southwest of Manchester. Two of the four attending members of the Guard paid for the lunch. Colonel Francone and Captain Rourke were happy to pay for everybody's lunch, especially for the three representatives from R&P.

Papers drawn up by the R&P lawyers' and cleared and approved by the JAG office down at the Gap meant that the Dragon Slayers were going to the field every drill. It was a tremendous savings in time and money for the Guard. No more driving all the way to the Gap during precious drill time! And that's exactly what was printed in the local Manchester daily paper. Right under the picture of Colonel Francone and Captain Rourke beaming in their Class A uniforms presenting the Vice President, Project Manager and Land Management Officer a large bronze American Eagle atop a polished wooden pedestal with an engraved plate that states "The Pennsylvania Army National Guard proudly recognizes the vital support provided by R&P Coal Company to the readiness of America's Citizen Soldiers."

For two years CSC has been using the R&P local training area to good advantage. They do everything in the field. Rourke does most of his paperwork on the hood of his jeep. Company leadership meetings are held in the company Tactical Operation Center (TOC). Which consist of the First Sergeant's, Executive Officer's and Commander's Jeeps backing in toward each other with an old deuce and a half ton truck canvas tarp thrown up between them and a pole in the center to keep it up providing some protection from the elements.

But mostly the R & P area is a great place to have the platoons really get into training. Rourke divided the land into four different training areas. The platoons are usually assigned an area to get organized for training. Past training operations have been pitting platoon against platoon, but there are times that Rourke has them using the whole training area for company level operations.

All the company's leadership truly believes their soldiers work their asses off. The men are challenged to perform all their soldier tasks to Army standards. They enjoy the time in the 'Home Station Maneuver Box'. The company training is now as realistic as the training at any active Army post.

CSC morale is consistently high. This translates to a soldier being absent from drill as fairly non-existent. If somebody needs to miss a drill it is because they have to. More and more soldiers are searching for opportunities for additional schooling and training. Over half the scout platoon became Air Assault qualified. Most of the TOW Sergeants completed the TOW Master Gunners Course. Two of the TOW Platoon Leaders graduated from the Cavalry Scout Leaders Course at Fort Knox. Within two years Rourke has created a unit where his soldiers actually can't wait to come to drill.

Rourke is proud of his company and all the men in it. The NCOs really took the bull by the horns and readily accepted all the responsibility that Rourke gave them. It was tough on some of them the first eight months of Rourke's command. Four Sergeants left the company. They thought the grass would be greener someplace else. Someplace where the commander wouldn't hold them to such a high standard.

Rourke and the remaining NCOs were happy to see them go. To his credit, Rourke has learned that having a solid NCO corps is key to getting any and everything done correctly to Army standard. You have to trust them. Most every time they have to make a decision, it is the right one. He never second guesses them. Oh, there are times things don't go well, but the mistake is always an honest one. Rourke's attitude is, let's get it fixed and move on. We don't play the blame game here.

Rourke shows tremendous respect for his NCOs. He always asks their opinions about running company operations. He gets a hell of a lot of great ideas by asking. Implementing the ideas shows everyone that their opinions do matter.

Rourke's philosophy is the answer to any CSC problem is right there in the company. There is invariably somebody in the company that knows the answer. All you have to do is put your ego aside and ask. There are times he will ask the whole morning formation for an answer to a company problem. He listens to anyone that puts their hand up to offer a possible solution. With all the experience that the 126 men of his company have, many with active duty time, he always gets an answer that invariably helps solve the problem.

This is a great lesson for everyone. If the commander can ask for and accept an answer from a private, everyone should be able to. Rourke tells his leaders, "Everyone has value to our organization. It's your job to find it and use it."

Because he trusts his NCOs, Rourke gives them authority to run their elements. This is of course overseen by the First Sergeant. After Rourke arrived, discipline is never a big issue in the company. NCOs take care of all the small infractions. Rourke depends on their judgement to make the call. Minor discipline issues are handled within the platoons. Mostly with extra duty or assigning an unpleasant job to the soldier needing a little "corrective action".

Rourke tells them if you believe the infraction is important enough to bring to me, I will handle it. And it will probably be harsh. I'm the guy that takes away rank and pay. I'm not here to scold your soldiers. If they fuck up enough to see the commander, they're going to get punished.

Rourke never gets into or sticks his nose into what the Army calls "Sergeant's Business". If for example he and the First Sergeant are walking across the drill floor in the armory and a platoon sergeant, a section sergeant and Spec 4 are in an animated conversation, the First Sergeant might peel off to see if his expertise is needed. Rourke continues walking. It is "Sergeant's Business". And even then, if the Platoon Sergeant glances at Top and gives him the slight head shake or a look that conveys, "Not needed", Top will turn around and catch up with Rourke.

When Rourke was first commissioned an old sergeant told him that the NCOs are the company. They are the home town soldiers. These are the young studs that enlisted at eighteen and like being in the Guard and they stay for years. They grew up in their hometown Guard unit. They slowly moved up in the ranks to become the backbone of their units. The officers would only be around for a couple of years at most and they would be moving on from unit to unit so they could advance their careers. When Rourke analyzed and studied the Guard for a minute he realized 'old sarge' was right. If you want to make an impact on your unit work to make the NCO corps the best you can. That will be your legacy as a commander.

CHAPTER 12

"He who is not courageous enough to take risks will accomplish nothing in life." - Muhammad Ali.

Combat Support Company 2/220 Infantry
Manchester, PA.
Sunday, 23 April 1989
16:00 Hours
Final Formation

Rourke calls the First Sergeant to the front of the formation in order to take it. As they exchange salutes Rourke states, "The Company is yours, Top."

"Thank you, Sir." First Sergeant does an about face to address the company as Rourke makes a right turn and marches off the drill floor. First Sergeant then begins going through a list of items he wants to address to the troops about this drill and what he's anticipating for the next drill. Reminding them of tasks to be done and the times that need to be met. There is an announcement that he needs to see Sergeants Meyer and Hyde after the formation. Regular First Sergeant stuff for the final formation.

Rourke watching the entrance way to the drill floor sees an old friend standing with his arms crossed and a big smile across his face. Rourke extends his hand and greets him with a big smile of his own. "Bob, good to see you. You're looking good."

"Devlin, it's good to see you too. I guess you finally figured out how to run a formation."

"Not really. First Sergeant runs it. I just salute and act the part. Glad you could stop by. I was hoping you could help out."

"I don't know why… you more than anybody could have done this. You're just as good if not better than me."

"Yeah, but I think they get a little tired of me all the time. Getting a little instruction from a fresh face sometimes is better than an old one. Even though the information is the same."

"All the lieutenants in formation I see. And where do you want the class? I brought everyone a manual. I'll be using that to get them up to speed for your live fire in August."

"You'll be taking the lieutenants down to Pizza Hut just about 100 meters down the road from here. This is part of my ODP… Officer Development Program."

"No shit. You have your ODP at Pizza Hut?"

"Yep. Every Sunday after drill. It's a combination AAR for drill, what I want them to focus on, what they should be doing on their own time for self-development, how to handle different situations as a leader, and to do a little bitching and getting things off your chest. All with pizza and beer."

"OK, first who buys? Then who leads the way?"

"Don't worry, cheapskate, I'll buy when I get there. I've got to do a couple of regular after drill commander things before I can get down there. The XO, Lieutenant Bob Kiser, will lead the way."

Just then First Sergeant could be heard giving the final order to Fall Out. The formation quickly breaks up and all the lieutenants begin moving toward Rourke and Captain Robert (Bob) Wilmington, Field Artillery, 1/328 FA Battalion, who are still standing together at the entrance way. Once they all arrive, Rourke introduces Captain Wilmington to everyone and tells Lieutenant Kiser to lead the way to Pizza Hut and he will be there as soon as he can.

A few minutes later, six lieutenants and a captain walk through the Pizza Hut door. The good folks at Pizza Hut have already put together several tables in anticipation of the arrival of the Guard. The waitress is putting down napkins, silverware and glasses at the seven place settings as they come through the door. She asks, "Two pitchers of Miller Lite and two large pepperoni, right?" Everyone chimes in about the great service and assure she's right on the money with the order. All the lieutenants go to their self-imposed assigned seats leaving Captain Wilmington to take Rourke's seat at the head of the tables.

Wilmington looks down the table with a big grin and cracks, "Boy, you guys got this down to a system... a pretty good system."

Lt. Chuck Clegg, 2nd TOW, chimes in, "Yes, Sir, and the best part is we don't pay!"

Everyone laughs. Lt. Petrone explains that Captain Rourke buys the first round and the first two pizzas. After that everyone pitches in.

Wilmington tilts his head and asserts, "Right... a great tradition." lifting up his right hand and then exclaiming, "And... we're going to stay with it!" brings a laugh from everyone.

The waitress comes back with two pitchers of beer and sets them in the middle of the table. She announces the pizzas will arrive in a couple of minutes. Two of the closest lieutenants grab the pitchers and begin filling everyone's glasses as they pass them over. Lt. Jesse Gattas, Mortar Platoon, looks over at Wilmington and before taking his first sip of beer asks, "Hey, Sir, how do you know Captain Rourke?"

Wilmington, who starts to get out some cargo pocket size manuals he has in a small back pack that he carried from the armory, sits the pack back down on the floor. "Oh, I thought Devlin would have told you who I am and what I'm here for."

Lt. Foley speaks up, "Sir, Captain Rourke says our ODP today would be on Fire Support and maybe a little on calling for fire. He says you are a battalion Fire Support Officer for the armor battalion down in Johnstown. That you would be stopping by on your way home to help us out. And... he did add you never turn down free beer!"

Everyone again laughs. Wilmington with a big smile, crosses his arms, leans back in his chair and seems like he's getting ready to tell a significant story. "So, you want to know how I met your Captain Devlin J. Rourke. OK, listen up."

Wilmington leans forward putting his hands together with the fingers touching. He looks down the table glancing at the eager faces waiting for him to begin.

"Captain Rourke and I first met at Fort Sill, Oklahoma, at our Field Artillery Officer Basic Course... let's say... a couple of years back. We were in the same class."

Lt. Gattas asks with some wonder, "So it's true that he attended two resident officer basic courses?"

Wilmington nods his head, "Yep, he sure did. The only officer I've ever heard of attending two resident basic courses."

Everyone is looking at one another nodding their heads and stammering, "Wow, it's true."

Wilmington continues, "Let me tell you how it happened. Fill your glasses... I met Devlin on our first day at Sill. We reported into the school battery, which is the same thing as a company in the infantry, we just call them artillery batteries instead, goes back in history. Well it's the battery for all the basic course guys. Of course, the first day means a formation so they can put out all the information you need to get in-processed to the school and Fort Sill." Wilmington takes a swig of beer, takes a second to gather his thoughts and goes on.

"We're in this formation. There are about a hundred lieutenants in our class. We have this mass formation. I'm looking around just to see if I recognize anyone and I'm curious like everyone else. I see this guy in the back of the formation. He's standing out just a little more than the rest of us." Looking down the table Wilmington can see he's got everyone's attention. They're all leaning toward the head of the table taking in everything being said. "What makes him stand out is his uniform; his BDUs are worn and a little faded. The rest of us being newly commissioned from either OCS, West Point or ROTC, we have on brand new BDUs.

"So somewhere along the day we all get in a line for something. Probably to sign more papers, I can't remember. But anyhow Rourke ends up behind me. In the process of signing these papers I tell the guy on the other side of the table I'm from Penn State ROTC. So Rourke asks me where I live in Pennsylvania. I tell him Mercer County. He says he's from Bluffton.

"I look at his uniform. While everyone has brand new 2nd lieutenant gold bars on one side of the collar, Rourke has this faded light gold, more like yellow lieutenant's bar. And on the other collar he has the faded cavalry cross sabers. He's smiling, seems to be a pleasant guy, so I ask him what gives with the faded BDUs? I am guessing he is prior service enlisted.... But the faded gold bar meant he'd been commissioned for some time. This didn't make sense. Anyhow, I finish signing on the dotted line and Rourke finishes the papers so we step off to the side until the next item in the process.

"Rourke tells me he's a Cav guy from the Indiana Guard. He has moved to Indiana from Pennsylvania, for a woman of course. That the MTOE of his squadron changed from a Hotel Series to an up graded Juliet Series. That the Fire Support teams would no longer be assigned from the artillery but would now be organic to and be a member of the Cav Headquarters Troop.

"The squadron asks him if he wanted to become a Fire Support Officer after three years as a platoon leader. Rourke says sure... send me to school.... and they did. So, there he is standing in front of me at Fort Sill. I asked him how that worked.

"He explained that in the Guard each state gets its own funding for training. And that for everyone in the Guard going to a school the money comes out of the state's training budget. His state, Indiana, is willing to send him to artillery school even though he has already gone to armor officer basic. And... it didn't hurt that the state training officer, the guy with the funds, is the former Squadron Commander of Rourke's Cav Squadron. Apparently, the Indiana Cav gets whatever they want from the state headquarters training department. That's why Rourke's been to so many schools."

Wilmington stops to think, then continues, "Your commander has been to the Tank Commanders Course out at Gowen Field, Idaho, the Scout Commanders Course at Ft. Knox, Kentucky, the NBC Course at Knox... not to mention all the KPUP training he's been to."

Lt. Petrone asks, "What kind of student is Captain Rourke?"

Wilmington laughs out loud. "Oh, Devlin made a name for himself at Sill. Not in a bad way... just in Devlin's way. He is a pretty good student, but Devlin made an impression on the Artillery School." Everyone is giving Wilmington the 'well go on explain' look.

"Let me give you an example." Wilmington drains his glass and passes it down the table to be refilled from the pitcher.

"Artillery basic is primarily divided in two parts. One part is learning how to shoot the guns. Everything it takes to run an artillery battery. What goes on at the gun line, what goes on in the fire direction control center, all about the different types of ammo, just everything about the shooting end of artillery.

"The other part is what happens at the other end of the shooting. The impacting of rounds on the ground. That's the fire support end of it. In school it's required, in order to qualify, that you have to successfully complete six live fires, calls for fire, on the hill. That means going out to an observation post, an OP, on one of the hills that surround the Fort Sill impact area and trying to hit a piece of junk in the impact area. Now, I told you we had about a hundred guys in the class.... But the class is broken up into 25-man sections. I was in Section 3. Devlin was in Section 4, the married guys section. Devlin was going through a divorce at the time but was still officially married on the first day of basic." Wilmington chuckles, "Anyhow that leads to another interesting story for another time.

"So, each section has a Gunnery Officer, usually a Captain, in charge of training the lieutenants for fire support. One captain and 25 young eager brand-new lieutenants for each section. Devlin had a captain, I can't remember his name, let's call him... Hard Ass, for his gunnery officer. This is Hard Ass's first officer basic class he's assigned to teach at the school. He's a newbie instructor. Therefore, he wants to set the tone for his students. So, he's a hard ass... and a pain in the ass for everyone. Actually, all the Gunnery Officers are pretty much a bunch of dicks to all the lieutenants. They have an attitude that they're there to mold the newly commissioned young officers into artillery warriors. This really means they do it by being a bunch of dicks.

"It's eventually no surprise to anyone in the class and the faculty that Devlin is Cav and going through artillery basic. Captain Hard Ass puts a little more pressure on Devlin in class just to test him. In the classroom he'd write a gunnery problem on the front board and point to Devlin and ask what answer the Cav has for the problem. I wasn't in the class with him but everyone says Devlin stood up well.

"OK, back to calls for fire. The way it works is that the section would catch a bus at the BOQ in the morning and drive out to one of the OPs, meet up with their captain, and start the calls for fire.

"The captain would identify a target out in the impact area then have all 25 students identify it and transpose the location onto their maps. After everyone identified the target location, the captain would then select the lucky lieutenant to conduct a call for fire on that target. The procedure is to announce it by the captain saying 'Your Mission Lieutenant... Whoever.' It is a little dramatic, but it did make everyone pay attention, and put a little more pressure on the selected student. There is no posted roster or logical sequence by which students are to be selected. The theory being all the lieutenants needed to pay attention because you never know when your name was going to be called.

"Remember I told you, you had to have six calls for fire missions to complete this requirement. Because of the randomness of the selection of students, some students got selected more than others. This particular day Devlin is with his section up on the hill right beside my section with our instructor. Being up on the hill meant sitting in the grass on the hillside and watching your classmate calling in adjusting rounds, trying to get within 50 meters of the target in order to qualify as a hit on the target. The artillery impact area is essentially littered with old rusted junk tanks and armored personnel carriers as the targets.

"The atmosphere on the hill is pretty laid back. Between the calls we would lie around in the grass snacking on fruit or candy bars and drinking water from our canteens and bullshitting each other about sports, women or cars... same ole bullshit guys do everywhere.

"OK, this particular day on the hill, Devlin by this time, has already successfully called in four missions. His captain has called Devlin's number more than anybody else's. There might have been two or three guys that had just as many but not more. Most guys had just called two missions. Consequently, Devlin is pretty confident that he wouldn't be called again for a while. I mean the rest of the class needs to catch up, right?

"So... this is going to be "Picture Day" for Devlin. Devlin took his Cannon AE-1 camera with zoom lens... out to the hill instead of his binoculars... he did take his map. He takes pictures of everyone and everything on the hill. His classmates do a little posing, he took shots of rounds hitting the impact area... he is enjoying himself. Now, he isn't making a big deal about this… Just sitting in the grass taking pictures. Whenever the instructor called out the target location Devlin would follow along with the rest of his class. Nothing unusual here.

"But… Captain Hard Ass got wind of what Devlin was doing and noticed that Devlin didn't have his binoculars. So, the next mission, after the captain had identified the target and all the students had identified it on their maps… You guessed it. The captain announces. 'Your Mission Lieutenant… Cavalry.'

"Devlin looks up at the captain. Hard Ass is grinning like the "Grinch who stole Christmas" looking at Devlin like, '*I just busted you*'! What are you going to do now?

"Devlin could have panicked. But he didn't. He could have asked a fellow classmate to borrow his binos. But he didn't. He looks down at his map. Worked out the grid location. Looked back at the target to reconfirm and then called out the mission to Captain Hard Ass. The captain acts as the radio operator to send the call to the firing battery. 'Alpha 11 this is Bravo 22, adjust fire grid 563786, over.'

"So… Devlin is telling the artillery battery fire direction center, the FDC, he has a fire mission and he'll be adjusting the impacting rounds onto the target at the map grid he just gave. The next radio message he sends is, 'Request shot and splash, over.' This means he wants to know when the round has left the tube, the shot. The FDC will call over the radio. 'Shot, over.' And Devlin will reply with 'Shot, out.' and ten seconds before the round impacts the ground, the FDC will announce 'Splash, over.' And Devlin will announce 'Splash, out.' At that point you should be putting your bino's up to your eyes and looking for the impact of the round in the vicinity of the target.

"Now, in an adjust fire mission, according to the book, you get to make three adjustments before you ask for "Fire for Effect." Remember you adjust your rounds with only one of the guns at the battery. Once you've made all your adjustments and you think the next shot will hit within 50 meters of the target, that's when you say Fire For Effect. At that point all the guns, all six, will apply the same gun data from the adjusting gun, the direction and elevation to all the guns, and they will all fire on the target. That's the normal course of action, but here at school they only fire one round for the Effects rounds… saves money.

"So... Captain Hard Ass receives the radio call, 'Shot, over.' And Devlin replies, 'Shot, out.' and a minute later he announces 'Splash, over.' and Devlin replies, 'Splash, out.'

"Every one of Devlin's classmates is staring at Devlin. He lifts up his Cannon AE-1... with zoom lens, puts it to his eye and waits for the impact. Everybody is freakin' out. Rourke is using his camera to fire this mission. The round impacts short of the target. Devlin turns the barrel of the zoom lens like that's going to help.

"You see, inside Army bino's is a set of scales left and right and up and down. These help you determine range and distance. You need them to make add or drop range and the left and right adjustments from the impacted round... to the target. You can make adjustment with the naked eye... but you've got to be really good. The only thing the camera's zoom lens really does is magnify the impact. No help in adjusting. Devlin knows this... but it's... the self-confidence attitude he's displaying.

"Devlin sees the impact, studies his map, makes some computations in his head, and calls out his adjustments. 'All this is B22, direction, niner zero mils, right four hundred add six hundred, over.' Hard Ass relays the adjustments. Devlin is going to bracket the target. With these large corrections his next round should be over and to the right of the target. It just becomes a process of making the bracket smaller and smaller with the adjustments.

"A couple minutes later we get 'Shot, over.' Then a minute later we get 'Splash, over.' Devlin lifts up his AE-1, with zoom, to check out the impact location.

"By now the word has spread all over the hill, over to my section with me and my 24 classmates. It is like, 'Hey, No Shit... Rourke is using a camera to call for fire!' Devlin sees the impact, compares the location with his map, makes some more computations and calls out his next adjustment. 'All this is B22, left two hundred, drop four hundred, over.' Every lieutenant is on his feet including my section. The expectation or anticipation is sky high. Devlin remains sitting crossed legged with his map in his lap. He seems pretty cool and collected.

"Old Hard Ass, who doesn't appear to be very thrilled about the situation announces, 'Shot, over,' Devlin says, 'Shot, out.' We all wait. And wait and wait. Then it's, 'Splash, over.' Devlin says, 'Splash, out.' Everyone is intently staring in the impact area. The round hits. Short of the target, which is expected, and almost in line, meaning the left or right adjustment needs to be a minor one.

"Devlin has one more adjustment round before he calls for "Fire For Effect." Everyone is trying to figure out what the best adjustment should be in order to set up for the Effect round. The hill gets quiet; we're all waiting for Devlin's next adjustment to be called out.

"Devlin declares in this no bullshit command voice. 'All this is B22, right five zero add one five zero, Fire For Effect!' Now this is BOLD! The hill is stunned! What's he doing? He's got one more adjustment! He's blowing it! Shit, he's going to fail. Captain Hard Ass is smirking as he relays the call to the battery FDC. Everyone is talking. Bets are being placed. This is like... with no time left on the clock... and it's pouring down rain... and your kicker needs to make a 49-yard field goal to win the game... by one point.

"Then the call came from the FDC, 'Shot, over.' Devlin says, 'Shot, out.' The anticipation is almost unbearable! We wait and wait. Then, 'Splash, over.' Every single set of Binos went up to everyone's eyes. Devlin just stood up and watched.

Wilmington stopped and gravely surveys every lieutenant all sitting on the edge of their seats around the table. And then he breaks out in a huge smile. "He hit the target! I'm Not talking about getting in the 50-meter target range... I'm telling you it is STEEL ON STEEL! He hit the top of the Tank! He hit the Target. That's a one in a thousand shot with artillery. The bright orange, yellow, red flash is amazing. A normal round hitting the ground sounds like a Ka-boom. This is like a KA-RACK! He hit it!

"The hill is stunned, in shock for about ten seconds. And then all hell broke loose! Everyone is jumping up and down, guys were thrusting their fists in the air, yelling, 'Fucking A! Un-fucking-believable! Can you believe this... He HIT the Target.'

"Finally, after a couple of minutes everybody calmed down. Everyone is looking at your commander. Now the mission isn't over till the observer tells the battery it's over. Devlin turns and faces Captain Hard Ass and says, 'Target, cease fire, End of Mission.' Hard Ass is shaking his head in disbelief... but he's smiling.

"It is like Devlin, with that wild Call for Fire mission, told all those asshole Gunnery Captains, 'We're also officers in the United States Army… We got skills and abilities too! Show us some respect. Quit being Dicks.'

"That weekend Devlin never bought a drink. And he got shit faced drunk. The Cav had rescued the lieutenants. And for the remainder of our time at Sill, there was some easing off from the gunnery officers. They were still dicks… but not as big."

Another pitcher is ordered, and a medium pizza. Captain Rourke walks through the door. "Did I miss much? I should have warned you guys… Captain Wilmington is an Artillerist."

Everyone puts on quizzical looks and shrugs their shoulders as if to say, "What?"

Lt. Foley asks. "What's an artillery… ist?"

Rourke smiles and explains, "It's a fancy name they call themselves, for their real title of "Cannon Cocker". But it truly means he'll skate out of paying for anything. It's really an art form the way they slide out of a restaurant and leave the poor Infantry holding the bill. I've witnessed them doing it many times down at the home of the cheapskates they call Fort Sill."

Wilmington laughs. "This coming from the guy that represents the branch that steals your beer, sweet talks your girl behind your back… and makes love to your horse all night. The… Cavalry!"

Rourke chuckling, offers his hand. "Fuck you, Bob."

And Wilmington smiling, gladly shaking it. "Fuck you back, Devlin."

"Well, have you gotten anything done?" Rourke asks while pulling up a chair.

Wilmington replies. "Not really, just telling war stories to break the ice, and drinking some beer and eating a little pizza."

"OK, you want to get started? What have you got for us Bob?"

Wilmington reaches into his pack and starts to pull out a bunch of manuals. "Gentlemen, I have Field Manual 6-20-20, Fire Support at Battalion Task Force and Below. Take one and pass the rest around. These are for you to keep… and what the hell… you might as well read them too!"

For the next hour Captain Wilmington goes through the FM chapter by chapter selecting the parts that are most applicable to the Dragon Slayer platoon leaders. And it is a learning experience for all of them. They delve especially hard into Chapter 2, Fire Support Planning and Coordination at Company Level.

Rourke personally feels that the use of indirect fires, both mortars and artillery, are the most misunderstood and underutilized asset by the infantry on the battlefield. The infantry relies on the artillery to provide it with Forward Observers and Fire Support Planners to help them on the battlefield and complete the operations orders.

Because of Rourke's additional experience and knowledge in indirect fires he, more than most infantry and even armor officers, understands what the artillery and mortars can do and how important it is to apply those capabilities into your operations orders. Having an "outside expert" give you input into your plan isn't even close to developing the plan inside your own head with the same knowledge.

There really isn't much originality or "design" theory put into operations orders. Most of the ones Rourke sees are more cookie cutter Op orders with an addendum or extra paragraph for fire support added on to the plan. Almost like an afterthought. The Army realized this and tried to fix it by adding a sync matrix into the Military Decision Making Process (MDMP) used to develop the operations orders. But this is used by brigade and division staffs way more than a lowly captain down at the company level.

CHAPTER 13

"The way to grow any organization is to grow the people in that organization." – John Maxwell

Combat Support Company 2/220
Manchester, PA.
Friday, 19 May 1989
06:45 Hours

Rourke knocks on the door frame of his First Sergeant's office door. The door is wide open but Rourke wants to be polite and he needs Top's attention anyhow. First Sergeant Donald Johnson is leaning back in his chair with his feet up on his desk and is reading the latest Army Times. He glances around from behind the Times to see who is knocking on his door. The First Sergeant puts down the paper in the same instant he drops his feet to the floor. "What's up, Sir?"

Rourke points down at the cover of the Army Times. "Looks like the President is sending more troops to Panama. Does it say how many?"

"The article says 1,900 combat troops." Top replies as he folds the paper to expose the article for Rourke.

He reaches out and takes the paper from his First Sergeant. He carefully scans the article and the picture of soldiers loading on to Air Force C-130 Transports, "This place has been heating up for a while. Think we're headed for a confrontation? Do you think they'll call up any Guard units?"

Johnson crosses his arms, drops his head, peers over his glasses and gives Rourke the *'you got to be kidding'* look, "I'm not sure about a confrontation. This Noriega guy is getting really goofy. He's a dictator getting out of control. We've got a lot of people down there. Dependents and civilians, I mean. If he moves on them… then all bets are off. Do I think they'll call up the Guard… Nope!"

Rourke tilts his head, leans back against the door. "Why not? We're all one Army… Right!"

Johnson laughs, "Right now that's the Only game in town for the Army… They are Not going to invite us to come play with them."

Rourke tosses the paper back on the First Sergeants desk, "You're probably right. Anyhow I came to ask about lunch today… Is it MREs or hot meals from the cooks? Do we need to break training for lunch?"

Johnson stands up getting ready to go out to the first formation, "The platoon sergeants wanted to go with MREs and asked to have a good hot meal ready for tonight before night ops."

Rourke nods, turns to walk out the door, "Good plan."

Johnson cleared his throat in that *don't leave quite yet, we've got one more thing to talk about*, kind of throat clearing noise. Rourke turned back around tilts his head and inquires, "Yessss, something else?"

Johnson gives him a pained gaze, lowers his voice, "All is not happiness in the land of the Dragon Slayers… we have a few disgruntled Slayers. They don't like all the extra time that's required this year… They signed up for the standard one monthly drill weekend and two weeks of annual training… according to them that is."

Rourke leans back against the door frame, "How many and who?"

Johnson sits down on the corner of his desk, which puts him three feet from Rourke, "The biggest bitcher is Sgt. Carstead from the 2nd TOW Platoon… and then a couple of young troops throughout the company."

Rourke crosses his arms, drops his head and goes into some deep thought for a couple of minutes then asks, "You talk with anyone else about this?"

Johnson nods, "Well actually Sgt. Donnelly brought it to me a couple of days ago."

"So, you and Rob talked about this?"

Johnson nods again, "Yea, we talked about it… Rob says fuck him, get rid of him. He's never been a fan of Carstead."

"What do you say?"

Johnson thinks for a couple of seconds, "I've never been a fan of Carstead either. I don't necessarily say… fuck him… but it wouldn't bother me if he found greener pastures elsewhere."

"How much time does he have on his current enlistment?"

"Two more years… I checked. I also called a friend of mine over at the Army Reserve Center across town. They'd take him… if you sign a release from the Guard and give him a good NCO Evaluation Report.

Rourke clenches his jaw and shakes his head, "This either pisses me off … or disappoints me because not everyone wants or has the devotion most of our soldiers have. I haven't figured it out yet." Rourke pauses, "Tell Carstead I want him out and in the Reserves by next drill. I'll do the release and write a glowing evaluation by this Wednesday… Get word to the others… that if they find another home in another unit… I'll sign the release. But it's up to them. They may have to travel many, many miles to another unit and get slotted in a position way below their current grade and position. This is on them and knowing what I know about other units… and even our own… that's exactly what will happen. Nobody gives up a slot you've been saving for one of your good troops for some new guy transferring in." Rourke now grimaces, "Top, what the hell happened to all my Merry Men?"

"Not to worry… it's just a couple of knuckleheads."

Forty-five minutes later the Scouts, Mortars, and Headquarters section receive and are assigned their new Humvees in the motor pool. Like kids at a birthday party, the soldiers show much anticipation. Hey, getting new stuff is always fun. Though technically these Humvees aren't new. They are requisitioned from or appropriated from other Combat Support Companies and Quartermaster Companies in the 28th Division. The good news is that the Dragon Slayer's NCOs have the drivers identified and were tested and licensed this past month using the company's TOW Humvees.

Thanks to Sergeant Ron Mason, Company Mechanic, who is the official company vehicle tester and license issuer, came in on his own time and met with the drivers on their own time and got it done. The whole thing took five, four-hour days. Everyone was paid for their time, but for convenience sake in submitting for payroll, this testing all took place on one day during the week. It really helps having soldiers that believe in and support their Guard unit. Otherwise this whole process would have taken months to schedule in order to work with everyone's personal available time. Rourke and the First Sergeant agree that somehow Sergeant Mason will be taken care of down the road.

Both the Scouts and Mortars have their "new wheels" parked outside the armory. Soldiers are running back and forth into the armory and working on vehicle load plans for all the equipment that has to be arranged and packed for field use.

Rourke walks out of the armory and walks to the first Humvee in line. His best guess is that his driver Specialist Josh Tibbs has his new wheels parked as the first vehicle. There is nothing to load and Josh would have gotten his vehicle out of the motor pool first. Rourke opens the back door, throws his satchel in the back and then opens the front and slides in.

Rourke looks over at Josh, "Hey, needle dick, how do you like the new wheels?"

The relationship between a company commander and his driver is all based on what the commander wants. Rourke knows he will be spending a hell of a lot of time with just his driver. He was told a great driver is worth his weight in gold! The best advice he got about getting a driver is pick one that's smart, can apply common sense, and uses initiative to take care of issues before you even know it. Josh is that driver.

He is an engineering student at the local Manchester College pulling a 3.8 GPA. He is a good-looking kid, about 6' tall, 190 lbs, light brown hair, blue eyes. Rourke and Josh spend quite a lot of time talking about current events, sports, and going into deeper subjects whenever they seem to pop up. Josh always holds his own in all the conversations even if they are controversial. They have good conversations in that jeep.

Rourke could have established the relationship as being very formal. With Rourke as the "Captain" and Josh "The Specialist 4th Class" or Rourke could have had Josh recognize him as "The Commander" and Josh's position as merely "The Driver". But Rourke advanced the relationship of big brother toward his little brother. With mutual respect shown and practiced by both.

A big part of selecting a commander's driver is trust! That driver, in the course of sitting beside the commander for hours and days on end, is going to see and hear things that the rest of the 126-man company will never hear. Conversations between the First Sergeant, the XO, the NCO corps, the lieutenants, and conversations outside the company with members of the battalion and others. The commander has to trust that information would never leak out into the company. These past two years, Josh has heard and seen quite a lot. He knows just about as much about the company as Rourke. Even though his fellow soldiers try to pry information out of him Josh never betrays that trust.

Josh is not only a driver; he is Rourke's "Executive Assistant". There are four radio networks that Rourke wants to monitor. His own company command net, the mortar net, the battalion command net, and one of the selected platoon's net. He also bounces around on the battalion fire support net and the S-2 Intel net. Rourke does a lot of listening and tracking events on his map. Josh very quickly learned radio procedures and how Rourke keeps track of the battlefield. Josh is amazed at everything Rourke can track while both reacting to and directing his soldiers proactively.

In order to maintain radio contact with everybody it becomes Josh's responsibility to answer a radio call whenever Rourke has a conversation happening on another net. Josh always answers any incoming calls with Rourke's radio call sign, Black Six. Josh typically answers an incoming call with, "This is Black Six. Send your traffic." Everyone in the company recognizes Josh's voice and knows it is Josh and not Rourke. But they also know Josh is trusted to receive the information and that it will be passed to the commander as soon as possible.

There are times Rourke steps out of the jeep and is actually talking face to face with someone in the company or a battalion staff officer or the battalion commander himself and can't answer the radio call. There are many times Rourke is working a problem on one or even two nets and he has Josh answer the calls from a third net and tells Josh what to answer. After spending two years with Captain Rourke and knowing how Rourke tactically operates, Josh can handle just about any routine radio request by himself. This comes in handy during annual training when Rourke needs to take a quick twenty minute cat nap in the middle of the day. Rourke knows Josh will handle company radio calls and that if battalion wants him, Josh will wake him and provide a briefing on what they want. Rourke considers Josh worth all the gold in Fort Knox.

So, Josh glares at Rourke and gives him a disappointed *'I can't believe you asked me that question'* look.

Rourke is grinning even bigger and asks again, "Well… how about it needle dick… you like the new wheels?"

Josh averts his eyes to the front window, slowly shakes his head, looks back at Rourke and answers in a slow, deliberate and sarcastic voice, "Why it's just great to see you, Captain Rourke. And yes, I am very pleased with the Humvee. And… as far as dicks are concerned… Just two nights ago mine is standing straight up, hard as a US Steel 12-inch pipe… being straddled and slowly being worked… by a hard bodied 21-year-old, long blond hair, swim team co-ed while I held on to and cupped my hands around the most beautiful pair of 36C breasts." Josh still staring down Rourke, now smiles and asks, "When is the last time you had a pair of 21-year-old 36Cs in your hands?"

Rourke leans forward, feeling like someone just punched him in the stomach. He has this *'you really hurt me'* expression on his face. "Damn Josh… I tried to be funny. You… You are just down right Cruel! … My God…That's Painful!"

Rourke sits straight up in his seat, shows a slight trace of a smile. He knows Josh did an excellent job of countering his "needle dick" insult with one hell of an imaginative insult himself. You've got to respect that. And the co-ed blond swimmer story is probably true. "Let me say two things before we go. One… I believe I was 23 the last time. And Rookie… There is no more free pussy after college. Just keep it in mind."

"I've got one more year." Josh gloats then reaches for the switch to crank the engine.

Rourke reaches to grab his map on the back seat. "I know. Don't rub it in… It's not nice to us older folks. Now get us out to the company TOC area, please."

Local Training Area
R & P Coal Company Land
Company TOC location
Friday, 19 May 1989
09:20 Hours.

Rourke arrives at the company TOC location twenty minutes later. He wants to set up in a small open area. After all the platoons park their vehicles in the wood line surrounding the field, the demonstration area is about the size of a basketball court. He is going to once again use this space to present to the company a couple of new counter-recon techniques. This is going to be a walk-through training session much like a football or basketball coach walking his players through some new plays added to the playbook. Rourke will individually place soldiers on the field, have them move and demonstrate what should happen during the operation. This is always a great way to show and rehearse actions for everyone to understand.

Participation by everyone is high. Questions and answers are significant and meaningful. The exchange of ideas and concepts is productive and creates an atmosphere of positive learning. Helmets and web gear come off, rifles are slung around their backs, getting comfortable is important, they might be here awhile.

It is encouraged for anyone to raise their hand in order to add to the discussion. On many occasions a soldier with a different experience will add to and improve the technique or method being demonstrated. This is where Rourke believes the company leadership is at its best. There are no egos involved. Rourke's philosophy, that everyone has value and a leader's responsibility is to tap into it, is always borne out during these walk-throughs.

Rourke draws some diagrams on how he wants to position the platoon's sections during the counter-recon fight. Instead of drawing football's X's and O's, Rourke uses the army's standard symbols for the different elements in the company. But the process is the same. There are primary positions and secondary positions that cover engagement areas and arrows showing moves to additional locations after some hopefully predicable events. They are similar to the diagrams of football plays that show initial blocking assignments with arrows showing moves for everyone's individual assignment toward their execution of the play.

Rourke asks Josh to get on the company net and call in all the platoons to include the mortars. He wants everyone to understand the counter-recon missions that CSC will implement. In the meantime, Rourke finalizes the finer points for the walk-through.

In twenty minutes the last platoon pulls into the TOC area. After they back their Humvees into the shade of the woods, take off their gear, get out their notebooks, pull out their canteens, the company is ready.

"Alright everybody listen up." Rourke starts while striding to the center of the field. Everybody turns to observe and give their full attention to their company commander. Rourke begins, "Throughout military history, we've seen the most successful unit operations are those where the scouts have done a thorough job of informing the commander what he is up against... prior to the battle. Their recon ability is in direct proportion to their success. This provides the commander the opportunity to align his forces to best combat and defeat his enemy." Rourke slowly turns in a half circle to address all his soldiers. "That's why every unit has scouts... or Cav scouts, out front working hard to get that... that on the ground true picture of the enemy.

"Now that being true..." Rourke takes a second while searching for the right words, "therefore, a unit can also add to its success by eliminating the scouts from their opponent. The scouts doing the reconnaissance are always described as the eyes and ears of the commander. And that's true. Poke out his eyes, and blow out his hearing, then he is... in essence... deaf and blind. What that does is improve your chances on the battlefield." Rourke holds up his right hand in front of him with the thumbs up sign and asks. "Makes sense... right.... everybody agrees?" All the company soldiers are nodding their heads looking around to confirm everyone agrees.

"If you haven't heard yet... the Scout platoon will be with us for the whole rotation... We will be operating as the battalion's Cav Troop... With four maneuver platoons... and of course our four-deuce mortar platoon." Rourke once again takes the time to inspect all the way around the company to confirm everyone understands. "Gentlemen, our battalion commander wants us to blind the JRTC OPFOR for ALL of our operations!... I'm going to go over our counter-recon operations. We're going to be actively hunting down the OPFOR scouts and killing them… Before they can help their commander… I want to emphasize we are going to hunt down their scouts… and kill them!… Got It!" Everyone is getting pumped up and they all enjoy that.

"I want to go over two counter-recon methods we're going to use. The Army really doesn't have an official published doctrine on the "How To" execute counter-recon operations. If you've got anything to add or any questions… you already know to speak up. This will eventually be "The Dragon Slayer" way. No one leaves here not understanding what we're going to be doing… Right?

"When we go on the offense… we'll put together hunter-killer teams within the platoons. Everyone will then be given an area to "Go A Hunting" in. We'll go over those techniques first. Then in the defense we'll set up a two-line screen. The first line will be to identify OPFOR recon elements…then notify the killers on the second line for them to use quickly established engagement areas to finish off their scouts." Rourke continues to check for his soldiers to nod and acknowledge their understanding. "Alright give me the 1st TOW Platoon out here. I'm going to get them lined up as hunter-killers."

Rourke spends the next two hours doing walk-throughs with all the platoons on both methods of the Dragon Slayers Counter-recon missions. This includes a serious talk from everyone about the use of mortars and artillery fires. There are excellent questions and discussions on mounted and dismounted operations, on communications between elements, on coordination of movements and logistic support while way out front of the battalion. Finally, there are discussions and attempts at demonstrating what night-time operations will be like.

The rest of the long weekend is solely dedicated to all the platoons working on the counter-recon missions. Platoons rotate through the different training areas using different orientations. They do some force on force and finish with a company size counter-recon mission. Rourke feels good about the training. He is confident everyone understands the concepts and could successfully undertake the mission. Now they need time to practice, practice and practice some more.

Rourke knows that one of the key reasons he has such an outstanding, tactically proficient company are his lieutenants. Out in the field, they are good, really good. And he thanks the "draw and selection" from this year's lieutenants' draft.

The "Draft" is now a two-year-old procedure or practice that Colonel Francone started when he first arrived. Rourke believes that the colonel is one hell of a smart man. So, when he explained to the battalion that he wanted to oversee the growth and development of the battalion's lieutenants, Rourke knew it was going to be a good thing for the lieutenants and the battalion. The term "The Draft" is just a natural name that fit the process. The NFL has their draft. Now the battalion has their own.

It started on the last day of Rourke's first annual training with the battalion. It was the day before they were to convoy home from Fort Pickett, Virginia. The Battalion Commander, the battalion XO, the S-3 Plans and Operation Officer, and the five company commanders met in a small room inside the headquarters building.

Everyone arrived on time exactly at 15:00 hours. The colonel was standing right outside the door welcoming everyone with a smile and a handshake. No one knew why he called the meeting, so everyone had a quizzical look as they shook the colonel's hand.

LTC Francone laid out his goals and objectives for the program. As the colonel stated, "I want our lieutenants to grow both for their own military careers and to improve our battalion with experienced and knowledgeable junior officers. I've seen too many times a young lieutenant is wasted by staying in the same company doing the same job for years. When he finally moves up to captain he is limited in his view of what he can accomplish and should be accomplishing because he never had any other opportunities for varied experiences."

Francone went on explaining, "The battalion is truly a multifaceted organization that is designed and organized to put combat power where and when it is needed on the battlefield. We have a lot of assets and battlefield operating systems to synchronize and to utilize. Most lieutenants really don't have a clear picture of how we work. I want to change that. These young men need to get out and experience all of a battalion's slices. They need a taste of the challenges that other elements of the battalion go through. It's important to see how other leaders work and make decisions.

We're going to do ourselves and the battalion a big favor. We're going to develop our young lieutenants into top-notch leaders."

Wow! Everyone was blown away. And everyone was thinking, 'How are we going to do that?' Colonel Francone continued with, "This is how we're going to do it."

He paused and glanced around to ensure everyone had his full attention. "The rules are simple… First, no lieutenant will stay in the same position for more than two years. … Got that?… We want him to experience multiple jobs. No lieutenant will stay in the same company for more than three years… Got that? … We want to expose him to different leaders. I believe we have our lieutenants for approximately six years before they make captain. That means a possibility of at least three different jobs and three different companies." Francone smiled, "That means plenty of opportunities to make those young lieutenant mistakes." He pointed around the room. "And plenty of opportunities for you commanders to provide them excellent guidance."

What a great concept. Captain Young from Alpha Company spoke up, "This is great sir, but how do we make it work? I've got five lieutenants, and one of them lives in West Virginia. If we assign him to another company he might have to leave the battalion because of the driving distance. And by the way, he's my best lieutenant."

A thoughtful Francone nodded his head, "Yea, I know. We will have to consider each case and make the best decision we can. But I believe we can do better by our young leaders." Francone stood up, walked over to the tripod mounted paper stand, picked up a marker, "Major, please pass out the two pages listing the lieutenants with their currents assignments. And give me one."

Francone looked down at the sheets and ordered, "We're going to start with Alpha Company. We're going to go over each lieutenant… how long they've been in their current job and how long they've been in the company." Francone pointed to the A Company Commander, "Carson, your 1st Platoon Leader, Lawson, what have we got?" Carson pondered for a second. "Lawson's been a rifle platoon leader in the company for three years now."

Francone raised his hand in a wait a minute gesture. "OK, he definitely needs a new job and a new company." Francone questioned Carson, "Can he travel?"

Carson replied, "Yes, Sir. He lives in Armstrong County. He could make all the other companies."

Francone then asked, "How would you rate him as a platoon leader?"

At that point it dawned on Rourke that if he worked this right he could get rid of any duds or weak lieutenants and try to pick the better ones. This was good old horse trading in the best tradition of trying to get the better horse. Let the buyer beware. If you've got a horse that stands tall and looks great… you don't necessarily volunteer that he needs constant direction or supervision. Or that out in the field he couldn't find his ass with both hands and a flashlight! Commanders still need to have their loyalties with their own company. Surrounding yourself with the best people is a principle you shouldn't ignore.

Rourke had a dud lieutenant. He tried working with him. But he knew this guy would be better off in some sort of technical field where he didn't need to work around or lead troops. He really did suck.

The problem was he was only in the TOW platoon leader's position for two years and in the company for two years. That meant Francone could decide to just change his job by sending him to the scouts or heavy mortars and keeping him in the company. Rourke had to nonchalantly volunteer this dud for another job in another company without raising any suspicion from the other commanders.

Sometimes it's better to be lucky than good. During the course of moving the battalion's lieutenants around, swapping this guy for that one, the assistant S-3 for Air Operations position opened up. The current lieutenant was going to Charlie Company as a mortar platoon leader. Rourke then spoke up, "Hey I think I got the perfect guy for air ops. If he spent this next A.T. in the Three Shop, he would be ready to move to a rifle platoon leader's position after that. He'd have anti-armor from my company, battalion staff in Headquarters Company, and then line company experience."

Once again everyone peered around for agreement. Everyone nodded, mumbling that, yea that sounded good. Francone then flipped over another page and wrote Lieutenant Shift from CSC goes to Headquarters as the Assistant S-3 Air. On the outside Rourke was nodding and appearing to be the serious commander doing essential business. On the inside, Rourke was jumping up and down in exhilaration. He just got rid of one of the biggest dud lieutenants he ever knew, but to make it even sweeter is the S-3 Air worked directly for the Training Officer. And that would be that "Ass Hole Swoon". Fuck you, Swoon… I hope Shift drives you fuckin' crazy."

The trading and swapping went on for three hours. Everyone seemed pretty happy with the results. Everyone felt like they were helping the lieutenants and the battalion. Time would tell. After this next year all the commanders would realize they could end up with some pretty shitty lieutenants if they didn't stay on their toes. Rourke realized he did well this first time. He got rid of the dud, picked up what he considered a B plus and a solid grade A lieutenant.

The next draft got cut throat and Colonel Francone had to end up being the final decider on many of the swaps and trades. It was tough. It seemed all the commanders had done a little scouting of their own. They had been asking their NCOs what the word on the street was for some of the lieutenants. They came to the draft and already had it in their minds which ones were the ones to avoid. But in reality, it did help the lieutenants and it did help the battalion.

After all the moves were decided, Major Dye, the S-3, would write out the new assignments with a marker on the big tripod tablet, carry it outside the building and set it up for everyone to see.

Every lieutenant in the battalion hung around the outside of headquarters building waiting for the new postings on the tripod. After the major firmly set it up and walked away, the lieutenants ran to see how their immediate future had changed. They all studied the posting, finding out their new positions and those of their fellow lieutenants. Some walked away feeling as victors with raised fist. Some felt disappointed they didn't get what they believed was the right position. But they had to keep in mind there is next year; and next year they could be the victor.

CHAPTER 14

"Soldiers can sometimes make decisions that are smarter than the orders they've been given." - Orson Scott Card

R&P Local Training Area
Saturday, 24 June 1989
20:30 Hours

The radio comes alive. "Black 6, this is 5, over."

Rourke reaches over and picks up the hand set wondering what the XO wants. "Hey 5, this is 6, send it."

"Can we meet, over?"

Rourke thinks for a second. "Roger, what about the TOC location, over?"

"Roger that, I'm ten mikes out, over."

Rourke replies. "See you in ten, out."

Rourke hangs up the hand set, looks at Josh and asks, "Wonder what's up?"

Josh shrugs, "We'll know in ten minutes." Josh pulls the Humvee out from under a set of trees on a small hill overlooking training area 3. The mortars are practicing setting up a quick firing position. Josh pulls out and drives down a dirt trail no bigger than the Humvee. He makes a left turn onto another trail that leads uphill and is being washed out by the rain. Traction is getting difficult. The vehicle slides left and right up the mud road with Josh finding some solid parts to gain traction. It is a fight but one that Josh is slowly winning.

Rourke extends his left arm pressing his hand against the front dash to keep from getting tossed around while Josh manhandles the Humvee.

Rourke asks Josh, "How many days has it been raining now?"

Josh still fighting the steering wheel and concentrating on keeping them moving forward laments, "Six days!... Six solid days without any let up... A fuckin' miserable six days."

Eight minutes later Josh pulls into the company TOC location. He parks right in the middle of the small open field. This is not a tactical meeting. No sense pulling into the trees and searching for concealment. This is going to be a face to face meeting with the XO. Just as Josh stops, the XO's Humvee comes in from the opposite direction, pulls directly in and parks right beside Josh facing the opposite direction. As everyone starts to nod their acknowledgement to each other the First Sergeant's Humvee pulls in and parks on the other side of Josh.

Since it is going to be too awkward to sit in their Humvees and try to carry on a conversation by yelling out the windows, Rourke, the XO, and First Sergeant all get out in the drizzling rain and meet in the front of Rourke's Humvee.

First Sergeant Johnson speaks. "Heard you guys on the command net... Just wanted to crash the party and wanted to talk with you, Sir."

Rourke leaning back against the front of the Humvee nods at Johnson and banters, "Always welcome, Top, the more the merrier and you know misery loves company"

Rourke looks at Lieutenant Kiser and asks, "What's up Number One?"

Kiser seems to struggle for a moment, glances at Rourke, turns his hands up to catch some rain and contends, "I think we need to call it a day." Kiser looks down, shifts his weight from one side to another, and looks back up at Rourke. "I don't think we're getting any training value out of," Kiser spreading his arms out, glancing up at the sky, showing total frustration, "this shit."

Rourke crosses his arms and looks down to contemplate Bob's frank assessment.

First Sergeant Johnson speaks up, "Sir, that is exactly what I wanted to speak to you about. You've always said that we don't need to practice misery; the Army gives that to us naturally. This is misery."

Kiser steps forward closer to Rourke. "Think for a second, I know you want to squeeze every ounce of training time out of our drill weekends... But we're not getting anything accomplished here. Sir, everything is soaking wet... everything. You're soaking wet. I'm soaking wet. Everybody is soaking wet and Cold! We've been cold, soaking wet for over 32 hours now. Nobody has gotten any sleep. We went half the night last night with only a couple of hours sleep. Nobody can sleep in this shit. Most, if not all, of the drivers slept sitting up in the driver's seat. Everyone else tried to find a dry spot. There aren't any! Let's Endex, drive back into the armory and just have everybody crash on the drill floor. At least we'll be dry and warm."

Rourke stares at Bob, nods his acceptance of Bob's appraisal of the situation. He turns to Johnson, "Top?"

Johnson puts his hands on his hips, "The XO and I are in total agreement... Sir, I know you push these guys farther than any other commander. And I know you do it because you believe in them. You have more confidence in your men than any other commander. And they have proven they deserve your confidence. But right now, I believe it's time to call it a day."

Rourke puts his head down, this is critical decision time. He just had his two most trusted advisors, the two men that have been providing him with good solid advice and some damn good counsel, advise him to end the training day.

Rourke glances down at his watch, crosses his arms and apprises both of them, "Alright, it's 20:30 hours. I wanted to conduct a couple more field problems." Rourke pauses for a minute thinking some more. "Let's do the company level defensive counter-recon set up that we did yesterday. I just want everybody to roll into their positions, report in that they're set, call Endex, and have everybody head to the hardball by platoon and back to the armory. I'm thinking we should Endex before 22:00 and be on our way. Sound good?"

Both the XO and First Sergeant nod their approval and both agree it sounds good. First Sergeant says he's going to head out now for the armory to get everything ready and to have the cooks prepare plenty of hot soup and coffee for the company.

Rourke walks back to the passenger door, reaches in to grab the hand set and tells Josh to switch the radio to the company command net. Rourke depresses the push to talk button and speaks, "Guidons, Guidons, Guidons." This lets all his platoon leaders know this call is for all of them. "I need all elements to cease current operations and move to the TOC location for further instructions... break... Confirm, over."

Each lieutenant, in established sequence, reports they heard and would comply.

Rourke gets back on the radio. "This is an admin assembly with headlights on. Safety first, Black 6, out."

The last of the platoons roll into the TOCs small field just before 21:00 hours. Rourke calls all the platoon leaders over to his Humvee. Rourke surveys his guys, all standing there still in the drizzling rain, all in their green rubberized rain suits, with cold water running off their helmets and down their necks. Rourke feels proud of his lieutenants. Tough men. They've never complained. Rourke really does push them and challenge them to make smart decisions and to continue to think through all their options. Rourke is convinced they are becoming damn good leaders.

Just as they gather in a small circle, Lieutenant Foley from the 1st TOW, smiles and roars with just too much enthusiasm, "Man I can't believe I'm getting paid for this!"

2nd TOW's, Chuck Clegg chuckles, "Trevor, you're an idiot."

Foley continues, "You can't beat this! Hanging out with the guys! Outdoors like real men! We got free weapons. Driving around in four wheelers. Shit, man, there are guys that pay good money to do this kind of stuff! We get paid to do it!"

Mortar platoon leader, Jesse Gattas, gapes at Foley in mock disgust, "Trevor, you really are an idiot."

At this point Rourke interjects, "Alright listen up. One more mission. I want you to brief your guys on setting up in the defensive counter-recon mission we did yesterday afternoon." Looking around to ensure he has the full attention of everyone. "Yesterday we were pretty fresh and not so cold.

Tonight, all I want you to do is find your original position from yesterday. Just find your spots, call in when your platoon is set and then wait for the Endex call. At Endex, go with headlights on, driving out of the training area, hit the hardball and safely and I mean safely return, no hitting the hardball and flying up the road to the armory. Got it?"

All the lieutenants head toward their platoons to put out the word on the mission to let them know it is the last mission and everyone will be sleeping on the warm, dry, armory floor tonight.

Rourke's actual purpose is to exercise the lieutenants. He wants to have them find their assigned platoon locations in the dark. Rourke knows the soldiers will select the best individual position to fight from; he just wants his platoon leaders to find the right defensive sector to put the platoon in. This isn't intended to be much of a tactical deployment challenge. Just find your sector, get set in position, and then Endex.

At 21:21 hours, Rourke hears the worst radio call in his time in command. He recognizes Sergeant Callahan's voice in an urgent call, "Medic, Medic, Medic, real world, come to grid 378633 on Route Miller, just before the creek crossing, on the left side of the hill... Do you copy, over?"

"This is Medic, copy location. Can you send a Medevac nine-line message, over?"

"We're working one up now. Be advised we've got a rolled Humvee. We're trying to assess the status now, over."

Rourke is in disbelief for what seems like... forever. Rourke feels his heart pounding in his chest. He swivels his head over toward Josh. Josh immediately without looking back slaps the gear shift into drive and cries, "Got it." He knows exactly where the accident is and tears out across the field to hit the trail that will take him down to Route Miller.

Rourke reaches over and grabs the handset, "Red 1, this is Black 6, over." Red 1 is the call sign for the 1st TOW Platoon. They are the closest to the TOCs open field.

Lieutenant Foley immediately answers on the command net. "This is Red 1, over."

Rourke's mind is racing. *What do we need NOW?* "Red 1, get up to the TOC and establish a hasty Dust-off L.Z. Be prepared to bring in the Medevac. How copy, over?"

"This is Red 1, on the way."

Next Rourke calls the XO. "Black 5, this is 6, over."

"6, this is 5, send it."

"Are you close to the hardball, over?"

Executive Officer, Bob Kiser is monitoring the conversations over the command net and is anticipating Rourke's next request. The company leadership has talked several times in the past about what to do if they had a medical emergency out in the training area. The company has one guy qualified as a medic from active duty. Sergeant Roper is now a TOW Gunner with the 3rd TOW Platoon. But he is the go-to medic for simple medical incidents that pop up from time to time. The company has a standard issue medic bag which Roper keeps with him all the time.

The training area is too far from the armory to establish any kind of radio communication. What they need is a landline into the training area. They all agree that is never going to happen. The Guard isn't going to pay for a landline into the woods to be used maybe a couple times a year. So, they decide when needed, they would send somebody the two miles up the county road to the 24-hour convenience store to call for whatever help is required.

"Hey, roger, I'll be on the hardball in two mikes and on the phone in ten, over."

Rourke continues working the radio, acknowledging the XO's transmission and next asking for Lieutenant Clegg of the 2nd TOW Platoon. "Thank you, 5... break... White 1, over."

Clegg with an immediate reply, "This is White 1, over."

"White, get up to the hardball and be prepared to receive any type of ground ambulance, over."

"Roger, break, do you want me to be prepared to escort them down to the site, over?"

Rourke considers that for a second, "Roger, send your guys on a quick route recon down Miller to see if we had to, that could work, over."

Rourke goes back to the XO, "Black 5, 6, over."

"Roger, I copy, Red for Dust-off and White for ground transport. I'll be at the phone in five mikes, over."

Rourke replies. "Good copy, I'm coming up on the site now, will inform soon, out."

Josh turns a bend and is carefully driving up to the roll-over site still about 100 meters away. What a shitty night. Still raining, still cold, straining to see through the rain-glaring windshield with the wipers working hard keeping it clear, Rourke worries this could be bad.

The meeting with the XO and the First Sergeant rushes into Rourke's thoughts. They both recommended to end the training right then. He wanted one more mission. Plainly this was one too many. Guilt and his own disappointment in making the wrong decision is starting to creep into Rourke's mind. Rourke knew his wanting to push his guys further superseded a correct evaluation of the risk. This accident is his fault!

Rourke knows this is the Scout Platoon because he recognized Sergeant Callahan's voice on the initial call for the medic. There are three Humvees with their headlights on, surrounding and illuminating a Humvee up on its four wheels and appearing to be in reasonably good shape. Men in green rain suits are moving all around, on top of, and climbing inside the lit-up Humvee. Another Humvee is setting off ten meters to the right of the vehicle cluster with its flashers on. This is probably the 3rd TOW Humvee with the medic, Sergeant Roper.

Josh decides to pull up five meters behind Roper's Humvee, sort of out of the way, in case there needs to be more room for other vehicles. Rourke jumps out and runs over to the illuminated vehicle covered in mud and the focal point of all the action.

Rourke makes it inside the ring of lights and recognizes the Scout Platoon Leader, Mark Fugate, standing over a rain gear clad soldier sitting up on two 5-gallon jerry cans stacked together. Sergeant Roper is on his knees working on the soldier's legs.

Rourke knows that there are at least three men in each Humvee. He reaches out and grabs Fugate's arm. Fugate half turns to face Rourke. Rourke leans in to Fugate, asking as if he is afraid of the answer, "What's the situation?"

Fugate sees and hears the anxiety and even fear Rourke is feeling. This is just how Fugate felt not more than five minutes ago before he arrived at the location. Knowing exactly what Rourke wants to hear first Fugate explains in a slow and deliberate voice, "Sir, there were three in the vehicle. Maskell, sitting right here," Fugate points down to the soldier on the jerry cans, "is the only one that got hurt. Roper thinks it's a broken leg. The other two are in Sergeant Callahan's Humvee over there." Fugate points to a Humvee sitting about twenty meters farther back with its flashers on. "They're both a little shook up, maybe some bumps and bruises, but still OK."

Rourke feels like a 1,000-pound weight has just been lifted off him. The total look of relief that springs from Rourke's face makes Fugate smile. Rourke relaxes his neck letting his head fall down and stammers, "Holy fuck, thank God. My thoughts we're racing a thousand miles a second. What the fuck would we do with a death?"

Fugate agrees, "Sir, I'm sure when the call went out everyone in the company was wondering that same thing."

Rourke suddenly looks up at Fugate, "Shit… can you put out a net call that all we have is one soldier with a broken leg?" Rourke gazes down at Maskell, "That we'll transport to the hospital. And that everybody is to hold in place right now."

Fugate nods and reassures, "Good idea, will do." He turns and jogs out of the light toward his Humvee.

Rourke squats down next to Specialist Anthony Maskell and Roper. Maskell looks at Rourke and groans, "Hurts like hell, Sir." Maskell then assures Rourke, "I'll be alright, Sir, I'll certainly be ready in six weeks." Rourke's heart sails at this young soldier's loyalty and enthusiasm then his heart breaks that he was the root cause of his injury.

Rourke smiles at Maskell then turns his gaze to Roper, "What have we got?"

Sergeant Roper looks up at Rourke, "Without an X-ray, I'm only guessing it's a broken leg. I'm going to splint it and transport him to the hospital E.R. in my Humvee. Sound good, Sir?"

Rourke nods and assures, "I'll call your Platoon Leader and let him know what you're doing. And thanks."

Roper stands up, grabs hold of Maskell's arm. Rourke instinctively steps around Maskell, grabs his other arm and says, "Ready, lift." This gets Maskell up and on his good leg. Between them they walk Maskell to Roper's Humvee and put him in the back seat on the passenger side.

Maskell pulls himself to the door and apologizes to Rourke, "Hey, Sir, I'm sorry about this."

Rourke leans in putting his hand on Maskell's shoulder, "Hey, Tony, it's called training. You've just given us an opportunity to train for casualty evacuation at the JRTC."

Maskell smiles, "I'm just glad it isn't practice for graves registration."

Rourke laughs, "Me Too!"

Rourke walks back to the rolled Humvee. Sergeant Callahan who is standing off to the side supervising the work going on, hears someone walking through the muck coming up behind him, half turns, "Hey, Sir, I think we dodged a bullet on this one."

Rourke stops right beside Callahan, scans over the rolled Humvee, crosses his arms and asks, "How did this happen?"

Callahan points up the bank. "There's a small trail about twenty feet up that runs along the hillside. These guys used the same trail yesterday. What happened is because of the six days of rain running down this hill, that trail just became weaker and weaker, especially the edge. Maskell's crew was slowly driving down the trail when the whole right side collapsed. The bank is kind of steep right here. There is no time for the driver to attempt any type of recovery. The Humvee just did a quick dip to the right and the law of physics took over. They did a complete 360 slow motion roll down the bank. What slowed them down is the hillside is nothing but mud. Thick, deep mud. Once the right side hit the hill it sank in which kind of slowed the momentum. It continued to roll onto its roof and again sunk into the mud and then onto its other side and then finally rolling over and landing upright on its wheels."

Rourke considers this then asks, "Damage?"

"Well it is covered with mud, but what we've been able to make out is some damage to the front fenders, cracked fiberglass, the windshield is cracked pretty badly, but that can easily be replaced. The mirrors are gone. The electrical system seems to be alright, all the lights work; the engine won't start, probably because all the fluids in the engine just got turned upside down. I believe Sergeant Mason will have it up and running by tomorrow afternoon."

Rourke nods his head in acknowledgement. "What about vehicle recovery?"

"We have some tow straps for platoon self-recovery. Sergeant Koloski has driven towed Humvees before and Sergeant Barns has driven the towing vehicle before. We'll have the rest of the platoon front and back with flashers on. The last vehicle will be mine, with two strobes hooked on the back. We're only going to be going 35 all the way to the motor pool."

Rourke agrees, "Sounds good. The XO is still hanging by the phone. I'll call him and have him call the State Police and ask for an escort up the hardball."

"Will they do that for us?"

"Yeah, they help us whenever they can, besides we let them play ball in the armory every Wednesday night... for free."

Callahan turns to face Rourke. "Sir, I just want you to know this accident isn't anybody's fault."

Rourke puts up his hand to stop Callahan. "Doug, I completely understand the circumstances. Just one more question... Wasn't there anyone in the top turret when it started to roll?"

Callahan reaches up takes off his helmet, rubs his head, puts his helmet back on glues his eyes on Rourke, "Well, Sir, I know this is still technically a tactical movement... and somebody should have been up and manning the 60. But Specialist Maskell decided that based on the situation and the mission requirements he dismounted the 60, put it inside, shut and locked the turret cover, and was sitting on a sleeping bag in the center of the vehicle watching the driver when it rolled."

Rourke once again puts up his hand. "Doug, Tony Maskell made a decision based on considering all the factors of the current situation and executed that decision. And because he did... we just have one guy with a possible broken leg... instead of pulling a dead soldier out of the mud on that hillside."

Rourke stops and gathers his thoughts. "What Specialist 4th Class Anthony Maskell did was consider his men when making that decision. There was no need to have anybody manning a machine gun in the open turret in this rain when all they needed to do is move to their assigned position and call in they were set. It was a good decision. If Captain Devlin Rourke had used and applied the same judgment as Maskell, a little over an hour ago... we wouldn't be standing here in the rain right now with a rolled over Humvee."

There is a long minute where both men just stand there staring at the Humvee. Finally, Callahan interrupts the silence, "Sir, I'm going to get this recovery operation going. I'll see you back at the armory."

Rourke puts his hand on Callahan's shoulder. "Don't worry, your guys are good… this is on me. I'll see you back at the armory."

———————————

Army National Guard Armory
CSC 2/220 Infantry
Manchester, PA.
23:30 Hours.

First Lieutenant Bob Kiser walks through the door of the upstairs conference room carrying his ruck sack over one shoulder, feeling worn out. He still has his wet rain gear on. He walks over to where Rourke is sitting at the head of the conference table. Rourke is just reaching down to take off his green, wet-weather boots. Kiser drops down into the chair next to Rourke. Rourke looks over, smiles and asks, "What have you got, Number One?"

Kiser takes off his wet helmet and sets it on the floor beside the chair. "First, I'm beat. What a fucking night! The good news. The State Police did show up and helped out a lot. They sent two patrol cars. Free basketball pays off." He takes a couple of deep breaths, "We got the rolled Humvee into the motor pool. Examining it, I'm surprised, it really doesn't look bad. All the vehicles are in and parked. Everybody first stopped by and unloaded their stuff into the armory, so the vehicles and the motor pool are secure."

Rourke finishes taking off his boots, stands up to take off his rain gear. "I did a walk-through of the armory. We got soldiers everywhere. The scouts took all their stuff down to their platoon room. 1st TOW is up on the drill floor along with 2nd TOW, 3rd TOW is down in the locker room getting squared away. I'm not sure where the mortars are but I did see all the tubes in the arms room. So, they're around somewhere."

Kiser bends over to start taking off his over boots. "You see Top anywhere?"

"Last I saw him was about a half hour ago. He has all the Platoon Sergeants over in the corner of the drill floor and they are going over the "Armory Sleep Over" plan. He'll crash in his office. He has a cot stored behind his door."

Kiser walks over to the far end of the table in anticipation of helping Rourke pick up and move the table against the far wall to make room for the Lieutenants to roll out their sleeping bags in the middle of the floor. "You see the LTs?"

Rourke drapes his rain gear over a folding chair he has set up in the corner and walks back over to pick up his end of the table. "Yea, they're working the arms room, weapons accountability and sensitive item security in the platoon cages. I expect them up here within the next half hour. Ready, lift."

Kiser walks back over to the chair beside Rourke's, reaches into his ruck sack and pulls out two beers. "As I was going by the Platoon Sergeant's room, Sergeant Hyde from 3rd TOW called me in and tossed me these two. Told me to share with the Old Man. They're cold."

Rourke reaches over and accepts the offered can. "This is going to taste damn good. Hyde needs a promotion!" They both pop the tops, raise the cans and in unison, "To the Dragon Slayers." Both take a hardy drink.

Kiser leans in toward Rourke. "How much shit you going to get from battalion?"

Rourke takes a breath, looks up to reflect on his reply, "I'm not sure. I hope the colonel just gets pissed. Says I need to get my head out of my ass and quit making fucked up decisions. But I think this is going to depend on the pressure he gets from up above. If they consider it a regular training accident… I think I could get the "get your head out of your ass" talk. If someone, probably in maintenance, I'm thinking brigade or division, wants to make a big deal out of rolling a Humvee… and we really don't know how truly fucked up the vehicle is, in the light of day after we clean it up, it might be really fucked up. Then there might be some sort of inquiry with a "report of survey" type investigation. Then it's my ass."

Kiser nods then confides, "I told Sergeant Mason down at the motor pool not to talk with battalion maintenance until he hears from either me or you."

Rourke nods, "I'll make the call to battalion first thing in the morning, I'm thinking around 06:30 hours, I know they've got their TOC operations running 24 hours during drills. I don't want the Colonel hearing this from somebody other than me."

Kiser nods, finishes off his beer, squeezes the can and asks, "What time is chow?"

Rourke finishes taking off his soaking wet uniform, hangs it over another folding chair, "I really don't know... I set my watch alarm for 06:00. You want up then?"

Kiser smiles while trying to get into his sleeping bag. "Nah, fuck it. I set my alarm to 06:10. I'm sleeping in for once!"

CHAPTER 15

"The power of people — combined and focused on desirable behavior — can make any unit a winner. And in the infantry, what it takes is weapon system proficiency, physical conditioning, and focused leaders and soldiers." - Brigadier General James E. Shelton

Muir Army Air Field
Fort Indiantown Gap, PA.
Friday, 21 July 1989
13:20 Hours.

After just landing on the only runway, the Boeing CH-47 Chinook helicopter taxies over toward the main terminal. It gets 100 meters away and pulls onto a yellow painted parking spot on the tarmac and shuts down. Two deuce and a half trucks and two Humvees immediately pull within twenty meters of the rear of the chopper. The chopper's rear ramp comes down and 24 ruck sack, laden Dragon Slayers walk off and over to the vehicles. All three of the TOW platoons and the Scout platoon are represented by these men.

Mortar Platoon Leader, Lieutenant Jesse Gattas, gets out of the lead

Humvee and salutes Captain Devlin Rourke as he approaches the vehicle. "How was the flight, Sir?"

Rourke returns the salute then gives him a disinterested shrug. Rourke goes to the back of the Humvee and throws his ruck and sleeping bag into the back. "Jesse, if you like getting bounced around in a very loud aluminum can for 30 minutes I guess it's all right. I think the guys enjoy the ride. It's different and they get to tell everyone they rode down to the Gap in a "Shit Hook" for training. That's kind of cool to say." As Rourke gets into the front passenger seat he asks, "How's everything going down here?"

Gattas jumps into the rear seat behind the driver so that he and Rourke can see one another. "We got down here OK. The convoy didn't have any problems last night. We pulled in about 21:00 hours. We stayed at area 12 motor pool last night. Motor pool guys took care of us. We had pizza with them. I called the company with a closing report."

Rourke interjects, "Yea, we got it. I stayed at the armory last night. Everybody showed up on time. We got to the airport just as the bird was landing. Simple as walking from the parking lot onto the back ramp. The crew chief had us all buckled in, in about three minutes. They never shut down the engines. Then before you know it," Rourke puts up his hands, "here we are."

Gattas nods and leans forward to ensure Rourke can hear him over the Humvee engine as they pull away from the Chinook and head out the gate to the road. "This morning I got to Range Control and signed for three mortar points and OP 21 on the hill. It's the one you wanted because of its size. We can get everyone up there for briefings or AAR's. That's where we're headed now. I did sign out a building in case it starts to rain or you want us to get showers."

Rourke half turns to face Gattas, nods in agreement, "Good call on the building. But I don't really want to use it. You know, once we open it and use it, we have to clean it and get it inspected before we can clear post? And that has proven to be a real pain in the ass more than once. We're "good to go" on staying up at the OP overnight, right?"

"Not a problem. Range Control says it's ours all weekend and they'll have a guy up to clear us at 09:00 on Sunday morning. The three mortar points should be all cleared by 10:00, so I'm hoping to be on the road by 10:30 and hoping to be back at the armory by 15:30."

Rourke smiles, "I'm hoping you're right. Where are your guys right now?"

"They occupied MP 37 at 10:15. The tubes are set, FDC is up. Sergeant Hamilton is working on the ammo draw from the ammo point. The radios are all up, we're on freq 38:20. Calls for fire will be on 45:30 per the SOI."

He takes a second, looks back at Gattas, "Did you or Sergeant Hamilton get a count on the ammo draw?"

"Yes, Sir. Rob got me the paperwork from the S-4 and handed it to me before we took off from the armory. And yes, we did get double the original request." Gattas rubs his hands together and loudly exclaims, "We are going to blow some shit up this weekend!"

Rourke laughs. "Blowing shit up is good. I just hope while we're doing that, we actually hit the target." Rourke grabs the hand mike from the front of the radio and hands it to Gattas, "Let your guys know we want most of them up at the OP in twenty minutes for the drill weekend mission briefing. I want everyone that can be there, to be there."

The Fort Indiantown Gap airfield and cantonment area is at the foot of the Pennsylvania Appalachian Mountains in central Pennsylvania, 30 miles northeast of the capital, Harrisburg. The training area is basically in a large valley between the two large mountain ranges directly to the north of the cantonment area. Blue Mountain overlooks the cantonment area and the top ridge of Second Mountain is the northern boundary for the Gaps training area. At this point in the Appalachian Mountains the ranges run more east and west rather than north and south.

The impact area sits in the middle of the valley and runs along a small ridge that tracks up the center of the valley. Like all impact areas, you can spot large old rusted armored vehicles placed in the area as targets. Most of the vegetation around the targets has been blown away after many years of direct and indirect firing into the impact area.

There are two hardball, two-lane roads that run east and west the length of the training area. Ammo Road runs along the top of Blue Mountain. The other, McLean Road, runs in the valley along the foot of Blue Mountain. Most of the entrances to the live fire ranges are accessed from McLean Road. There are four main large gravel tank trails that also run east and west in the training area. Two run along the side of each mountain range. These are used exclusively by tactical vehicles.

The valley and the training area are accessible through a natural gap in Blue Mountain range. Obviously, this gap is named Indiantown Gap.

Twenty minutes later Rourke's mini convoy from the airfield pulls off Blue Mountain's first major tank trail onto the narrow dirt road that leads to OP 21. The observation post is located on the north side of the Blue Mountain range and looks down into approximately the middle of the impact area. The actual OP is on a small ridge that sticks out of the mountain. The top of the ridge is flat and well shaded. You can park about fifteen tactical vehicles in and around the top edge of the ridge. This leaves a large open shaded grove area in the middle where Rourke can assemble the men from the mortar platoon and the soon to be "call for fire observers" that came with Rourke on the CH-47 chopper.

Rourke and Gattas both jump out in the middle of the OP shady grove area. The convoy also stops and soldiers start pouring out of the trucks and into the open area. Lt. Gattas tells his driver to move off and start a parking area about 30 meters away. Rourke motions to the next Humvee and points at Lt. Gattas's Humvee and yells, "Follow him!"

Peering back at the trail entrance Rourke can see the Mortar Platoon Humvees arriving. Gattas runs at the first vehicle and points to the opposite side of the grove. He wants them to be able to move out and back to the mortar firing point after the briefing.

The six mortar platoon vehicles back into the trees and the men dismount. Two of the mortar crews pull out large coolers from their vehicles and carry them to the center of the grove. Sergeant Eric Sharp smiles and salutes, "Gentlemen, compliments of the mortar platoon. Some cold beverages... sorry it's not the good stuff, if you know what I mean."

Sergeant Jeremy Miller from the 1st TOW platoon exclaims, "Thank you, mortar guys... and don't try and bullshit us. We'll be down this evening to your firing position to get the "good stuff"."

Everybody has a smile and chuckles over the exchange. Rourke steps forward with a wide grin, "There will be NO good stuff this weekend." He searches the face of Sergeant Sharp, "Isn't that right, Dragon Slayers?"

Once again everybody chuckles, smiles and offers their comments to each other about the possibility of the mortar's having some "cold ones" down at their firing positions. Most agree they wouldn't put it past the mortars to try something like that.

Rourke's personal feelings about his mortars is based on his years of experience working with mortar platoons starting in the Cav. Mortar men are a different breed of soldier. Or maybe, Rourke sometimes thinks, the Army made them that way in mortar school. They are typically the company renegades. At most mortar firing points Rourke pulls into, he could count on seeing every soldier wearing a different combination of the uniform. There actually isn't an enforced standard uniform. Some guys would have their shirts and web gear on, some would just have their shirts on, some would have no shirts on, and some would have no shirts and just their web gear. It is always like that. The only way Rourke could make out the difference between a regular platoon and a well-disciplined platoon is in the well-disciplined platoon most of the mortar guys have their helmets on.

Rourke also sees most every mortar platoon seems to have two footlockers stashed away in the bottom of a truck or a mortar track. One is filled with food, either canned or packaged. This is due to the mortars being forgotten, missed or not being found by the chow Logpac. Mortars get screwed out of a lot of hot meals over time. It isn't intentional; they are just always isolated in some remote mortar firing point. Rourke has Josh keep a case of MREs hidden in their Humvee for the mortars. First Sergeant also keeps an MRE case for the mortars.

The other foot locker has a large stash of X-rated dirty magazines. Rourke never figured out why and he never asks about them. Rourke asked Josh one time why he believes the mortars always have a shit load of "men's magazines" at the firing point. "Well, Sir, I really don't see any of these guys reading through "Great Expectations or War and Peace." He never brings it up to the platoon leader or the platoon sergeant. Some things just need not be brought up. Don't open up a can of worms that doesn't need to be opened. Besides, if he ever has an urge to peek at a dirty magazine, he knows where to go.

When talking to the mortar guys, you also have to understand that in each sentence that is uttered, there has to be the word "fuck or fuckin' or at least some variation of fuck". So, when Rourke drives into a firing position, he is always met by a mortar guy and the conversation goes something like, "Hey, Sir, good to see you, welcome to the mortars. We got everything fuckin' squared away. We're laid in… right on the fuckin' numbers. The ammo is prepped, and ready to fuckin' drop." About that time the FDC Sergeant would glance up to see Rourke talking to one of the gun crews, so he would yell out to everyone, "Hey, everyone, I'm not telling you again, to put your fuckin' shirts and fuckin' web gear on!"

Rourke loves to visit his company mortars in particular. Josh has given the mortars the moniker, "The Wild Bunch", after a movie of the same name, a movie that highlighted a gang of misfits and rebels. Whenever Rourke wants to visit the mortars, all he says is, "The Wild Bunch."

Josh would smile, shake his head and usually say something like, "I wonder what we'll see this time?"

The Dragon Slayer mortars are the best in the battalion. This is a proven fact and everybody recognizes it. Rourke sent three of his guys, including the platoon leader, to the Infantry Mortar Leaders Course, down at Fort Benning. The other companies only sent one each. This is an 8-week course that has a reputation for graduating the highest caliber of mortar men.

Staff Sergeant Ryan Stutsman, the chief FDC, is a natural wiz on the new Mortar Ballistic Computer. Stutsman is the primary instructor used by the battalion to teach the other three company mortar FDCs how to use their newly issued mortar ballistic computers.

In his civilian job, Stutsman is an accountant and financial advisor. He loves numbers. And he makes a damn good living at it. He always drives an expensive car and lives in the wealthier part of Manchester. During Rourke's first year, Rourke asked him while at a firing point, "Why are you a Guardsman? You don't need the money."

Stutsman just smiled as he swept his hand around the firing point and beamed, "I can't get this sitting in an office with a shirt and tie on." Rourke laughed and knew exactly what he meant.

After the mortarmen sit the coolers down in the middle of the group, Rourke tells everyone to have a seat, take off their helmets and get one of the cold beverages.

"I hope I have everyone's attention. I need to go over what I want to get accomplished this drill." Rourke turns in a small circle to wave everyone from the back side of the group to gather together to his front. Now he is facing a group of 50 soldiers, 24 of whom are his Platoon Leaders, a couple of Staff Sergeants, a bunch of Buck Sergeants and a few Spec 4s who are the observers that will be making the calls for fire.

Rourke wants to take advantage of this opportunity. Because of the JRTC mission, he now has twice as much ammo as a normal live fire weekend drill. He is going to use his mortar's live fire to train his guys how to call for fire. He chose the lieutenants because they absolutely need the knowledge to continue their tactical development.

The use of indirect fire is paramount for success on the battlefield. Rourke wants the young sergeants to learn this critical skill now. They are the future trainers for their platoons later on in their careers.

Within a regular infantry rifle company, there is assigned an artillery forward observer (FO) team, usually a two-man team for each platoon and a four-man team for the company headquarters. Even though it's considered a "common soldier skill" most infantrymen really never have a chance to call in live rounds into the impact area at real targets.

There are never any artillery FO's assigned to the Combat Support Companies. This is okay with Rourke. He wants to teach his guys the fine art of putting indirect fires onto the target. Rourke considers it an art. Selecting types of rounds, types of fuses, methods of engagement, mixing ammo types, and many more factors into a call for fire is like an artist working on a canvas.

Rourke has all the ingredients he needs, a high-performance mortar platoon that understands and can work every aspect of the ammo, fuses and mortar tubes, an FDC that can work wonders with the computer, and now a whole bunch of extra ammo!

"All right, is everybody good?" Rourke glances down at his notes for a second then looks back up, "The mission is for every one of the observers to properly call in at least two missions. One daytime, the other for illumination and High Explosive, HE for night."

Rourke turns and faces a little to the right to see the mortar crews, "For the mortars, all your fire missions will be close support fires. To maximize our use of fires, you'll be firing with two, 2-gun sections. We can get twice as many missions that way. This means running two FDCs.

This is no problem. We have Sergeant Puterka and Sergeant Stutsman both working the computers." Rourke can see everyone nodding their heads in agreement, "There won't be any moving of the mortars tonight. We won't move them till tomorrow afternoon. I really believe the focus should be on getting our observers trained on rapidly working up their calls for fire and then getting their calls into the FDC."

"Sergeants Sharp and Massie won't be moving their sections or occupying the next mortar firing point till we're all satisfied our observers are squared away." Rourke looks at both section sergeants and asks, "You got that, Eric and you, John?"

Sergeant Sharp replies, "Yes, Sir, John and I will be ready to move. We already have a plan worked out with Lt. Gattas and the platoon on moving the ammo and the tubes. We're going to run it as a deliberate occupation mission."

Rourke nods, "Good, any problems get the word out obviously to your LT and Platoon Sergeant Hamilton, and get word up here to us on the OP. Just keep us informed. Like everyone else I hate sitting around wondering what's going on. Got that?"

Both Sharp and Massie nod, "We got it, Sir."

Rourke continues talking to everyone, "Now up here on the OP we'll be learning how to call for fire. But I want at some time this weekend to be able to send some guys from up here, down to the mortar firing point to observe and participate in firing our heavy mortars." He looks at the mortar platoon, "I want them to understand the process of getting rounds down range. It's important they understand the teamwork and coordination it takes for indirect fires to work." Rourke orders, "Just don't have them drop one round and consider that good enough… but understand that everyone should drop at least one round to give them the real-life experience of holding a 22-pound high explosive mortar round about four feet in the air for a couple of seconds before it launches back out the tube at 100 miles an hour."

He gives the mortars a devilish smile, "Please be careful with the TOW guys. I hope no one shits their pants trying to hoist that live round up to the top of the tube! And please go over the procedures for a "hung round"." He looks over at the observers to explain, "A hung round is when you let go of the high explosive round at the top of the tube. You hear it slide down the tube… and then… Nothing happens. There's now a high explosive round… with its propellant… sitting at the bottom of the tube… usually a hot tube. It kind of gets the heart pumping." The observers all glance around at each other showing some uncomfortable looks. The mortar platoon members all chuckle at Rourke's remarks. They love that Rourke truly understands and appreciates their challenges, hard work, and dangers at the firing point.

Rourke tells the mortars they're free to go and to get up on the fire net when they're ready to receive calls for fire. He calls over to Mortar Platoon Sergeant Hamilton, "Hey, Gordon, make sure we control the flow of observers down to the firing point. I don't want to overwhelm the firing point. Work with the guys up here to coordinate the flow."

Sergeant Hamilton nods with confidence and answers, "We got it, Sir."

Rourke turns back to the Observers and looks to Lieutenant Foley, "LT, you got your team ready to go?"

Foley walks up to the front of the group, squares up to Rourke, salutes and teases, "Yes, Sir, not to worry, the Warriors of 1st TOW Platoon have this, Sir." Foley then breaks into a big grin. The rest of the group lets out some good-hearted banter and razzes Foley for a minute. Foley puts up his hands to quiet down the crowd. "Now that I have your attention, let me give you guys a briefing on how this, the observer training, is going to be run. I'm the OIC for this mission."

He points to two men off to his right, "Sergeant Eikenberry and Sergeant Robertson come on up. These are your primary trainers. Both have vast experience in calling for fires during their careers. I'll brief you on the operation up here, what you're going to do, and where you're going to go, chow plan, getting down to the firing point… even where you're going to piss. They'll brief you on how they want you to call for fire. They've got hand outs and they're going to set up a sand table over by the edge of the OP. They brief you after me."

Rourke is pleased with Foley's plan for this weekend. He assigned the Call for Fire Mission to Foley two months ago. The back brief he got last month from Foley was really impressive. Rourke has only made a couple of suggestions for Foley to consider putting in his plan. Obviously, he has used some references and training manuals to put together a solid plan in a short period of time. Using his two TOW section sergeants as the instructors is right in line with the principle of war, "Unity of Command". These are his guys, responsible to him, not some committee that would do a half-assed job because nobody is in charge.

After the briefings, the observers split into two groups and move over to the edge of the hill. There are two small sets of aluminum bleachers that Sergeants Eikenberry and Robertson have the groups pick up and move closer to the edge. Then they have each group scratch out a sand table in front of the bleachers. Using a couple of entrenching tools and some plastic toy tanks they brought they are able to make a primitive replica of the impact area. PRC-77 manpack radios are set up at the end of the bleachers with the handset clipped onto the straps. All observers are required to use the radio and call their own calls for fire. It is important they get used to talking with the FDC by themselves.

Both sergeants do an excellent job of describing all aspects and parts of requesting fire. It is obvious they studied Field Manual, FM 6-30, Observe Fires, intensely the last two months. Their hand-outs include calls for smoke, illumination, and high explosive. They decided to focus on the two most important fire missions: Adjust Fire Missions and Immediate Suppression Missions. After everyone gets the actual call for fire radio procedures down, they will move on to Effects of Indirect Fires. This is asking for specific types of rounds and different fuse settings to really put a hurt on the enemy.

Rourke wants the lieutenants to make their calls first. This is to put a little pressure on them to do well and set an example for the rest of the men. This also means they will finish first so Rourke can take them aside and work on indirect fire planning. He especially wants to get into Quick Fire Planning. He knows he will not get an artillery Fire Support Team to help him with planning fires for the company. He knows that because his platoons will possibly be all over the battalion's sector that it will be impossible for him to do a complete company plan. Therefore, he has to rely on his Platoon Leaders to come up with their own plans that Rourke can consolidate and submit to the Battalion Fire Support Officer, so he can get it to the mortars and the artillery before any operation.

Lieutenant Foley makes the first call and the first round goes down range at 16:10hrs. Lieutenant Clegg calls for his fire mission from the other set of bleachers three minutes later. Because the missions are so close together both groups can observe the rounds hitting the impact area minutes apart. This makes for a natural competitive setting. Everyone gets into the spirit. It is platoon representative against platoon representative or even bleacher against bleacher. Who can hit their target in the least amount of adjusting rounds and who can call in to the FDC in the quickest time. This makes for some great training intensity. Everyone stays focused and in the game. Sergeants Eikenberry and Robertson do a fantastic job of skillfully pointing out mistakes as a way of having everyone learn.

After the four lieutenants finish their calls for fire, Rourke has them move back off the OP and in toward the parked vehicles. They pick a shady spot, sit down and pull out their "FM 6-20-20 Fire Support at Battalion Task Force and Below" manual. Rourke reminds them of the ODP class given to them by Captain Wilmington. They go quickly through the manual hitting the highlights. Rourke has them open to chapter 2, 'Planning'.

Rourke begins, "Because of the nature of our mission and the way we will conduct our operations… You guys really have to have your shit together. You'll be working independently from the company and out there on your own. You'll have your weapons and whatever indirect fires you can get. As an old Cav platoon leader, I will tell you that indirect fires should always be used first. As soon as you squeeze a trigger of a rifle to put fire on the bad guys, they know immediately where you are. Now you're in a fight! Don't get into a fight until you have all the advantages. Use your indirect. Let steel rain down from the sky first. Create confusion within the enemy ranks first." Rourke glances all around turning up his hands with a gesture that asks, "Am I right?"

Lieutenant Petrone from 3rd TOW asks, "Is calling for an adjust fire mission going to be fast enough to put a hurting on the OPFOR? Especially before they find us?"

Rourke observes Petrone, "Good question. The answer is sometimes yes and most times no!" He let that sink in, "Good and I mean good fire planning is going to be key to our success. You guys have to plan your fires way before the OPFOR gets there. Which means you need to plan targets on likely enemy avenues of approach and on locations critical to our security. You should be establishing engagement areas to kill the OPFOR. Most of these will be initially by map recon. And then follow up with putting your guys on the location to cover it."

He looks at everyone to ensure they're getting it. "Most likely I'll ask you to pick three targets to provide for responsive and effective fire support. Our mortars and the artillery will enter those target locations into their computers. The data will be already computed for the guns, making it a hell of a lot quicker to fire on the targets. That's twelve targets from you guys and I'll most likely pick three for the company. In the big scheme of things that's a lot of targets for a company. But I believe we can get those approved for our missions."

Pointing to his map, "Another smart thing to do is keep a list of your own preplanned targets in your map case. What I mean is to pick an additional target and not submit it for the fire plan but write down the grid on your map so you don't have to figure it out in the heat of battle. Call it an immediate suppression mission. Got it?"

Rourke continues, "I'm pretty sure our company will have priority of fires and I'll select the platoon that will have priority within the company. That all depends on the missions the battalion gives us... But with the focus on counter-recon we should start out having priority most of the time."

Rourke reaches into his satchel and pulls out some operations orders to be used as training for the fire planning, "I put together these fill in the blank operations orders so you guys can practice fire planning. This first one is a defensive counter-recon mission. Using your current Gap maps and the op order, give me a quick-fire plan. You guys have twenty minutes. Then you'll brief the group on your plan." Rourke smiles, "Then the rest of us will tear it apart."

Everyone chuckles and Lt. Petrone taunts, "Yea, good old Army training. You get extra points for embarrassing your fellow platoon leaders!"

In two hours time Rourke is pleasantly surprised at the progression of the fire planning training. All the lieutenants really put forth a great effort to understand and practice the principles of indirect fire planning. They go through two different missions. The discussions that follow each briefing are insightful and add to everyone's knowledge. It is obvious that the lieutenants studied on their own since their ODP with Captain

Wilmington at Pizza Hut. After the final briefing and discussion, he feels extremely confident in his lieutenants and knows they are now ready.

At 19:00 hours Rourke calls for an end of the fire missions. He asks the observers and Sergeant Hamilton to have some of the mortar crews get up to the OP for an AAR. After everyone congregates in the shady grove, Rourke steps in front of the group to congratulate them on doing a great job so far. He then turns the AAR over to Lt. Foley.

Foley jumps up and strides over to the middle of the group and asks, "Did everyone get a chance to call for a mission?" Everyone nods. "Did everyone get a chance to rotate down to the mortar point?" Everyone again nods. "Did everyone get a chance to break into their delicious MRE's for evening chow?" a lot of groans and comments about what soldiers refer to as 'Meals Rejected by Ethiopians'. Foley continues by pointing to the back of the grove, "The sleep area is behind the vehicles. It's roped off by engineer tape. No moving vehicles tonight. We don't need to have anyone run over."

Foley calls over to Sergeant Hamilton, "Sergeant Hamilton can you give us a briefing on the learning ability of our observers to becoming mortarmen?"

Hamilton standing off to the side of the group takes a couple of steps forward. Hamilton reports, "Most guys were able to drop at least two rounds. Then they rotated over to the ammo and got to set some fuses, hump some rounds and then over to the FDC to watch the FDCs do their work. I'm pretty sure they all got an appreciation of what we do… all day… in the hot sun." Hamilton, reaches up, scratches his head, "I did ask if anybody wanted to transfer over to the mortars… Surprisingly nobody took me up on it."

All the observers start to mumble out loud about "not in this life time… they got my respect… that shit isn't easy… I'll stay with TOWs."

Sergeants Eikenberry and Robertson both go systematically into their portion of the AAR. They ask some probing questions of the observers to ensure everyone feels confident in the basics of calling for fire. Everyone agrees they could now confidently call in a fire mission and hit the target. Tomorrow will be some fine tuning and getting fancy with mixing rounds and getting different effects on the target. A big part of tomorrow is going to be instruction on the use of smoke rounds. The artillery considers this the thinking man's ammunition. And there is a good reason for that. Tomorrow Rourke will be leading the class on using smoke on the battlefield. Smoke can be your best friend or your worst enemy if you screw it up. Having your own smoke screen blow back into your position so that you can't see your enemy could be deadly to your own men.

After the AAR, the company gets ready for night time illumination missions. Once again Eikenberry and Robertson will be teaching the basics of lighting up the target and if they have any time left they will be putting HE on the lit-up target.

Rourke feels really good about the training so far. They make excellent use of the time they have in the training area. The instruction by Eikenberry and Robertson is excellent. Foley's rotation plan is running smoothly. No problems down at the mortar point. Most of the observers are able to get an adjust fire mission called. It appears it will be even better tomorrow. They have all day Saturday and most of Saturday night.

Tomorrow night Rourke is planning an indirect fire demonstration by combining illumination, white phosphorus smoke and HE in a show of what their very own Dragon Slayer's heavy mortars can do to a target within minutes. He likens this to a fireworks grand finale. This will give the Wild Bunch a chance to do a little showing off. Rourke feels they deserve it. Rourke asks Sergeant Hamilton to bring up the two youngest mortar guys to watch the demonstration from the OP. It is paramount these youngsters understand that in the great scheme of the battlefield, how important their platoon is. And a great way to end training on a high note.

Sunday morning, they will clean up the OP and the Mortar Firing Points. The newly and highly trained observers will be trucked back to the air field to catch the CH-47 chopper and fly back to Manchester. The Mortar platoon will finish up turning in whatever they need to turn in and will be convoying back to Manchester by 10:30 hours. When Rourke gets into his sleeping bag at midnight he is feeling pretty damn good.

Fort Indiantown Gap
Mortar Training
Saturday, 22 July 1989

Saturday starts out great. The observers are up early and eager to start learning more calls for fire stuff. They are pumped! The mortar platoon is also up early and ready to put steel on target. Radio checks are done. New frequencies are dialed in. No problems! First rounds go down range at 08:20 hrs. The lieutenants are put back into the call for fire rotation. So of course, the competition starts between the lieutenants, their men, and the other platoons.

At 11:40 Rourke who is standing off to the side of one of the bleachers watches his guys having a good time calling for fire and most importantly "learning" this critical skill. Sergeant Eikenberry holding up a radio handset calls over to Rourke. "Hey, Sir, Lt. Gattas wants to talk to you."

Rourke walks over to Eikenberry, takes the handset and says, "This is 6, send your traffic, over."

"Black 6, this is Catapult 1. This message is in the clear... break... Range Control just drove into the firing point and says our First Sergeant called them to deliver a message, break... We need to get PFC Tommy Elmore back home as soon as possible, break... His family in a car accident, break... Call back on his departure, over."

Rourke replies, "Roger, got the message, break... you have all the wheel assets, you'll have to pull one off mission, break... with a driver to get Elmore back home, over.

Gattas replies, "Roger that, I've got enough to continue to cover all our requirements, over."

Rourke, after thinking for a quick second, "Catapult, put Elmore and a driver in one Humvee and drive it up here to the OP. I want to put a Sergeant in with them for the drive back, break... I want you to bring your vehicle up here to escort them back down to Range Control, break... so Elmore can call home to let them know he's on the way, break... and for you to call Top and let him know their departure, over."

Gattas replies, "Roger, on the way, see you in ten mikes, over."

"Roger, I'll have your sergeant ready, out."

Rourke turns to Eikenberry to ask, "Ben, which one of our sergeants is pretty much squared away on calling for fire?"

Eikenberry thinks for a couple of seconds, "I'd say Gabriel Barnes pretty much has this down. He called in some great illume last night and his HE rounds are quick and on target."

Rourke looks up into the bleachers and spots Sergeant Barnes sitting on the back row and yells out, "Gabe, I need to speak to you."

Barnes stands up and weaves his way down the bleachers to Rourke, jumps off the last bleacher bench and asks, "What's up, Sir?"

Rourke reaches out and puts his hand on Barnes' shoulder to explain, "Young PFC Elmore from the mortars needs to get back home. Top called to let us know Elmore's family was in some sort of car accident." Rourke shrugs, "We don't know how bad… but Top wants him home. The mortars are bringing him up here right now in a Humvee with a driver. I want you to jump in, make sure PFC Elmore gets back safely. I don't feel good about sending two young PFC's in a single Humvee on a five-hour drive through Pennsylvania back to the armory… with this heightened sense of urgency… without a little NCO supervision… if you know what I mean?"

Barnes nods and looks right at Rourke, "Sir, I got this. I'll get him back safe and sound. I'll just need to pick up my stuff over at the sleeping area."

Several minutes later two Humvees pull into the OP. They drive in a large circle so that they face the exit ready to go. Lieutenant Gattas jumps out of the first one, walks over to Rourke and reports, "I got PFC Elmore and PFC Colandrea in the second Humvee. I explained the situation to Elmore. He's nervous and anxious as can be expected. They have all their gear. The vehicle is fueled. We shouldn't have any problems."

Rourke nods and calls to PFC Elmore, "Tommy, come over here for a second."

Elmore steps out of the Humvee and quickly walks over to Rourke, "Yes, Sir?"

Rourke reaches out and puts his hand on his shoulder and advises, "Tommy, first you're going to have Sergeant Barnes going with you guys. He knows the way and will make sure you guys don't let lost. Second, you're going to stop down at Range Control to call home and get an update on your family's situation and let them know you're coming home. Then you're going to be taking off from there. Travel quickly, but safely… got that? I hope everyone is OK and this is just a case of some scratches and small bruises." He looks right into his eyes, "Hang in there, Tommy. We'll get you home."

After some more instructions to Lt. Gattas and Sergeant Barnes, both

Humvees pull out of the OP at 12:35. Rourke is satisfied that they will get Elmore back home by 18:00 hrs.

Fifty minutes later Rourke glances up to see two Humvees pulling into the OP. Reading the bumper numbers Rourke can see they are both the mortar vehicles. Rourke is thinking, 'Man this is odd, should be only one returning'.

The first Humvee pulls up between the bleachers where Rourke is standing preparing to give his class on the use of smoke. Lt. Gattas slides out of the vehicle with a big grin, walks up to Rourke and salutes. Rourke returns the salute and is now smiling. He asks his mortar platoon leader what happened.

Everyone on the OP stops what they're doing in order to listen to Lt. Gattas.

Gattas places his hands on his hips and starts with, "Sir, we went right down to Range Control to make the phone calls. Mine is to Top to get the actual low down on the situation and Elmore's to his family." Gattas stops for a second to gather his thoughts then continues, "Range Control offices are closed. All their personnel are probably out in their trucks running around the ranges and training areas, so nobody is manning the office. So, I figure to run up to Post Headquarters and use the duty officer's phone to make the calls." Gattas moves his hands out to his front with palms up as to say, makes sense right. Rourke's smile gets a little bit bigger and he inquires, "OK, then what?"

Gattas puts his hands back on his hips and continues, "On the way to Post Headquarters we start to go past the airfield. I look over and there's a Huey sitting by itself on the tarmac outside of operations. There's a guy sitting in the open door. I thought what the hell. So, we swung around and drove up to the gate. I told the security guy we wanted to get a guy back home for an emergency... he says sure and then let us in. We drove up to the bird. The guy sitting in the door is the crew chief. We ask him where he is from. He says the Cav Troop down in Jefferson. They are down here at the Gap for a Squadron meeting and that the Cav commander, the pilot, and the XO, the co-pilot, are on their way back to the Huey to fly back home. I ask if they have any room. He says sure but we have to ask the commander. A couple of minutes later the two show up. The Commander says, sure he would take both Elmore and Barnes and drop them off at the Manchester Airport.

"They said they have to pre-flight, then flight time would be about 45 minutes. I told Barnes to go with him… I thought it would be a good idea for him to be with Elmore. After doing their 10-minute pre-flight they took off. That is about 30 minutes ago. I then ran over to the flight operations building and called Top to brief him on the situation. Top says no sweat, he would have them picked up right when the bird lands."

Rourke reaches out and whacks Gattas on the side of his upper arm and exclaims, "Well done, LT. Great use of initiative. Our men should be in Manchester in less than 30 minutes from now."

The rest of the men in the bleachers call out praise for the lieutenant's decision. Way to go, LT! Good thinking! Way to make it happen, LT! Gattas turns toward the bleachers and gives everyone a big smile and a thumbs-up.

Rourke smacks Gattas one more time on his upper arm and congratulates, "Good job, Jesse. Feels good taking care of soldiers, doesn't it?"

Gattas replies, "Yes, Sir, he's a good troop." And then changing to a serious look, "Top did say his father is in a bad way. He wasn't wearing his seat belt. His mother is bruised up, but mostly OK."

Rourke nods and says, "Alright, don't you have a platoon to run?"

A couple of minutes later, Gattas with both his Humvees pulls out of the OP and heads back down to the mortar firing point.

Sunday morning when Rourke wakes up at the OP, he assesses the Dragon Slayer training during the whole weekend has been superb. He knows his mortar platoon is better. They put a lot of rounds down range, a lot of different types of rounds. They completed every fire mission flawlessly. The newly trained observers also did a great job. They now understand how to call for fire, and especially how important indirect fires can be on the battlefield. Rourke gets that rare feeling of total satisfaction.

Now the next mission is to get everyone safely home. The observers will be flying in a CH-47 Chinook and the mortars will convoy back in their Humvees to Manchester.

CHAPTER 16

"Perfection is not attainable, but if we chase perfection
*we can catch excellence." --*Vince Lombardi

Headquarters, 2/220 Infantry
Army National Guard Armory
Bluffton, PA.
Sunday, 22 October 1989
12:50 Hours.

Captain Rourke and First Sergeant Donald Johnson walk into the
battalion conference room and are met with greetings from all the other
commanders and first sergeants waiting for the briefings to begin. The
white board on the far wall has a hastily written greeting… "Welcome –
Battalion Train Up AAR", and in much smaller letters at the bottom, "no
excuses or whining!" Johnson, going to the chair he'd been assigned with
a paper name card on the table, yells out, "That's right Dragon Slayers in
the house… but you need not get up… keep your seats."

Of course, this starts a little uproar with everyone in the room. Good
natured ribbing of Rourke and Johnson is consuming some of the energy
in the room. This finally settles down to everyone discussing the subject of

the meeting. After a couple of minutes Colonel Francone walks in followed by his staff and the battalion sergeant major. Naturally everyone stands and waits for the inevitable command to sit back down from the colonel so they can start the meeting. Which he gives.

Francone glimpses around the room, smiles and says, "I want to thank everyone for getting here today. This will be the final time we get together before our little exercise down in Arkansas."

Everyone repeats the phrase, "Little exercise, yea, right. Just a little exercise."

Francone continues, "Today we have two objectives. One is to pass out the battalion operations order and the JRTC maps with overlays. The battalion staff will brief you on the operations order. This will give you a chance to spend the next month developing your own company orders. You'll give me the back brief on the next Friday's drill. That should be November 17th at 15:00 hrs."

He looks to see that he's understood by the commanders, "After we get everything worked out Friday, you should be able to have your companies run through your company orders and do some rehearsals on Saturday and Sunday between loadings." Francone spreads his arms as if to say, '*right, everyone agrees*', and then he continues, "But let's start with a small briefing on the status of your troops and your equipment. We pretty much know what they are but we want some solid numbers so we can make some last-minute corrections and improvements. I also believe it's important that we all know the battalion's overall status. The staff will then brief you guys on the load up process for this next month. Then we'll open it up for questions. I'm sure you guys will have some." Francone glances over at the staff and says, "I hope we have the answers for you. Let's start with Alpha Company. Carson, you have the floor."

Each company goes through their briefings providing the latest updates on their soldiers and their equipment. The most intense briefings are on the training status of each platoon. Commanders give a number value, from one to five, to each collective task at which the platoons are supposed to be proficient. The number five is to represent the platoon is totally proficient. Commanders give out very few fives. Most tasks get a four with some threes. There aren't any real surprises. Nothing that would fit into the category of a "war stopper". There are a couple of minor problems which Francone directs the staff to take care of.

Next comes the staff. After three intense hours of everyone focusing on the staff's briefings, Francone stands up and walks to the front of the conference room, glances around looking directly into everyone's eyes, "Gentlemen, I want to thank everyone for coming." The group nods in unison. Francone breaks into a smile, "Like you really have a choice!" This brings a burst of hearty laughter from the whole room. After hours of determined and steadfast attentiveness, the laughter acts as a well-deserved release of pent-up tension. Francone continues, "I feel pretty good about the battalion and our chances at the JRTC. We've worked hard… everyone in the battalion… please pass on to your guys that I appreciate that. But the job's not done. We've got to load the battalion, move to Arkansas, pick up our equipment and then deploy into the maneuver box… and then." Francone straightens up his posture, places his feet solidly shoulder width apart, puts his hands on his hips and announces, "We Then Beat the Shit Out of the OPFOR!"

Everyone jumps to their feet and cheers on with, "Yea… Beat the Shit Out of the OPFOR!"

Rourke jumps up with the same enthusiasm as his colleagues, shouts out just like everyone else, but he is truly thinking, '*if we break even… it would be a small miracle*'.

CHAPTER 17

"Never neglect small details, even to the point of being a pest. Moments of stress, confusion, and fatigue are exactly when mistakes happen. And when everyone else's mind is dulled or distracted, the leaders must be doubly vigilant. Always check 'small things.'" - General Colin Powell.

Fort Chaffee, Arkansas
Staging Area
Friday, 1 December 1989
10:00 Hours.

Fort Chaffee is an old military base left over from its beginning at the opening of World War II. There is an east side cantonment and a west side cantonment area. Both are made up of the wooden two-story barracks building that are typical of the World War II era military construction. Fort Chaffee hasn't been used as a major base since the end of the war. It was used as a holding area for thousands of Cuban Refugees in the mid 80's but reverted back to idle use after that. The post is mostly abandoned and being slowly torn down with some salvage of electrical wire and copper pipe by local contractors.

The Arkansas Army National Guard maintains the fort. It is now mostly used in the summer months for Reserve and National Guard annual training. A small portion of the post cantonment is being utilized by the JRTC operations.

Captain Rourke and his Executive Officer, 1ˢᵗ Lt. Bob Kiser, are standing on the south side of the large, designated staging area in the east cantonment area. They are both trying to stay out of the way and occasionally helping out when needed. This could entail jumping into a vehicle to move it or helping unload or cross loading equipment in all the vehicles being moved down from the north side after being unloaded from the many trucks lined up at the debarkation point.

As far as Ft. Chaffee Logistics Department is concerned, Rourke is designated as the Officer In Charge or OIC, of the staging area. This is because the Army always wants, at least in name, an officer to be held accountable, but in reality, this is NCO business. The men up at debarkation are being led and directed by the battalion Logistics Chief, SFC Robert Colandrea, and the South side staging area by Operations Chief, SFC Gary McCallister.

To Rourke, the situation appears to be running smoothly and efficiently. The many different crews led by other NCO's are working hard and coordinating their efforts so that the battalion's vehicles are properly lined up and ready to roll the next morning.

Rourke and Kiser are standing out in the open watching all the activity going on. Kiser has a clip board and occasionally flips through some of the papers to check some detail that needs checking. Both Rourke and Kiser turn after hearing a vehicle coming up to them from the debarkation area located about 100 yards from them. It is McCallister. He pulls up next to the pair, drops the window to address Rourke, "Hey, Sir, there's a captain from Ft. Chaffee Log Office that wants to see you."

Rourke looks a little puzzled, "What does he want?" After a slight pause, "Is this good or bad?"

McCallister leans forward, puts his head on the steering wheel, sits back up, stares back at Rourke and surmises, "I don't think this is for receiving the award for best unloading. I kind of get the impression the captain is a little upset." McCallister let that sink in and then asks, "You want a ride up there? It's right where they're unloading with the crane."

Rourke shakes his head, "No thanks, it's only a couple of minutes walk. Maybe he'll cool down by then. Thanks anyhow, Gary... By the way what's the captain's name?"

McCallister looks up for a second searching his memory, "I believe it's... Morel. Yep Morel." McCallister let loose a sly little smile, "Good luck, Sir."

As McCallister drives off, Rourke looks at his XO, "Wonder what the hell is up Morel's ass?"

Kiser gives him the, "I don't know shrug" as they both start walking toward the large crane that is set up on the far side of the debarkation site. Kiser is wondering what is up with the Ft. Chaffee logistics staff. He is also wondering if this is going to be sorted out with pleasantries between the two captains or is this going to be a confrontation.

Kiser has seen Rourke work some magic when it comes to unscrewing a problem by using charm and finesse when dealing with an agitated fellow captain. He has also seen Rourke go toe to toe with an unreasonable fellow captain on a few occasions. What impresses Kiser is that Rourke always seems to get the better of the situation. Kiser is thankful that he has Rourke as a mentor in showing just what method to use in any given situation. The outcome is always the same. Rourke gets what he wants. Rourke never backs down.

Sometimes his fellow captain is happy to help Rourke resolve the "problem". Occasionally there is a great reluctance by the captain to help resolve the problem. Sometimes the conversation ends with a "Glad to help you and your men out, Captain Rourke. It is a pleasure working together to solve this mutually difficult challenge". And then a few times it ends with, "Fuck you Rourke! I'm giving this to you this time, but you better, never need help from me again, Dick!" Whatever the method, the outcome is always Rourke getting his way. This means the men of CSC get a better deal than if they had a commander that isn't willing to get in there and do some scrapping for them. Kiser is now contemplating what method or technique he is going to see with this next "captain on captain" encounter.

They head for the big crane on the far side of the compound. The crane is used to off-load shipping containers, large boxes and even vehicles sitting atop the many flatbed trailers. The tractor trailers are lined up in one huge single file line that zig zags around the north side of the compound. Each patiently waiting their turn to move up to be offloaded.

As Rourke and Kiser approach the offloading site they spot several groups of soldiers standing around or working around the trailers. These are obviously the ground crews effecting the securing of the cables, chains, or nylon straps used by the crane to pick up the load to swing it off the trailer.

By the unit patch on their shoulders, most of the soldiers appear to be from the Ft. Chaffee logistics department. A few soldiers are from Rourke's own battalion. The closest four-man crew with their backs to Rourke is standing off to the side observing another crew's efforts to hook up to the next trailer's shipping container. Rourke and Kiser head there to ask about the whereabouts of Captain Morel.

After walking a little closer and looking a little closer, it isn't actually a four "man" crew. The closest soldier is a tall female. Rourke guesses she is probably 5' 9". She is wearing a pair of standard issue tan colored thick leather work gloves. She has a set of crane nylon straps draped over her left shoulder. What gives her away is the standard female hair bun on the back of her head secured under the hardhat she is wearing and the attractive shaping contours of her uniform.

Rourke smiles to himself and is thinking, *'If I could use a little charm on this young lady... I might get a little Intel about this Captain Morel... Maybe find out where he's from?... What he likes to do?... Maybe he's a Pittsburgh Steelers' fan?... If I could get something from her... just to get a little edge when I start a conversation with Morel'.*

Just as Rourke steps next to her from behind, there is a loud crash up on the trailer being unloaded. Everyone's attention goes immediately to the trailer. Apparently, the crane tried to pick up the container and dropped it back down onto the flatbed. It is about a one-foot drop. Dropping 3,000 pounds one foot onto a flatbed makes a terrible noise. Now everyone's attention around the unloading area is focused on what is happening on the trailer. This includes Rourke and Kiser standing side by side with Rourke next to the female soldier. Rourke, while still focused on the activity of the offloading crew, uses his right hand to tap on the left arm of the female next to him and asks, "Hey troop, have you seen Captain

Morel around here… apparently he has some burr under his saddle and thinks I can fix it."

After some time watching the off-loading crew get the shipping container re-hooked to the crane, Rourke realizes he didn't get an answer to his question. He turns to observe the soldier. She has done an about face and is standing squared up with feet shoulder width apart, hands on her hips, glaring straight at Rourke from under the hardhat visor. Rourke is impressed. She is attractive. He is definitely captivated by her. He takes a small step back to get reoriented and steps right into Kiser. Rourke mumbles, "Sorry, Bob, didn't mean to step on you." The only thought now in Rourke's mind is, *'Damn… this could get interesting'!*

She starts talking. Well it is more like lecturing him. A really stern lecture. Rourke is baffled; everything up to now has seemed to be going so well. His brain is now trying to catch up to her. He glances down onto her uniform collar. On the left side is her assigned branch. It is transportation. On the right collar are the two black bars of a… Captain! Rourke immediately gawks at the name tag sewn above the right pocket. In standard black lettering it displays, Marcell. The next thought in Rourke's head is, *'Shit!… This is Morel?… McCallister… he knew this captain was female! That son of a bitch set me up!'*

Rourke quickly gathers himself as best he can. This situation has him back on his heels. Holding up her right gloved hand toward Rourke's chest, she takes a small step forward into Rourke's personal space to emphasize her point. Rourke takes another step back. This time he didn't step on Kiser. Kiser has moved off to the left of Rourke to get a good view of what is going on.

Rourke suddenly hears, "Yes, Captain Rourke, I do have a burr under my saddle and it was put there by your battalion." Normally this would put Rourke right into the verbal thick of things. After all she just sort of disrespected his guys. But Rourke sure isn't himself. She keeps going, "You are the OIC of this Operation… are you not? Yes, you are! And you are required to have three unloading crews here at this spot at zero eight hundred hours. There is only one crew from your battalion here. My soldiers are here to give your soldiers a 30-minute train up in unloading. My soldiers have a lot more to do. But now they're stuck here because your soldiers didn't show. I'm already shorthanded. SOCOM, the Southern

Command Logistics in Panama has just appropriated one of my logistic teams for another one of their exercises. We are falling behind schedule!" She then half turns and points to another crane sitting 50 yards away with its boom down and locked in place. "If your other two... required... crews were here we would be operating two cranes and getting twice as much done."

At this point Rourke is finally focusing in on the problem. Yea, she is beautiful, but Rourke is still the OIC and this needs at least a reply. But he doesn't have one. He has no clue as to why there are two crews missing. He looks at Kiser appealing for some help. Kiser just shrugs and gives him a blank stare.

Captain Marcell waits for an answer, doesn't get one so she continues in a voice best described as frustrated, "The name is Marcell. It's spelled; Mike, Alpha, Romeo, Charlie, Echo, Lima, Lima. Got that? This needs fixed. You, as the OIC, need to fix it."

Rourke is getting a little more composed and answers with, "Captain Marcell, first I'm sorry about the name. I was told Morel... so I thought it was Morel. I now stand corrected and believe me it won't happen again." Rourke tries a little smile hoping this along with the apology would soften Marcell's mood. No smile in return. She is not going to soften.

He puts up his hands, "Listen, Captain Marcell," Rourke starts out and is going to try some truth telling in hopes of getting this cleared up, "I'm not sure why we haven't got all our people here. But we are a good battalion and I'm sure there is a reason for why we haven't got everyone here. If you could give me a little time, I could get you an answer. And... I didn't even know there is a schedule."

Marcell still seeming to be pretty adamant and uncompromising demands, "Captain Rourke, I really don't care why your people aren't here... I want you to get them here... as soon as possible. And why as the OIC you don't know or even have a schedule shows some considerable weakness on your unit's effectiveness." With that she abruptly turns and walks away.

Kiser is dumbfounded. He has never seen any captain get the better of Rourke. After she is out of ear shot Kiser swears, "Man, she smoked your ass!"

Rourke glares back at Kiser, starts to say something, stops himself, throws up his hands and mumbles, "Let's find Sergeant Colandrea and the missing crews."

They start walking toward a Humvee on the far side of the unloading area which appears to be centrally located and the logical place for running operations.

As they walk, Kiser can't help thinking about what he just witnessed. Why did Rourke get so... rolled over by Captain Marcell? Is it because she immediately took the offensive and Rourke couldn't somehow recover? And why couldn't he recover. The more he thinks about it and the more he analyzes the conversation, a smile slowly spreads on his face. Rourke, the guy that never breaks just got bettered by this... hard-hitting female captain. Kiser's smile is now ear to ear. He is thinking, '*What's the word... Smitten! Yes, Rourke is Smitten by Captain Marcell.*'

Kiser, with his new-found knowledge is going to do exactly what every guy does when they see a friend of theirs has been bested by a woman. He is going to give him a little, humorous, well-intended grief!

So, Kiser starts, "Hey, Captain Rourke, you OK, I mean you feeling alright?" Rourke just continues walking. Kiser continues, "Devlin, I'm serious. The way she just handed you your ass. Really, I've never seen you get beat up like that. Are you sure you're OK? We can find a medic."

Rourke still walking to the Humvee simply explains, "I feel fine... she just has a point... and I was letting her vent and voice her frustration."

Kiser, feeling he now has the upper hand, "Bullshit... Devlin, just admit you're a little taken with her."

Rourke stops, takes a deep breath, gazes up to form his thoughts, looks back at Kiser, "Bob, I can't deny... yes...she is a beautiful babe. Even you have to admit that."

Kiser smiles, crosses his arms, nods and agrees, "Yea, she's hot. But you've got to get focused. This will be the biggest event of our National Guard careers. You're not an eighteen-year-old private in the 3rd week of basic training... and pining over the only girl friend you ever made out with."

Rourke nods, "First of all, I'm not pining over her. And I got to tell you... I have a lot more respect for logistic officers that wear leather gloves and hard hats on the job site." He gazes toward the Humvee and orders, "Bob, find out what happened to those two crews. I know there's a practical reason the battalion failed to meet this commitment. I'm going back down to the staging area." Rourke glares directly at Kiser who is still grinning, "No... I'm not trying to avoid another run-in with Captain Marcell. Yes, she really did verbally beat me up. And by the way... thanks for all your help while I was getting beat up. Thanks for watching my six... XO! Let's just say... for right now, I should give her a little time to cool down."

Kiser chuckles as he replies, "We both know before you reach the staging area, you'll be wondering what it would be like to share some drinks and "make out" with her back home on your couch."

Rourke smiles, hangs his head down and admits, "Damn, thanks a lot pal, if I wasn't... I will be now."

Before Kiser turns to start off to the Humvee he says, "I'll find the two crews and get them over here... and Devlin, in all seriousness, she is hot. And she is probably pretty squared away, and might be a great catch... but, we need to stay focused... just get her number."

CHAPTER 18

"War makes extremely heavy demands on the soldier's strength and nerves. For this reason, make heavy demands on your men in peacetime exercises." – German Field Marshall Erwin Rommel

Fort Chaffee, Arkansas
Battalion Staging Area
Saturday, 2 December 1989
06:00 Hours.

Rourke walks over to his Humvee, opens the back door, throws his gear in the back, glances up and asks Josh, "Are we ready for this?"

Josh shrugs, holding the pragmatic viewpoint utters, "Well we better be… I guess we'll find out in about two hours."

Rourke looks at him, nods then looks at the company of men loading their gear in their vehicles all around him, and then announces for everyone, "Hey, give me a Dragon Slayer huddle right here. Pass the word. Huddle at the commander's vehicle."

It takes a couple of minutes to get the whole company to gather around Rourke's Humvee. He motions with his hands and tells everyone to take a knee. Rourke smiles, slowly surveys all his soldiers, everyone showing eagerness and anticipation as to what is coming.

Rourke nods in approval, and then begins to speak to them, "I'm not going to be long. Just a few words. Our LD time is 07:00 hours." He pauses for a couple of seconds, "You are a very good company. You are some of the best soldiers we have in the Army. We will face challenges we've never faced before as a company, as the Dragon Slayers. You will do well. There will be some setbacks... and maybe they will beat up on us for a time. But because you are very good... we will learn and quickly recover... and then do some beating of our own." Rourke can see his soldiers nodding. He sees the determination in their eyes. There is a resolve there.

He continues, "We probably won't have an opportunity to get together again as a company. You'll be working within your platoons. You'll be spread out over the battalion's AO. You need to depend on each other within the platoon... but also don't forget to help your brother platoons out there with you. As I know you will." Rourke stops for a couple of seconds, puts his hands on his hips, "Make good decisions, and make them quickly. Think faster and move faster than the OPFOR. Make them react to you. If you're confused or unsure about doing something or following a course of action... ask the Dragon Slayer next to you. I know for a fact... he's a pretty smart guy, between the both of you... you'll get it figured out. Finally, your focus and your mission are to kill the OPFOR. I really don't care about holding terrain or fancy maneuvers or scoring style points. Remember you're acting as a cavalry troop. We have a covering force mission. We provide early warning by fighting a covering force battle if necessary. Don't get decisively engaged. Don't get in a fight you can't get out of. If you have to, run away... then come back and fight another day."

Rourke shifts his stance, continues to gaze around at everyone, "They're out there right now. There will be a small element out in the box watching us move into our positions. Remember security is always number one priority." He nods, is pleased with their bearing and poise, looks around again to make eye contact with his soldiers and then as a matter of fact says, "Let's kill those fuckers."

There is no jumping up and yelling or cheerleading or raising of fists. Everyone quietly stands up and moves off to their vehicles to complete their load of equipment and final preparations.

Rourke calls out, "Let me see the platoon leaders for a couple of minutes please." Rourke proudly looks at who he feels is the best group of lieutenants there are anywhere in the Army. He starts to talk, "Well, you have your operations orders from me and have written and briefed your own. I heard everyone's briefing and I'm pretty happy and maybe slightly impressed with what I saw. You all have your own AOs, but you'll be working pretty much side by side in the battalion sector. Try to stay off the radio as much as possible. The OPFOR will intercept you to try and gain Intel and then will jam you to interrupt operations. We know each other. We know our voices. Keep to one quick sentence. Don't use a call sign unless you have to. If someone asks for your call sign… It's the OPFOR Intel trying to put the puzzle together. Don't give them a free piece." Everyone is nodding in acknowledgement.

Rourke continues, "Cross talk to pass info on to each other, use our codes and prowords. Everyone has the company freq. We jump frequencies every 24 hours starting at 19:00 hours. I want us using a clean freq for night operations. We may jump at any time if I feel we've been compromised. If you get lost on the radio and don't know the new freq. Which should never happen by the way. Get over to freq 30:30 and say "Roger that". Josh will encode our newest freq and pass it to you as four letters." Rourke watches them all waiting for acknowledgement from everyone. "Maintain situation awareness of everyone. All your brother platoon leaders. You may get a call telling you to move west of TRP 34. If you're the only platoon east of TRP 34, obviously I'm talking to you. Keep your head in the game. Get sleep when you can. I mean that! You all have great drivers and crews… get a cat nap in whenever you can. I will! … I'll be where I think I can do the most good. I don't plan on getting into any firefights."

Rourke swings his arm and points toward the XO, Bob Kiser, and continues, "Bob will be working his ass off getting you everything you need on the LOGPAC. Don't piss around getting your resupply. Bob will use the most efficient method to get you resupplied. He may come to you or he will tell you to meet up with him. Follow his lead. Get your stuff, give him your next log report and then hustle back to your mission." Rourke again looks to ensure they get it, "Don't get hung up on the little shit, let your platoon sergeant do his job, he'll take care of the important small stuff. Put your guys in the position to kill the OPFOR… And like I told everybody, don't get in a fight you can't withdraw from… Don't get in a fight for your lives. Being in the Cav is being very good at fucking with the enemy. Live to fuck with them another day. We are the battalion covering force." He gazes around one more time and with a big smile exclaims, "Good luck and good hunting!"

The meeting breaks up with everyone quickly moving out. Rourke notices a captain standing ten feet away who obviously has been listening. What really caught Rourke's eye is he is holding one of the company's M60 machine gun mounts fabricated especially for the Dragon Slayer's Humvees.

He is smiling. He walks over to Rourke puts the mount in his left hand and offers his right. Rourke reaches out and shakes it. He introduces himself, "Hi, Captain Rourke. I'm Captain Chancy, Tim Chancy. I'm your company's primary OC out in the Box. I'll have a couple of others working with me on my team. We'll stay out of your way. You won't even notice us. We've been doing this for fourteen rotations."

Rourke drops the hand shake, gets a glimpse of the mount, smiles and asks, "Tim, I'm Devlin. I know you OCs are very professional. What can I do for you?"

"Devlin, we might have a little problem." Chancy holds up the mount, "You see this isn't an Army issue item." Chancy inspects it, "Your guys built or made these back home… I talked with one of your sergeants… who let me borrow this one."

Rourke crosses his arms tilts his head and asks, "What exactly is the problem?"

"These aren't MTOE items for your type of unit. Your Humvees are… according to the MTOE only supposed to be Anti-armor TOW mounted Humvees. Your sergeant tells me you guys have fabricated these M-60 machine gun mounts for every Humvee in the company. That these mounts fit exactly into the TOW launcher base. This gives you the ability to go from tank killer to infantry killer within minutes… and of course back again within minutes."

Rourke straightens up getting ready for a fight. "Tim, why is that a problem? We are a combat arms unit getting ready for all types of battle conditions and situations. I would think you would applaud our ingenuity."

"Well the trouble is that when this field problem was agreed to by your battalion and the JRTC Operations Group back in June, we... meaning everybody, agreed to use the battalion's MTOE as the baseline as to the kind of battalion the OPFOR would be fighting. And now listening to your talk with your troops and your leaders... I now know this isn't going to be a conventional type of fight for the OPFOR. I'm thinking of not letting you use the mounts."

Rourke drops his arms, puts his hands on his hips, spreads his feet and goes into an obvious defensive stance, glares right at Chancy and slowly begins, "So you're telling me because the OPFOR might be at a slight disadvantage... because they are under the assumption... that the unit they will be fighting is an ordinary combat support company that is strictly for anti-armor fighting... So, they've been planning for this battle all along knowing exactly what type of unit they will be facing." He lets that sink in then continues, "Oh... that sounds fair to all the incoming Blue Forces."

This time Chancy changes his stance putting the mount against his hip, looks up to think, "Well, I don't think that's ever entered my mind... Never really thought about that. Good point."

Rourke sees he might have a chance to win this, "You know the OPFOR are US Soldiers also. Don't you think we kind of owe it to them to provide them some training challenges they haven't seen previously? ... I mean think about it... They know exactly how to prepare for their battles knowing the precise makeup of their enemy." Rourke again lets that sink in, "We'll give them a little taste of... better training opportunities." He could see Chancy once again shifting around and now showing signs of a little smile. Rourke continues on, "And anyhow isn't the philosophy of the JRTC that this is the place to be able try out new tactics and work on non-doctrinal operations and ideas? This is described as a place where units can be free to challenge the norm... You're supposed to be able to make mistakes here without any career repercussions. I mean that's what you've been advertised as... Right?"

Chancy is now grinning from ear to ear, puts up his free hand and capitulates, "Alright Devlin, you've made your point. The mounts stay in play. I'll return this one to its owner." Chancy is now nodding in agreement, "Good argument... and you're right on all counts... This is going to be a notable two weeks!" Chancy steps forward and again offers his hand. He smiles, lowering his voice, he leans in closer to Rourke and whispers, "I shouldn't be saying this… I'm not taking any sides here… but… the OPFOR really needs an ass kicking. I hope you guys can do it."

Rourke leans in even further and squeezing Chancy's hand a little harder confides, "Tim, they haven't seen anything like us… We're going to try like hell."

As Chancy starts to walk away he turns and asks, "Devlin what's with all the concertina wire on the back hatches of your Humvees. It looks like you've got enough concertina to encircle the whole fort… I've never seen that with a CSC?"

Rourke explains, "We pull that stuff out and run it in places we don't want the enemy to go. We either use it to impede a dismounted avenue into one of our TOW fighting positions or we use it to try and channel the enemy into a kill zone. We've got it set up so it can be easily pulled off as the vehicle moves out. You'd be surprised at how fast we can emplace it."

Chancy, shakes his head and exclaims, "I bet I won't be!"

Fort Chaffee Cantonment Area
Line of Departure for the Maneuver Area
07:00 Hours.

The 1st Platoon leading all the Dragon Slayers crosses the LD right on time and promptly heads for its assigned area in the maneuver box. The plan is pretty simple. The execution is going to be tough. Rourke has asked for and was given a large forward area to conduct recon and counter/recon operations. The rifle companies are each establishing defensive positions in approximately three-kilometer square areas. Rourke has an area ten kilometers wide and six kilometers deep. This is a little over six miles by almost four miles. Within his zone Rourke has established areas of responsibility using standard map graphic control symbols for his four maneuver platoons.

After consultation with the S-2 Intel section, S-3 operations and the battalion commander, the Dragon Slayers have identified four different enemy avenues of approach coming into the battalion area. Two are dismounted approaches and the other two are possible vehicle mounted approaches. Rourke has set up four forward observation posts that are to be manned by the scouts. The scouts are organized into four sections each having responsibility for watching an avenue. This establishes a screen line across the whole front of the battalion. They are going to act as the hunters by patrolling and hiding alongside the approaches and then calling back to the TOW platoons who will then be the killers. No enemy reconnaissance elements are to be engaged from the scouts on the screen line which reduces the chance of the scouts detection. Even with indirect fire, the scouts will compromise their own positions and maybe even the mortar and artillery elements while only getting small returns in OPFOR kills.

The 1st TOW, now divided into two sections will be working with the 1st and 2nd Scout sections. The 2nd TOW sections will be hooked up with the Scouts 3rd and 4th sections.

Third TOW has the mission of sweeping from behind 1st and 2nd TOW platoons back toward the rifle companies searching for OPFOR recon or observation posts already established in the battalion's sector. Their tasks are guided by an enemy template that Rourke and the S-2 have worked up on possible enemy recon locations. The hope is that by stealth and walking up from behind the enemy, 3rd TOW can catch a lot of the OPFOR off guard.

1st and 2nd TOW has to establish engagement areas or EAs along the enemy avenue two kilometers behind the Scouts. Engaging the enemy this far from the scout screen line, Rourke is hoping this will give the enemy a false idea of the battalion's actual front line. Rourke wants the scouts to remain undetected for the whole operation, thus providing the battalion and the Dragon Slayers a complete picture of enemy elements entering the battalion sector with enough time to react and even surprise the enemy.

Both 1st and 2nd TOW platoons have responsibility for one enemy mounted EA and one dismounted EA. TOW missiles, machine guns, along with mortar and artillery fires will play a big part in destroying OPFOR mounted elements. Intel analyses predict two T-64 tanks and two BMPs will make up the enemy recon moving along both mounted avenues. A total of four tanks and four BMPs.

The dismounted EAs are actually harder to set up. Because of vegetation, wooded and hilly terrain trying to get walking OPFOR soldiers inside an EA is going to be difficult. The EA is actually a large L shaped ambush site. With claymore mines, machine guns and the Dragon Slayer's own mortars ready to provide indirect fires, along with the element of surprise, those elements will have to do the job.

Both TOW platoon leaders have organized their platoons into a four TOW Humvee killer team for the vehicle mounted avenue and a two-machine gun Humvee killer team for the dismounted avenue.

Rourke has taken two Humvees, a TOW mounted and a machine gun mounted vehicle from the Scouts and put them with him. He has Josh mount an M-60 machine gun up on the roof of their vehicle. He isn't planning on using it. But in a pinch, either one could jump up in the turret and provide some fire. Rourke believes it is better to have it and not need it, rather than needing it and not having it. He is using the same philosophy having the other two scout Humvees with him. Keeping a little firepower in his back pocket is always a good tactic to practice. His three vehicle Humvee Quick Reaction Team sets up between the 1st and 2nd TOW platoon sectors, approximately in the middle of the company sector.

Based on the current situation paragraph in the operations order, Rourke believes they have about eight hours to get their sectors ready for any kind of OPFOR activity. After eight hours, it is going to be OPFOR challenging them with sniper, quick hit and run attacks on logistics assets, and getting harassed with mortar and artillery fire. This will start in the evening and go on all night. Rourke believes they will be interceding with small, five or six-man teams in order to hamper the battalion from setting up their positions and, just as importantly, getting a good night sleep.

By 11:00 Rourke receives a cryptic "found and occupying their assigned sectors" message from all the platoons. Now the hard work is beginning. Rourke knows the priority of work will be: 1. A security sweep on their areas to either kill or chase out any OPFOR hanging or snooping around their areas. 2. A recon of the area to find the ideal observation and fighting positions. 3. Putting together a plan based on the terrain and positioning which will best accomplish their platoon's mission. 4. A rehearsal to test the plan. 5. Then finally making any modification to the plan.

Rourke has already talked to both Lt. Foley, 1st TOW and Lt. Clegg, 2nd TOW about the importance of putting a deception plan in place. "You have to assume that the OPFOR will have somebody, if only two guys, that will be watching you. Try moving your vehicle around to confuse those observers where your actual positions are and what your plans are.

Third TOW which hasn't received a dedicated sector, starts their counter-recon operation using Humvees and dismounted soldiers to start sweeping back toward the company areas.

Now that Rourke has been out in the maneuver box for a couple of hours, he gets a good feel for the terrain. It is wooded but not heavily like back home in Pennsylvania. The leaves on the trees are gone this first week of December, which helps visibility. But that works both ways. We can see each other moving a long way off. Camouflage is now a bit more difficult for both. The folds in the rolling terrain will need to be used to hide, as opposed to hiding behind a big bush. The maneuver map provided to everyone for the deployment shows a couple of large tank trails, a couple of single lane dirt roads and a couple of trails or large foot paths. But Rourke can see that over years of use there are many more single lane dirt roads and many large trails. Trails large enough to run a Humvee down with no problem. Rourke was concerned about mobility of all his vehicles in the woods of Fort Chafee. But it appears that isn't going to be as big a problem as he feared.

———————◆—◆—◆———————

CSC Area of Operation (AO)
Covering Force Mission
11:30 Hours.

Spec Chas Ferguson loves being an M-60 machine gunner. He loves carrying it. He especially loves firing it. And everyone in the company pretty much agrees he is the best shot with it. The M-60 weighs 26 lbs. without ammo. Most soldiers will accept being assigned the M-60, but not very many ask to carry it. Spec Ferguson won't carry anything else. He has no problem carrying it. Ferguson is 6'2 and 230 lbs. In high school, he was an all-conference linebacker. So, adding about fifteen more pounds of ammo to his load is no problem either.

Spec Ferguson, PFC Nathan Puterka, assigned as the machine gun ammo bearer and Sgt. Jon Anderson, section sergeant, all from the 2nd TOW platoon are headed for what they believe will be the first machine gun ambush location. The location is pointed out by Platoon Sergeant Rob Donnelly to the section, by way of Donnelly pointing north from the second machine gun location and telling them, "Move up there about 100 meters, find a good position, dig in, camouflage, and then I'll be up there in a little while to give you your instructions. Keep in mind you should find a position that allows the OPFOR to walk by you unnoticed and walk into our machine gun here. Allowing you guys to get them from behind. And don't forget to have a way of getting out of there. Got it?" Off they go.

After walking for some time, Puterka asks Sgt. Anderson, "Hey Sergeant, shouldn't we be there already? I'm pretty sure we've been walking long enough to cover 300 meters much less 100 meters."

At this point, Anderson stops, gazes around and sheepishly stammers, "Well, I might have gotten a little turned around."

Ferguson shifts the M-60 to readjust the weight from the carry sling across his shoulder, chuckles and asks Anderson, "Shit, Sergeant, we got lost just walking 100 meters, didn't we?"

Anderson looks at Ferguson, smiles and with a conciliatory expression agrees, "Yea, I guess we need to back-track and get re-oriented and try again."

Puterka puts up his hand, "Hey listen... I hear some digging and some talking... I bet we walked in a circle and that's Sgt. Morgan digging in their gun. Hopefully Sgt. Donnelly won't be there to chew our asses."

Anderson starts toward the noise, "Sounds like thirty meters over this little hill, let's go... we can get re-oriented and get back on track. If we see Sgt. Donnelly I'll take the heat."

Ferguson stepping right beside Anderson warns, "I know you will... like you've got a choice?"

As they crest the hill they see four men in a small opening, two are in a small pit with entrenching tools digging. There are boxes and a bunch of 5-gallon jerry cans scattered all around. The other two standing on the edge are holding canteens and appear they have just finished their turn at digging. They have a conversation going about their favorite football teams making the playoffs. None of the four notices Anderson, Ferguson or Puterka now standing side by side just fifteen meters away. And it's a good thing too. It takes a second for the three Dragon Slayers to comprehend that these four are the enemy! Spec Ferguson acts first. He swings up the M-60 like a rifle, clicking off the safety, sighting down the barrel and pulling the trigger in one very swift motion. The adrenalin is pumping into

Ferguson. He doesn't feel the massive recoil of the M-60 pounding into his shoulder. The noise brings both Anderson and Puterka out of a state of surprise and back to reality. They both bring up their rifles and fire. Ferguson has fired off about twelve rounds, comes off the trigger, re-sights and fires off about twelve more rounds just to make sure.

The fight is over in twenty seconds. All four OPFOR solders are resigned to their fate and the MILES alarms going off on their harnesses and sit down. An OC, who has been leaning against a tree about 30 meters away, walks over, nods his head and says, "Nice attack."

Sgt. Anderson quickly takes control of the situation. "Ferguson, get down in overwatch. Puterka with me. First we search the dead and then secure the area."

Ferguson immediately goes to the ground in a prone position and flips up the bipod legs on the front of the M-60. Anderson approaches the two soldiers on the left and Puterka goes to the two on the right. All four OPFOR soldiers play their new roles and lay all the way down as if dead. The OC stands by to observe the actions of the Blue Force.

Platoon Sergeant Donnelly is standing fifteen meters away from his Humvee wanting to ensure it is in the perfect position to be hidden but able to put effective fire on the enemy. He also needs to be able to move out quickly to a supplemental position in order to add further fires to the EA. He pivots around and turns his head to the left, favoring his good ear. Did he just hear machine gun fire? Yes, there is another burst. The direction is toward Sgt. Anderson's position. Two thoughts popped into his head. First his guys are in a firefight and second, he needs to get everyone up there right now. Any plans for setting up an ambush are over. Any hope of surprise is over. The OPFOR is now aware of them.

Donnelly frantically waves to his Humvee driver, Spec David Gram, to pull out. They are going somewhere fast. Gram leans back to yell up to the gunner, Spec William Gorman, "Bill, hold on."

Gram hits the gas pedal and they shoot out of their hide position to pull up next to Donnelly. Gram never really stops. Donnelly jumps in and yells to Gram to drive over to pick up the other two Humvees over at their hide positions. Within a matter of minutes Donnelly has policed up the other Humvees, gets them loaded with everybody at the ambush site, and is moving toward where Donnelly believes Sgt. Anderson and his men should be.

———————————●◆●———————————

Anderson finishes searching his first dead OPFOR soldier and starts to search the second. He notices this one is a Staff Sergeant. That raises the hairs on the back of his neck. Staff Sergeants lead 12-man squads! They don't dig holes. They normally supervise digging holes. This dead man search is going to be thorough and meticulous. Immediately Anderson is getting a little resistance from the "dead" OPFOR. When he tries to roll him over the Staff Sergeant doesn't completely roll all the way over. Anderson suspects he is trying to hide something. This makes Anderson even more determined to do a complete search.

Bingo! In the dead sergeant's right cargo pocket Anderson finds a folded map. A quick glance and he knows he has some important Intel. Anderson looks over at Puterka to see that he has just finished his second dead soldier. With just a hint of excitement Anderson calls Puterka over. Anderson stares right at Puterka and orders, "Nate, take this map back to Sgt. Donnelly and then guide him back here. I think we got something kind of big here. Can you find your way back?"

Puterka nods his head, smiles and calculates, "Yea, I can be there in fifteen minutes."

"OK, Chas and I are going to reposition ourselves for any kind of counter attack. We're going to move over to that little dirt mound in that clump of small trees. Bring Sgt. Donnelly up from the rear over that way. Got it?"

Puterka nods, "I got it." He stuffs the map into his left cargo pocket then takes off running back toward the 2nd TOW platoon ambush site.

Puterka gets no more than 80 meters on his way back when he hears Humvees coming through the woods. He steps behind a large evergreen bush to wait and see. Is this friend or foe? After a minute, he recognizes Bill Gorman in the turret of the first Humvee. Puterka jumps out waving his arms. Gram pulls up next to him putting him right at the passenger door so he can talk with Sgt. Donnelly.

Donnelly looks at Puterka, opens up his hands, tilts his head forward and asks, "Well Puterka, what's going on?"

Puterka leans on the door frame and begins explaining the situation. "First, I guess we got a little lost. We walked and walked. Then we heard some digging and some guys talking. We thought we had walked in a circle and it was Sgt. Morgan digging in his gun. So, we walked up this little hill... glanced down and right in front of us were four OPFOR guys digging a hole."

Once again Donnelly nods and says, "OK, keep going."

"Well, it is so sudden... we just opened up on them. Got them all. So, Sgt. Anderson and I start searching them with Chas providing overwatch. Sgt. Anderson found this map on a staff sergeant. He told me to take this back to you and bring you up here. He and Chas are setting up a position across from where we shot them." Puterka stops for a second, pulls out the map, hands it to Donnelly, and points back toward the site, "We're only about a football field away."

Donnelly examines the map. There isn't a whole lot on it. He is hoping for some maneuver graphics or troop locations. But what he notices is a logistics symbol right there at the firefight location. Donnelly asks, "Any supplies in the hole?"

Puterka thinks for a moment, "Nothing in the hole but there are small stacks of wooden and cardboard boxes and some jerry cans around. We didn't really have a chance to search the area Sgt. Donnelly."

Donnelly slides out of the Humvee, looks back at the other two Humvees, waves and then pumps his fist in the air for everyone to dismount and come running. Once he gets everyone around him he takes a knee which means for everyone to take a knee. He glances around and begins, "Listen up; I believe that Sgt. Anderson and his guys accidently ran into a group of four OPFOR digging in a supply cache. We're quicker so we killed all four. Sgt. Anderson got this map off of one of the dead, a staff sergeant. You know and I know staff sergeants don't normally dig holes and normally are in charge of at least twelve or more guys."

Donnelly looks around to ensure everyone is following his logic and then continues, "I think the staff sergeant sent most of his guys back to get the rest of the supplies for the cache and he stayed to ensure the hole or multiple holes are getting dug." Donnelly can see everyone nodding so he continues, "I doubt if any more OPFOR guys are currently around. They would have put up a fight to overwhelm our three guys. They are probably getting their supplies or humping those supplies on their way back." Donnelly stands up and reaches into his Humvee and pulls out his map case. He kneels back down and waves Sgt. Morgan over to kneel next to him. He glances around once again and begins, "OK, here's what we're going to do. We're going to move up about 500 more meters from here and set up a new ambush site. I'm hoping to catch these returning OPFOR guys before they reach their cache site. They should be tired from humping all their shit… and their guard should be down because they don't expect to see us this far into their territory."

He pulls out his map, takes a second to run his finger over the map and points to a location he's selected for the ambush site. "We're going to set up right about here. I'm going to guess we should expect at least a 30-man platoon. So, the ambush site needs to be big. We'll need to stand off at least 100 meters before we open up with the guns. I want to use arty and mortars to initiate our attack. We get any closer and we'll be victims of friendly arty fire. We've got three Humvees. If we can keep the guns mounted on top and quickly move around the engagement area… maintaining fire on their asses we could do some substantial damage."

As he looks around he can see everyone nodding and buying into the plan, "After the fight, we move back to this cache and pick up everything we can load into the Humvees and move back to our original site. That's the plan… everybody got it?"

Donnelly reaches over and grabs Sgt. Morgan by the shoulder. "Tommy, get out your map. You and your driver race back to here." Donnelly is pointing to his map, looking over at Sgt. Morgan to ensure he is following along on his map, "From there call the LT, use the code word *Castle*. This is a throw away code word that will only be used once. Castle means meet me at the following location. Then send a TIRS location to meet him another 500 meters down this trail towards him. Got that so far?"

Donnelly stares straight at Morgan, "The OPFOR has great intercept and direction-finding stuff. I'm betting they don't know we've got their northern most cache… so that's why I don't want you to transmit till you're all the way down here." Donnelly points to the spot on the map, "Let the LT know our plans on this new ambush site and… give him the OPFOR map. Point out the symbol for cache is right here and there are two more cache symbols right here and here." Donnelly points out the locations for Sgt. Morgan on the OPFOR map. He then points his finger at Morgan to emphasize, "I know the commander will want to get his hands on this map like right now! Make sure the LT understands that. After you do that, get your ass back here as soon as you can… I mean fly! You'll have a spot you'll need to fill when you get back here. Got all this?"

Sgt. Morgan understands, "I got it." He points to his driver, gestures a come-on wave, and runs back to his Humvee. His driver hits the gas and they do a quick turn around and are headed back within a minute.

Donnelly looks around at the rest of his guys and to Puterka says, "Jump in with me. We're going to rush up to Sgt. Anderson, pick them up, and then move out to our new ambush site."

CSC Area of Operation
13:10 Hours.

Sgt. Morgan meets with Lt. Clegg about 30 minutes later. The LT brings another Humvee with him. Better to travel in pairs in enemy country. Morgan arrives first. He does his best to hide his Humvee then waits for the LT to arrive. After stepping out on to the trail and waving him down, Clegg's driver along with the other Humvee, pull off the trail and also try to hide as best they can.

Morgan runs over to Clegg's Humvee just as the LT steps out. Sgt. Patterson from the other Humvee runs up to get included in the conversation. Morgan stops at the front of the Humvee, pulls out his map and the OPFOR map, and spreads them across the hood.

Clegg tilts his head with a quizzical look, "Sergeant Morgan, I noticed you transmitted to me over the company net and not our platoon net. Is this something the company needs to know?"

Morgan nods, clears his throat, "Yes, Sir, I know the commander heard my call and knows that we probably have something going that he is going to want to know about. I sent it as a sort of heads up. Let me give you the scoop on what we've got going on."

Just then over Clegg's radio on the platoon freq they hear a spot report from the scouts who are set up about three kilometers in front of Sgt. Donnelly's sector. "White, Green 3, Three Zero, Romeo, Romeo, Delta, Grid 112814, Sierra Whiskey, Time now, over."

Both Morgan and Clegg study their maps. The scouts supporting Sgt. Donnelly's Ambush mission who are three and a half kilometers out in front of Donnelly just called in that the OPFOR has a platoon of about 30 dismounted infantry soldiers with rifles, rucks, and Dragon anti-tank missiles, are now three kilometers away heading southwest.

Morgan looks at Clegg, "Sir, let me get started. We've got to get going here."

For the next ten minutes Morgan gives Clegg the updated plan on the ambush and what has happened at the OPFOR cache location and the importance of the OPFOR map. Finally, Clegg glances up from the maps then looks at Morgan and says, "OK, I've got this. You need to get your butt back to Sgt. Donnelly and take Sgt. Patterson's crew with you. You guys are going to need the extra firepower."

Lt. Clegg also aware of the expert radio intercept capabilities of the OPFOR jumps in his Humvee and makes a quick radio call to Captain Rourke using another throw away code word for 'meet me at' then uses the TIRS location code for the exact position. The call takes ten seconds.

Rourke, who has heard Sgt. Morgan make his call to Lt. Clegg over the company net, knows he will be getting a call rather soon. He also assumes it would be in the 2nd TOW sector so he has Josh and his two Humvee QRFs slowly drive toward them hoping to save some time. It does save time. Within twenty minutes of Rourke getting the radio call from Clegg they are pulling in together off the same trail from opposite directions.

The leaders all dismount and head toward the Commander's Humvee. Gunners in the turrets swing their guns around to face out to provide security and protection. Just as everyone gets to the Humvee, Rourke's radio goes live with a report from the 3rd TOW that they have engaged and killed four OPFOR. Josh grabs the hand mic and acknowledges the message. This little message puts smiles on everyone's faces. Rourke peers around and warns, "Don't get too cocky. It's only 14:30 on the first day. The OPFOR will be spending most of its energy moving tonight to get all their real assets in place. What they currently have in place has been watching us. They're just waiting for the right time to jump our asses."

At this point Lt. Clegg steps forward and advises, "Sir, the reason I called to talk with you is our situation in our sector." Rourke nods in understanding. Clegg continues, "Sgt. Donnelly's guys happened to walk up on the OPFOR digging in a cache about 300 meters from their planned ambush site. They had a quick firefight and killed all four OPFOR. None of our guys got hit. They searched them and came up with this map." Clegg lays the map on the hood, "We took it off of a staff sergeant. It shows the location of the cache site they were digging in, and two others."

Rourke picks up the map to examine it, "Chuck, do you believe this to be real and not a ruse or fake map used to deceive us?"

Clegg puts his hands on his hips, thoughtfully observes Rourke and considers, "I don't think so. I honestly believe this is a dumb luck circumstance that we just fell into." Clegg reaches over and points to a location on the map, "Sgt. Donnelly believes this is the real deal. He's moved his ambush site up to here, about 800 meters further north than the original. He thinks he can catch the OPFOR going to this cache. I gave him an additional Humvee for more firepower. The scouts sent us a message that we have an OPFOR infantry platoon probably moving to the cache site now. I'm hoping Sgt. Donnelly can be ready for them."

Rourke looks down to intensely study the map. He leans back against the Humvee's brush guard, crosses his arms and then points a finger in the air and says, "Everyone follow along for a minute. Check me on this." All three of his leaders lean in just a little closer.

Rourke begins, "Let's assume, and I know that isn't a good thing to do, but let's make some assumptions. That we did just happen to run into these OPFOR guys. That they have no clue we are so far north. So, they let down their own security and left just four guys behind to get started on the cache. One is a staff sergeant who probably never planned to go further into the maneuver box. That's why he has a logistics map on him." Rourke could see everyone nodding and agreeing with him so he continues. "Let's assume they still don't know we killed their guys and have their map of the caches. Rourke pauses, "That the platoon headed for Sgt. Donnelly is actually humping supplies for the cache stocks and will break up into smaller elements and continue on into the box tonight for their follow-on missions."

Once again, a radio in Rourke's Humvee can be heard breaking squelch on the speaker. Everyone immediately looks inside the Humvee. It is one of the scout sections reporting that there is an enemy platoon with rifles and rucks and Dragons moving toward the 1st TOW sector. Josh calls out that it came over the 1st TOW freq. Rourke spins around and unfolds his own maneuver map on the hood. Everyone now crowds around with the two section sergeants leaning over Lt. Clegg and Rourke trying to get a peek. Rourke speaks, "Their current location and direction of travel would probably have them missing the 1st TOW platoon dismounted ambush site." The radio speaker comes on again with Sgt. Winters replying to the scouts that he copied.

Rourke studies both the OPFOR map and his map for several minutes. After formulating a plan, Rourke holding the OPFOR map, turns back around to face the three Dragon Slayers and starts to lay out the new plan. "I truly believe that the OPFOR really doesn't know what we now know. I believe this second set of OPFOR troops is headed for this second cache site right here." Rourke takes out a map marker from his shirt pocket to use as a pointer and circles the site on the OPFOR map. "The only problem is that Platoon Sgt. Winters is set up in the wrong position." Rourke considers the Sergeant right in front of him and says, "Gabriel, come here, pull out your map. I want you and Woodley to mount up and get to this location. This is about 500 meters in front of the second cache site and hook up with Sgt. Winters to establish an ambush site. I'm using the same theory that Sgt. Donnelly is relying on. They don't know we have their map."

Rourke pauses, gathers his thoughts, "Sgt. Winters will have no idea why we selected this new site. Give him the low down on what's happening. I'm going to call him and have him pick up everything and move to this new location and meet with you. It's going to be dark in two hours. I hope we can pull this all together. Gabriel, what's your call sign?"

Sergeant Gabriel Barnes quickly replies, "Green 4". To make clear his instructions he asks, "Do you want me to go to the new ambush site and wait for Sgt. Winters or you want me to hook up with him on the way to the new ambush site?"

Rourke replies, "Go to the new ambush site, we don't have a lot of time. Whoever gets there first will have to start planning and setting up the engagement area. This is where you start earning your pay, young Sergeant. Once you hook up with Sgt. Winters give him the low down on the current situation. Once you spring the ambush move back to the OPFOR cache site and try to find any supplies you can. Load up what you can, blow the rest, and move back to the original ambush site for tonight. Got It?"

Sgt. Barnes confidently replies, "Yes, Sir, got it." He looks at Spec Vince Woodley and says, "Let's go Woodley." They both turn and run to their Humvees. Within seconds they are heading to the new ambush site.

Rourke steps to his side of the Humvee, reaches in, grabs the handset to call Sgt. Winters. He tells him to pick up and move to the new location and meet with Green 4 with new instructions. Sgt. Winters acknowledges and confirms he will comply.

Rourke throws his arm around Lt. Clegg, "I think we're going to do some serious damage to the enemy. You and your guys are doing well, my young Jedi!"

Clegg chuckles and asks, "What about the third cache site?"

Rourke turns back to the Humvee hood to ponder the two maps. Studies them once again and decides, "I'm going to call Lt. Petrone." Rourke pauses for a second and continues, "I'm going to try and meet with Jim to see if he can't put some of his guys on this third cache site. This is more or less in his sector. But I still want him running some of his guys throughout his sector. I believe even if they don't find and engage the OPFOR, they, the OPFOR, will be spending a lot of time tracking and working to take out the 3rd TOW."

Clegg asks, "Does Jim know he's the shiny object that's supposed to keep the enemy occupied?"

Rourke nods and reveals, "Yea, we talked about it before we left home station. He's already reported killing an OPFOR three-man team. I'm interested in how he is able to do that. We had talked about different tactics. I let him decide on which one or ones he wanted to try based on what kind of terrain he found in his sector."

"Sounds like Jim's going to be a busy guy for the next 24 hours." Clegg states.

Rourke looks at Clegg, "If we're successful this evening, I bet tomorrow morning you're going to become pretty busy yourself. The OPFOR has no idea he's got the whole CSC up here in his usually "safe" zone. But he will realize it by tonight. His S-2 is trying to paint a true picture right now.

Once he figures that out, they'll try and get rid of us with their limited but effective armor vehicles tomorrow. Be on your toes, Chuck."

"Yes, Sir, I need to take off and get back to my guys."

Rourke nods and says, "Good hunting, LT."

Clegg turns and swiftly moves to his Humvee rotating his wrist in small quick circles, giving the driver the start it up signal. Rourke moves to the passenger side of his vehicle, reaches in to grab the handset, glances at Josh and requests, "Put me on the 3rd TOW freq and what's the next code word for, 'meet me'?"

Within twenty seconds Rourke is on the radio with Lt. Petrone. They set up a meeting location and both say they are moving to get there. Rourke has no idea where Petrone is at that time but knows he will be face to face in about 45 minutes.

———————◆●◆———————

CSC Area of Operation
16:15 Hours.

Thirty minutes later Josh pulls off the trail and finds a good hide position and backs up into a little gully. Rourke gets out with his M16 and walks back the fifteen yards over to the trail to flag down Petrone who is soon to arrive. A couple of minutes later, Josh steps out of the vehicle, cups his hands around his mouth and calls out just loud enough for Rourke to hear, "The mortars just got a call from Sgt. Donnelly for HE and smoke. Rourke takes a glimpse back and shows a thumbs-up. He then checks his watch and surveys the sky trying to judge how much light they have left. After another five minutes, he sees a Humvee coming down the trail. As he steps out onto the trail, Josh again calls out that Donnelly is in direct contact! Once again, Rourke checks his watch. If things go right, he should be getting word in 40 minutes from Sgt. Winters about his ambush.

Petrone's vehicle pulls up next to Rourke. Petrone slides out with his map, looks back into the Humvee at the driver and points up the trail. The driver nods, eases the Humvees 50 meters further up the trail to take up a security position off to the side. Rourke looks back up the trail and sees an additional two Humvees pulling off the trail about 100 meters away. Both taking up security positions. Petrone looks at Rourke, smiles and boasts,

"I call it rolling overwatch. They stay about one to two hundred meters behind. I'm doing it with the other section too."

Rourke leads the way back to his Humvee. They both lay out their maps on the hood. Rourke says, "Let me give you the low down on the company's situation and what I want you to do."

Rourke spends ten minutes explaining what happened and what is now happening with everyone in the company. Rourke glances at Petrone and clarifies, "This third cache site is yours. I'm not sure if there is anything there yet. I believe it's more of a proposed site that is supposed to be supplied tomorrow. This one is about two and a half kilometers further south than the other two, which are," Rourke smiles broadly, "supposed to be supplied tonight."

Petrone, who is studying the map, glances up at Rourke, "You want me to check it out and set up an ambush?"

Rourke shakes his head, "No, I think after tonight the OPFOR is going to know we got their logistic map from their Staff Sergeant. They might send somebody down to recon and see if they can pull an ambush on us if we are waiting for them. They will want to ambush the ambushers, so to speak. I was thinking if you could set up an observation post far enough away, but still able to at least call in some fire, we might get a little lucky. I know the OPFOR has used this site before. We are all creatures of habit... even the OPFOR... I know. I used to be one. That location might have been used before as a cache or an assembly area or at least a rendezvous location, but I'm guessing it will be used again... It's at a perfect distance to our front-line companies." Petrone deliberates over his map and nods. Rourke continues, "Why don't you do a drive by tonight just to locate where it is... so tomorrow morning... like BMNT early tomorrow, you find the perfect OP location and sit on it for 24 hours."

Petrone looks up from his map and confidently states, "We got this, Sir. I'll try to find a standoff location where we can use our TOW site to keep an eye on it. That should keep us far enough away to prevent getting exposed."

After the briefing and exchange of ideas, Rourke turns and leans back against the brush guard and asks, "How did you get those three OPFOR guys?"

Now it's Petrone's time to smile, he chuckles a little and then begins explaining, "I guess these three studs thought they could take on a machine gun Humvee by themselves. We are running with the rolling overwatch. They obviously didn't see the two Humvees 100 meters back. They opened up on the lead with M16s at about 80 meters. Our gunner returns fire with his 60 and reports the three to his front right at 80 meters. The overwatch vehicles hit the gas, break to the right, and shoot through the woods, and begin opening up with their 60s. This is too much for the three studs. They probably never imagined they would be charged by three machine gun firing Humvees at... I would guess 30 miles an hour, through the woods. Well, like I said, I guess it was too much for them, so they got up and started to run for what they believed are thicker woods. But we closed so fast we gunned them down before they got twenty meters."

Rourke asks, "Have you decided to do any dismounted hunting?"

"Well we thought about that... Me and the NCOs... after considering the lack of vegetation and the rolling terrain... the ability to see pretty far off, we felt we really wouldn't have that much of an advantage. Even if we could silently walk up on them, most likely they would get a couple of shots off at us after the fire fight started. I decided that the cost to us... would be too much." Rourke nods his head in agreement. Petrone continues, "So we decided to use the rolling overwatch and throw a couple of new tactics in the mix." Petrone crosses his arms, leans up against the brush guard and continues to explain. "We figure that after our killing the first three OPFOR they would get the word out about our one up and two back traveling tactics and make adjustments. So, we added three new ones... the sprint, the about face... and the rolling thunder!"

Rourke turns to face Petrone with a big grin, obviously enjoying Petrone's war story and teases, "OK, General Rommel, The Fox of Fort Chaffee, what are these new tactics?"

"Well, the Sprint is where we kick it into high gear and go tearing around the woods at a rather high speed." Petrone goes on to explain, "The purpose is to use speed as security, we're moving so fast they can't get an ambush set up, and then secondly, maybe with a little luck, run up on an OPFOR team unable to get hidden or get out of the way before we're on top of them." Petrone pauses, "the About Face is pretty simple. We just quickly reverse course, do a turn around and head back the way we just came. The hope here is that we catch an OPFOR team thinking it's safe to pick up and move since our Humvees have just driven past them." Petrone readjusting his stance, takes a second to gather his thoughts, "Now the Rolling Thunder... is when we get the whole platoon together, all six, and then go cruising through the woods acting all intimidating and mean and looking for a fight."

Rourke, who has been enjoying his 3rd Platoon Leader describing his own original and creative tactics then asks, "Well, Rommel, do you think you'll be successful in killing the enemy?"

Petrone looks down to contemplate his answer, gazes at Rourke after some earnest reflection and says, "I believe we can do a little damage... If we can catch at least two more elements and kill them plus having Humvees driving throughout the sector will put the OPFOR on notice that they need to stay hyper-vigilant around here. If they're reporting us to their S-2 each time they sight us tearing through the woods, he must be a very busy guy... maybe we can add some confusion to their well-conceived plans."

Rourke reaches out and smacks Petrone on the arm, "You and your guys are doing well. I hope you'll be able to kill two more teams. With what the rest of the company is doing I think we'll be giving the OPFOR a run for its money."

Just then the radio comes alive. It is SFC Donnelly with a situation report. He estimates fifteen enemy KIA but sadly he lost a Humvee and four of his guys. They recovered the four bodies but had to leave the Humvee. He moved back to his original ambush site and is setting up for night operations. Rourke is disappointed in losing a Humvee. He knows he will be losing people. Just losing four to the enemy losing fifteen isn't bad. Actually, it is really good. So far, the OPFOR has lost 22 and the first day isn't even over.

Rourke looks at Petrone, "Jim, that's all I've got. You need to move out and get busy for tonight's operations."

"Yes, Sir, I'll keep you informed. Maybe we'll get lucky again tonight." At that Lt. Petrone turns and jogs up the trail to get back to his Humvee.

Rourke moves to the passenger door, slides into the Humvee, looks over to Josh, "Let's hook up with Lt. Foley over at 1st TOW."

Josh looks over and smiles, "Is the big old captain scared to be out here all alone?"

Rourke grinning now, "As a matter of fact I don't want to get caught out here and get either killed or worse, get captured. The embarrassment would be enough for me to kill you for getting us in that situation... I mean literally kill you... beat you with a... something. So yes, I want to snuggle up to the 1st TOW platoon and use their security." Rourke takes out his map, puts his finger on the 1st TOW location and asks, "You got it?"

"I got it." He kicks over the engine, pulls out and heads back north at a fast clip. Josh is using speed for security.

When they get to what Rourke believes to be half way there the radio breaks squelch. It's Sgt. Winters asking for fires on the battalion fire control net. He's in contact with the OPFOR and has started his fight with artillery fires. Rourke and Josh look at each other with the same '*I hope this goes well*' look. Rourke leans over and switches one of the radios over to the 1st TOW freq. Sgt. Winters should be sending his situation report over his own net to Lt. Foley. They drive on both listening for the next radio message from Sgt. Winters. There it is. Sgt. Winter's driver is sending a contact report. They've sprung the ambush. Rourke is thinking this should be over in about ten minutes.

Rourke stays on the net and listens to the battle that unfolds on the radio, most of which is one of the vehicle commanders directing machine gun fire or directing the movement of the Humvees. Rourke breaks into a cautious grin when he hears a command to, "***move 50 meters to your right and get those guys running north!***"

After a couple of minutes, it is over. Sgt. Winters gets on the radio and says they are executing, "Maple Tree" at this time, code for leaving the battlefield. They are not going to search the dead or do a body count. They aren't the infantry. There isn't going to be a consolidation or reorganization on the objective in order to get ready for a counter attack. They hit them like a Cav unit, now they are getting the hell out of there.

Rourke, while studying the map points to the left and tells Josh to pull over. Josh pulls the vehicle over and finds a gully to back into. The squat hills on either side of the gully are about twelve feet high. Rourke knows the 1st TOW platoon should be around here somewhere close. Josh grabs his M-16 and scales the hill on his side. Crawling the last few feet in order to conceal himself, Rourke jumps out and cautiously moves up the trail. After about fifteen meters he hears someone quietly call out, "Hey, Sir, over here."

Rourke glances to his right and notices a soldier lying on the ground behind an immense tree. Rourke runs over and lies down on the same side of the tree. Rourke recognizes Staff Sergeant Eikenberry, "Ben, good to see you. Do you think your guys can find a place for us for tonight?"

"No sweat, Sir, I'll put you and your driver over by my location." Eikenberry leans over on his side, points up the trail and explains, "Move your Humvee about 60 meters up the trail and then turn off to the right. I'll have a ground-guide for you. We'll move you another 60-80 meters further into the woods. I've got a hole you can drop your vehicle into for the night. And it appears like we've only got about five more minutes of light. So, let's move, Sir."

After getting their vehicle into position, Rourke asks if he can be led over to Lt. Foley's position. In 25 minutes, he is face to face with his 1st TOW platoon leader in a small depression in the ground. Both leaders sit down facing each other with their legs crossed Indian style. Lt. Foley has his map sitting in his lap with a small, red-lens flashlight ready to give his commander a briefing on his platoon's current situation.

The first question Rourke asks is, "Trevor, how did Sgt. Winters do?"

Foley leans a little more toward Rourke and starts his briefing, "First he has two KIAs and three WIAs. He got them all off the battlefield and back to the medics for evac back to battalion. I know the XO got involved with the evac somehow. I didn't get the details, but Bob worked the evac with the battalion medic team and also removed the dead. Winters advised it saved him a lot of time with what little assets he has. He lost a Humvee to a Dragon missile. Right now, he's hunkered down in his original ambush position."

Rourke nods and asks, "How'd we do against the bad guys?"

"Sgt. Winters says that as he was pulling out his dead and wounded and pulling equipment and weapons out of the Humvee, he counted twelve dead OPFOR. They pulled out their wounded as they were running out of the ambush kill zone."

Rourke nods as he starts to put together all the events that happened on their first day, "Trevor, let me give you today's run down." As Rourke verbalizes the day's events he begins putting it together as if he is the

OPFOR Intelligence Section. "Let me run this by you and see if it makes sense to you." Rourke pauses to gather his thoughts, "Without a doubt... they now...*Rourke looks at his watch...* it's 18:20 hours... know that the 2nd Battalion 220th infantry has its Combat Support Company way up here in no man's land. Where normally a Blue Force infantry CSC would be back watching and patrolling the Main Supply Routes, and in overwatch positions of armor avenues of approach to protect the rifle companies."

Foley leans back and puts his hands on the ground behind him. "Well what do you think they'll do?"

Rourke puts his hands on his knees, gazes up to ponder for a minute and then looks back at Foley, "Right now the OPFOR commander, his operations guy, and his Intel guy are huddled together studying a map... probably the S-2 map with all the locations of our actions and an overlay of all the sightings of our Humvees throughout the maneuver box." Rourke nods as if to agree with himself, "Yep they know we're here. And they are a little bit pissed." Rourke opines to Foley, points with his index finger, "They got surprised today; they got a bloody nose... I mean they got a real bloody nose. They know we're here. They've got to get rid of us. I bet the commander and his command group figure if they can get rid of us tomorrow... they then have free reign to destroy the rifle companies with their armor tomorrow night or the next day for sure."

Foley is nodding, "If they wipe us off the face of the earth... they own our battalion."

Rourke asks Foley, "Could you add Sgt. Winter's section to your own tonight... and have them ready to take on armor first thing tomorrow morning? ... I'm thinking of pulling both Winters and Donnelly off their dismounted avenues to bolster both yours and Chuck's armor avenues to add more to your EA's. What do you think?"

Foley shakes his head, leans forward putting his arms on his crossed legs, turns his hands up, "Sir, it's too late. I really don't think I could integrate him into our plan at this late date. We really couldn't find fields of fire for his TOWs tonight. And I really doubt if Chuck, over at 2nd TOW, could do it either. The best case would be them driving around the perimeter of the EA trying to find a good position... Maybe causing some confusion with the OPFOR armor... But most likely just getting blasted by their armor."

Rourke contemplates Foley's logic, nods in agreement, "Alright, this is what I'm going to do." Rourke lays out his plan, "I'm going to have Sgt. Winters and Sgt. Donnelly hook up together, establish their own quick EA behind Chuck's. I'm going to have Jim with four of his 3rd TOWs also establish an EA behind you. Hopefully this will provide us a defense in depth posture. Whatever gets through you and Chuck should get picked up by Sgt. Winters and Lt. Petrone."

Foley nods his understanding and asks, "When are you going to make this happen?"

"I'm going to have them moving at 04:30 hours. I'm sure they can put together a plan and be in place no later than 07:00 hours."

CHAPTER 19

"If you find yourself in a fair fight, you didn't plan your mission properly." - David Hackworth

CSC Area of Operation
Covering Force Mission
Sunday, 3 December 1989
04:30 Hours.

Rourke wakes up with Josh lightly shaking him. Josh leans in closer and whispers, "Sir... rise and shine, Sugar Muffin. We got to get moving."

Rourke unzips his sleeping bag, pushes himself up to a sitting position attempting to get the fog out of his head, looks at Josh with glazed eyes and asks, "What time is it and how come your up so bright and bushy tailed?"

"I've been up. I volunteered for the last watch with some of the 1st TOW guys... It is only the right thing to do... and it's 04:30 hours."

For the next fifteen minutes Rourke and Josh pack away their gear, take down the cammo net that they threw over the Humvee, roll it up, and store it on the back of the vehicle. They both work on getting the radios up and ensuring they are all set on the right freqs. It goes smoothly. They work as a team in the dark. Neither one has to utter a word. They have done this dozens of mornings. Finally, Rourke walks to the front as Josh slides into the driver's seat. Josh starts the engine. Rourke flips on his red-lens flashlight holding it at waist level and pointing down to the ground, making it visible only to Josh. Rourke turns, starts walking, and begins ground-guiding Josh out of the woods and back onto the trail.

Driving at night is always tough. Rourke learned while in the Cav not to use the vehicles blackout drive lights. The whole purpose for the blackout lights is to throw light out and down so it would provide enough illumination to allow the driver to safely see. The problem is this spot of light right in front of the vehicle in the black of night, tends to have drivers get fixated on just that spot of light. This results in drivers unable to use their natural night vision to take in their surroundings. They therefore drive a lot slower.

Rourke learned that unless it is absolutely pitch black, there is enough ambient light to see a trail or the outline of a tree line and to use the shadows and the different shades of black to negate the need of blackout drive lights. Many times, in the Cav, Rourke would actually duck down lower in the commander's hatch trying to scrutinize the distant horizon in order to determine the silhouette of the terrain up ahead. Rourke taught all of the company to drive without using their blackout drive lights.

Josh is pretty damn good by now. Rourke can see Josh moving his head slightly left and then right bringing his night vision into play and looking for silhouettes of the trees lining the trail. They are on the move to hook up with Lt. Petrone.

Rourke concluded that the armor avenue approach being covered by Lt. Foley and now backed up by Lt. Petrone is the most important and the most likely to be fought over by the OPFOR.

———◆━◆━◆———

CSC Area of Operation
06:10 Hours.

The hook up with Lt. Petrone happens 30 minutes later. It is getting lighter. The briefing to Petrone is quick and thorough. Petrone voices one concern while pointing to the map, "Sir, I understand that I'm to backup Foley. But I just don't have a lot of open terrain back here behind him. I've got some… but if they break through his position with say three armor vehicles… I don't know if I've got the battle space to engage all of them. The terrain and woods prevent me from getting even decent short shots, let alone any long shots."

Rourke studies the map, nods without looking up, asks, "If you do get three vehicles… you know tanks get killed first, right?"

"Oh yea… we've got our priority of fires squared away. I'm just saying if they're moving fast we might not get them all."

Rourke looks over at Petrone, directs him to follow along on his map, and explains a plan, "OK, let's say they do get three or even four vehicles into your EA." Rourke moves his map marker around to illustrate his plan. "Take your concertina wire… all of it and set it up here… use it to discourage any vehicles from running to get to this trail. That leaves two escape routes out of your EA. If they take this one… it runs them up to Sgt. Winters and Donnelly's EA. You call them; let them know they got company on the way." Petrone nods his understanding. Rourke continues, "If they… and I'm really hoping there is only one vehicle left… If they get to this trail by this wood line… your only shot is to move a TOW Humvee out in the open to this point and try to shoot him in the ass as he heads toward the rifle companies."

Rourke stops to consider another thought, "As soon as Trevor lets you know his fight is over and you've got… so many vehicles headed your way… start calling in smoke… lots and lots of smoke, both mortar and arty." Rourke looks at Petrone, "Don't let the enemy get any ideas where your guys are… Have them roll into a big cloud of smoke. It'll certainly slow them down and help you get off your short shots while they're trying to find a way out." Rourke grins, "What the hell, throw in some high explosive with the smoke… it might add to the confusion."

Petrone smiles, puts his hands on his hips and speaks with confidence, "Alright, 3rd TOW is on it. Not a bad plan… we'll make it work, Sir!"

Rourke slaps him on the arm, "Good luck and good hunting, Jim."

Petrone nods, turns and jogs back to his Humvee.

At 09:05 Rourke looks at his watch and is wondering why the OPFOR hasn't attacked yet. He has selected a hide spot between Lt. Petrone and Sgt. Winters areas. Josh found a perfect spot to drop the Humvee into, a low-lying depression only big enough for the vehicle, with two little hills on either side, just tall enough to conceal the Humvee on either side. Rourke lies on his side just below the crest on one hill, and Josh does the same below the crest on the other. Both have their M-16s and are glancing out providing security for their position. The radio speakers are turned down just low enough for only Rourke and Josh to hear.

1st Lt. Kiser with a trailing Humvee pulls up to Rourke's Humvee, stops and Kiser with another soldier get out. Kiser signals the soldier and points to Rourke. The soldier nods and runs up to take Rourke's place and mission of local security. Rourke slides partially down the hill, stands up and meets Kiser at the front of Rourke's Humvee. Both Humvees move off to take up security 50 meters away then shut down. Both vehicles are equipped with M-60 machine guns on top.

They lay their M-16s on the hood. Rourke asks, "What brings you up here this early? Not that I'm unhappy to see you."

Kiser smiles, "I brought the Logpac up a little early. I've got them hidden about two klicks back with good local security. I haven't heard anything for a while. Just like you, I expected a battle by now. So, I preloaded the Logpac with additional ammo and fuel. I guess we just wait."

Rourke changes his look to that of concern, "Bob, why haven't they attacked by now? They know approximately where we are. I would have thought… they would have conducted an attack by now.

Kiser leans forward and grabs hold of the brush guard with both hands, pauses for a long minute, "Think back to our time with the OPFOR at the NTC… Remember if we didn't conduct a… Hasty Attack… usually within four hours, we would take the time and plan a Deliberate Attack. A lot more detailed and thorough. With a complete picture of the enemy from the scouts. Right down to each enemy vehicle position. It took a while but was always worth it."

Rourke is remembering and nodding agreement, crosses his arms on his chest, drops his head and contemplates what his XO just said. Finally, he looks up at Kiser, "You're right. We should be under a hasty attack right now… what they're doing is finding and plotting every position we have. We've been sitting in place and waiting since about 08:00. It'll probably take them another hour to be satisfied they have 95% of our vehicles located. They don't want to take any chances. They want to kill us all in this one attack… After all, we are all in relatively one area. They don't have to hunt us down throughout the whole maneuver box... Once we're gone, the rifle companies only have Dragons to fight off any armor. That's no match."

Kiser nods, "I agree, any idea when this is going to start? And can we now counter-punch?"

Rourke looks up at Kiser, "Just like the NTC, when they cross the LD, their vehicle commanders will have exact enemy locations to attack... of course using the best attack avenues they already know." He pauses and then continues, "They will also hit our locations with artillery fires... for best results, those fires will hit ten minutes prior to the armor arriving there. Just like the NTC, they want either killed, neutralized, or totally confused vehicle crews when their armor arrives. We never gave them a chance to reorganize for the battle after the arty prep." Rourke now grinning, "Remember how easy it was for us?"

Kiser chuckles, "Yea, it was intense and we always had the upper hand... What are we going to do now?"

Rourke pulls out his map and lays it on the hood. He studies it for a couple of minutes and then answers his XO's question, "I really don't want to send radio messages out to the platoons giving them all kinds of instructions. The OPFOR will pick up on it and then make adjustments." Rourke traces his finger across the top of the map, "Bob, I'm guessing this is probably their LD... right along here. That's about fifteen minutes away from our 1st and 2nd TOW platoon EA's. That's also right where our scouts are. I haven't heard anything indicating our scouts have been spotted. So, with any luck they should give us the word when they pick up enemy armor up around here."

He looks at Kiser, "When I get the word from our scouts about OPFOR armor... I'm going to put out a net call and instruct all elements to move to their alternate position... Telling them to move with an urgent... MOVE RIGHT NOW command! This is where that disciplined training comes in... I know our guys have primary, alternate, and supplemental positions. It's our SOP. I'm hoping they move their asses fast enough to get out from underneath the arty."

Rourke and Kiser talk a little bit more about the upcoming battle, and how Kiser is assigned to bring up the Logpac and resupply the company. They have a plan. Both feel pretty good executing it. Finally, the XO advises, "Sir, I've got to get back. I've got to take care of those things we've talked about." Kiser put out his hand, "We're going to kick their asses... And don't you get killed... I'm not ready for command yet."

"Bob, you more than anyone else, are better prepared for a command right now." Rourke then adds, "I'm going to try like hell, not to get killed!"

Kiser turns and jogs down to his Humvee.

11:12 Hours.

The scouts in front of Lt. Foley and the scouts in front of Lt. Clegg both report armored vehicles moving fast down the armor avenues of approach. They make the reports over the company net. Everybody gets the reports. The number of vehicles is of special interest to everyone.

Sgt. Callahan in front of 1st TOW reports two T-64 tanks and two BMPs. Sgt. Davis in front of 2nd TOW reports one T-64 and three BMPs.

Rourke who is standing beside the Humvee grabs the handset and quickly replies, "Roger that, out." Rourke unkeys the handset takes a couple of breaths, represses the push to talk button and commands, "Guidons, Guidons, Guidons, execute River Bend at this time. Execute River Bend Now! Six out." Rourke then waves and calls over to Josh, "Come on, Josh, we got to get out of here!"

Josh slides down the hill, throws his rifle inside the Humvee, jumps in and starts the engine. Rourke jumps in the passenger side, lays his rifle alongside Josh's in the middle of the vehicle. Josh slaps the gear shift into drive, hits the gas and makes a sharp left turn. As they pull out Josh glances over at Rourke, "Why are we leaving? It is a great place to hide."

Rourke looks back over at Josh and declares, "Josh, believe me... we needed to get out of there! They know who we are and where we are."

After traveling 300 meters down the trail back toward 3rd TOW, they pass a JRTC pickup type Humvee going the other way. Rourke glances over at Josh and asks, "You know who that is, right?"

Josh looks back, "No... is that an OC?"

Rourke laughs, "No, Josh, that is a fire marker. He's the guy that acts as the impacting rounds of artillery and mortars. The back of his Humvee is filled with artillery simulators and smoke grenades. He gets a radio call

from the indirect fire control cell on where to go and drop his artillery…
and… he has a MILES God gun for killing anything within the target
radius of the impacting rounds. Now guess where he is going down this
trail?"

Josh suddenly realizes, "Holy shit, he is going down there to kill us."

"That's right, there is… without a doubt… an OPFOR team somewhere
down there that spotted us and called in our location to their fire support
folks. They are going to take us out as part of their overall fire plan."

Josh nods, "Good call, Sir… Saved our butts."

"Let's go another 500 meters and find another hide position about 50
meters off the trail. That should leave that OPFOR team about a thousand
meters back there… that's enough space for us… for a while"

Rourke pulls up his map and studies it. He lets Josh find their next
hide position. Rourke is trying to evaluate the Intel report the scouts sent
everyone. *They have two tanks and two BMPs going down avenue one and
they have one tank and three BMPs going down avenue two. I know they have
more armor. They're probably trying to overwhelm us by attacking on both
avenues at once. They'll probably have a second echelon to follow their guys
with the most success.'*

———————————————

Staff Sergeant Ben Eikenberry, 1st TOW platoon, has been lying on his
stomach inside a little clump of evergreen trees for the last two hours. He
is by himself acting as the lookout for his TOW Humvee that is hidden
about twenty meters behind him in another clump of evergreens. He is
getting cold. He has plenty of clothing and has even laid out his foam mat
to keep the cold from seeping up from the ground. But lying on the ground
for hours still brings on the cold monster. Eikenberry knows he needs to
get up and move around a little bit just to get the circulation going. He's
been putting that off for a while because he knows the OPFOR is out there
searching for them.

During the first thirty minutes on his stomach, he is running through
every possible scenario they could be subject to when the enemy armor
shows up.

Earlier they had picked out the alternate and supplementary positions.
They had actually driven into each position in order to become familiar

with these locations and ensure he could still cover his portion of the EA from each. He feels he has every one of them covered. They had emplaced all their concertina wire using 18-inch tent pegs. Eikenberry has placed it all within a hidden trail opening off to the left of his position. If they try to sneak down this trail they will have to get out and clear the wire first. His crew placed it in a small stream bed that runs across the middle of the trail. It is low enough that if a driver isn't paying attention he could run right into it.

Eikenberry knew from experience that having concertina wire wrapped around your road wheels and drive sprocket is a bitch. It could actually stop your track vehicle. Even worse it takes hours with a pair of wire cutters to clear it from the tracks. Experienced crews know this and will do anything to avoid running into wire.

In preparation, Eikenberry even has his crew kneeling over all the scenarios as he draws them on the ground with a small stick. He isn't pleased with his portion of the EA the lieutenant gave him. To his credit, Lt. Foley admits he is giving him the worst position. But to try and make up for putting him in the lousy position the LT swears he believes Eikenberry is the guy who can make it work. Just as he is finishing up the battle position and his plan to fight the enemy, Lt. Foley pulls up. He gives the LT a quick rundown on the plan. Foley is pleased, smacks Eikenberry on the arm, and says, "That's great, now kill every one of them you can. I'll be in my battle position trying to do the same." With that Foley jumps into his Humvee and hurriedly drives off.

With the prepared battle position work done, it is now time to wait, watch and listen. Eikenberry spends much of that time reflecting on this past year, his first year in the Guard. It makes him smile with pride. He is now an Army National Guardsman. What really makes him smile is that he never thought that a little over a year ago he would have even considered becoming a weekend warrior. When he thinks about it, he is actually proud to be a Guardsman and particularly proud of his unit, *'Fuckin' A... I'm a Dragon Slayer'.*

———◆◆◆———

Lt. Clegg, 2nd TOW is feeling pretty good about his platoons EA set up. Clegg is thinking, *'Going against armor is pretty tricky, oh hell, it is downright dangerous. The only advantage the TOW missile system has over armor is stand-off range. The TOW can fire on an armor vehicle at 3,750 meters away. The whole concept is to shoot at them over two miles away and then run like hell. Getting into any kind of toe to toe fight is pure suicide. Thinking in the rock, paper, scissors vein… steel beats fiberglass every time'.*

When he had first come to CSC, one of the first "Pizza Hut" officer development programs was how to use TOWs in the close-in fight. After a pretty lively conversation and of course guidance from Captain Rourke, the Dragon Slayers came up with some anti-armor rules to live by.

Rule 1. Never present yourself within the 45-degree arc of the track commander's front observation area. Rule 2. If you're limited to within 900 meters range, take nothing but flank shots. Rule 3. Rear shots are best of all. Get behind them when you can. Rule 4. Tanks are always first priority. Rule 5. When mounted, quickly move from your hide position to your firing position. Fire and then move to another hide position. Rule 6. Dismounted positions should always be for rear shots after the armor vehicle has driven past. Trying to run away on foot afterward isn't going to cut it. Stay hidden. Rule 7. Be aware of your intended target's wing man. His mission is to find you. And he is searching. Rule 8. Always use your indirect fire assets, both mortar and artillery. They should precede your TOW firing. Rule 9. Use your concertina wire, anti-tank mines, or any combat engineer assets available. Rule 10. There is nothing wrong with running away. Don't die trying to hold a bad position. Use your speed and live to fight another day with a healthier advantage.

Clegg is sure he has used all the rules to set up his EA. He has four crews. Three are set up for flank shots and one is dismounted on the reverse slope of a steep hill. He set up the Humvee that belongs to the dismounted crew as a decoy at the far end of the EA. The hope is that the OPFOR will focus on the partially exposed Humvee sitting in the wood line and not take the time to search for everybody else.

Clegg has been sitting for hours now. He knows his soldiers are going to become complacent just sitting and waiting. Even though he has been feeling anxious this first hour, he is now getting impatient. He has gone over every possible scenario he can imagine and coming up with possible actions to take for each one. Now he is just thinking, *'Fuck this… I hope they just show up in the next ten minutes. I'm starting to fall asleep. Anything is better than this waiting'.*

CHAPTER 20

"As long as military units are made up of people, people will be their most important ingredient. What a unit commander must do is capture the imaginations of those people, harness their energies, and focus their actions on the unit's mission. It is that focus – combining desired actions – that will provide the teamwork necessary to the unit's success." - Brigadier General James E. Shelton

Covering Force Area
1st TOW Platoon Engagement Area (EA)
11: 34 Hours.

Eikenberry hears a small commotion back at his Humvee which causes him to glance back. He sees his driver, PFC Henry Smith, jump out of the vehicle desperately waving for Eikenberry to come running. He is up, grabbing the foam mat and running in a second. Eikenberry gets to the front of the vehicle when his driver calls out, "We got a code word and the command to do it now." Eikenberry stops, reaches into his shirt pocket to grab a little cheat sheet of code words. Eikenberry put all the code words on a small sheet of paper he has ripped off a 3 by 5 pocket notebook. He figures if he gets shot he could be quick enough and stuff it in his mouth, chew it and swallow it before the OPFOR can find it on him.

Eikenberry finds the cheat sheet and asks, "What is the word?"

"Execute River Bend Now." The driver exclaims.

Eikenberry scrolls down the list, finds it, looks up at everybody and yells, "We got to go now. Smitty, take us to the alternate firing position."

Everyone is loaded and moving within a minute on their way to the alternate position 500 meters further north. The radio broadcast comes back on with a situation report from the LT, on the platoon net, "Two tanks and two BMPs at grid 082810 moving south."

They had gone about 400 meters when they heard artillery simulators going off about where they had just come from. Eikenberry stares back to see large clouds of smoke starting to build at their last position. He shakes his head in disbelief, *'We just missed getting creamed'*. Eikenberry glances over at his driver, "Smitty, put us in the hide position and then get ready to move to the firing position quickly. We just moved closer to the oncoming enemy."

Covering Force Area
2nd TOW Platoon Engagement Area (EA)
11:40 Hours.

Second TOW Platoon Leader, Lt. Clegg, hears the scout report on the company net. The OPFOR is rolling on both avenues. He copies the grids for both armor forces. He starts to get mentally prepared for the fight. An old feeling comes over him. He felt this many times before. He smiles, just a little bit. It reminds him of standing at the ten-yard line waiting to receive the kick for the opening kickoff back in high school. He knew as soon as he caught the ball, all those anxious feelings would simply disappear. He would automatically convert to a kickoff return man with the laser focus on getting past the opposing team. The smile disappears. Now is the time to get laser focused.

He picks up the radio handset and is going to pass on the scout report to the platoon when the radio comes alive. It is the company commander, "Execute River Bend Now... Execute River Bend Now!" This is on the company net. This goes out to everybody. Clegg realizes after receiving the scout report that Rourke wants the whole company moving.

Clegg barks at his driver, "Crank it up. We've got to get out of here now. Head to the alternate firing position."

Clegg speaks into the handset, "All stations this net. Execute River Bend at this time... Execute River Bend Now." The vehicle is now bouncing around so much that Clegg has to tell the driver to slow it down a bit. He puts his hand on the dash to steady himself, brings the handset back up to his mouth and broadcasts the next message to his men, "One tank and three BMPs at grid 095812 moving south." He knows his platoon crews are also moving, rather he hopes they all got the message and are moving to their alternate locations. He knows once they get there, they won't have much time to get ready for the OPFOR armor that is also moving fast.

1st TOW Platoon, Engagement Area
11:44 Hours.

Eikenberry thinks Smitty is going to drive past their alternate position, he yells out, "Smitty, it's here on the left."

Smitty starting to brake calls back, "I got it, Sergeant... the hide is right there." Smitty stops the Humvee. Eikenberry jumps out and starts running forward to the firing position. Smitty cranks the wheel all the way to the right, slaps the gear shift lever into reverse, watches his mirrors and hits the gas again. The hide position is back in a clump of evergreens. The firing position is about 30 meters to the front and in a depression four-foot deep that provides some good concealment for the Humvee when they fire.

Eikenberry jumps down into the depression and lunges against the front of the hole. Bringing up his binoculars and resting on his elbows he starts to scan the EA.

The first thing he notices is the smoke and the flashes of artillery simulators going off at a couple of different locations around the EA. He guesses these are the locations of his fellow platoon mates. Or rather he hopes these are their locations prior to moving to their alternate locations.

He shifts to his left and starts scanning, looking further north. He is scouring for movement. There is no way the OPFOR is going to be running right down the middle of the EA on their way to the rifle companies. They should be moving from tree stand to tree stand with their wingmen on overwatch.

Suddenly he sees movement. Looking through the binos he picks up a BMP that slips behind a stand of trees. While still viewing through the binos he sees some other movement further to the east. About 300 to 400 meters away from the first BMP, he spots another one. That means the two tanks are in overwatch probably somewhere about 300 meters behind. The BMPs are going first to scout out any Blue Force locations. Eikenberry knows this is where his patience and confidence in his fellow platoon members comes in. He is the farthest TOW in the northern section of the EA. He has to wait till the BMPs go past and further wait until the tanks are parallel to his location before he can take a flank shot.

Artillery simulators and smoke start landing inside the EA. Eikenberry knows that Lt. Foley has called in the fire mission. He guesses the timing is going to be fairly accurate. The smoke will be building into a thick smoke screen by the time the BMPs and tanks get into the center of the EA. He knows that once they are in the center that Foley will call for both more smoke and then some HE which will compel the armor to drive with their hatches closed, forcing them to maneuver buttoned up.

The BMPs make a quick jump out of their current positions and race to their next positions. As they stop, they begin to traverse the BMP turrets using their high-powered gun sights to scan for the Blue Force. Eikenberry sees one of the tanks lurch out of the wood line and make his own dash for its next position. Eikenberry is surprised by the tank. He is only 300 meters away. This one is way too close to fire on without being seen. Eikenberry decides to search for the far tank and wait till the far tank has gone past so he can hit him with a right rear shot.

What amazes him is the speed in which they not only move from position to position but how fast they are moving through the EA. Just guessing he figures they could be out of the EA in five minutes. He has to admit that being in this alternate position probably put him in a good location to see the whole EA.

Unexpectedly he sees the strobe on the closest BMP go off. *Damn! One of our guys got one.* Less than 30 seconds later he sees the closest tank's main gun simulator go off in a flash with a smoke signature.

Following the main guns orientation, he sees a strobe going off in the far wood line. *'Damn! They got one of us'.*

More smoke is now falling in the EA. He is checking for the far tank now. The closest tank is moving too fast into and out of covered and concealed positions for him to get a shot off. The tank is now 400 meters further south of his last position. He will be somebody else's problem now. The far BMP is obliterated by the cover of smoke. Eikenberry is searching an area where he hopes to find the other tank. Bingo, the tank is parallel with his position and now quickly moving to another position. Eikenberry stands up, jumps out of the hole, gives Smitty the get here now wave and yells out, "Smitty, come on... Go, Go, Go!"

Eikenberry jumps on top of the roof of the Humvee just as it settles into the four-foot-deep hole. He grabs his gunner's shoulder with his right hand, leans into Sgt. Lawson and extends his left arm pointing out the tank that is moving from the left to right. Eikenberry speaks in a slow controlled voice, "Cory, you see a tank about 900 meters out, moving south... about your... two o'clock now?"

Lawson moves his head to put his right eye against the sight, traverses the launcher to the right, "Yea... I got him... He's slowing up a bit... he's searching for a covered position. As soon as he stops I'm going to nail him."

Eikenberry leans back off of Lawson to give him space to do his work. Ten seconds later he hears Lawson slowly whisper, "You're mine."

There is a flash and a small bang followed by a stream of white smoke that comes out from behind the launcher as Lawson presses the trigger. Lawson is holding the launcher sights on the target to ensure a missile kill. Several seconds later the tank's strobe light goes off.

Eikenberry and Lawson both throw their arms in the air and yell out, "Yes! We got that OPFOR bastard! Yes, we did!"

Eikenberry jumps off the roof to smack Smitty on the arm and continues the celebration, "That was some damn good driving, Smitty."

Smitty replies, "Thanks Sergeant, and that was a great shot by Cory... but don't you think we should move?"

Eikenberry looks at Smitty, still smiling and acknowledges, "Yea, you're right... back out and pull over to that small hill... over there about 80 meters from here." Eikenberry then grabs ahold of Smitty's arm, "Wait... let's all load up and move to the supplemental position and get ready for anything else. I'd feel safer moving there. There's too many OPFOR fuckers around here."

———————————

2nd TOW Platoon Engagement Area
11:50 Hours.

About ten minutes after pulling out of their primary firing position, Lt. Clegg's crew is pulling into their alternate position. They back into their hide position. On the way there he has made the call to the battalion fire support team to fire on his preplanned targets with smoke. He has given them a long linear target in order to saturate the middle of his EA. He wants to get word that he has armor in his EA before he calls for high explosive to force the enemy to button up. After that he wants quick smoke from the Dragon Slayer mortars. Their smoke would be thicker and build quickly and cover completely.

Clegg jumps out and runs up to the firing position to check his EA. He can see puffs of smoke and bright flashes going off at three of the platoons' abandoned firing positions including his. He shakes his head and thinks, '*Holy shit... glad the commander got us all out of there*'.

He has a PRC-77 radio in a ruck sack with him and is on the platoon freq. After watching his smoke rounds impacting in the EA, he gets a call from his dismounted TOW guys. From their hidden position they spot two BMPs. Clegg tells them to send the grid locations and their direction of travel over the air in the clear. He wants everyone in his platoon to know where the OPFOR is and to focus on tracking them. He is aware of the OPFOR radio intercept and jamming expertise. He is betting he can get his gunners to take out all the targets, have everyone switch platoon radio freqs, before the OPFOR radio interceptors find him and start to jam his radios.

The TOW crew, led by Sgt. Sean Meyer, positioned 300 meters to his north calls over the platoon freq that they spot the tank. It is actually sitting a little behind the dismounted crew about 100 meters off to their east. This means Clegg can account for two BMPs and the tank. They still need to account for one more BMP. All the OPFOR armor is moving from concealed position to concealed position quicker than anyone anticipated.

Clegg broadcasts over the net, "All elements… if you've got a shot take it now." Clegg is afraid they will be through his EA before they can fire a shot.

The next radio traffic is cross talk between his crews. They are assigning themselves targets and letting everyone else know. Both of the other Humvee TOWs take shots at the two known BMPs. Clegg has his binos up and is looking first at the known BMP locations, waiting for the strobes to go off and then searching for the missing BMP.

There is one strobe on the closest BMP. One kill, and by now it is obviously one miss on the far BMP. Clegg knows his crew with the miss is reloading, he hopes they can get another shot before they are spotted. The crew with the kill is already backing out of its firing position and moving to its next position using cover and concealment to get there.

Just then Clegg sees movement to his left front. It is the missing BMP. They see the flash and smoke signature from Sgt. Meyer's Humvee, making an immediate left turn, hitting the gas, racing across the EA's open space, they are now in hot pursuit. They have the scent and like a bloodhound they are charging after Meyer's vehicle. Clegg grabs the radio handset and just about yells into it, "White 3… you got a BMP on your ass… take action."

Clegg stands up and waves anxiously to his Humvee to move up and into their firing position. His gunner, Spec Steve Paulson stands up in the hatch and asks, "Where Sir?" Clegg now standing in the front of the repositioned Humvee raises his arm and points to the BMP racing across their front, "See him running… about two o'clock at 700 meters? Steve… you've got to see him!"

Paulson quickly puts his head against the sight and yells out, "Yea, I got him… he's moving fast… Wait he's slowing down… He stopped… he's firing at somebody. I'm taking the shot."

With a flash and a bang Paulson fires off his missile. He holds the sight picture on the target till he sees a bright yellow strobe go off.

Clegg immediately yells out, "Great shot… now let's get the hell out of here." Clegg runs over to the passenger side jumps in, and hollers to the driver, "Go… that tank is still out there."

After travelling 400 meters to their next position, Clegg gets a radio call from his dismounted crew still hiding on the back side of the far northern hill, "We got the tank. Got 'em with a rear shot... Need a little help, over."

Clegg knows the "need a little help" is a request for the dismounts to get their Humvee back. Clegg answers, "Yea, we got you on the help request... break... I'm looking for another BMP unaccounted for... anybody?" The only reply he gets is from the dismounted crew with a, "Negative on the BMP... and I see two of ours with strobes... sorry."

Clegg talking to himself murmurs, *'Shit, we lost two'*. He picks up the handset for the radio set to the company net. He knows Sgt. Donnelly, now teamed up with Sgt. Winters, will be monitoring. "White 2... One BMP in route to your location... how copy, over?"

Donnelly, in his typical confident voice replies, "Roger that... We'll take care of him, over."

Clegg smiles, "When you get your work done... execute Candy Corn on my command, over."

"Candy Corn" is another throw away code for "meet me at a time and place to be designated later". The missing BMP is now Sgt. Donnelly's problem. Clegg has to get a couple of things completed. Like getting his dismounted crew their wheels. Then getting a handle on his platoon situation. It isn't looking good.

The last thing Rourke wants to do is be a pain in the ass to his platoon leaders. He talked to several Vietnam veterans who complained about their leaders flying around overhead in a helicopter directing the squads, platoons and even companies on the ground. It ultimately created more problems by usurping the authority of the leaders on the ground. Instead of directing their own squads and platoons they simply became a conduit for orders literally coming from above.

When Rourke first became a Cav platoon leader, he had a troop commander that was a bit of a micro manager and lacked self-confidence. He was not sure of himself and consequently never felt in control of the situation. He was on the radio asking for an updated situation report every five minutes. Rourke many times wanted to reply, "When something changes... I'll give you a call. Otherwise quit asking every fuckin' minute!" But of course, he never did. Rourke was pretty happy to get his new troop commander seven months later, a solid captain that turned out to be a good mentor to all the lieutenants.

But he felt the battle had gone on long enough with him basically in the dark. He and Josh had been flipping through all the platoon freqs, the fire support freq, the mortar freq, and monitoring the company command freq in order to try and stay on top of the current battle. Now is the time to get a current situation report from everyone. If he can positively influence the battle he feels he must do it now. He sends out a net call, first to change the company and platoon freqs, and then to have the platoon leaders prepare an encoded situation report giving Rourke the true picture on what equipment, weapons, and men are left. He wants it fast.

Rourke begins pacing outside his Humvee. Josh remarks, "Hey, Sir... I wonder if this is how the battalion commander does his waiting while standing by for a situation report from you?"

"Hey, funny man... If you must know they teach us this pacing technique at our officer basic course. This is not typical pacing... this is special officer pacing and don't ask me to explain it. I'm not allowed to. Now if you would agree to become an officer... I could let you in on the secret."

Josh nods, "Nice... No way... I got bigger plans."

The company command radio breaks squelch, "Six... you got more coming... three BMPs and two tanks. Same, same, over." It is Sgt. Callahan from the 1st Scout Section in front of the 1st TOWs. This is the second echelon and they are coming down the 1st avenue of approach at the same speed as the first OPFOR group did.

Rourke takes three steps, slides into the Humvee, picks up the handset, starts to talk then stops to think for a couple of seconds. Rourke is trying to put together his tactical situation. But is at a real loss as to what he has and where it is.

After evaluating what he knows and what he doesn't know, Rourke speaks into the handset, "Hey, Green, can you help us out on this?" Rourke wants Callahan to try and engage some of the OPFOR armor with his scouts. This is not in the original plan. The scouts are to stay hidden throughout the operations and provide important Intel. Having them fire on the OPFOR will compromise their mission. But Rourke feels he needs the help. He only hopes that Callahan can do the "Jedi mind reading" with him and understand Rourke wants him to change his mission and help kill some of these OPFOR vehicles without going into a long explanation on the radio.

Jedi Callahan replies, "Roger that… will work the problem."

Rourke feels slightly better. If the scouts can kill even one vehicle it will help. Several seconds later the situation reports start coming in on the new company command net. Josh already has a small note pad open ready to copy the encoded reports.

After getting them all, both Rourke and Josh double check the decoded messages. The run down is 1st TOW lost two Humvees, 2nd TOW lost two Humvees, Sgt. Donnelly lost a 2nd TOW Humvee due to the initial enemy artillery fire. Rourke has to shake his head, *there's always one guy who doesn't get the word'*. 3rd TOW didn't lose anyone and the Scouts are still 100 percent. Rourke has to admit it isn't too bad. It could have been a lot worse.

The run down on the OPFOR is: 1st TOW Platoon killed one tank and two BMPs, 2nd TOW Platoon killed one tank and two BMPs, Sgt. Donnelly/Winters killed one BMP, 3rd TOW Platoon killed one tank. That accounts for both armor elements. The Dragon Slayers got them all.

So now the next battle matches up with 1st TOW Platoon having two Humvees and 3rd TOW Platoon having four Humvees going against the next echelon of three BMPs and two tanks coming down the 1st armor avenue of approach.

Rourke calculates they have a couple of minutes before the OPFOR 2nd echelon will be in the 1st TOW platoon EA. It is too late to move anyone from the 2nd TOW or the Donnelly/Winters team to have any effect on the upcoming battle. Rourke is fairly confident everyone is aware of their situation. He reaches for the handset, "Red, Blue… you got this… use your assets… good hunting, over." Rourke just confirms to them the fight is all theirs, there is no help coming.

Foley answers first, "This is Red… good copy… we're working it, over."

Petrone answers next, "This is Blue… good copy… Red, give me a heads up when you can, over." Petrone is hoping for Foley to give him a situation report, like when he should expect the armor on his doorstep.

Foley again answers, "Roger Blue, will do… working with Catapult at this time, out."

Rourke, like everyone else in the company, is waiting for word on the company net on how the next battle is going to go. Just then the radio breaks squelch with the voice of Sgt. Callahan, "Six, Green, over."

Rourke replies, "Six, send it."

Callahan again, "We got a heavy… couldn't catch anyone else, over."

Rourke smiles, speaks into the handset, "Roger, copy… got a heavy… that'll help, thanks, Six out."

Rourke is feeling slightly better. The OPFOR has three BMPs and one tank going against six TOW Humvees.

1st TOW Platoon Engagement Area
13:25 Hours.

Lt. Foley can't help but feel overwhelmed right now. He is by himself on the east side of the EA while Sgt. Eikenberry is over on the west side. He picks up the mic for the radio set on the platoon freq, "Hey Four, let me know when you see them… send out their position if you can…I'll do the same, over."

Eikenberry comes back, "Roger that… the count is 3 and 1, correct?"

"Roger, 3 and 1… I'll buy if we get them all."

Eikenberry laughs out loud, looks over at his driver and spits out, "Smitty, you got to love our LT. We're going to be lucky not to get killed ourselves, let alone do some damage to the OPFOR."

After Eikenberry's first kill from the alternate position he has the Humvee move to their supplemental position. When they get there he promptly recons the firing position; doesn't like it. Immediately walks back to the vehicle and tells Smitty to drive back over to their primary position. Eikenberry knows he is taking a chance going back to the primary. The OPFOR has already fired on it with artillery earlier. But it is still the best position to overwatch the EA. They put the Humvee in the hide position. Eikenberry crawls up to the firing position. With his binos in hand, and a PRC-77 radio, Eikenberry conducts a search of the northern side of the EA.

A minute later he spots the smoke signature of the exhaust of a BMP speeding south. He knows the other two have to be on line across the EA.

He guesses the tank is probably 400 meters behind and probably in the center of the EA so he can overwatch and provide cover fire for all three BMPs.

He does another bino search and spots the second BMP. Picking up the radio handset he calls over to Lt. Foley, "One... got two BMPs... grid 084805...break... grid 088804... over."

Foley comes back, "Roger, good copy... We have one heavy at grid...085810... I'm moving to get a shot on him... break ... can you get a shot on others, over?

Eikenberry checks again through his binos to assess the location of the two BMPs. Picks up the handset, "I'm moving for a better shot." He stands, picks up the ruck sack with the PRC-77 and starts to jog back to the Humvee. Right when he is twenty feet away he stops. Does he hear an engine? Is it a BMP engine? Holy shit. Yes, he does. Damn! The missing BMP. He continues to slowly walk to the Humvee tilting his head and trying to locate the exact position of the BMP. It is close. He glances up at his gunner, "Cory, you hear that?"

Spec Lawson stares to his left and stretches his head toward the sound. After a couple of seconds, Cory whispers, "Yea, it's a BMP, but he's not moving our way... He's like gunning his engine... like he's stuck and trying to get out."

Just then it dawns on both Eikenberry and Lawson at the same time. Both break out in big grins and look at each other, Lawson snickers, "He's stuck in our concertina wire!"

Eikenberry throws the ruck sack in the back and jumps into the passenger seat, "Smitty pull out and take a left... we have to go further west and circle around this sucker and shoot him from the rear. There's a spot about 500 meters from here. We've got to go, Smitty... come on, hit it." Smitty punches the gas pedal and they dart out of the hide position.

———————◆—•—◆———————

Foley wants the tank. He told his crew they should let the BMPs go by; he wants the tank. He points out the tank location to his driver and asks, "We have to move further north. Can you take us through the woods and get us up there about 800 meters, break out of the woods to put us on his flank?"

PFC Bill Gorman nods and says, "Yes, Sir, I think so."

Gorman selects a little trail leading back into the woods that first appears to lead them north. After traveling 100 meters up the trail, it makes a sharp right turn to the east. He stops. Everyone searches down the trail to see if it breaks back left so they can continue north. Foley cries, "Shit... That's the end of this trail going north. Gorman you're going to have to break some new ground and get us through the woods here."

Gorman, scanning for a way to enter the woods, simply says, "Yes, Sir, hold on."

He finds a spot, hits the gas and takes off. Later on, Foley has to admit that Gorman did a terrific job of running their Humvee through the woods making a trail where there was none.

Gorman is working hard on the steering wheel and alternating between hitting the brakes and hitting the gas, going between big trees and driving over little ones. Foley, sitting in the passenger seat is as the old saying goes, "holding on for dear life".

Finally, Foley believes they have gone the necessary 800 meters, so he tells Gorman to take a left and get back to the EA. Foley is hoping to break out of the woods and be a little bit behind the tank which should have moved forward to its next position.

When they break out of the woods there are three problems. The first is they hadn't gone 800 meters; they have gone only 600 meters. Second the tank hadn't moved. Third, they came out of the woods and there isn't any cover or concealment. They break out into an opening that overlooks the EA. They are now in front of the tank and with their bursting out of the woods into the opening it easily gets the attention of the tank commander.

Foley immediately locks eyes with the tank commander 200 meters away. Foley is just a micro second faster realizing what happened. Foley screams, "Fuck! Back in the woods!"

Gorman slams the shifter into reverse and hits the gas. Holding the steering wheel straight, he is hoping he will be able to shoot back into the woods exactly where he has come out. Gorman can hear Foley yelling, "Shit... he's traversing his turret... He's going to shoot us... Shit... he's going to shoot us!"

They are now fifteen meters in the woods when Foley sees the flash of the main gun simulator affixed to the top of the main gun. The Humvee strobe goes off once, signifying a near miss. Gorman is now working like a mad man backing the vehicle further into the woods. He is using both mirrors, checking back by leaning and hanging out of the driver's side steering in reverse. Foley on the other side is leaning out looking back and yelling, "You're good on my side... you're still good on my side. Keep going!" The gunner on top, staring into the EA starts yelling, "He's coming... The fuckin' tank is coming. We got to get out of here."

After backing up another 30 meters Gorman finds the new trail that he had broken just a minute before. He makes a sharp left turn and furiously drives back down, later to be named in future war stories, the "Gorman Trail".

After traveling another 300 meters through the woods Foley has Gorman stop. Foley jumps out and walks 30 meters toward the edge of the woods and listens. What he hears is the tank working its way down the woodline searching for Foley's Humvee.

Foley jogs back to the vehicle, looks at both the gunner and Gorman, "The tank is running down the woodline looking for us. We're about 60 or 70 meters back in the woods. He'll never see us... and even if he did, he couldn't shoot us... no clear shot... and we'd move anyway... on the other hand we can't shoot him either. We're stuck."

Foley reaches in and picks up the handset, "Hey, Four... sit rep, over."

Eikenberry immediately comes back, "One...Four... We got a BMP... The other two kept going... you get the heavy, over?"

Foley replies, "Four... One... negative on the heavy. He'll be moving on also... I'll notify Blue, out."

Foley glances in at Gorman, "Bill, switch me over to the company net."

Foley makes the radio call to Lt. Petrone, "Blue, Red, over."

Petrone comes back, "Red, this is Blue, over."

"You've got two and one on the way, over." Foley wonders if everyone on the company net can tell from his voice he feels total disappointment.

Petrone comes back again, "Roger... I copy two and one, out." Foley could tell from Petrone's voice, that his fellow platoon leader is now all business.

CHAPTER 21

"Its hard to beat a person who never gives up" - Babe Ruth

"I've missed more than 9,000 shots in my career. I've lost almost 300 games. 26 times, I've been trusted to take the game winning shot and missed. I've failed over and over and over again in my life. And that is why I succeed." -Michael Jordan

3rd TOW Platoon Engagement Area
14:40 Hours.

Lt. Petrone puts down the handset. He is standing outside of the passenger door with his left arm lying across the top of the frame and has his head against his arm. He is thinking about his new situation. His platoon is all that is standing between the OPFOR armor and the battalion's infantrymen behind him. He wishes that Trevor could have taken out another armor vehicle but that didn't happen. He reaches in to pick up the handset again, leans in and asks his driver to switch the radio to the fire support net. He asks fire support for smoke, lots of smoke in the EA. With only his four Humvees to battle the remaining OPFOR armor, he wants some assistance with a smoke screen. Petrone knows he needs some luck and is praying for something to fall out of the sky and give him some. He reaches in and pulls out his map. Wishful thinking isn't going to get the job done. Time to go to work.

The radio comes on. His farthest TOW Humvee, led by Sgt. David Hyde, reports sighting a BMP entering the EA. A few seconds later Hyde's crew reports seeing the other BMP entering the EA but way off to the east. And then a couple of seconds later again they report that it appears that the BMPs are not travelling down the middle of the EA, but are swiftly working their way down the sides of the EA.

Petrone thinks about this for a couple of seconds. *'Damn, they changed tactics, they're not trying to get somewhere... they're now hunting. They're hunting my Humvees. The smoke that's landing down the middle of the EA... to hinder their movement is probably going to hinder our ability to spot them across the EA. I need a new plan... fast'.*

Petrone gets back on his platoon net. "Hey two and three, you need to take care of the BMP on your side... break... four you're with me... everyone watches for the heavy. Call him out if you see him." It is the best Petrone can do. With Platoon Sergeant Stewart and Sgt. Hyde working the west side, Spec Zack Lewis and himself working the east side, he is hoping they can dispose of the BMPs quickly.

Sgt. Hyde sees the BMP approaching and moving fast. He is outside the Humvee about 30 meters forward leaning against a big tree. He turns, runs back to his vehicle, jumps in and tells his driver, "Johnny, we got to find a place in the woods to hide till this guy goes by. He's gon'na find us... Johnny we've got to hide out... let's go."

Within a matter of minutes Hyde's Humvee is working its way through the woods seeking a place to hide in a location that an armored BMP couldn't come crashing through the woods to kill them. This requires them to be at least 60 meters back from the woodline. They find a spot that has five big trees lined up that provide ideal concealment. Hyde slides out and slowly walks twenty meters back toward the woodline. Just close enough to catch a glimpse of the BMP creeping along the woodline. Hyde barely discerns the two figures on top of the BMP turret using their binos to search the woods for any sign of the Blue Force. Hyde's reaction is to lie even lower in the sparse plot of evergreens where he is concealed. Hyde stops breathing when the BMP stops and starts traversing its turret left and right.

The two figures on top are pointing and Hyde could just make out over the engine noise they are talking. It is apparent that they have seen Hyde's Humvee skirt into the woods somewhere around there. They are searching. It seems like forever for Hyde, but finally they back out of their position and make a left turn to continue south.

Hyde, when sure they had really driven further south, and aren't waiting to surprise him when he comes back out, slowly gets up and walks to his vehicle.

Johnny speaks as soon as Hyde sits down in the passenger seat, "Damn, Sgt. Hyde, I thought for sure they saw us and were going to come charging in on us."

"Yea, I was kind of shitting my pants thinking the same thing for a couple of minutes there." After a long pause, Hyde comes up with a new plan. He explains, "Johnny, I'll ground-guide you back out to the woodline… stay back far enough, if I start waving you back, you move back. Got it?"

Hyde gets all the way back to the edge of the woodline and raises his right hand in a fist, signaling for Johnny to stop. His Humvee is still fifteen meters back in the woods. It has been a good fifteen minutes since the BMP started searching for Hyde's vehicle. He drops to one knee and listens. He hears a slight engine noise down the woodline. This is probably where his Platoon Sergeant, Sgt. Stewart, is located.

He checks around. He looks north hoping to see the tank. No luck. He brings up his binos and searches the woodline across the EA hoping like hell he'll find the other BMP and tank. He sees neither. What he sees is the smoke that landed in the middle of the EA thickening and drifting east to completely cover the south-eastern portion of the EA. If there is an OPFOR vehicle down there it is going to be hard for his guys to find it.

He again inspects south down his side of the EA. He sees nothing. He drops his head down and thinks to himself, 'OK this is where the rubber meets the road. As much as I don't really want to… I've got to go a little bold here'. With that, Hyde stands up and runs into the EA. He is running and looking south trying to find the BMP. He gets about 60 meters into the open and that's where he spots it. He immediately drops to one knee. It is approximately 400 meters away partially pulled into the woods. He focuses on the BMP's movements. It appears to be working in and out of the woodline like a dog that has an animal cornered. Hyde realizes it is Sgt. Stewart's crew that is the trapped animal.

Hyde stands up, stares back at his Humvee and begins yelling and waving for it to come forward. Hyde makes the tough decision to expose his crew in order to kill the BMP that is on his Platoon Sergeant's ass. He is hoping to be so fast he will make the kill then get back to cover and concealment before he gets killed.

Johnny, who comes roaring up to Hyde, slams on the brakes. Hyde looks up at his gunner, points south and yells up to him, "Marcus, he's at 400 meters... can you find him?"

Spec Marcus DeCastro looking through his sight yells back, "Yea, I see him... he's firing at somebody in the woods."

"Marcus, kill him... quick!"

Hyde hears the missile fire then sees the white smoke blasting out the rear of the tube. He turns back and watches for a couple of seconds till the BMP's yellow strobe goes off.

Hyde, who is feeling like a guy with his pants down around his ankles in the middle of a shopping mall, quickly jumps into his vehicle, glances at Johnny and is just about to scream, *"Let's get the hell out of here."* when the strobe attached to the hood in front of the passenger's seat goes off in a steady pulse.

Hyde takes off his helmet, holds it in his lap, tilts his head back and shouts out the only thing that conveys everyone's feelings, "Fuck!"

He climbs out of the passenger's side, throws his helmet up on the hood, scans north and sees the OPFOR tank 300 meters away and really moving. The tank is going so fast it is kicking up a rooster tail of dirt that is as high as the tank. It is going to be passing right by Hyde's vehicle. As they speed past, both the loader and the tank commander are sneering down at Hyde's crew. They both have big grins and are shaking their heads with that *'You're such a dumb ass'* look. For a couple of seconds Hyde thinks they are right. That was kind of a dumb ass move. He then looks up and sees his gunner, Marcus, thrusting up his right arm into the air and giving them the finger. It makes Hyde smile.

He turns around, leans against the vehicle, and examines the EA. He sees further down south another yellow strobe going off in a sure steady pulse. He reaches in to grab his bino's. Peering through the thick smoke he makes out the shape of a BMP. The guys over on the east side got the other BMP. He searches the whole east. No other strobes. The LT and Spec Lewis are still alive.

Lt. Petrone is looking through his binos at the west side of the EA. He is having a hard time seeing through the dense smoke he is standing in. He tried the radio a minute earlier to reach either Sgt. Stewart or Sgt. Hyde. There is no answer. The coordination between him and Spec Lewis worked well. They trapped the BMP between them. Just a minute ago they both got a shot off but Petrone really didn't know which one made the actual kill. If asked, he of course, is going to give the credit to Zack Lewis. Petrone is confident Zack is going to be a fine NCO in the near future. This kill at the "great JRTC experience" should help his reputation down the road.

After searching for a couple of minutes he picks up three strobes. Sadly, he identifies two of them as his guys. He knew the tank had gone down the west side of the EA. With both his guys killed over there, the tank has a clear path down to the battalion rifle companies. He has a little guilt creeping into his head. *'Shit, it is my platoon that has the responsibility to stop them'.*

He then reaches in and picks up the handset to make the call to the commander letting him know the tank is loose and on the way south to the battalion.

The call is short. Cpt. Rourke is matter of fact when he gets the situation report. He wants his three TOW platoons, after sweeping the battle area for their dead and wounded, to all meet at a central location to quickly consolidate and reorganize in order to get back out on the covering force mission, to hunt down the tank and to start working on the OPFOR dismounted infantry. Petrone pores over his map. It is going to take at least twenty minutes to get to the consolidation site after working another twenty minutes on the dead and wounded issues with the battalion medics. He calls Trevor on the company net to ensure Rourke hears that he wants them to hook up and then move together to the consolidation site. Traveling with four machine gun Humvees is safer than just two. This will add another ten minutes to the time. But everyone knows it is the better decision.

15:35 Hours.

Rourke gets off the radio with Petrone. He hears Petrone making arrangements with Foley to meet up and travel together to the consolidation site. Smart move. Hell, he didn't even think about that. He turns to look at his XO. "Number One... I know the platoon sergeants will be giving you the scoop on their personnel... get the dead and wounded back as fast as you can... the sooner we get them back to the rear the sooner we get them back in the fight."

Kiser is nodding, "Top's on the ball with this. He's waiting in the rear and working with the S-1 to make this work." After a couple of seconds Kiser asks, "I don't monitor the battalion, have you called in a situation report lately?"

"Yea, we're good. Actually, Josh sends in a report periodically to Sgt. McCallister in Ops. Josh just sent the message, 'We have an OPFOR tank on the loose... headed to the rifle companies.'"

Kiser glances down at his watch. "Hey, Sir, I got to go. I've got to meet up with the medics and the support platoon guys. I called in everyone's log reports to Top and Supply Sergeant Burke. They're putting together the Logpac. My turn around time is going to be pretty short. I figure it'll be a middle of the night Logpac for the platoons... You need anything else from me?"

Rourke tilts his head up, thinks for a second, "Nah, nothing from you... keep doing what you're doing." Rourke grins and sets his sights on his XO, "If anyone back there asks... tell them the company is doing well. I've got to sit down and figure out some things. I'll try to catch you tonight with the Logpac... and watch your ass out there."

With that Rourke slides into his Humvee and takes out a note book to do some figuring. After summarizing all he has in the company he reaches for the handset and leans over to switch the radio freq to the scouts. The call is short, "Green One, this is Six, over."

"Six, Green, over."

"Green, need to see you… and bring three to give up, over."

You could tell the disappointment in Lt. Fugate's voice. Nobody wants to give up three of their Humvee crews while still in a fight. But he knows the TOWs paid a price for all their work killing the OPFOR armor. Three pretty much meant he is giving one crew to each of the TOW platoons to help them get back to fighting strength.

Fugate speaks into the handset, "Roger that 6… Wilco on three… six zero mikes, over."

"Copy, thanks… Six out."

Fifty minutes later, Rourke hears several Humvees pulling into the little opening 25 meters in front of his vehicle. He sees Lt. Petrone jump out of his Humvee and run toward him. What makes this odd is that Petrone has the biggest grin across his face. Obviously Petrone is happy about something. Before Rourke can ask, Petrone calls out, "Hey, Sir… Third Platoon didn't let the battalion down… we got the tank!"

Naturally this brings a big smile to Rourke, "What?… How the hell did that happen?" Josh, sitting in the driver's side, jumps out and quickly moves around the front in order to hear Petrone's story.

Petrone stops in front of Rourke who also gets out of the Humvee. Petrone rests his arms on his M-16 at his waist, which is suspended by the sling around his neck, throws his head back a little and exclaims, "Remember my two guys… I put out in an overwatch position to keep an eye on the third OPFOR cache site?" Rourke, guessing where this is going, smiles even bigger and presses, "Well I know we talked about it… but I didn't know exactly where you put them."

"Well we searched around for a location where we would be out of the way… but still have a good view of the site. We picked a spot that is elevated, wooded and about 500 meters away. It is 30 meters off one of the major trails running back to the battalion. You couldn't see it from the trail… it is in a clump of evergreen trees and a bunch of ferns." Rourke has to laugh a little just looking at Petrone who is excited and animated using his hands and arms still resting on his rifle.

Petrone never stops his explanation, "Well, we knew the best way to keep an eye on the site is a TOW sight. So instead of just giving them the sight… we set up the whole TOW dismounted system on the tripod and left two missiles. We weren't planning to fire them… we just dumped out the system and missiles to make more room inside the Humvee. We also… of course… left them a PRC-77 radio." He takes a quick breath, "Well, they're sitting there and a tank goes cruising by behind them on the trail… Well they know we don't have tanks and they know we've been fighting up here to kill all the armor… so they know this one got away. They pick up the TOW system and a missile… literally run it out to the middle of the trail… set it up… in record time… by then the tank is about 300 meters down the trail. They shoot it in the ass!" Petrone, with a sense of pride declares, "Yes, Sir… Third Platoon finished them off."

Rourke relays to Josh, "Call battalion. Tell them we got the tank."

Josh flashes a thumbs-up and says, "Way to go, Third TOW! Good job, Sir." then moves back around the vehicle to make a quick call to Sgt. McCallister.

Rourke looks at Petrone and marvels, "Wow LT… that's good for us that… luck… just fell out of the sky. We could sure use more like that down the road."

Petrone nods, "You've just got to pray harder, Sir."

<hr />

16:50 Hours.

Rourke never expects to see all his platoon leaders at one time during the first four days, but, this last 24 hours was pretty crazy. They form a small huddle in a group of trees after walking about 50 meters from Rourke's Humvee. Each finds a small tree to sit by and lean against. Rourke looks over all of them. They are tired. They have been going since before they crossed the LD back at main post. The excitement of participating in the JRTC experience is starting to wear off. Rourke knows that adrenalin has been driving them since crossing the LD.

Last night they should have gotten some sleep, but with Rourke's own past experience he knows they hardly slept. Burnout is going to happen soon if they don't get some sleep. The situation has drastically altered. He needs to make changes to the original operations plan.

Before he gets started Rourke spots a figure walking toward the group. When he is within ten meters, Rourke recognizes him. It is Captain Tim Chancy, the OC for his company. He speaks to him, "Tim, I guess it's good to see you... Do you need anything in particular?"

Chancy shakes his head and replies, "No, Devlin... this is just part of the OC process... I'm going to sit in on your meeting... pretend I'm not even here."

Rourke, understanding the importance of the OC's role more so than the lieutenants, glances at Chancy, nods and points to an open spot in the circle and continues his meeting.

He starts with looking around smiling, and begins with, "All the company has done a fantastic job since hitting the maneuver box. Make sure you tell your guys I appreciate everything they've done." Rourke glances up at the sky, "It'll be dark in less than an hour. So, whatever we do will be done in total darkness. We're all tired... tired soldiers mean mistakes and possibly safety concerns. Soldiers get hurt when we're all tired. Therefore, I want to limit any movement of vehicles tonight. We're still doing the mission of covering force... we're just changing the method and using a different technique.

Rourke brings up his field note book, runs his finger down the page. "Let's go over the company's situation and check to see if what I have is what you have. 1st TOW, Trevor, you've got what?"

Lt. Foley starts, "Well I lost two and Sgt. Winters lost one, I got three, left with one scout... so four." He moves on to Lt. Clegg.

Clegg nods and glances over at Rourke, "I lost two and Sgt. Donnelly lost one, I got three left." He motions to Lt. Petrone.

Petrone is watching Rourke, "I lost two in today's battle and lost one last night for blown engine. The XO drug it back on the last Logpac... I forgot to tell you earlier... so I'm running with three, once I pick up the dismounted OP back on the trail." He finishes and passes on to Lt. Fugate.

Fugate picks up with, "Well I started with ten... Sir you took two... then gave those to Sgt. Winters... He lost one this morning to artillery fire... So, I've got eight... but you told me to bring three... so I'm down to five."

Rourke acknowledges and begins, "OK, 1st TOW with three and one scout... 2nd TOW with three... 3rd TOW with three... Scouts with

8." He stops for a minute then continues, "Mark, your scout with the 1st TOW stays with them… Give one to 2nd TOW and another to 3rd TOW and I want one with me." Rourke scans all around. Everyone is nodding in understanding. Rourke's eyes settle on Lt. Fugate, "Mark, sorry to have to take from you… but we have to share the wealth or… the misery… however you want to look at it."

Fugate smiles, "Well, Sir I kind of look at it as… trying to improve the TOWs with better quality soldiers."

Almost in unison the three TOW lieutenants belt out, "Fuck You… You're such a dick!… maybe if your guys could fight once in a while… bunch of pussies."

Rourke with a big grin raises his hands to indicate everyone to settle down. He stares at Fugate and chuckles, "That is being a dick… try not to be such a dick… at least the rest of the time we're here… thank you."

He announces, "New plan for tonight. I'm assigning the three TOWs their own areas across the front of the battalion. Scouts will be staying in place forward to continue to act as early warning… they're still hunting and the TOWs are still killing." Rourke continues, "I'm pretty sure we've killed all the OPFOR armor… not one hundred percent… but highly confident it's all gone… so now we start working on the dismounted infantry. Which means we start getting dismounted… starting tonight. Once I give you your area… find a good hide place, set up your security… run some short, dismounted patrols around your area and make sure everyone gets some sleep… quality sleep." He stops and gazes at each lieutenant to ensure they understand. To reinforce the point he explains, "The real reason I'm taking a scout crew with me is to ensure both Josh and I get some sleep tonight. Splitting up the night watch among six is better than just two."

After Rourke pulls out his map and makes the area assignments he speaks a few minutes about the Logpac and alerts everyone to try and anticipate their next couple of days requirements. The meeting breaks up. The lieutenants head back to their vehicles. On the way they do a little coordination among themselves along with some joking and ribbing each other before loading up and moving out.

Rourke, still sitting against the tree, reaches around to his canteen on his left hip, pulls it out of its cover and takes a long drink. It is getting dark now. He can just barely make out Captain Chancy's face. He reaches out his hand holding the canteen to offer some water to his guest. Chancy smiles, puts up his hand to show he doesn't want any, "No thanks, I appreciate the offer… but I have a little cooler of sodas back in my Humvee… One of the perks of being an OC."

Rourke nods, "I know I'll get the whole back brief and lessons learned at the AAR… but since you're still here… how we doing?"

Tim lets out a little chuckle, "I really can't say much… You're right; my portion of the AAR will cover what you guys will have done by that time… I am taking copious notes. I know you've seen my team roaming around up here… mostly staying out of the way and doing that observing portion of the OC job." Chancy leans forward bringing his knees up, putting his arms on them and clasping his hands together, "I'm really not supposed to say anything that might give you an advantage… but… I will say… you know all the OCs meet and talk throughout the exercise…I will say you have got everyone talking… including the OPFOR. They have not seen anything like you guys and they are not prepared for you. I personally think it's great. They need a whipping… getting one every once in a while is good for keeping the ego in check. They're getting their egos checked."

Chancy rolls to one side, puts his hand down and starts to get up. He stands, gives a quick point of his finger, "Devlin, just keep doing what you're doing… shit… I've learned a few things from you guys myself. See you at the AAR." With that Chancy turns and walks back toward his Humvee parked further down the trail from the rest.

Rourke leans his head back against the tree and thinks, *'Damn, I'm tired… but I feel good. Chancy didn't have to say a word. But he did tell me we're kicking the OPFOR's ass. I bet they were more worried about Christmas leave for their guys than taking on the National Guard. They're probably short people due to letting some go home on Christmas leave or even scheduled some to leave while we're still here. They forgot… never underestimate your enemy… they'll screw you every time. Chancy just told me… we're doing a pretty good job of screwing them'.*

Rourke rolls to one side, pushes up with his left arm and stands up, rearranges his web belt and gear then walks back to his vehicle.

He gets to his Humvee, tosses his map and rifle in the back and sits on the seat. Josh slides into his driver side and relays, "Hey, Sir, you got a call from battalion… you got a meeting tonight… like in one hour. I think we should get going now, it may be a little hard to find in the dark."

Rourke reaches up to take off his helmet, rubs his head and in the process feels his hair. With the dirt and sweat of the last two days it feels like fur from some dog's back. He puts his helmet back on, takes a deep breath, looks over at Josh and asks, "Was this for only me or everybody?"

"It is for all the commanders… and the rifle companies got encoded FRAGO's to be ready to move."

Rourke nods, "Well that's interesting… I guess the commander is wanting to make a move on the OPFOR… OK, let's saddle up and get moving and we need to pick up a scout Humvee on the way out of here."

Josh reaches across the Humvee with a large white Styrofoam cup of steaming hot coffee, "Made us both a cup of joe after I took the call from Sgt. McCallister… two creams and no sugar… figured we need the caffeine and the warmth."

Rourke takes the cup and raises it in salute, "Josh you're a good man… I was going to say something tremendously funny but I'm too tired to even think… so thanks, I appreciate this."

Josh takes a big drink of his coffee, switches the cup to his left hand, puts the vehicle in drive with his right and then switches the cup back to his right in order to drive the Humvee one-handed down the trail.

CHAPTER 22

"Battles are won by slaughter and maneuver. The greater the general, the more he contributes in maneuver, the less he demands in slaughter." - Winston S. Churchill

2nd Battalion 220th Infantry TOC
19:00 Hours.

It takes them the entire hour to find the battalion link up location. It is pitch black dark. They stop a few times while Rourke and one of the scouts run up and down the trail attempting to find the entrance. The location itself is at least 100 meters back off a trail in a heavily wooded and swampy area between a couple of small rolling hills. In the dark this would probably make a perfect hideout for the old west's "hole in the wall gang". They are guided by a Headquarter's Company soldier with a red flashlight into a small vehicle parking area under camouflage netting.

After backing in, Rourke gets out and asks the guide which way to the meeting. The young soldier steps within arm's reach, points to his right and whispers, "Sir, the TOC is about 50 meters that way." The soldier then walks away to his left in order to help the next vehicle get situated.

Rourke takes a couple of small steps while scanning forward, hoping to see a glimmer of light to help guide the way. Nothing to be seen. He is just going to have to stumble his way to the TOC. Maybe with a little luck, he will hear somebody talking which will help him find the way. After what he guesses is 30 meters, he stops, turns his head and strains to hear anything. He takes a couple more steps. There, he can hear something. It is a portable Honda generator for the TOC. He follows the sound and won't need to softly cry out for a little help like others have done trying to locate the TOC at night. Twenty meters later Rourke opens the tent flap to the blacked-out exterior entrance and then enters the TOC tent through the main flap. The bright light is startling. There are three, single, four-foot-long fluorescent lights hanging by parachute cord on three sides of the tent. There are about twelve, folding chairs set up in the middle all facing a large map board on the far side of the tent.

Sergeant First Class Gary McCallister is standing in front of the map making some additions or changes to the symbols scattered over the map. Part of his duties is to maintain the current situation of all the battalion elements on the map. Another part of his job is to find a location to put in the TOC.

Rourke goes over to comment on McCallister's ability to complete that task, "Gary, I got to hand it to you... you do know how to find the most secure areas to put in the TOC. I bet the OPFOR couldn't find this place and they've been here for years."

"Thank you, Sir. I kind of have a knack for this. Back home I have two hide locations the wife still hasn't found."

Rourke chuckles, "Yes, the fun part is staggering and stumbling through the woods and swamp and only tripping and falling once." He holds up his mud-covered hands as proof, "See, only once for me... I'm sure there will be some who bite it more than me."

Gary is enjoying the conversation, "Why yes, Sir, based on past experience... I would venture to say we have at least three others who will surpass your single mark."

As if on cue, the tent flap flings open and in steps Captain Swoon. The left side of his uniform is covered with a new layer of black swamp mud. He glares at McCallister and fumes, "Damn it, can't you TOC guys hang one freakin' chem light on the front of the tent?"

McCallister glares at Swoon with a straight face and retorts, "No, Sir, we have a night light discipline policy approved by the commander."

Swoon standing in the light, examines the damage from the mud, voices his disgust and frustration, and asks McCallister, "What do you suggest I do in the mean time?"

Keeping a straight face McCallister answers with, "Maybe you could change uniforms or… let that one dry and just shake it out."

"Sergeant McCallister, I now stink to high heaven."

McCallister nods in agreement and pleads, "You are correct, Sir, and please… don't sit near the front, I'm sure the Battalion Commander would rather not smell that during the briefing." With that he turns back to work on the map.

Rourke, who is standing at the map board right beside McCallister, looks over at him to see a slight smile. He lowers his voice and asks, "Now, Sergeant McCallister, what kind of advice would you call that given to Captain Swoon?"

"Why, Sir, that's known as professional courtesy advice… There is no way the Colonel likes Swoon sitting anywhere near him… stink or not."

Rourke smiles, "I'm not sitting by the little stinker either. See you later."

The tent is filling up. All the company commanders are there along with the primary staff officers. Everyone is shaking hands and joking around like they haven't seen each other in days. Which they hadn't.

LTC Francone followed by CSM Daniel Morando abruptly enters the tent. Francone commands everyone to grab a seat. It's time to get started. Francone walks to the map and asks McCallister if everything is up to date. McCallister nods, "As of five minutes ago, Sir."

"Thanks Gary… When is the TOC going to jump?"

McCallister reaches up to put a bunch of map markers in his right shirt pocket and answers with, "Sir, we're jumping the TOC immediately after this Op Order brief. I think we're making a pretty big Intel signature with everyone here. It'll take the enemy awhile to put all the sightings together and any radio intercepts… but I don't think we should take any chances."

Francone nods, "I agree. I'm hoping this doesn't take long." Francone uses a tag line from an old battalion in-house joke, "Yea, one hand grenade could take us all out."

McCallister laughs, "Sir, might not be a bad thing... hanging out in the rear for a couple of days... showers, hot chow, chilling, reading the paper... just enjoying Arkansas."

Francone assures him, "That's not for me Gary... I'll take this Army misery any day."

McCallister chuckles while moving off to the side to sit and be in the perfect location to assist anyone using the map.

Francone turns to face his soldiers and begins, "Gentlemen, I really want to make this quick... there will be no Military Decision Making Process... no three different courses of action to pick from... no synchronization matrix. Take some good notes... cause this is it." Francone contemplates the information in his own field notebook, looks up and starts, "First some assumptions. The OPFOR has used all of its armor. Thanks to the Dragon Slayers they're gone... during the battle against the armor they moved a lot of their infantry past our covering force and are now down in our area."

He moves off to the side of the map to point out the two areas. "Devlin had his hands full with killing off the armor and the battalion is very grateful for that... he didn't have the resources to also hunt down and fight the OPFOR infantry. However, the covering force did have some success initially against their infantry. So much so, I believe the armor attack on the covering force was to eliminate them so they could have free reign throughout the area... Our guys prevailed instead. I think the enemy is now off balance. Let's take advantage of that."

Francone fixes his gaze at the three rifle company commanders sitting in the front row. "Time now for our infantry to start earning their pay. Keep in mind that our initial mission is Defense... we are to hold this ground. So right now, we're going to reposition our defenses. At 06:00 hours I want all three rifle companies to rapidly move forward three kilometers... that's 3,000 meters and then reestablish your defensive posture... dig in... then after two hours, I want you to be prepared to move quickly forward another 3,000 meters and again reestablish your defensive positions."

He switches sides in front of the map board and sweeps his hand along the map to illustrate the movements. "Remember my guidance way back in March... and remember all the training done every drill weekend... this is where we put it into practice."

From the back of the tent someone speaks up to question Francone's tactics, "Jim, I really don't mean to interrupt but this seems a lot like an offensive operation... and that isn't your mission. Your mission is defense." Everyone turns to gaze at the surprise speaker. Rourke immediately recognizes the small group standing in the back as the battalion's OC team. The speaker is a Lieutenant Colonel that is Francone's counterpart. He sees Captain Chancy standing with the group. Rourke assumes they are all the company OCs as well. They had quietly come in right after Francone had moved to the map board in the front. With their focus on the battalion commander no one had noticed the OCs coming in.

Francone feigns surprise, shifts his body, and lifts his hands in the, 'What... I really don't know what you're getting at' gesture. He explains the differences, "Bob, as the commander I have the right to re-position my troops if I feel it will put me in a better situation... I never used the term Movement-to-Contact... nor did I designate objectives... or routes to any objectives... all of those are offensive terms for offensive operations. I'm simply having my companies reposition to better ground to better repel any offensive attack by the enemy."

Everyone in the tent is smiling including the OC team in the back of the tent. The chief OC speaks again, "Alright Jim, it's your exercise... let's see how the repositioning goes."

Everyone in the tent knows that officially, yes, you can call this a repositioning, especially using the two hour pause in the middle and using the term "Be Prepared" to move again. This term provides flexibility to any operation. Technically, the first repositioning could be the completion of the whole operation. By using the term in his briefing, Francone could claim he chose to move to even better ground after reconsidering the first position.

But everyone knows the battalion is going on the offensive. This is a 6,000 meter Movement-to-Contact with a pause in the middle. Everyone remembers the commander's guidance. We are going to be moving and moving and moving and then moving some more. Everyone also remembers the drill weekends for the rifle companies consisted mostly of conducting Movement-to-Contact operations. Francone, after spending considerable time at the companies all those months, knows they have Movement-to-Contact down pat. And the most important piece of guidance is to "Kill the OPFOR". He feels that now is the time to move on the OPFOR using one of the battalion's strengths and yes, to kill the OPFOR.

Francone isn't quite finished, "John, I want you to give your best platoon from Charlie Company to Devlin. He's going to need the three squads to help him continue to disrupt the enemy infantry moving back and forth in our... Defensive... sector." At the word, *Defensive*, Francone stares back at the OC group and smiles. They smile back. Francone continues, "Devlin, you've given each of your TOWs a sector to cover, right... adding a 12-man squad to each one of them should help."

Francone looks back at Captain Bynum, "John, see if you can't get them loaded up on some trucks and moving to Devlin's locations by 05:00 hours. I would like to have them also working when the battalion starts its repositioning... at 06:00 hours. I'm guessing our moving is going to force some of the enemy to move... Work out the link up details after this meeting with Devlin." Francone surveys the group to see that everyone understands the briefing. "The staff is here for any of your questions... that's all I have... and good hunting."

The briefing lasts another fifteen minutes, mostly questions from the rifle company commanders on coordination of supplies and the use of arty and mortars for the operation. The battalion Fire Support Officer announces that the companies now have priority of fires. Rourke's covering force mission is secondary in the battalion's battle plan. He has done a quick-fire plan and passes out the planned targeting overlays to the commanders. Rourke gets one, reads it, and knows it doesn't apply to him so he gives it back. He is hoping his platoon leaders remembered to work up their own fire plans because he sure forgot to mention it.

Cpt. John Bynum walks over, puts his hand out, "Devlin, I understand you and your guys did a super job up in the covering force battle."

Rourke reaches out and shakes hands, "John, you say that like the battle's over for me. It's not... I'm afraid you infantry guys running through the woods are going to create all kinds of havoc with the OPFOR. And then they'll start running through my area... and taking a toll on my company."

Bynum steps in a little closer, lowers his voice, "Devlin, what do you think of the new plan?"

I think the commander believes the OPFOR has underestimated our battalion. They're back on their heels and he's going to use you grunts to run up on them… and steam roll over them. Now I'm guessing here but… that two-hour pause is a deception. It'll take the OPFOR Intel two hours to figure out where we initially stopped. They'll try and send more guys down to engage you… and that's when you guys pick up and do another… three klick Movement-to-Contact."

Rourke pauses for a couple of seconds to let that sink in then continues, "John, if you guys are as good as I think you are… this thing might be over by tommorrow evening. You're going to do a lot of killing tommorrow. I hope most of it is shooting the enemy in the back as they try to fall back and regroup… because you guys are moving too fast for them." He takes another couple of seconds to think, "John, I know you're the reserve company but if I were you, have your guys ready to jet up to the front of either Alpha or Bravo companies if they stall out for even a minute. The Colonel will have your company on a short leash… when he says go… you guys need to fly."

Bynum nods, "Oh we've got Movement-to-Contact down… and we'll be right up on Alpha Company's ass during the move ready to go when called." Bynum asks Rourke to step over to the map, "Devlin, show me where you want my platoon to link up with your guys. I'm giving you my 2nd platoon. The platoon leader is kind of new… he was with headquarters last year… he spent all this year learning… but the squad leaders are strong. That's why I put him with the 2nd Platoon."

Rourke points at the map to a location in his area off the main trail coming from the battalion, "You'll have three trucks from the Support Platoon… a squad in each truck. I'll have each of the TOW platoons send a rep to meet them there. They'll grab one of the trucks and take it to their area and then release the truck to come back to the battalion."

Bynum leans in to take a closer look at the map, "OK, I got the spot… we should be there at 05:00 hours. By the time everybody is hooked up and where they're supposed to be… it should be around 06:00 hours… right when the battalion kicks off on the repositioning." Bynum smiles and turns to Rourke, "Don't get my guys killed, Devlin… take good care of them for me."

Devlin reaches up and grabs hold of Bynum's shoulder, looks him in the eye and swears in an overly dramatic voice, "Not to worry, John... I'll love them like my own."

Bynum nods, "Yea, that's what I'm afraid of... now I've got to go and take care of a hundred things." As he turns to exit the tent he sees Sgt. McCallister with his back turned. He half turns back to Rourke and speaks loud enough for McCallister to hear, "I only hope I can find my vehicle within the next couple of hours. Damn, Gary keeps putting the TOC out in the middle of absolutely nowhere and has the parking area... seems like two miles away... and it's always on the darkest night."

A grinning McCallister turns around and quips, "Captain Bynum, I would have thought, you being a super infantryman, you would shoot an azimuth from the vehicle parking area to the TOC in the daytime... you were here today... walk the distance... so that at night you could shoot a back azimuth and walk back using the pace count." McCallister opens both hands, shrugs and asks, "Right?"

Bynum looks at McCallister, "Oh yea, using that compass thing we carry around." He then looks at Rourke and asks, "Is that how you do it, Captain Rourke?"

Rourke looks at both with a serious expression, "Gentlemen, I am a Cavalry Trooper; I always know where to go and how to get there. I don't require the use of one of those infantry devices that constantly shows the direction to north."

McCallister nods, points to Rourke's hands and asks, "I suppose you got all that mud up to your forearms while changing your horse's shoes tonight?"

Rourke drops his head, grimaces, obviously doesn't have a comeback, glances back up, smiles and stammers, "Gentlemen, I must be moving on." With that he strides over to the tent entrance to make a stealthy getaway.

Once Rourke gets outside he takes a couple of minutes standing there to establish his night vision. He makes it back to the Humvee to find Josh sleeping sitting up with his head against the steering wheel. He slowly slides into his seat and softly calls over to Josh, "Josh, wake up man... we got to get rolling."

"What... What time is it? Where to?" Josh reaches up and rubs his head, "I think I've got a permanent dent in my forehead."

Rourke looks at his watch, "It's almost 21:00 hours and we're going back."

Rourke has Josh find the link up point and pull into a hide position along with the scout vehicle. He broadcasts a message to the TOW platoons to send a vehicle to the link up point at 04:30 hours. It is now 22:10 hours. Rourke, Josh, and the four scouts get together and determine the "stand the watch" schedule. They give Rourke the choice of going first or last. That way he can get the most uninterrupted sleep. Rourke sighs, "Thanks, I can feel the love." He takes the first watch.

CHAPTER 23

"In every battle there comes a time when both sides consider themselves beaten; then he who continues the attack wins." – General Ulysses S. Grant

CSC Area of Operation
Monday, 4 December, 1989
04:25 Hours.

Rourke feels one of the scouts shaking him awake with, "Hey, Sir, time to rise and shine... you want cream or sugar in your coffee?"

Rourke sits up in his sleeping bag, rubs his head feeling the fur on top, and thinks to himself, *'Man, I could use a shower'*, wipes his eyes in an attempt to see the scout clearly, "Really, you guys got coffee?"

"Yes, Sir, Josh just got his first cup a minute ago. We got a little pot over by the Humvee... cream or sugar or both?"

"Just cream, please. I got to start spending more time with you scouts." With that Rourke pulls his legs out of the bag and rolls to his side to push himself up. The scout walks away and comes back with a Styrofoam cup of steaming coffee with cream. Rourke reaches out and eagerly takes the cup, "Thanks... Man, I need this...Damn, how cold is it?"

"Sir, we have a thermometer hanging in the vehicle… it's 35 degrees… at least it's not freezing yet."

Rourke takes measured sips from the cup, "It feels like freezing… fuck… I'm freezing. We need the sun to come out."

"That's not for a while yet, Sir. If you need any more come on over and we'll give you a free refill… after that it's going to cost you."

Rourke finally starts to fully wake up, "What's the price for the third?"

"Four tickets to get the hell out of here. We're not fond of Arkansas, Sir." He turns and walks back to his vehicle.

Rourke carefully sets his coffee cup down, rolls up his sleeping bag, puts on his web gear, picks up his rifle, picks up the cup and walks over to his Humvee. The first TOW Humvee pulls into the small opening. A minute later the other two TOW Humvees pull in. Rourke walks over to them, softly calls the men to gather around. He gives them a five-minute briefing on the battalion's plan and that Charlie Company is giving them three squads. They are waiting for three trucks to show up any minute. They are each to take a squad and start working everyone through the woods in an attempt to catch the OPFOR moving around. All acknowledge the big plan, their part in the overall plan, and that they will pass this info to their lieutenants.

The three trucks pull in a short time later. All three TOW Humvees quickly match up with a truck, pull out of the opening and head back to their areas. This leaves one lone soldier standing in the middle of the opening with a large ruck sack at his feet. Rourke has Josh pull up next to the soldier. Rourke jumps out and offers his hand, "You must be Lt. Heller, right?"

Heller reaches out and shakes hands with Rourke, "Yes, Sir, first name is Dan."

"OK, Dan, throw your stuff in the back of the vehicle and sit behind the driver… that's Josh by the way… so we can talk easier."

Heller tosses his ruck in the back seat, his rifle in the middle within easy reach, and then climbs in.

Rourke can tell Heller isn't too enthusiastic about being there so he asks, "Hey, Dan, you OK… you seem a little out of sorts."

Heller glares right at Rourke with a disgusted expression, "Hey, Sir, you took my platoon off me."

This throws Rourke off for a minute then he understands the lieutenant is right. He realizes he would be just as pissed as Heller if they took his troops.

"Dan, let me explain something to you. I didn't take your platoon off you... your commander didn't take your platoon off you... The battalion commander directed your commander to give one of his platoons to my company to increase my dismounted infantry capability. I'm sorry. If we would have had more time we might have come up with a better plan... but right now this is the situation. You're going to have to suck it up for the time being... in the meantime do what you can to help me. You'll get your time in the fight.

05:45 Hours.

Rourke finds a pretty good hide position close to the middle of the covering force area for his vehicle and the scout vehicle. They throw camouflage netting over the vehicles, set up two OPs on either side of the vehicles. Rourke is sure his part in the next phase of the covering force battle is going to be minimal. He tells everyone in his small party that now is the time to hide, stay low and quiet, and not go searching for a fight. If the OPFOR walks by and doesn't see us, let them walk by.

At 06:00 Rourke and Heller are sitting in the Humvee listening to the battalion command net on one of the radios. There is no radio traffic. This is exactly what Rourke expects. The battalion is very good at radio listening silence discipline. At the LD time, everyone simply gets up and starts moving forward. He switches over to Alpha Company command net. If there is going to be any action it is probably going to come from Carson Young's company.

It doesn't take long. Fifteen minutes later Alpha's lead platoon is in contact with an enemy element of squad size. Rourke hears Carson direct his 2nd Platoon to move to the left of the 1st Platoon's flank. He knows that normally a platoon would maneuver and try to overwhelm an enemy squad size element. But Carson is going to move a whole platoon into them. One squad against two platoons, it is going to be over quick. Rourke hears Carson tell his 3rd Platoon to move in behind the 2nd and be prepared to assume the lead of the company. The radio on the battalion fire support net breaks squelch broadcasting a call for fire. It is Alpha Company Fire Support Team calling for fires. Rourke guesses the fires aren't for the current fight but to prep the next suspected enemy location.

He figures Carson is going all out moving rapidly to his next position. The OPFOR now knows he is moving. Carson is going to use his momentum to try and roll over the OPFOR. He is going to lay down artillery and mortar fires right in front of his moving company. Hopefully this will kill some of the enemy and also create a little confusion right before his infantrymen get there.

Rourke stares over at Heller to get his attention and then back to the radio, "Do you understand what's going on?"

Heller glances at Rourke, nods and summarizes, "I believe that Captain Young is trying to steam roll over the OPFOR. If his 1st and 2nd platoons take too much time… he's going to shoot the 3rd Platoon into the lead in order to maintain momentum… and if they get hung up on the next engagement… he'll have the closest platoon maneuver on the enemy to support the 3rd… and then shoot the remaining platoon back into the lead. He's using his indirect fires to keep the enemy off balance till he engages them with his grunts."

After ten minutes, Rourke is tempted to go down to the Alpha Company platoon nets and listen in on the direct fire action. But he decides to switch over to Bravo Company and catch any action going on there. This will give him a feel for how fast the battalion is moving. Everything over at Bravo seems pretty quiet. After listening another ten minutes Bravo starts receiving indirect fires. They run into some enemy troops that are willing to fight and then run. This is a delaying tactic. Rourke has used this many time himself in the Cav. Engaging your enemy so they take the time to deploy and maneuver their forward forces, only for them to attack a position that just minutes before was abandoned, slows down the enemy profusely. Do that several times in a row and you've really slowed down their momentum.

Colonel Francone has apparently used those same tactics in the past. Rourke hears Francone calling Charlie Company Commander on the battalion command net. The instructions are short and quick. Charlie

Company is to race past Bravo Company and continue the move to the new defensive position. Bravo Company is to continue the fight on their own.

Rourke checks his watch. It is 08:20 hours. He can't believe how much time has passed. Rourke looks back over to Heller and asks him to switch the radio to Charlie Company net. Heller leans over the radio, spins the dial, stops on the appropriate freq, glances back at Rourke and laments, "These are my guys... wish I was there."

Rourke smiles, "Yea, I know... Don't worry, there's going to be plenty of battles for you to get killed in... Just relax on this one."

Next, they both hear Captain Bynum direct his company to "drop your rucks". This is a sure sign that they are going to be moving fast. The next directive is the M-60 machine guns are to come to the front. Heller looks at Rourke and remarks with some delight, "I'll bet Captain Bynum is going to use a lot of lead to plow through anything that gets in his way."

At 09:15 Rourke gets a call on his company command net from Lt. Fugate, the Scout Platoon Leader. It is a situation report that informs Rourke the scouts are seeing a lot of infantry moving south, and he has individually informed his brother platoon leaders on the enemy's location and direction of travel on their nets. He thanks Fugate and asks him to report again in an hour.

Rourke thinks for a couple of seconds, speaks into the handset again to make a net call. He forgot to mention this morning to the guys that picked up Heller's squads to pass on that the rifle companies now have priority of fires. He is trying to figure out how to use some kind of encoding, couldn't come up with anything, so just sent in the clear, "All stations this net... we no longer have priority of fires, out."

Rourke has Heller switch again to the battalion net. At about 10:00 hours Rourke hears traffic that indicates the rifle companies are settling in and establishing their defense. Rourke is impressed. If the OPFOR Intel guys are picking up the company's and battalion's radio transmissions they are certainly going to buy into the deception. Rourke has to admit that the ruse is done well. There is just enough Intel leakage on the radio to make the OPFOR work to figure out what the battalion is doing but not enough to make it obvious.

The updated situation report is called in by Fugate. The report mentions more enemy infantry moving south following a couple of previously used trails. Most of the foot traffic seems to be on the far, east side of the battalion boundary. After thanking Fugate, Rourke decides to call each of his platoon leaders on their nets and get a situation report on their activity. All report some sporadic contact, mostly long-range shooting at each other. Rourke gets the feeling that his guys might have killed a couple of OPFOR but it is mostly harassment of OPFOR movement.

Next, he calls the battalion S-2 and talks to Captain Easton. He gives him a situation report based on what he got from Lt. Fugate and his other LT's. Using short cryptic sentences, Rourke hopes he conveyed that the movement south of large numbers of enemy infantry coincides with the battalion stopping for the appearance of repositioning their defense. It appears that OPFOR is buying the deception. They are moving more troops into a position better able to strike the battalion.

Easton replies with, "Roger, good copy... good confirmation." Easton did get it and apparently agrees with Rourke's appraisal.

CHAPTER 24

"In the absence of orders, go find something and kill it." – Field Marshall Erwin Rommel

12:00 Hours.

At noon, Rourke and Heller are listening to the battalion and Alpha Company's radio nets. Once again there are no transmissions which would have announced the moving of the battalion to its next defensive position. Rourke looks over at Heller and asks, "Do you think they're moving yet?"

Heller smiles, "Sir, I'd put money on it."

Rourke asks, "What do you think the OPFOR is doing now?"

Heller glances up for a second, "Right now their OPs are peering through their binos and freaking out. They're seeing two rifle companies with about 140 grunts each just stand up and start walking right at them. But knowing the battalion I would imagine they get up and start running toward them... It would sure freak me out."

For the next two hours, Rourke and Heller listen to the radios. They bounce between the battalion command net, the different companies' nets, the fire support net and even the battalion Intel net. Rourke keeps one of the radios on his own company command net in case his guys need anything.

Rourke also takes the opportunity to evaluate Lt. Dan Heller. After all, there will be a lieutenant draft sometime in the future. Why not get a little insight into Heller before then? Rourke is impressed with Heller. Rourke's first impression is that Heller cares. He cares about his soldiers, he cares about the mission and he wants to have leadership responsibility for his platoon. All good traits he seeks in his lieutenants. An additional bonus is that Heller is smart. He is able to promptly deduce what is happening on the battlefield by listening to the radio. Rourke has asked him some tough questions about tactics and the use of direct and indirect fires. Heller knows his stuff. After sitting with Heller all morning, Rourke knows that at the next draft he will make a serious pitch to pick up Heller for the Dragon Slayers.

At 15:00 hours Rourke asks his platoons to send him a situation report. At 15:30 Rourke assembles the encoded sit reps into one for the company. Rourke charges Josh, with the help of Heller, to work up a coded sit rep that will be sent to the battalion.

The basic message is the platoons engaged in a continuous running battle with small OPFOR elements who are trying to move back and forth into the main battle area against the rifle companies. Rourke makes it clear that they aren't doing a lot of damage or killing a lot of the enemy, but they are upsetting any timetables and plans the OPFOR are trying to implement. He knows the OPFOR commander is probably getting pissed that he has to run his guys through this gauntlet of renegade Blue Force soldiers to get anything done.

Rourke calls for a meeting with his platoon leaders at 16:15 at his location. He wants to formulate a plan for the night and wants input from his lieutenants.

Captain Tim Chancy, Company OC, drives by Rourke and parks his Humvee about 80 meters down the trail, gets out and walks back to Rourke. They shake hands. Chancy smiles and says, "Devlin, I'm going to tag along for a while… got to keep up the notes you know."

Rourke answers, "Tim, I'm having a meeting with the platoon leaders over there in the woods… waiting for one more… you know you're always welcome in the Dragon Slayer family meetings."

The scout platoon leader, Lt. Fugate, pulls in last. Rourke gives them all a follow me wave and walks 50 meters away from the vehicle park area. When they are all sitting, Rourke looks over at Fugate, "Mark, you've been tracking all the scout sighting's since we started this whole thing... What's your best guess as to what the OPFOR is doing?"

Fugate sitting cross legged, drops his head to gather his thoughts, picks up a little stick and starts tapping it against his boot, "Sir, they're using mainly three dismounted avenues of approach into our area... and most of that traffic is moving down the far eastern avenue... into Jim's sector. The other two... we see mostly five-man fire teams... the one avenue going into the 3rd TOW sector is providing twelve-man squads and a few times even more... I haven't kept track of the firefight action... but I assume Jim's getting a lot of fighting done or at least pretty much has engaged a lot more."

Everyone shifts their gaze to Lt. Petrone who is resting his arms on his crossed legs. He turns his hands up and clarifies, "I've been in just as many little fights as the 1st and 2nd TOW platoons... nothing more and nothing bigger."

Rourke looks back at Fugate, "Mark... you're saying Jim's getting twice as many enemy soldiers as the other two?"

Fugate leans forward, interrupts Rourke, "Sir... at least twice as many... I'd say more like three times as many."

Rourke asks Petrone, "Jim, are they getting past your guys without you knowing it?"

"Sir, anything is possible... but with the addition of one of Dan's squads..." Petrone nods at Lt. Heller, "They are pretty good by the way... I don't really believe they're getting past us."

Rourke glances all around, "OK... where the fuck are they?"

Petrone reaches to his left and picks up his map case, brushes off some dead leaves and twigs, glances back at Rourke and announces, "The Black Forest."

Everyone now reaches for their own map case. Rourke, with a show of uncertainty and disbelief asks Petrone to please explain the "Black Forest".

"Alright, everyone find grid square 1280. It's right on our battalion's border with the notional battalion on our right... Everyone, see on the map it's colored all green for vegetation. But there's no way of telling how thick the vegetation is." Petrone looks around to ensure everyone understands and then continues, "Guys, it's thick… I mean like the Hurtgen Forest thick. You know the incredible battle fought by our Division in World War II. The one where we got the shit kicked out of us?" With a little sarcasm he adds, "I'm sure you all have read about our own Division's history." Then he continues, "My guys have scouted all around this… It's only about 600 meters wide and 800 meters long. There are no tank trails or vehicle trails going into it… except on the north side… there is one little trail just big enough for a jeep. It's the only one in and the only one out. My guys came up with the name… The Black Forest… a couple of my guys were stationed in Germany… go figure."

Rourke rubs his chin and asks Petrone, "If you had to guess… how many?"

"Sir you could easily hide two companies in there… but based on what Mark says went by the scouts… I'd say there's a company of infantry in there. Probably a squad or two got by us and headed down to the rifle companies to give them some grief… But, best guess is a company in the Black Forest."

Rourke then asks, "I take it you felt it best not to take your guys into the forest?"

"Shit, Sir… I've got four Humvees that can't get in there. One squad of grunts… Once again Dan, pretty good grunts to go into the Black Forest against a whole company… that knows the forest like the back of their hands… No Sir, I didn't think it fit my mission." Petrone pauses, smiles at Rourke, "I hope at least you read what happened to our Division when they went into the Hurtgen Forest?"

Rourke is concentrating on his map, "Yes, I did…it was bad. Point well taken, Jim. Now what do we do about this?"

They all sit there in silence for a couple of minutes till Rourke speaks up. Rourke looks around and starts with, "Our covering force mission is to disrupt and delay the enemy moving through our sector. We've been given great latitude to accomplish this… And so far, I believe we have done that." Rourke gathers his thoughts, "I don't know why… nor… can I figure out why the enemy has at least a company of infantry in the Black Forest? But we know they're going to be used here in the very near future. Our mission is to disrupt and delay... which includes this enemy company... So, that's what we're going to do."

Rourke looks at Lt. Heller, "I told you you'll get your time in the fight. Tonight, is Your time."

Heller is taken by surprise. The only thing that comes out is, "Sir?"

Everyone around the circle chuckles and adds a few good-hearted jabs, "Welcome to the Dragon Slayers... Now you're going to earn your pay. Welcome to the world of no sleep and no pity. You'll soon wish you were back at Charlie Company."

Rourke raises his hands to bring everyone back on track, "Listen up, everyone... We're going to move both of Dan's squads from the 1st and 2nd TOW platoons over to the 3rd TOW with our vehicles. Starting with everyone going to 1st TOW and moving them... then the squad at 2nd TOW gets moved. Dan you're going with Jim over to his 3rd TOW platoon to start formulating a plan. Your plan. Ask Jim for anything he has to help you."

Rourke looks to ensure Heller understands so far and then continues, "My guidance is that you are to infiltrate the Black Forest with your three squads. Your mission is to disrupt and delay the enemy in the forest." He gets up on his knees, leans toward Heller to emphasize the next point, "You are NOT to become decisively engaged. Don't attack the enemy in the forest. If you try that, he'll wipe you out. I want you to use small hit and run tactics in the forest to keep them awake all night... to keep them moving and wasting time and manpower trying to kill you. Don't bunch up... and always have a way out if the fight gets even a little close. Do you have any questions?"

Heller is smiling, "What time do you want me to start?"

Rourke checks his watch but has to press the light button on the side to see the dial, "If you can pull this all together by 23:00 hours and cross the LD then... the LD being the woodline of the Black Forest... that would be great. If you're having problems or can't make it, call me to keep me informed. If you pull your planning and prep together prior to 23:00 hours... use that time to get you and your guys some sleep. Even an hour will help. Cause you're going all night... call it quits at 06:00 and move your platoon back to 3rd TOW's position."

Lt Clegg from 2ⁿᵈ TOW asks, "Do the rest of us still have the same mission tonight, Sir?"

Rourke replies, "Yea, Chuck, do some patrolling around your area. Don't get in a fire fight. If you run into any of the enemy, use your indirect fire. Everyone... if you run across any large groups of OPFOR get on the company net and let everyone know. If it's a large group, I suspect they're out there hunting for us and hoping for a fight." Rourke chuckles, "Remember, sometimes it's better to run away and then come back to kill them on better terms another day."

There is a pause as everyone lets Rourke's guidance sink in. Then a voice from within the now dark circle of leaders speaks up, "You know, Sir... according to the Infantry School at Fort Benning... that's not the official mission of the U.S. Infantry."

Everyone bursts into laughter. Rourke is trying to subdue his laughter and splutters, "Yea, that's no shit. But they are words to live by... Dan... You're making yourself into a fine Dragon Slayer. Now everybody, time to get to work. Chuck... Josh and I will be bunking up with your guys tonight."

The meeting breaks up. The young lieutenants hurriedly move out to continue their work. As they walk away, Rourke can hear them talking among themselves in order to coordinate their actions for this evening's mission.

As Rourke gets to his Humvee, he feels a hand grab him on the shoulder. He turns and makes out the outline of Captain Chancy. He is a little surprised and asks, "Tim, I didn't realize you were still here, what's up?"

"I want to say your company is really impressive. I mean that. I've seen a lot of companies come through here. But you and your guys work together better than most."

Rourke mulls that over for a second, "Thanks, Tim... Now could you use that somehow to get me a pay raise or maybe a shower?"

This time Chancy chuckles, "No...wish I could. I just wanted you to know I'll be hanging around the 3ʳᵈ TOW platoon's area tonight taking more notes."

Rourke replies, "I'll be moving over that way also. Maybe I'll see you there."

Chancy reaches up and hits Rourke on the arm. "I hope not. If you do then I'm not doing my job." He walks past Rourke and wanders up the trail to his vehicle.

Rourke stares into the dark in the direction of Josh who is leaning against the brush guard, "Hey, let's pack up and move over to 2nd TOW area to get some sleep. We can't stay here… not with all this vehicle traffic moving in and now moving out. I'm surprised we haven't been hit with any artillery fire yet."

Josh walks over to the driver's side and slides in. Rourke takes two steps and slides in the passenger side. Josh simply states, "We're packed and ready to go." Josh points to a white Styrofoam cup sitting on top of the radio with steam escaping from the top. Rourke picks up the cup of coffee. He raises the cup in a salute to Josh, "Josh, thank you. I really appreciate this."

Josh reaches up to the dash and starts the engine. He pulls the gear shift back to drive, hits the gas pedal, drives a short way out of the woods, and makes a right turn to head towards the 2nd TOW platoon area.

About 300 meters down the trail they are passed going the other way by a JRTC Fire Marker in his Humvee pick-up truck. Josh and Rourke immediately look at one another. Both grin and laugh at the same time. Josh exclaims, "Damn, you know they're going to get us one of these times."

Rourke cheerfully replies, "Nah… not if we keep moving… I hope."

After driving a bit more Rourke asks, "Do you know where the 2nd TOW is located? Because I don't. I mean I gave them an area but I don't know the exact location?"

Josh nods, "I got with the other drivers. They pointed out the exact locations for their platoons on the map."

Josh drives them to the 2nd TOW secure area where a soldier with a red flashlight guides them to a hide position 40 meters in the woods. As soon as the vehicle stops, Josh and Rourke jump out and start their routine nighttime set-up. It is fast and quiet. After putting up the camouflage net, Sgt. Donnelly walks over, "Looks like you guys are set for the night. You need anything from us tonight?"

Rourke steps closer to Donnelly, "You want to work us into your guard mount tonight?"

Donnelly replies, "Sir, if you don't mind... yea we could use the extra bodies for watch... I'll give you your pick... first or last?"

Rourke confesses, "Damn that is supposed to be a rhetorical question... you are supposed to say... Nah, Sir, this is 2nd TOW. We don't need any help."

"Sir, I'm a platoon sergeant with a hundred years of experience... You should know by now that none of the platoon sergeants are going to turn down free help... no matter who it's from... even the battalion commander... you'd have better success with a young buck sergeant trying to impress the commander... I'm like, way passed that, Sir."

Rourke reaches up and grabs Donnelly on the shoulder then confesses, "Rob, you're absolutely right. I should have known better... I'll take the first watch and you should have known I always take the first watch. Lead the way to your command post... Old Sarge."

After telling Sgt. Donnelly to wake him at 06:00, Rourke pulls the first watch and then wakes Josh to take the second. As soon as Rourke zips up his sleeping bag he gets warm. Within a few minutes he is fast asleep.

———◆–◆–◆———

2nd TOW Platoon Area
Tuesday, 5 December 1989
06:00 Hours.

Rourke feels Donnelly gently shaking him awake; he opens up his eyes to darkness. He assumes it is Donnelly kneeling over him, "Thanks for the wake-up, Rob... I got it from here." He hears Donnelly move around the Humvee, wakes Josh with a slight shake and tells him, "Josh, it's 06:00 hours. Time to get up, Sunshine."

At 06:30 Rourke is sitting beside Lt. Clegg and across from Sgt. Donnelly. They are all sitting in a close circle on large logs and drinking hot coffee. It is still dark.

Rourke lifts up his left arm and presses the light button on his watch to check the time. He asks Sgt. Donnelly what the plan is to get the Charlie company guys back into the 3rd TOW area.

Donnelly takes one more sip of coffee and begins explaining the plan, "Sir, I coordinated all this with their platoon sergeant, Sgt. Walters, last night. Right now, I've got two of my guys about 200 meters out to the east at a link up point waiting for two of their guys to move in and make the link up. Once everything is good with link up signals… their platoon will follow our guys back into our area. We have three squad areas within our perimeter for their three squads. They dropped their rucks and sleeping bags last night in those three areas. Each squad leader knows their area and will set up sleeping areas and post guards as part of our platoon security plan."

Lt. Clegg interjects with, "After talking with Lt. Heller, his Platoon Sergeant, Sgt. Walters and of course Sgt. Donnelly here… and no further guidance from you… we thought it would be a good idea to put the troops down for six hours this morning and into the afternoon. To catch up on their sleep. My platoon is going to take responsibility for everyone's security."

Rourke takes a drink of his coffee, surveys both Clegg and Donnelly and agrees, "Sounds like a solid plan… I really don't have anything in mind for the company… just continue the mission… which everyone will do until I get further guidance from battalion."

Clegg then asks, "What do you want to do with Dan and his grunts after they get some sleep?"

Rourke thinks that over for a minute, as he takes a couple more sips of coffee and says, "We'll go back to the original plan and have one squad assigned to each of our platoons to beef up our dismounted mission… We'll have the other two squads conduct combat patrols back to their assigned platoons… our 1st and 2nd TOWs… maybe they'll get lucky and run into the OPFOR and get a couple of kills out of it."

Donnelly then asks, "Sir, how did the battalion do on its little… move the battalion forward mission?"

Rourke replies, "Rob, I don't know… I know the real mission is to try and run down the OPFOR and kill as many as we can as fast as we can… I just don't know how successful we were. I was listening on a couple of the battalion nets… I'm just guessing here, but I would say the rifle companies got into quite a few firefights… and I know they took a bunch of casualties doing it."

Clegg slowly stands up, turns to face the noise he hears and signals, "I hear them coming in… about 30 meters out." He then reaches into his pants left cargo pocket and brings out a red chem light. He snaps it, shakes it and holds it at waist level. Five minutes later his two men step within ten feet and quietly announce, "Hey, Sir, we got them right behind us."

Donnelly quickly moves past the two men and makes contact with Sgt. Walters. Rourke and Clegg can hear the two professional NCOs softly talking and conducting their sergeant business. Then Sgt. Walters quietly calls in his squad leaders to provide them with their new instructions. Within minutes all the soldiers have moved out to their assigned squad locations. All is now quiet and then Lt. Heller steps up to Rourke and Clegg still standing side by side with coffee cups in their hands.

Rourke puts out his hand. In the growing light Heller can just make out the extended hand. Heller reaches out, shakes hands with Rourke and states, "What a night, Sir."

Rourke says, "Dan, there's a log to sit on just off to your right... have a seat. Let's hear what happened this morning."

Clegg sits down on the log across from Heller. He reaches behind the log and brings up a thermos of coffee, "Got a thermos here... Dan, it's straight black but it's hot. You want a cup?"

"Hell, yes. Thanks, Chuck... I can really use a cup right now."

Rourke reached across with his cup extended, "Chuck, warm me up."

Clegg deadpans his response with, "Sir, you want a hug... or some more coffee?"

"That's real fuckin' hilarious... just fill it up, funny man." Rourke replies with a touch of fake annoyance.

Rourke shifts his weight on the log and asks Heller, "OK, Dan, how did it go last night?"

Heller, holding the cup with both hands to keep them warm, takes a quick sip and begins, "Sir, the plan was pretty simple. I divided the platoon into three... each squad got its own area. Then each squad divided into its two fire teams. The lead fire team would move in toward the center of the Black Forest trying to find the perimeter of the OPFOR company. The trail fire team would act as support and provide a base of fire to cover the retreating lead fire team that was being chased by the OPFOR. Once the lead team passed the support team they would set up for the now retreating support fire team. They established a rally point and if the team got broken up while running through the woods in the pitch black... And it was pitch black... they would meet up at the rally point and do it again."

Another sip of coffee, "At the first rally point meeting they all called me and gave me the grid location of the OPFOR perimeter in their area. By 01:00 hours I had a picture of where they were. They were pretty well spread out. They know not to bunch up. I then called in some indirect into what I believed was the center of the company every 45 minutes. I doubt if I hit anything... but I think I met the mission of harassment and disruption.

Rourke asks, "Did you do that all night?"

Heller grins and continues, "Well that was the plan. Apparently the OPFOR didn't get the plan. The original plan only worked twice. The bad guys must have figured out that was our plan... So, they came up with their own. Their plan was to go out and hunt us down like dogs and kill us so they could get back to sleep."

Clegg then interjects with a sarcastic remark which makes Rourke and Heller smile, "Those bastards... coming up with a... Counter-Plan!... I hate these OPFOR guys."

Heller looks over at Clegg, shakes his head and continues, "I'd say that about 03:00 hours it went from us fuckin' with them to them fuckin' with us... and this consisted of them sweeping a platoon... or more... through an area looking for us... and us... having to try and slink away without getting caught. Every time one of our fire teams would stop for a breather... they would set out some trip flares. That worked well at first. After tripping a flare the OPFOR would all hit the ground and wait for a firefight to begin. Well, after the second one, they knew we were just using them to try and slow them down... so they began to just ignore them. First squad realized the OPFOR was just blowing through them so on the fifth trip flare set-up... they set up an ambush." Heller takes a large gulp of coffee.

Rourke takes a drink of his coffee then asks, "OK, good for first squad... How did that go?"

Heller continues, "Well, not so good for either first squad or the OPFOR. We lost six guys... we think we killed about fifteen of theirs... maybe more... The problem is they had more than a 40-man platoon. Our guys are guessing a platoon plus at least another squad. And they know exactly what to do in an ambush. The six remaining guys said they were lucky to get away."

Rourke then asks, "Dan, what is your platoon casualty count?"

Heller glances up for a second, "Ah, first squad lost six, second squad lost three and third squad lost two... I couldn't even guess what the OPFOR casualty count is." Heller raises his right hand, pointing up in the air to emphasize the point, "I'm sure we accomplished the mission. No way they got any rest... chasing us around the Black Forest all night."

Rourke asks, "How do you feel?"

Heller sighs, "Tired... but I feel pretty damn good. It felt good running my own operation. Usually my platoon is part of the company operation, but tonight it was all second platoon. The men did extremely well... morale is high. We kicked ass."

Rourke nods, "You guys did do well. Thanks... now you need to go get some sleep. You got a place laid out?"

Heller replies, "Yes, Sir. Sgt. Walters has a place by him over by second squad... We always do a little AAR after all the operations we do." Heller stands, hands the cup back to Clegg and apologizes, "Hey, Sir, I'm sorry about acting like a little bitch when you picked me up yesterday morning. That whining about losing my platoon... and you telling me to relax, that I would get my turn. Well, tonight I got my turn in spades... Thanks."

Rourke advises, "Go get some sleep LT. This isn't the end by any means."

As Heller walks away Rourke reaches over to Clegg with his cup, "Hey, Chuck, can you give me a last refill? I think I need to go after this one."

Josh walks up just as Rourke drains the last of his coffee, "Sir, we got a message from battalion. Another meeting... again all the commanders."

Rourke asks, "Is this the new battalion TOC location?"

Josh showing a hint of doubt stammers, "I don't think this is... It's too far forward... seems to be close to Bravo Company... starts at 09:00 hours. We should take off for it by 08:30 hours."

Rourke nods, "Let's get going. I want to run by the other two TOW platoons this morning."

CHAPTER 25

"Only if you reach your potential as a leader do your people have a chance to reach their potential."
– John Maxwell

Battalion TOC location
Tuesday, 5 December 1989
08:55 Hours.

Finding the link up location isn't any easier in the day light than the night. Rourke is glad that they left his area at 08:30 as Josh had suggested. They have the grid location. Which means they know where they are going but they just don't know how to get there. Finally, Josh says he is cutting into the woods and working his way to the link up point that is 200 meters away.

At about 150 meters in they spot a soldier off to their right front waving to them. Josh makes the adjustment and drives right to him. It is a headquarters company soldier that walks up to the vehicle driver side. With a grin he teases, "Hey, Sir, good to see you and you too, Josh. You guys aren't lost, right? The meeting is about 50 meters over there. You can park your wheels over there in the vehicle park area... and when you leave you can take the trail out of here that everyone else took to get in here."

Rourke reaches back and grabs his satchel and map case, then jumps out and starts walking toward the meeting. Josh takes off his helmet, stares at the soldier, "No, Tony, we aren't lost... we didn't know about the trail... so we had to break some new ground. We Dragon Slayers do that a lot. Jump in and show me the parking area."

At twenty meters out, Rourke can see the battalion command group and the company commanders sitting on the ground in a large semi-circle in a small clearing. All their backs are turned his way. He is coming up from behind them. There is the standard tripod mounted map at the head of the semi-circle.

As he breaks into the clearing, he interrupts in a voice just loud enough for the back rows to hear, "Shit, one grenade could kill you all."

Everyone turns to see Carson Young smiles and pointing to an empty spot next to him wisecracks, "Devlin, are you lost... or practicing that Cav sneakiness?"

Rourke walks between several soldiers and sits down beside Captain Young. Rourke gapes at Young and replies with some fake smugness, "I always practice the best tactical approach to any area... using the same trail like the rest of you guys... is just not tactically sound. The OPFOR probably knows exactly where we are. No thanks to everyone using the same trail."

Captain John Bynum sitting in front of Rourke half turns and notes, "So you were slightly lost."

Everyone breaks up with a little laughter. Rourke just sits there smiling and refuses to answer.

From off to the right, about fifteen meters, Rourke can see Colonel Francone in a conversation with his OC, the Lieutenant Colonel that Rourke had seen during the last battalion operations order brief. They appear to be in deep conversation then Francone turns and walks to the map board with the OC trailing him.

Francone looks over the group that is sitting and waiting his guidance. Francone smiles, swings his arm toward the OC and announces, "Gentlemen, I've just been informed by Colonel Jeltsen that as of right now we have... a change of mission. That means the first part of our operation is over... and we will now receive a new mission for the next part of our JRTC exercise. All the companies will withdraw into their assigned assembly areas to prepare for the next mission. The OC teams will be conducting AARs when everyone is back at their assembly areas. Our command group and company commanders' AAR will take place at the AAR building near the cantonment area." At that point Francone glances over to Jeltsen and queries, "Colonel Jeltsen, have you got any more?"

Jeltsen steps to the map board and points to a spot on the map, "Gentlemen, the temporary AAR building we will be using is located right here, just east of the cantonment area. It's a big white metal building... built like a warehouse. There's a parking lot on the west side. Enter the building on that side. There is a sign that says, JRTC AAR Facility. It's painted on a 4 x 8 sheet of plywood out front... can't miss it. The AAR will start at 11:00 hours... that's two hours from now. Commanders have your XO's and First Sergeants with you. There is assigned seating, so find your seat and then relax. We'll have coffee for you. Bring an MRE if you want to eat... we'll break for lunch. Any questions?"

There are none. Colonel Francone steps back into the center of the group. "Thanks, Bob, we'll all be there."

Colonel Jeltsen nods and walks off to the vehicle park area. Francone stands there and waits till Jeltsen is gone. He then inspects his men and smiles, "Colonel Jeltsen tells me the Chief of Operations for JRTC is calling a halt to this mission a little early. Normally this defense mission goes on for another 24 hours. But the Chief felt another 24 hours is not going to provide us with any additional lessons." Francone can see everyone seems to be a little anxious. They are wondering if that is a good sign or bad news. Francone put his hands on his hips, gazes out to the group and beams, "I'm pretty proud of you guys. According to Bob... the battalion did well. We surprised a lot of people. Yep, I'm pretty proud of our battalion... and you should be too."

Francone pauses for a minute then continues, "Don't let that go to your heads. We still have another mission to accomplish... at less than 100 percent strength in personnel and equipment. So, let's concentrate on our next mission. See everyone at the AAR at 11:00 hours... don't be late."

As they approach the entrance to the AAR building parking lot, Rourke checks his watch. It is 10:05 hours. They are 55 minutes early. He points to the left and says to Josh, "Pull in and park in the back. We're early so maybe we can catch twenty minutes of sleep."

Josh backs into an open space in the back between two OC Humvees. Actually, the back of the parking lot is filled with OC and JRTC operations Humvees. They are all inside preparing for the AAR. Rourke steps out and stretches.

Josh steps out; he starts to walk toward the double door main entrance and says, "They say they will have coffee in there. I bet they'll have donuts too. We're early enough that they'll still have them out for the AAR prep guys... You want any if I find some, Sir?"

Rourke replies, "Josh if you can escape with a donut or two... I'll take one."

Rourke then sees a single side door toward the back of the building open up. A soldier walks out toward the parked Humvees. It is Captain Chancy. He walks up to the vehicle parked to the right of Rourke's. He recognizes Rourke, throws his hand up in a little wave, reaches into the Humvee and yells over to Rourke, "Hey, Devlin, you want a cigar? I got a box here. You smoke cigars?"

Rourke yells back, "Yea, I'll take a cigar. Are they cheap or expensive?"

"They're Free! So, does it really matter?"

Rourke replies with, "Well... if you put it that way... I guess it really doesn't. Yea, I'll take a free cigar."

Chancy walks around his Humvee to hand a cigar to Rourke who is already sitting in the passenger seat facing out. Rourke points to the back seat, "Have a seat and make yourself at home."

Chancy sits down facing out with his legs stretched to the ground.

Chancy lights up his cigar then passes the lighter to Rourke. Chancy takes a puff on the cigar and advocates, "Nothing like a good cigar after a good field exercise."

Rourke takes a puff on his cigar and asks, "Yep, good cigar, but was it a good field exercise?"

Chancy is wondering how to reply when the single back door opens up and another soldier walks out. Rourke glances up and immediately recognizes Captain Marcell from the first day off-loading incident, or more like Rourke feels, not so much an incident, more like a verbal scrap and one that he lost. Rourke also appreciates she is still striking.

She walks past them to the vehicle parked on the left of Rourke's. Both Rourke and Chancy half turn in their seats to follow her movement. She reaches inside and picks up a field notebook placed in the middle of the Humvee. She turns, walks to the front of Rourke's Humvee, turns to face both men, smiles and asks Chancy, "Tim... I didn't know that you cavorted with the Blue Force before the AAR?"

Chancy takes the cigar out of his mouth, grins then jokes, "Cavort... you know that's a big word for us infantry types. Does that mean... like... hang out with?"

Her smile gets a little bit bigger and she steps closer to the two men, leaning against the fender. "Yes, I guess that is a big word for you infantry types."

Rourke takes the cigar out of his mouth, smiles and retorts in gleeful triumph, "I knew what it meant all along, of course I'm not infantry."

In mock excitement Marcell exclaims, "Well, well... what are you, Captain?"

Rourke puffs out his chest, raises his nose in the air and proclaims with a corny southern accent, "Why, Ma'am, I'm a Cavalry Officer... at your service."

Chancy jumps upright out of his seat and declares, "Miss Olivia... It is my pleasure to introduce to you Captain Devlin Rourke of the Pennsylvania Militia. And Captain Rourke, Sir. It is my honor to introduce to you Captain Olivia Marcell, currently residing in the confines of Fortress Chaffee, Arkansas."

Both Rourke and Marcell laugh, look at each other and at the same time announce, "We've met."

Marcell looks down at her notebook in her right hand, moves it to her left, extends her right hand towards Rourke and says, "This is a lot better meeting than the last one."

Rourke stands up, readily takes her hand and replies, "Yes, it is... and I'm sorry about us screwing up the off-loading on day one."

Marcell nods, "That was days ago... It got fixed. I believe your XO was able to round up the required crews." Rourke is struck by her blue eyes. They let go of each other's hands. As she turns to walk back to the building she says, "See you two at the AAR… don't be late."

Both Rourke and Chancy sit back down on the Humvee seats. Both put their cigars back in their mouths and silently watch Captain Marcell walk back to the building. Rourke asks, "Why is she here at the AAR… her shoulder patch says she belongs to Fort Chaffee… and not to you JRTC guys?"

Chancy explains, "She's substituting for one of our logistic OCs. He getting ready for Christmas leave. She's done this a bunch of times… and I got to tell you… she's a better OC than the guy she's subbing for."

Rourke guages Chancy and asks, "She knows her stuff?"

Chancy nods and sighs, "Oh yea, she's good… you'll see that in the AAR." He then pauses, points to the back door and reveals, "I will tell you… that woman almost ruined my marriage."

Rourke with a look of surprise and wonder slowly turns to Chancy and cries, "You… and Olivia… did the deed?"

Chancy gets a pained look on his face, "No… Hell no… Not even close… as much as… never mind."

Rourke then demands, "You can't end a statement like that. What do you mean she almost ruined your marriage?"

Chancy pauses for a couple of seconds and then resumes, "OK, here's the low down on Olivia… Only because I saw the look on your face when you saw her. Oh yea, she is attractive alright."

Rourke takes the cigar out of his mouth, blows a cloud of smoke in the air and says, "Yes, it's not hard to admit… I am attracted to her."

Chancy chuckles, "Oh you poor bastard… you and every other guy on this post. But I have some bad news. She doesn't date soldiers."

Rourke gives him a quizzical look, "What?"

Chancy reaches out with his cigar hand and flicks the ashes off, puts it back in the side of his mouth and begins to talk, "She doesn't date soldiers… and no she isn't a lesbian… every single soldier and probably a couple married ones have taken a run at her. I know that she has dated a banker and an architect over at Fort Smith, the town outside of Chaffee. But no soldiers. Olivia has her sights a little higher than the rest of us."

Rourke asks, "Where is she from?"

"I think she is from Indiana. She went to a Division II school there.

She played basketball and ran track. I believe she was small college all-American in basketball. As you can imagine just by looking at her, she has no problems with PT tests. Those very long legs of hers help her pass most of the guys during PT runs. She is one hell of a jock... so to speak. She plays golf with the Post Commander and two other guys. They have this co-ed team that travels all around the area and competes in tournaments... and they mostly always win... makes the Post Commander very happy. She's smart too. She's got one of those, *'Cum Laude - I'm a really smart cookie degree',* with her bachelor's in engineering."

Rourke nods his understanding then asks, "Well how did she almost ruin your marriage?"

Chancy without taking his eyes off Rourke pulls the cigar out of his mouth, and recalls, "OK, it was about five months ago. Just on a whim and because I'm such a romantic guy... I called up my wife and asked her if she would like to go out to dinner and a movie. This is on a Monday and I suggested for the upcoming Friday. That we should get a babysitter. I have one kid... a three-year-old son... and to make reservations at the fancy restaurant, La Ture's, downtown Fort Smith."

Chancy pauses, blows out some smoke and continues, "We get to the restaurant at 19:00 hours... right on time... we're seated at a nice table... the waiter comes over... we order drinks, appetizers and the main meal. They have great steaks by the way. The drinks come and the appetizers arrive. My wife... and by the way... my wife is a pretty good-looking babe herself... as a matter of fact... I've been accused of having money because of her. There have been guys that say there's no way I could have gotten a girl like Audrey without having money."

Rourke is grinning, puffing away and enjoying Chancy's little story but is getting impatient so asks again, "What's this have to do with Olivia?"

Chancy gives Rourke a sideways look. A look that warns, *'don't interrupt me'.* So, he continues, "At about 19:30 hours, Olivia and her date walk into the restaurant. First... the date is this tall, Hollywood handsome... blond hair, perfectly cut and styled... wearing a perfectly, tailored, gray Italian suit with a blue silk tie...I mean one sharp looking guy. Not that I'm not killing it in my J. C. Penny off the rack standard blue blazer with a cotton polyester light blue shirt and patriotic red white and blue tie." Chancy gives Rourke the, *'you know what I mean look'.*

Rourke nods, "Sadly, I have the same killer suit."

"Then there's Olivia." Chancy tilts his head back and closes his eyes, he smiles as he remembers the moment and again continues, "I swear to God... when she walked in I heard that song from the Hollies... *Long Cool Woman in a Black Dress*. I swear to God I know I heard it and every other guy in there heard it too. It is like divine intervention... only in our heads."

Rourke busts out laughing and starts singing, "*Saturday night I was downtown, working for the FBI, Sitting in a nest of bad men, whiskey bottles piling high. Bootlegging boozer on the west side, full of people who are doing wrong.*"

Chancy puts up his hand to signal Rourke to stop so he can go on. "So, as I'm sitting there opposite Audrey, my wife, at the twelve o'clock position. The entrance is off to my left at the nine o'clock position. We're about three quarters the way in the dining area. Olivia walks in and of course takes a look around while her date is taking care of the maître d, and waiter. She spots me staring at her... she smiles and gives me a little wave... one of those... nice to see you, fellow co-worker kind of wave. When she's happy... having a good time... I swear her smile can light up a room.

"I wave back. Audrey turns to see who I'm waving at. Audrey sees it's Olivia... They've met before at a couple of the unit get-togethers. They both wave to each other. I'm not sure... but I'm pretty sure Audrey did a visual sweep of the room and took notice that every guy in the room is... gazing... at Olivia. And damn, you couldn't blame them. She is tall... I would guess 5'9" or 5'10"... she's wearing three-inch black, high heel pumps, black stockings, a black,sleeveless cocktail dress that goes to mid-thigh... a silver belt at her perfect waist... that sets off the perfect set of." Chancy raises both hands to form cups over his chest, closes his eyes again, blows out another puff of smoke, and continues the narrative, "She's wearing a small silver chain necklace with a couple of diamonds in a little heart shaped ornament with matching ear rings. She has long... kind of a light, golden-brown hair that reaches below her shoulders. She has a modest amount of make-up on... something that made her seem to glow."

Rourke takes the cigar out of his mouth, and with some obvious doubt, questions Chancy's choice of words, "Glow... she seemed to Glow... Is that what I'm hearing? She was radioactive?"

Chancy rolls his eyes, takes exception at Rourke's doubt and continues,

"Well… glow might not be the right word… but she sure stood out… just standing there. She is the most beautiful woman in that restaurant… other than my wife. The waiter takes them to a table that puts them at my 11:00 o'clock… remember that Audrey is right across from me at my 12:00 o'clock.

Chancy takes a drag on the cigar, blows out the smoke, and starts to chuckle, "About twenty minutes later… I alter my casual gazing of Olivia. I glance at my wife… my lovely, beautiful wife of five years. I don't know what made me notice her at that time… maybe it is some sort of self-survival innate… thing… but I look at her… and she's giving me… *that look!*" Chancy is nodding to himself and remembering the incident like it was yesterday.

Rourke pushes himself off the seat, stands up, gazes at Chancy and asks, "What look… what is… that look?"

Chancy stands, stretches, stares directly at Rourke and slowly replies, "The look that says… *You look at that woman one more time… and the last time you saw my pussy… is going to be… the last time you saw my pussy!* I got the message. From that point on I kept my head down… talked about how great the meal was… and that we need new tires for the car… all during the next week I did the dishes a couple of extra times… just to make sure I wasn't in the dog house."

Rourke laughing sits back down and wonders, "Olivia, the long cool woman in a black dress, almost upset your marriage… just by her appearance… and she doesn't consider dating soldiers?"

Chancy puts up his hand and clarifies, "Wait a minute… I said she didn't date soldiers… I didn't say she wouldn't *Consider* dating a soldier… I just don't think she's seen one that appeals to her… or… maybe she just did."

Rourke asks, "What are you talking about? We just shook hands… politely at that."

Chancy explains his hypothesis, "I believe she is checking you out. She has never stopped by just to be sociable to me… It's always been a polite wave on her way to wherever. She's not going to talk with any old captain… The captain she would show interest in would have to be unique or exceptional. That's you, Devlin. She stopped to converse with us… I'm telling you… if it was just me… it would have been a wave and maybe a

'Hi, Tim' on her way back." Chancy stops to collect his thoughts, "I told you all the OCs talk… she's heard more about you than any previous company commander going through JRTC. You have made a notable impression on the JRTC Operations Staff. She knows damn well you are a Cav Officer… That's how we talked about you… The Cav Captain in the infantry battalion."

Rourke stands up, puts his hands on his hips and contemplates his next reply, "Tim, thanks for the compliments. It's nice to hear about my Army accomplishments…but what I really want to know is… do you think she could be interested?"

Chancy glances down at his watch, "We've got to go. AAR starts in five minutes. You need to find your seat… It's up front with the other company commanders." Chancy lifts up his left leg and puts out what's left of his cigar on the sole of his boot, smiles at Rourke and says, "Enjoy." He walks past Rourke to head for the back door. Rourke takes one more drag of the cigar stub, lifts up his left leg, puts it out on the sole of his boot and stuffs it in his pocket to throw away inside. He then weaves his way through the now mostly filled parking lot to head for the double doors at the front entrance.

CHAPTER 26

"After a battle is over people talk a lot about how decisions were methodically reached, but actually there's always a hell of a lot of groping aound." - Admiral Frank Fletcher.

JRTC AAR Building
Tuesday, 5 December, 1989
11:00 Hours.

Coming through the doors Rourke sees it is a big warehouse. He enters the front of the building but it is actually the back of the AAR assembly area. The post engineers built an arena type area taking up three quarters of the building. There are temporary plywood office spaces and storage rooms built along most of the walls. This is where the AAR prep work is done by the OCs. Rourke goes to the front of the seating area to find his seat. On the way he stops to briefly talk to his XO and First Sergeant who have assigned seats a couple of rows behind the front row. Each row has eight folding chairs set up with enough space between them to plunk down a soldier's gear on the floor without creating a hazard. He guesses there are seven or eight rows. The last three rows are set up on a two-foot-high platform with three step stairs on the ends and one in the middle. There are a couple of portable TV VHS camcorders mounted on tripods up there.

Rourke finds his seat on the front row. A piece of tape with CSC Commander written with marker is attached to the third folding chair from the end. He is sitting next to Charlie Company's Commander, Cpt. John Bynum; next to him is Bravo Company Commander, Cpt. Andy Daugherty; then the Battalion Commander, LTC Jim Francone; the Battalion Fire Support Officer, Cpt. Marty Bowman; Alpha Company Commander, Cpt. Carson Young; then Headquarters Company Commander, Cpt. Dale Walker. The second row is all the battalion staff officers to include the battalion XO and Sergeant Major. The third and fourth rows are the companies' XOs and First Sergeants. The last couple of rows are soldiers of the battalion service support elements. The OCs sit mostly in the back with some standing along the sides of the rows.

Rourke sees to the front of him a 4 X 8 white board off to the far left. He guesses it is to be used to add notes and lessons learned. There are two big white screens directly to his front. One is used to project video or images from a computer. The other is used to display overhead transparent slides that are made up by the OCs. The projector is currently showing the first slide. It is the agenda for the AAR. Off to the right is an oversized 4 X 8 map of the whole maneuver box area. Hanging down from the ceiling is a 2 X 6 wood placard with the definition of an AAR on it; *An AAR is a professional discussion of an event, focused on performance standards, that enables soldiers to discover for themselves What happened, Why it happened, and How to sustain strengths and improve any weaknesses.*

At exactly 11:00 a full bird colonel steps to the front of the assembled soldiers. "I want to wholeheartedly welcome the soldiers from the 2nd of the 220th infantry to your first AAR here at JRTC. My name is Col. Vance Harrison… I am the Chief of Operations. I want to introduce myself and welcome you here at the JRTC. My job is to make sure we correctly run the JRTC and ensure the units that come here… leave here a whole lot better. The JRTC has been the Army's primary trainer for infantry units since '87. We provide exceptionally realistic and relevant training to prepare units and develop leaders for the challenges of combat operations."

Harrison sweeps his hand across the front of the audience, "Your battalion and your leaders have been the beneficiaries of unparalleled opportunities to train your collective skills in a tough, realistic setting against a professional opposing force. I will tell you… you have done well so far. And you have learned more than you currently realize. It will take some time but down the road you will understand how much you've grown as teams and individually as leaders. You need to keep up the pace for the next exercise so you can come out of the JRTC as a complete battalion ready to take on any future challenge… including combat." Harrison finishes with, "Keep up your hard work. I'll now turn you over to your battalion Observer Controller, LTC Robert Jeltsen."

Jeltsen who is standing off to the side, walks to the center, removes the agenda slide and drops his first slide, "Thank you, Sir… I just want to quickly go over a few definitions for everybody. First is what an OC is and what we do." Jeltsen picks up a transparency slide and drops it on the overhead screen. It displays the definition; *Observer-Controller (OC). Army Soldiers selected to provide feedback to JRTC rotational units and have a duty to the training unit and the Army to observe unit performance, control engagements and operations, teach doctrine, coach to improve unit performance, monitor safety and conduct professional AARs. OCs are required to have successfully performed their counterparts' duties. They constantly strive for personal and professional development and are well versed in current doctrine, tactics, techniques, and procedures.*

Jeltsen waits a minute to ensure everyone has read the slide, picks up the next slide and drops it on the projector; *Opposing Forces (OPFOR). Professional Army organizational unit which conducts combat training operations as an opposing force to provide realistic, stressful, and challenging combat conditions for Army units at JRTC. The OPFOR is an uncompromising threat unit that provides the challenge of a real-world conflict by using doctrinally generic tactics and provides a level of realistic collective training, which cannot be duplicated at a unit's home-station. The OPFOR is a dedicated, permanently stationed US Army unit that is highly skilled, both individually and collectively, at executing threat force doctrine and TTPs.*

After several minutes Jeltsen turns off the projector, "These are the two entities that make the JRTC what it is. You've done home station training using STXs and FTXs to try and prepare for this training but only here at JRTC can you get the complete package." Jeltsen takes a couple of steps to the left, puts out his hand and introduces the OPFOR Commander, "2nd

of the 220th. I would like to introduce the second part of that package… the commander of the OPFOR, LTC Charles Schulberg."

LTC Schulberg moves to the front, steps by Jeltsen and says, "Thanks, Bob." He turns and faces the assembled. He stands there for a couple of minutes and scans over the men of the 2/220th Infantry. He nods and then bemoans, "So, you're the ones! I was going to say something else. Something not so generic, as the ONEs." Schulberg cracks a little smile, "So, you're the ones that made my life… let's say… challenging for this first mission."

The battalion responds with small grins growing on everyone's faces. They're starting to think, this might not be so bad.

Schulberg slowly paces back and forth. He's very comfortable in front of a group or class. He's a good speaker. He stops in the center, turns and begins, "Up until a day ago… I was one pissed off OPFOR soldier. I was pretty mad… not just at you… I was at first… pissed off only at you… but soon I realized I was pissed at my guys also. The source of my anger was the circumstances I found myself in… My guys were being frustrated. Frustrated at every turn. It seemed that no matter what we did… it didn't or wouldn't work… at least the way it did in the past." He resumed pacing again, "You guys really gave us a different perspective… starting on day one. We've never quite seen the use of battalion assets the way you've used them."

He stops in front of Francone, gazes down, "Colonel, you've done an excellent job with your battalion." Schulberg smiles, "I'm not going to say you somehow beat us but… you provided us with many challenges to overcome." He pauses, stares up at the ceiling, shakes his head and continues, "Challenges every single freaking day. Normally, at the first AAR, I just give the OPFOR mission and a couple of highlights that the Blue Force should focus on… and then I leave and let the OC's lead the AAR…but today I'm going to sit in the back with my operations officer and do a little learning myself. Don't be surprised if from time to time I ask a question or two." He turns to Jeltsen, points to the back of the classroom to indicate that's where he'll be and concludes, "The AAR is back to you, Bob."

Jeltsen walks to the front of the room and drops a new slide onto the projector. "Gentlemen, we're going to examine the last couple of days through the lens of the Battlefield Operating Systems... the BOS. Knowing that you guys already know them, this slide is just a quick reminder what we'll be talking about."

Rourke looks up on the screen and sees the BOS slide listing all seven systems; Intelligence, Maneuver, Fire Support, Air Defense, Mobility and Survivability, Combat Service Support, and last, Command and Control. Rourke knows from experience that all BOS are not equal in all operations nor do they apply for all tasks. The hard part is to synchronize the BOS to ensure total military power is coordinated and directed toward accomplishing the mission.

Jeltsen continues, "Now normally we would just follow the sequence on the slide and start with each subject matter expert to give their own quick appraisal as to what they thought and how they felt the battalion did. Then the OC for that system would take over and facilitate a conversation on what actually happened. But because of the way the battle played out... we're going to change up the sequence a little. There is a whole lot of Blue Force action on the maneuver side... I believe most of our conversations will be focused on that. So, I want to start with Combat Service Support. We have limited time... so let's sort of get this out of the way... Not that it's not important... There is just a whole lot more maneuver. So, let's have OC, Captain Marcell, start out the AAR with the guys providing the beans and bullets... the logistic support for the battalion."

Marcell, who has been standing behind and off to the side of Rourke, confidently walks past him up to the projector stand, takes off the slide and drops her own on the screen. Rourke can see it contains four headings: Arming, Fueling, Fixing, and Manning the Force.

She turns to face the room. She is standing right in front of LTC Francone. She smiles, looks at Francone and states, "Sir, as the primary OC for your logistic guys, I want to let you know they did well. We're just going to take some time and explore the reasons they did do well, and maybe figure out how to work on a couple of things... they need to improve."

Francone chuckles loud enough for everyone to hear, "Why Captain Marcell, that's the nicest way anyone has ever said... let's review all your screw-ups... maybe there's a way we can fix them."

Everyone in the room breaks up laughing. If there are any anxious feelings, they are now gone. From this point on in the AAR, there is a feeling that everyone is here to genuinely provide helpful advice and to improve the battalion's performance.

Then for a brief second, in an unconscious move, Cpt. Marcell glances at Rourke and smiles. Rourke who has been fixated on Marcell the very second she walked passed him, instantly smiles back. She turns her head to focus on the rows further to the back, and asks her first question, "Captain Morley, you're the S-4 right?"

Captain Pat Morley, who is in his second year as the battalion S-4, quickly replies, "Guilty as charged."

Marcell's next question is the beginning of a one-hour review into the workings of the battalion logistics, "Let me ask you how did you, or what is the method you used to select the location of the field trains?"

Rourke has to admit she is an excellent OC, not only in her knowledge of logistic operations, but her control of the interaction between all participants. There is a lot of learning going on. Rourke picks up a couple of things that he wants to talk with his XO and First Sergeant about.

From what Rourke could see, the battalion field trains made three jumps to three different locations. Picking up and moving all the support elements is really difficult. They have a lot of vehicles and equipment. Packing up and unpacking during every move was time consuming. Oh, by the way, they still had to continue to provide support to the battalion, which they did. And just to add another level of difficulty, two of the moves were at night.

Most battalions have gotten in the bad habit of trying not to move them until they're compelled too. Unfortunately, that usually starts with getting hit with enemy artillery fire resulting in losing people and equipment. But the 2nd of the 220th Infantry field trains were able to avoid that. All this effort by the logistics guys, meant they always had Rourke's and every company commander's admiration. The commanders hardly ever complained about not getting what they needed. The Logpac system was sometimes slow, but it worked.

The biggest hit on the logistics is that the Logpac seemed to always be late. It was recognized in the AAR that was actually due to the movement of the field trains. It was put to the commanders that either get your stuff late or not get it at all. The commanders all said they could work around late Logpacs. Nobody wanted to take a bigger chance of losing the field trains to an OPFOR attack. Rourke was concerned about the battalion losing a fuel truck to an enemy ambush on a returning Logpac from one of the rifle companies. He wanted to talk with Lt. Kiser about any impact that could have on CSC operations. He knew in the very least it would mean an order for the company not to run their vehicles for using the heaters only. He could just imagine all the drivers sitting inside partially opened sleeping bags while driving.

There is a problem with the MRE's. The battalion is going to run out of food in two days because someone forgot to place an order two days ago. The S-4 guys are trying to work a fix but it isn't like just going to the warehouse back on main post and picking up the required amount. This is war and the OCs are making the battalion play it all the way. Francone finally ordered the battalion on just two MREs per day for the next two days until they can catch up with a required MRE draw.

Rourke wants to talk with his XO about getting five of the M-60 machine guns repaired and back in the company. The NCOs have been doing a good job of cross leveling weapons after every firefight or battle. If the platoon lost a Humvee, the good M-60 was quickly pulled off and was used to replace broken ones on operational Humvees. The broken one went with Lt. Kiser on the evening Logpac. The M-60s are old machine guns. Most of the battalion's guns actually saw service in Vietnam. They were refurbished several times. The Army recently decided to buy a new model as a replacement. Rourke could only guess when they would come to the National Guard.

Rourke wants the status on getting replacement Humvees required to get back up to 100% or as close as possible to 100%. Listening to the AAR, he isn't feeling too hopeful that will happen either. A problem Rourke never thought about is that the support guys have to also take care of their own equipment and vehicles. Which, due to all the movement, are now being stretched more than ever before. Two Support Platoon trucks broke down. The mechanics are up to their necks in broken support vehicles including their own. Waiting for new parts is going to kill the battalion.

The lesson everyone is learning and that is brought out by Captain Marcell is that everyone takes it for granted that putting in the "right" paper work for a replacement is the answer. That is just half the problem. Having assets to go get it or understanding how and when and where to receive it is more difficult if you've never actually had to do it. All these years of driving back into main post to pick up what you need isn't going to cut it at the JRTC.

The bottom line is that the battalion support guys are slowly falling behind in providing support for the battalion. Everyone is learning. It just isn't going to be fast enough. It isn't going to get better real soon.

Captain Marcell finishes up her portion of the AAR by asking LTC Francone if he has any questions or has anything to add. Francone answers by replying he appreciates the feedback and knows everyone in the battalion will be working harder to get the glitches and errors corrected. Marcell ends with a thank you and walks over to sit on the end chair one row behind Rourke. LTC Jeltsen walks to the front and drops the next slide on the projector. It simply states LUNCH! He clasps his hands together, grins and says, "How about everyone take 60 minutes and enjoy a wonderful MRE... of your choice." He then looks at Francone and suggests, "Colonel Francone, I'd like to buy you a cup of coffee over at the OC break room."

Rourke stands up and turns to face Cpt. Marcell, Can I offer you an MRE... of your choice... there's a whole case, with all the delicious varieties, in my Humvee."

Marcell stands, smiles, shakes her head and declines, "No thanks, Captain Rourke. You're going to need every one you now have... remember you're down to two a day... besides I brought a lunch. It's in the refrigerator in the break room."

Rourke smiles, "Maybe I could have some of your lunch... I could save the MRE for a later time... like when I'm starving in two days."

As Marcell walks past Rourke on her way across the room she says over her shoulder, "That isn't allowed... but maybe someday we could share a lunch together."

Rourke wants to come back with some quick repartee, something witty and funny, but he has nothing. Showing frustration by holding up his hands he simply says, "Yes, I would like that." He watches her walk to the break room door and go in. He shakes his head and thinks to himself, '*Real smooth Rourke... Yea... real smooth. You really made quite an impression there... boy you're so suave*'.

Rourke hears his name called from behind. It is his XO, Lt. Kiser,

"Hey Captain Rourke, since you're not going to have lunch with the... OC. Why not break a little bread with me and Top?"

"Wipe that grin off your face, Lieutenant... and you too, First Sergeant. Actually, I was hoping she would turn me down... I was just being polite. I really enjoy sharing our time together... eating those delicious MREs on the hood of a Humvee."

CHAPTER 27

"If you train hard, you'll not only be hard, you'll be hard to beat." - Herschel Walker

"A smart man makes a mistake, learns from it, and never makes that mistake again. But a wise man finds a smart man and learns from him how to avoid the mistake altogether." - Roy H. Williams

Jeltsen holds open the break room door for Francone. As Francone walks in, he says, "Thanks, Bob." Jeltsen follows him in and points to a table off to the side that is already occupied by the OPFOR Commander, LTC Charles Schulberg. There are six other OCs sitting around the room at various tables unpacking their lunches. Captain Marcell is sitting with another OC at the table next to Schulberg.

Schulberg pushes an already hot cup of coffee aside, stands up and offers his hand to Francone, then signals Francone to take a seat. "Jim, right?... please call me Chas."

Jeltsen picks up a pot of coffee from the counter, grabs two cups, pours the coffee then walks them over to the table. He sets one in front of Francone, sits down and begins explaining the situation, "Jim, we don't normally do this… inviting the Blue Force Commander in for a cup of coffee… as a matter of fact this is the first time."

Francone raises his cup and toasts, "Well I guess I'm honored then."

Schulberg starts with, "Jim, I asked Bob if I could talk with you here in the break room. I didn't want to take up valuable AAR time asking some questions about your battalion."

Francone nods and queries, "Chas, what is it you're interested in?"

"Jim, you have been more successful than most of the battalions coming through the JRTC… and you have been the most successful National Guard battalion… ever." Schulberg smiles, "That doesn't mean we're not going to beat your asses this next mission… but I would like to know a little bit about how you prepared for JRTC… and in particular… using your Combat Support Company as a cavalry troop. You've broken some new ground here… the Army would like to know how you did it."

He takes a sip of coffee, "A couple of months ago, I was asked to write a paper for the magazine, Military Review, published by the Command and General Staff College at Fort Leavenworth. I was going to write about the typical lessons learned by battalions passing through… but you've given me a new twist or new insight at how to prepare for our training here at the JRTC. Maybe I can pass some of your good ideas on to the rest of the Army. Of course, I will give you full credit as the co-author."

The six other OCs in the break room are slowly and quietly eating and have focused their full attention on the table with the three LTCs. They're all thinking, *'as a professional soldier, this conversation I'm listening to… is going to be pure gold'.*

Francone puts down his cup, crosses his arms, leans back a little, gathers his thoughts and begins, "Chas, we only have a short time here for lunch… so I'll tell you what… at the end of the rotation why don't we sit down with my S-3 and the commanders and go over our training schedules we used for this past year." Schulberg nods in agreement. Francone continues, "I will tell you that we have a different philosophy than most units coming here."

Francone pauses, "The Army seems to be concentrating on developing processes… more concerned on the process of coming up with a plan. As leaders we're to oversee our staffs implementing the Military Decision Making Process… to come up with three different Courses of Action…

come up with the Sync Matrix for the Battlefield Operating Systems. The Army wants you to work through all this in order to come up with the best plan. Chas, I'll tell you right now… as National Guard soldiers we don't have a lot of time for going in depth and learning the finer point of all these processes… let alone trying to fully put them in practice… So, I decided that coming up with the plan to defeat the enemy is my job. That's why they made me an LTC and that's why they trusted me with a battalion. We do a quick and highly modified MDMP… basically we get two courses of action and I pick the one I like. There really isn't any staff recommendation… and I don't ask for one.

Our focus the whole year was to find and kill the OPFOR. We didn't have time to follow a process. Our process is to find the OPFOR and kill them… every single one of them. The S-2 was asked to do a hasty Intelligence Preparation of the Battlefield… an IPB and his best guess where the OPFOR was… we would confirm it or not… and then kill them when we found them. It is really that simple."

Schulberg grins and says, "Seems like you guys have streamlined the whole process."

Francone smiles back, "So, Chas, at the end of the rotation we all will sit down and talk about training and getting ready for the JRTC… but let me take the rest of the time to talk about my CSC." He looks up, searching for a way to start, looks down and smiles at Schulberg, "The Army 5th and 7th Corps in Germany each have a Cavalry Regiment providing them a covering force… used to shape the battlefield… and all Army Divisions have Cavalry Squadrons to help do the same. Brigades have Cav Troops to help the commander with his battle… As a battalion… why shouldn't we have the same assets and advantages as those other organizations? I think I can argue that being much closer to the fight… I really NEED a Cav Troop. So, as an infantry guy… I believe in the Cav mission… always have."

Francone stands up with his cup, turns and walks over to the coffee pot on the counter, looks back at the table, offers the pot up to refill either cup, both want refills. Francone walks back to the table, refills both cups, walks back to the counter and continues to talk, "Now this part of the story is more about fate." Leaning against the counter, "Captain Devlin Rourke was made the CSC Commander two months before I came to the battalion. That was just about three years ago. He is a Cav officer that transferred from a squadron in Indiana. When I showed up at the battalion Captain Rourke was already making a name for himself... in just two months... of course he was given command of the worst company not just in the battalion but in the brigade. During our first meeting during my first month... he asks me if he could turn the CSC into a light Cav troop. I guess this is where fate comes in. I believe in having a Cav troop for the battalion and now I have a Cav officer just transferred in... and he wants to create a Cav troop. But I know this is going to take a special kind of Cav officer to get this done."

He walks back to the table, sits down, "I've spent my whole National Guard career in the Infantry. I know good Infantry officers and I can pick out bad Infantry officers within a day of working with them. Captain Rourke is not infantry... So, before I agree with Captain Rourke and give him my permission. I need to find out if this young officer is truly special. Looking at his resume... it's impressive... all the training and schooling he's been to... is the most of any officer in the brigade. I checked. But I still need to know if he can lead. Because changing an Infantry CSC into a Cav troop is going to take strong leadership. He will be tested. Challenges in training, maintenance, personnel all the while selling this new concept to his soldiers... soldiers who have been in the Infantry for the past twenty years."

Jeltsen nods, asks, "Obviously you decided to go with Rourke... What did you do to make the decision?"

Francone takes a sip, "I dug into his Officer Evaluation Reports. His OERs from his recent Cav squadron. If I was going to pull this off... I needed an exceptional officer. Was Captain Rourke exceptional or just an average Cav officer in his squadron? ... He had three troop commanders. Two had written glowing reports... one had written an average report. There had to be a personality conflict there... knowing Rourke like I do now, it's not hard to imagine him pissing off a... let's say a flawed commander... so, I threw that one out. He had two different squadron commanders writing in the senior rater section. They both thought the world of him... but what really stuck with me was the last commander wrote in his section... the very first sentence is... *I consider Lt. Rourke the best platoon leader in my squadron.* I've never written anything like that.

You really have to mean that to put that in your section… and he also put him in the second stick man block of the senior rater profile. Rourke was the only one holding that position. He is an exceptional officer… the squadron's loss." Francone sits up straight, grinning and finishes with, "My gain."

Schulberg asks, "So, Captain Rourke is your secret ingredient or should I say… secret weapon?"

Francone replies, "That and the fact Rourke's had his Cav troop for three years now… I've been reading in Army publications this past year about units coming to JRTC and converting their Delta companies into scouts and trying to get more offensive minded with them. But they have all been about making those changes right before coming to the JRTC. Rourke's been training his guys for three years. Using a combination of Infantry and Cavalry… Mission Training Plans. We just didn't throw our CSC into being a Cav troop and operating Cav missions this year… His men know Cav operations… they may be MOS 11H, Anti-Armor Gunners, in their personnel files… But they are all Cav troopers… thanks to Captain Rourke." Francone looks at Schulberg and concludes, "And I guess you found that out recently?"

Schulberg smiles back, "Yes I did Jim. I appreciate your time and your explanation. But I haven't heard everything… I suspect you've got a couple more tricks up your sleeve… like moving your whole battalion… twice… with a two hour stop in between. In what Bob here says was a Defensive Repositioning… and NOT… an Offensive Movement-to-Contact Mission… Right?"

Francone raises his cup in a sort of salute to Schulberg, "Right."

Jeltsen clears his throat, then stands up, looks at his watch and states, "Gentlemen, we need to get back out to the AAR. I guess lunch is over… Jim, since I cheated you out of your lunch… go ahead and munch on your MRE during the AAR."

Jeltsen half turns and addresses Captain Marcell, "Olivia, since you've already completed your portion of the AAR, you can sit out the remainder if you'd like."

Marcell smiles, "Thanks, Sir, but I'll stay… I think I might be able to pick up some valuable professional knowledge… The 2nd of the 220th has provided everyone some… interesting… challenges."

At 12:55 hours the AAR building starts to fill back up. The front double doors are propped open and the participants come flooding back in from the parking lot. The large trash cans on either side of the doors begin filling with empty MRE packages as the soldiers pass by. Five minutes later everyone is once again in their assigned seats. Rourke sits down in his assigned seat with the two empty seats to his right and takes a moment to look over his shoulder to see if Captain Marcell is going to be sitting back down in her seat. She is approaching the chair from the back of the room. Looking directly at Rourke, she smiles and gives him a little wave with her left hand from her waist. Rourke leans back and asks, "How was your lunch?"

As she sits down, she answers, "Delicious, I had a salad, and you?"

Rourke nods, "I had the yummy chicken ala king downed by some perfect room temperature cherry Kool-Aid… yep… fit for a king."

Jeltsen walks to the front and opens up the AAR with a welcome back and then turns it over to Captain Chancy. Chancy, as the OC with CSC, the unit that actually got the battle started, is to facilitate the conversation with the opening actions by the Dragon Slayers.

He asks Rourke to explain how the first firefight is started by an accidental meeting of his men and the OPFOR. He has Rourke explain how fast they turned the captured map into actionable intelligence by setting up hasty ambushes. Most of the audience is surprised how the battle was started. They are also impressed how fast Rourke shifted his resources to maximize his personnel and weapons.

Chancy asks probing questions and remarks about the flexibility and versatility of CSC. Everyone can tell Chancy is impressed with the amount of initiative Rourke allowed his NCOs and platoon leaders. Rourke reiterates his belief in and trust he has with all his soldiers. Chancy credits that initiative with CSC's ability to control the action on the battlefield. On several occasions Chancy gives credit to Rourke's leadership in making tough decisions promptly. Chancy believes that every soldier in CSC is totally committed to their company and accomplishing the mission.

Chancy has Rourke explain and review the major battle against the OPFOR armor, on his positioning of his reorganized four TOW platoons. Finally, he has Rourke go over the battle of the "Black Forest" with his attached infantry platoon.

The OPFOR Commander, LTC Schulberg, occasionally asks Rourke some questions. It is apparent that Schulberg is most interested in CSC's ability to clearly communicate and work together. He realizes, just as Francone has told him, this is no pick-up team. These men have been working together for a long time.

At the end of Chancy's AAR, LTC Jeltsen walks up front, tells everyone to take fifteen minutes and grab a cup of coffee, that they would finish up with the battalion's, 'Repositioning of the Defense' action.

Rourke stands up and starts to turn in order to go to the back of the room where there are two large coffee urns set up for everybody. Captain Marcell who is sitting one row behind and on the end, stands, steps out to intercept Rourke, "Devlin, we have freshly brewed coffee in the break room... or would you rather have the mess hall blend in the back?"

"Fresh is always better... but is it allowed... for coffee?"

Marcell smiles, "Of course it is... for coffee. Your battalion commander had two cups during lunch."

Rourke steps aside making a sweeping motion with his arm and bids, "Please lead the way."

As Marcell passes by, Rourke looks over to his XO and First Sergeant. Both have grins ear to ear. Lt. Kiser, nodding his head, makes a fist and pumps it in the air a couple of times for encouragement and mouths the words, "*Go get some*" and then pumps the air again.

Rourke rolls his eyes back, shakes his head and mouths the words back to Kiser, "Grow up!"

Kiser's grin just gets bigger. He looks back at First Sergeant Johnson and quips "Come on Top, I'll buy you a cup of coffee... in the back."

Rourke follows behind Marcell on the way to the break room. '*He couldn't help thinking that this is the first time she called him Devlin and not Captain Rourke. Is the ice beginning to melt'?*

They enter the room and walk to the coffee machine. Marcell opens a cupboard and takes out two cups, sets them on the counter and asks as she pours, "Cream or sugar or both?"

Rourke replies, "Just a little creamer... and why are you being so nice to me, Olivia?"

She puts powdered creamer in both cups. She turns around and points to an empty table on the far side of the room, picks up her cup and walks to the table. Rourke grabs his and follows.

"I guess I'm trying to make up for our first meeting… when I really tore into you over the missing crews… I found out later it really wasn't anybody's fault… just a mix up caused by both units… poor communication… we shouldn't let that happen again."

Rourke takes a sip of coffee, "Olivia, I don't think we will. I think we can trust one another now… so that if anything gets in our way… we can approach one another and get it resolved… amicably." *All the while Rourke is thinking where is she going with this? Why the privacy of the break room? Am I to assume she is interested in me and wants me to ask her out? Or is it just what she says it is and wants to be nice to make up for the time she ripped my head off? Rourke, you need to be careful. One stupid word and this may not happen. Take it slow and try to be charming*.

Marcell tilts her head and smiles, "Amicably… my… I guess you're not Infantry. That's a big word for those guys."

Rourke smiles back, "Yes, it is a big word for my grunt brothers… whom I love dearly… But I've got to be honest. I've been saving to use that word in a sentence for the last three years… that is actually the last time I used it… and I suppose I won't get a chance to use it again for another three years."

She laughs and reaches over to touch his arm, "Devlin, fifteen minutes are just about up… we should get back to the AAR." With that she pushes her chair out and gets up to return her cup to the counter. Rourke follows her to the counter and then out the door.

They both get back to their seats just in time for Jeltsen to walk to the front and resume the AAR. This portion of the AAR has Rourke as a listener and a learner. This is about the fight the battalion rifle companies had on their repositioning move. Rourke knew it was intense but had no idea just how intense and in-depth it was. All the companies took a good number of casualties but they seemed to give better than they got.

LTC Schulberg still sitting in the back has to admit the OPFOR took a beating. He takes a couple of minutes to elaborate. The first move of three kilometers took the OPFOR by surprise and they had some small elements quickly overrun. The OPFOR used their artillery and mortars to good effect against the battalion. The OPFOR believed that their use of indirect fire was the reason the battalion stopped the first time. They assumed the battalion was going to dig in and continue holding the ground they has just gained.

The second move by the rifle companies completely surprised the OPFOR again. They were caught establishing new positions 800 meters to the front of the battalion. By the time they looked up, the rifle companies were once again overrunning the OPFOR. To make matters worse, none of the OPFOR re-enforcements hurrying forward knew they were heading into a full battalion of grunts running up on them. When they saw soldiers moving toward them, they assumed they were fellow OPFOR soldiers. Who would have guessed they would have moved 3,000 meters forward in the first place, let alone two hours later do it again?

The effects on the OPFOR were devastating. A key to the success was the battalion captured three separate sections of mortars that had decided to stay in their original firing positions. The six mortar tubes were all the OPFOR possessed. The only indirect fire remaining for their use was artillery. Too much use of artillery would make them susceptible to Blue Force counter battery fire. At this point, they had to be very careful how they used artillery.

It was reported that the reserve OPFOR company hidden in the Black Forest that spent all night running around trying to kill Charlie Company's Second Platoon, took too many casualties and was now too exhausted to have any effect in the main battle with the battalion.

After the last OC finished, Jeltsen came back up front to finish up the AAR and highlight the lessons learned. He informed the battalion that they would receive their new mission with the notional brigade's written operations order in their assembly areas in approximately one hour. He ended by asking Colonel Harrison to say a few words.

Col. Harrison walks to the front, crosses his arms and smiles, "Gentlemen, I'm very pleased with the first completed mission of the 2nd of the 220th Infantry. You've done well. All aspects of fighting... you've done well... and you should be proud of your efforts... however... the next mission is going to prove to be somewhat harder. The mission is tougher and you're now operating under 100% of men and equipment. I believe the battalion is somewhere around 75%. This will give you some additional challenges... After observing your first mission... I really am looking forward to you attacking this one. That's all I have. Good luck, gentlemen."

Everyone immediately gets up and stands at attention for a couple of seconds to demonstrate common military courtesy. LTC Schulberg walks over to Francone who is moving to the front doors. Schulberg smiles and offers his hand, "Nice meeting you, Jim. Sorry but now I'm going to kick your ass."

Francone takes his hand, smiles back and challenges, "Bring It."

Everyone within earshot is captivated. This is the ultimate picture of hard-nosed competition. Two commanders meeting in the center of the field, showing the highest respect, shaking hands, and vowing to bring their utmost to the contest. May the best team win.

Rourke stands up with the rest. He turns around, looks at Olivia. She looks back and confirms, "He's right... you're going to have a real fight on your hands... not only considering what the Colonel says... but now they know you guys. They know what to expect, no more surprises."

Rourke gives her a wicked smile, "Oh, they know about us... they got a good taste, but they don't know everything and besides, we have the most powerful weapon of all. Because we've already won... we now have absolutely nothing to lose. There will be no caution with us... there will be no risk avoidance. We'll be going right at them." Rourke finishes with an even bigger smile, "Make sure you stick around... this is going to be fun!"

"Devlin, it's my job to stick around. I'll be watching. You have been most impressive. I suppose you'll be up front again?"

Rourke nods, "LTC Francone and I talked about this months ago if this situation came up. We talked about what he wants to do."

Olivia drops her voice so only Rourke can hear, "Good luck, Cavalry."

Francone is waiting right outside the door. He gathers the company commanders together. "I want to meet with everyone in six hours at the battalion assembly area. Gary will have the TOC set up by then. I'm hoping to have the battalion operations order finished by then. In the meantime, get back to your companies. You know the drill. Reorganize and cross level weapons and ammo... and then prepare for offensive operations. You should have time to practice battle drills on Actions-on-Contact and Movement-to-Contact. Gentlemen, our basic fighting philosophy has worked... and we're not going to change. Remember and remind your men... we came here to kill the OPFOR. See you in six hours. It's just about 16:00 hours now. See you at 22:00 hours." With that Francone brings up his right hand in a salute signifying the meeting is over. Everyone returns the salute then breaks away and heads for their Humvees.

Francone calls out to Rourke before he gets a couple of steps away, "Devlin, can you get over to the TOC in three hours. We should have the brigade's operations order broken down and starting on our portion to create the battalion's operations order. I want you there as I prepare our order... remember our conversation a while back?"

Rourke smiles, "Yes, Sir, I remember... I'll be there at 19:00 hours."

On the way over to his Humvee, he is intercepted by his XO, Lt. Kiser. Kiser has a look of urgency on his face. He points to an open spot in the parking lot that would provide some privacy at least for a conversation. Rourke walks over with Kiser, turns to face him and asks, "What's up, Number One?"

"Sir, we'll be getting back some replacements for our men and three Humvees later on tonight."

Rourke looks confused, "That's good, right? We're getting three TOW crews with vehicles... that's great... and a little bit ahead of time... which is even better... Right?"

Kiser looks down to gather his thoughts, glances back up to Rourke and starts to explain, "Well, I got to tell you that Top and I kind of... gamed the system a little for this to happen this soon."

Rourke tilts his head and asks, "Gamed the system?"

"When the first reports came out that we were in contact with the OPFOR back on day one... Top and I decided to claim... or put in the paper work for replacements for three TOW Humvees and crews. We had talked before then, that no matter what the first fight was... we are going to get a little jump on the replacement system. That if we got caught... we would somehow claim confusion being... this being our first JRTC experience."

Rourke looks up in the sky right above Kiser's head like he's looking for an answer and contemplating what to do next.

Kiser continues, "Well nobody noticed. It's really taken for granted around here that the first battle is always won by the OPFOR and they usually kick the Blue Force's ass. Our guys at battalion just assumed the request was correct. The JRTC guys getting it from battalion didn't track the battle... they assumed the request was legit. They put it through... and the clock started on getting replacements through the simulated replacement system. We're getting ours about 24 hours early." Kiser takes a deep breath, looks back down waiting for Rourke's reply.

"Well, Lieutenant, we kind of have an ethical dilemma don't we. Do we not accept them for another 24 hours or... do we pretend not to notice?"

Kiser shuffles his feet, puts his hands on his hips and gazes at Rourke, "I don't know... I honestly don't know. I'm telling you so that if this blows up... you'll know what happened and who caused it."

Rourke moves his head to the side and with an inquisitive look asks, "What did Top say to all of this?"

Kiser takes another deep breath, takes his hands off his hips and opens up his hands in front of him, "Well, right off... Top says, Fuck 'em... If they're not smart enough to catch it... that's their tough luck... and this should teach those arrogant assholes a lesson on not assuming they're such bad asses they don't need to keep up with the battle because they win all the time... and then he ended with another... Fuck 'em."

Rourke starts to form a small grin. He bites into his lip just a little. He then crosses his arms, takes a solid stance and considers, "You know Top is a very experienced and wise man. I am by no means condoning such activities. And I hope that this will be a lesson for all concerned to learn. But we must keep in mind... Top relies on many, countless years of professional soldiering. Did I say he is a wise man? I believe we should defer to his wise judgment on this one case... keeping in mind this is a separate case and that this in no way sets a precedent for any future dilemmas... this is a onetime... thing... right, Lieutenant?"

Kiser shows a small grin, "Right, Sir... and I'm sure the lesson is learned by all concerned."

"OK, let's get down to the assembly area and get our guys ready for the battalion's offensive operations. And figure out who gets the three replacement TOWs tonight."

CHAPTER 28

"Desire is the key to motivation, but it's determination and commitment to an unrelenting pursuit of your goal - a commitment to excellence - that will enable you to attain the success you seek." - Mario Andretti

2/220 Infantry Battalion Assembly Area
Battalion TOC location
Tuesday, 5 December 1989
18:45 Hours.

Josh backs into an open spot in the battalion assembly area. Rourke who has gotten out to ground-guide Josh with his red lens flashlight, walks back to lean on the door frame on Josh's side. Josh turns off the vehicle, takes off his helmet to toss it off to the side, and turns his head to look at Rourke, "How long do you figure to be, Sir?"

"Josh, I'm guessing that working on the battalion order is going to take two hours... knowing the battalion commander. He knows what he wants to accomplish. The battalion staff will write it up and have it published by the time all the other commanders get here at 22:00 hours. No sense in us leaving just to come right back. So, I'm figuring you catch two hours of sleep… when I get done I'll be back to crawl in behind you and catch an hour before 22:00 hours. You might as well turn off the radios. The XO and Top are running the assembly area. If the battalion wants me… I'll be right in the TOC. Any questions?"

Josh teases with, "Yea, what's up with you and the OC Captain?"

Rourke takes a second to consider his answer, "Why Captain Chancy and I have a very respectful and professional relationship. We might be seeing him here… should I send him over for you to say Hi?"

Josh nods, "Nice deflection. If I see… the smokin' hot OC that I know we're both talking about… should I say anything to her… to help your cause, of course?"

Rourke steps back from the driver's door with a quizzical look, "What makes you think I've got any interest in the… smokin' hot OC?"

"Well, I first noticed the attraction at the AAR… when I went in to get coffee and donuts. I came out and saw you and Captain Chancy laughing it up with her… so I walked over to talk with a couple of other drivers… and drank your coffee and ate the donuts. Then when I went in to the building at the first break after lunch to get another coffee… to try and warm up… I ran into the XO and Top. I asked where you were. They started grinning and pointed to a door across the hall and said you two went into that closet ten minutes ago."

Rourke crosses his arms, puts on a, 'this kind of pisses me off', look on his face and asks, "So you think this outrageous rumor will go anywhere?"

This makes Josh smile and look right at Rourke to reply with, "Hey, Sir… The Dragon Slayers are a family. Which means we spread gossip like a family… which means I bet Top and the XO are down at the company assembly area laughing and exaggerating every little detail about you and smokin' hot OC… to all the platoon leaders and platoon sergeants right now. You know the platoon sergeants will eventually say something to the squad leaders and section sergeants and so on and so on." Josh holds up his hands and asks, "Am I right or am I wrong?"

Rourke shakes his head in apparent disgust. He turns to walk to the TOC. As he walks away, he says over his shoulder, "Josh, I'm disappointed in all this rumor mongering. We should be better than that." He stops after going ten steps, turns back to Josh and grins, "OK, she is hot. If I could be so lucky."

Josh leans out the door, "Well, I'm rooting for you, Sir."

Rourke makes his way to the TOC after getting directions from two soldiers. It is damn dark, but at least the TOC is in some decent flat wooded terrain and not hidden in a swamp like Sergeant Gary McCallister usually does. Rourke fights and finds his way into the TOC tent foyer, makes sure the outer tent flap is completely closed and then flings open the interior tent flap. Rourke's eyes are immediately struck with bright light coming from three light tubes hanging from the sides of the tent. It takes him a couple of seconds to make the adjustment.

He is called to the front by LTC Francone sitting on a folding chair in front of the map board. There is actually a small huddle of five men sitting on chairs around the commander. They have a folding table off to the side they are using for any writing. The S-3, Operations Officer, Maj. Charles Dyer, is standing next to the map board and using his pen as a pointer.

Francone waves to Rourke, "Captain Rourke, I've got a seat right here for you. We're just going over the brigade operations order... some pretty standard stuff for an offensive operation. Maj. Dyer is just about to go over our new area of operation." Francone turns back to the map board, "Go ahead, Charlie. What have we got?"

SFC McCallister has his operations guys do a hand drawing of the Area of Operation on a large sheet of tripod mounted presentation paper. This enlarged sketch makes it much easier for everyone to see. Dyer spends the next fifteen minutes going over the area and in particular the terrain and vegetation. The ground is really very similar to what they were just fighting on. Rourke notices three bigger and higher hills, a couple of streams and a ravine. These all seem to look like they could play a part in the mobility of the battalion. The wooded areas appear to be the same with about the average number of trails running throughout.

As Rourke looks at the new area, he does what he always has. He is looking at who can use the terrain to their advantage? There are several questions and a small discussion about the new area. Rourke feels until he can actually look at a piece of ground, all he is doing is speculating. After ten minutes of discussion Francone looks over and gives a nod to the S-2. Everyone's attention then turns to the Intel officer.

The S-2, Cpt. Morgan Easton, leans back in his chair, gathers his thoughts and then shakes his head, "Sir, I really don't think I can be any help to you for this next fight. For a couple of reasons... the first is... I'm trained to give you the typical enemy situation at this point and a template on how the enemy should be positioned on the battlefield. After sitting through our AAR with the OPFOR Commander listening, I can tell you this enemy will not now operate in a predictable manner. They know we use our CSC as a Cav troop. They will compensate for that. They understand our battalion's... character... our abilities... we are not the weekend warriors they presumed we are. They had their ego crushed. They have tremendous pride in themselves. We just gave them a good swift kick. They are... Not... going to take this lying down at the next battle. They will not be out there to help train this poor Blue Force battalion to become better soldiers. This time... they will be out there to beat the shit out of us. No, gentlemen, I can't predict any of their actions... other than they want to send us out of here not only defeated but... humiliated."

Maj. Dyer, who is sitting at the end of the table speaks up, "Morgan, that actually is a pretty good appraisal of what we can expect." Dyer smiles and continues, "I really enjoyed watching the hand shake between the Colonel and the OPFOR commander. I read this as... this is going to be a knockdown, drag out brawl with two titans going at each other. The gloves come off. Let's keep in mind what Morgan just said. They will next fight the enemy they just engaged... not the enemy they expected... or the enemy their S-2 had told them to anticipate. That's out the window. There's a reason the OPFOR commander and his S-3 sat there for the whole AAR. They are gathering Intel and searching for weakness. I just wonder what they found."

Francone sits there watching, listening and taking it in. He is enjoying the discussion. Then it comes time for him to take over the conversation. He stands and takes a couple of steps to the map, "OK, we've got the mission... conduct an attack to seize Objective Champion, no later than 16:00 hours on the 14th, in order to protect the brigade's right flank during their attack and seizer of the village of North Point, a key road and rail center. As you can see from the map... without us taking Objective Champion this leaves the whole east side of the brigade open to any counter attack. We need to secure Champion before the brigade starts their attack."

Francone takes a glance around to make sure everyone understands before continuing, "We're facing what size element Morgan?"

Captain Easton flips open a note book, "Sir, from what I can put together from my Intel sources it looks like a small battalion of approximately 240 Infantry. I think they'll run with three, 60 man companies... and a 60 man support company... and Devlin... I'm best guessing four or five BMP's and two or three T-64 tanks."

Rourke ponders, "So what you're saying is plan for six BMPs and four tanks."

Morgan flashes a thumbs up, "That's why you're so good, Devlin... prepare for the worst and then really prepare for the... let's say worser. Hey, it's now a new Intel word."

Francone points over to Dyer, "Charlie, what have we got for this mission?"

Sir, we have 330 grunts... if we cross level... that's 110 per company... with really no replacements for 48 more hours. Which is after the mission starts. Devlin, can you update us on the Dragon Slayers?"

Rourke looks down at his note book, "I've already cross leveled once. So, now I have the Scouts with five vehicles and the three TOW platoons with four vehicles each. That's seventeen Humvees and my XO tells me we're getting three replacement Humvees... with crews... this evening. Which brings me up to twenty Humvees for the mission... But the best news is that I've only lost three scout soldiers during the last fight...keeping the Scouts way forward and not having them engage is now paying off. So, we really have almost the whole scout platoon for the mission."

Francone gives Rourke a quizzical look. Rourke knows Francone wants to know how CSC is getting replacements so soon. Rourke lowers his head and looks up at Francone with the *please don't ask me the question* look. Rourke has used that look before a couple of times over the past three years. Fortunately, for Rourke and CSC, Francone has always picked up on it. Rourke is once again fortunate when Francone begins, "OK, we're in pretty good shape... let's take a look at the ground we'll be fighting on."

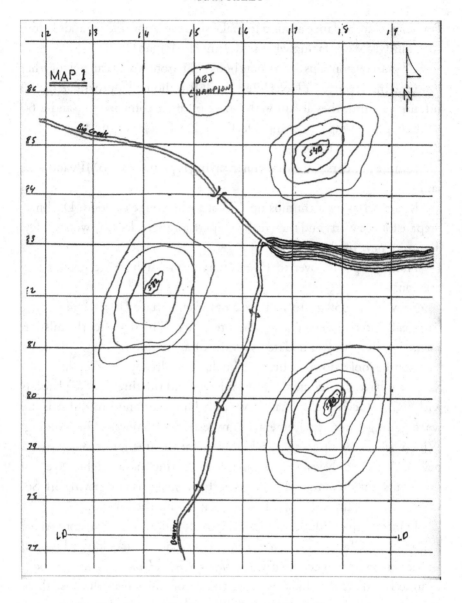

Francone reaches into the easel tray below the drawn map to pull out a collapsible pointer, pulls it to half its length and starts a terrain analysis, "I've looked at the map as I was reading through the operations order. This is going to be a little trickier than I first imagined. Within our Area of Operation there are three large hills. Let's call them hill 580, hill 532 and hill 540... or let's just call them 80, 32 and 40. That's going from the south to the north.

Hill 80 is two klicks right across our LD over on the east side. Hill 32 is about four klicks north, northwest from hill 80. Hill 40 is about four klicks north, northeast of 32. Between 32 and 40 is the Big Creek… that's its name and it really is… a big creek. It runs basically west to east. There is a bridge at 155840. A two-lane bridge. I would guess the bridge is the only way to get across the creek. If you follow the creek from the bridge about two klicks further east and a little south it drops into a steep ravine. The ravine continues on for several klicks out of our area. There is one feeder creek that flows into the Big Creek. That's Beaver Creek. It runs from the west side of our LD, predominately north east between hills 80 and 32. It meets the Big Creek right before the ravine, directly two klicks east of hill 32 at grid 164831."

Francone steps back from the map, turns to face the group, "Objective Champion at grid 153860, is a wooded area perfect for hiding a small enemy battalion… or several artillery batteries." Francone turns back to the map to point to the bridge, "Gentlemen, I'm just guessing here but I would say the most important piece of terrain or the key point… is that bridge. The two hills south of the Big Creek are important for holding ground… but I believe we need to focus our attention on getting that bridge. If the creek is high… and I believe it is… that bridge is the only way for us to get across and take Objective Champion to the north of it. We could get pinned down and massacred at that bridge."

Francone looks over at Dyer who is sitting on the table, "Charlie, do you see anything different?"

Dyer studies the map for an additional minute, "I am concerned with hill 80… it is 40 feet higher than anything in our AO. Owning that hill could be crucial to any operation we try to conduct. I would guess it has observation over the whole AO."

Francone nods and peers over at Rourke, "Devlin, have you got an opinion on this?"

Rourke stands up and walks to the map, studies it then turns to face the group, "I believe we should focus on hill 40. If we write an operation order that is focused on taking hill 40… I think everything else will fall in line. Hill 40 controls the bridge, Big Creek and Objective Champion. But to get the bridge we need to take hill 32… it controls the near side of the bridge… hill 80 can be isolated… it's four klicks from hill 32. Normally high ground is the most important piece of terrain... but in this case I don't think so." Rourke walks back to his seat.

Both Francone and Dyer study the map and run through Rourke's logic. Francone finally deduces, "What we really need is to know what we're facing on the ground. Devlin, why don't you come up with a zone recon plan for the scouts. This will be a dismounted recon mission... we have plenty of time. Oh, that reminds me, I was told that because we did so well so fast... we now have an extra day to prepare for this mission." Francone breaks into a wide grin, "A reward for kicking the OPFOR's ass, compliments of Colonel Hanson, Chief of JRTC Operations. Besides I think we threw their scheduling off for the next mission. They're using this pause to get reset."

Rourke suggests, "OK, Sir, how about we have the scouts do a zone recon and then stay in the AO and establish Observation Posts at key locations?"

Francone standing by the map says, "You know what?... I am tired. Since we have this extra day... let's take advantage of it. Gary, call the companies and let them know the warning order for tonight is cancelled... and the warning order will be given tomorrow at 14:00 hours here at the TOC. Let's give them a chance to get some sleep. Rourke, bring the zone recon plan and the OP plan at that time... Is that good for you?"

Rourke replies, "I'll have them ready, Sir."

CHAPTER 29

"Action is the foundational key to all success." - Pablo
Picasso

2/220 Infantry Battalion Assembly Area
Battalion TOC location
Wednesday, 6 December 1989
14:00 Hours.

The TOC is set up in its usual configuration for a battalion operations
order briefing. SFC Gary McCallister has his guys set up the Ops Map,
Intel Map and chairs per the SOP. There is a small folding table in the back
that holds a large insulated container of coffee along with some stacks of
Styrofoam cups, some sugar and powdered creamer. Rourke grabs a cup
before he sits down. All the commanders are there. Francone who has been
sitting and talking with Maj. Dyer gets up and turns to face the group. He
sees Rourke and asks, "Captain Rourke were you able to come up with a
zone recon and an OP plan?"

Rourke stands up and moves to the map and unrolls an overlay that
he places over the map, and opens his notebook to read from his notes,

"Yes, Sir, I think we've got a pretty good plan for both the recon and the observation posts."

Francone nods and signals Rourke to continue with the briefing.

Rourke steps to the side of the map, and addresses the commanders using his pen as a pointer, "We're going to conduct a dismounted zone recon of our whole AO. Starting at the LD and going all the way to the objective. The scouts are broken down into... five, 5-man recon teams and one, 5-man headquarters team. They'll be stepping off from the LD at 06:00 tomorrow morning. We'll have them spread or spaced across the LD about every 1,000 meters. They are designated as team 1 through team 5 and the headquarters team as team 6. Their radio call signs are all still prefixed as Green, followed by their team number. The maneuver plan is simple... just start walking straight north. So, what it worked out to be... is that eventually teams 1 and 2 will recon hill 32, team 3 will recon the length of Beaver Creek and 4 and 5 will take on hill 80. All the teams will then continue on north to recon the terrain... and then a portion of Big Creek. They will attempt to find the best way across... we will have at least one of the teams get across Big Creek and recon hill 42. They are all prepared to conduct a stream crossing... they have the necessary ropes and snap links to perform a crossing."

Rourke glances down at his notes, "What we'll get is a report on trafficability of any major trails, cross-country trafficability, suitable fording or crossing sites... any mines, or obstacles... locate any bypasses around mines or obstacles... determine enemy locations to a six-digit grid, enemy strength, their composition and activity." Rourke surveys the tent, "The OP plan is to... right now... establish three OPs... One is between hill 80 and hill 32... to monitor any traffic between them. The second is to overwatch the bridge. The third is to put one north of hill 40... keep in mind we'll maintain flexibility based on what the zone recon shows us. We are prepared to establish more OPs in support of the battalion's final Operations Order." Rourke closes his notebook, looks around and asks, "Any questions?"

Francone stands up and steps to the front, "Thanks, Captain Rourke, we should have a complete picture by tomorrow night... right?"

Rourke nods, "Yes, Sir, we're pretty confident that we'll have a picture to the S-2 by 20:00 hours tomorrow night."

Francone clears his throat letting everyone know to listen up, "This is your warning order, Gentlemen. This will be a three-phase operation. We'll be attacking hill 32 first. We'll show a demonstration to hill 80, with a platoon of infantry and a TOW platoon. I want hill 32 first... then if it's necessary we'll get hill 80... that will clear all the enemy south of the Big Creek. Alpha Company will be the main effort with Bravo Company in support. Charlie Company will provide the battalion reserve and the demonstration platoon in front of hill 80. After we take hill 32... I want Bravo to be prepared to attack hill 80 from hill 32."

He pauses for a few moments to ensure everyone is following, "Phase two will be... Charlie with support from CSC... be prepared to assault and take the bridge. Phase three will be... Alpha will then cross the bridge and attack hill 40 and simultaneously Bravo will cross the bridge to attack and take Objective Champion." Francone checks out everybody's faces, "Yea, I know, clear as mud. But it will give you the basic concept for you to prepare. Our scouts will give us the key information to write a solid plan. It may change some... but the concept will stay the same. Any questions for me?"

Rourke raises his hand, "Sir, I'd like to make the case for getting another infantry platoon assigned to the Dragon Slayers. My scouts will be dismounted... which means I'll have a bunch of Humvees available to mount up a platoon... it could provide the battalion an additional mobile asset along with additional firepower."

Francone chuckles along with everyone in the tent, "Captain Rourke, you're not trying to build your own empire... are you?... Don't answer that?"

Charlie Company Commander, Captain John Bynum, leans to his right to speak to Rourke sitting on the other side of Captain Young and asks with suspicion, "You wouldn't have any particular platoon in mind... would you?"

Rourke smiles, looks back at Bynum, "Well John, as a matter of fact I would offer up your 2nd platoon. Only because it makes complete military and tactical sense."

"And what sense is that, Devlin?"

Rourke replies with, "Lt. Heller and his men have already worked with us. We know each other now. CSC operates differently than the rifle companies. Your second platoon understands that. We have developed a solid working relationship and have trust in one another. Trying to establish all that with another platoon takes time... let's take advantage of what we have now... teamwork!"

Francone steps forward, pauses to consider Rourke's reasoning, "As much as we would all like to dismiss Rourke's argument... I believe he has a good point both on using the scout's Humvees and again using Charlie Company's 2nd Platoon.

Bynum shifts in his chair, looks at Francone, "Sir, with my 2nd platoon now going to CSC and you wanting me to supply a platoon for a demonstration in front of hill 80... that leaves me with only a single platoon to work with CSC to take the bridge."

Francone surveys the room, "Gentlemen, this warning order is to be used for planning on the general concept... John, just go with what we've got right now. Once we get a clearer picture from the scouts... we'll be making changes. Depending on what they see... there could be complete changes to our concept... but let's go with this for right now. Any more questions?"

There are none. Francone continues, "Gentlemen, we put the OPFOR back on its heels because we were so aggressive. Remember... we came here to kill the OPFOR... never pass up an opportunity to do just that. We have an objective to seize in this next mission. But try to kill as many OPFOR as you can on the way there... And one very important thing... We're going on a partial reverse cycle. What that means is our operation won't start at the crack of dawn, but will start later in the day. I want to equal out the playing field by doing a lot of our fighting and working in the middle of the night. They know the terrain, they know ambush sites, they can overwatch fields and danger zones... but at night not as much. They can't see us coming quite so far away. That's all I have. Gary will call you tomorrow evening for the time to receive the operations order... have a good day." With that everyone stands up and salutes. Francone returns everyone's salute and walks out of the tent.

Bynum gets up and steps toward Rourke, then says with a grin, "I can't believe you stole my 2nd platoon again."

Rourke smiles back, "John, first they are really fuckin' good. You should be proud of all of them. Lt. Heller is very good... and I'm going to nab him in the next draft. Second, I didn't steal them. They are assigned by the battalion commander… I just made a good argument that's all. And third, when can I get them to my assembly area? I want to start getting them up to speed on the Humvees."

"I could get them over there this evening. Do you want them to learn any night time driving?"

Rourke thinks for a couple of seconds, "OK, get them there this evening. They can't learn night driving in a couple of hours. I'm going to keep the scout drivers with their vehicles…but I will pull out some of your guys to recon with the scout teams. Walking with a ruck and a rifle is what they do best. If they can keep quiet while doing it… they'll add to our teams… let's get them hooked up with their teams and have them conduct pre-combat checks together this evening."

Bynum nods, "OK, Devlin, just take care of my guys."

"Once again, I'll love 'em like my own."

CHAPTER 30

"A true leader has the confidence to stand alone, the courage to make tough decisions, and the compassion to listen to the needs of others. He does not set out to be a leader, but becomes one by the quality of his actions and the integrity of his intent. In the end, leaders are much like eagles... they don't flock, you find them one at a time." – Unknown

2/220 Infantry Battalion Line of Departure, Grid 132773
Thursday, 7 December 1989
05:58 Hours.

Lt. Mark Fugate, Scout Platoon Leader, down on one knee, gets a glimpse of Rourke kneeling beside him and says in a hushed voice, "Happy Pearl Harbor Day, Sir."

Rourke grinning says, "You know we got our asses kicked on that day. I'm expecting exactly the opposite from your platoon."

Fugate scrutinizing the woods to his front, "Yes... but that was the beginning of the end for the enemy... same thing today."

"I hope you're right, LT."

Fugate lifts up his left arm, pulls back his jacket sleeve, glances at his watch, raises his right arm over his head and with a sharp forward motion signals his men to move forward. Two men get up and start cautiously walking north into OPFOR country. They're about twenty meters apart. Because of the scarce vegetation, and the wide spacing of the trees, Fugate wants to try having two-point men with the remaining three following 30 to 40 meters behind, also spread out wide.

After watching for a couple of seconds, Fugate stands, scans to his front, without looking at Rourke and quietly says, "See you in Tokyo, Sir." Then he starts forward with the other two also about twenty meters to each side of him.

Rourke waits and watches for several minutes until he can't see his men any more. He gets up and slowly walks the 100 meters back through the woods to his Humvee.

Josh, holding his M-16, who was leaning up against a tree 25 meters from the vehicle, walks over to meet Rourke. "I didn't hear any firing... so I'm assuming they got off OK?"

Rourke nods, "Yea, now we wait... all day."

Josh asks, "What radio freq will they be on to make their reports?"

Rourke replies, "Right now they're working for the battalion commander. They'll be reporting on the battalion Intel freq."

"What do you think our chances are they get all the way to the objective?" Josh asks.

"Oh, we'll lose some. Someone will walk up on a hidden OPFOR out post and get shot. But the rest will slide away and move around the enemy OP to continue the mission. The OPFOR Commander never asks what kind of experience our scouts have. He doesn't know most of them have years of prior active duty... that they're going to Manchester University on the G. I. Bill... They're experienced and smart. Just like you, Josh."

CSC Assembly Area
06:25 Hours.

Josh backs the Humvee into its hidden parking spot in the assembly area. Rourke slides out holding his map case, and starts walking to the 1st TOW Platoon area. That's where Lt. Heller's 2nd Infantry Platoon is getting trained on the finer points of using the Humvee for this next mission. On the way over he sees and waves to both his other two TOW platoon leaders to follow him. At the 1st TOW area he rounds up both Lt. Heller and Lt. Foley. He eyeballs at all four lieutenants, points to a clump of trees about twenty meters away and starts walking there. They all find a comfortable place to sit and lean against a small tree. Rourke spreads out his map case in the middle for everyone to see. He looks at both Heller and Foley, "How's the vehicle training going?"

Foley answers, "Real good… The NCO's are working well together… I think Dan's platoon likes working with us."

Heller nods, "Yes we do… you should have heard my guys at our company assembly area… man you would have thought the 2nd platoon had beat the OPFOR all by ourselves… a lot of bragging about the battle of the Black Forest. The other platoons have no idea what that is about… so they really couldn't counter brag with anything solid."

Everyone chuckles at that. Rourke continues, "I wanted to go over the map and do some wargaming on different scenarios we may run into. At least this will have us thinking on the same page."

Lt. Kiser walks up on the group after parking his Humvee some 30 meters away within the assembly area perimeter. He has a large thermos in his right hand, "I've got some hot… very hot chicken noodle soup here… get out your canteen cups for some of this delicious soup… it'll warm you to the bones." Two of the LTs reach back on their hips to retrieve their canteen cups from their covers. Kiser unscrews the top and pours out two cups worth of steaming soup for the LTs.

Rourke asks, "Bob, any chance you know the temperature right now?"

Kiser screws the top back on the thermos and replies, "Yes, Sir… you guys have probably noticed it's been getting colder day by day. We started in the mid-forties and today's high is only 35. With the sun being out most of the day and everybody moving a lot… we haven't really noticed. But, I just got done meeting up with our mortars. Gattas has been requesting a MET message from the artillery every day." Kiser notices not everyone knows what a MET message is, so he explains, "A MET message is short for a meteorological message. The artillery actually gets them from the Air Force meteorological sections. There are a bunch of weather elements that are factored into computing firing data for indirect fire like temperature, humidity, air density, wind direction… shit like that. They enter that data into their mortar ballistic computers so the rounds coming out of the tubes and flying a couple of miles in the air… hit the target. So, if you ever want a weather report ask Jesse."

Rourke nods and asks, "OK, what have we got for the next couple of days?"

Kiser glances around, frowns and confirms, "Temperatures are going to continue to drop everyday… at least for the next couple of days. Expect to be operating in the twenties for the next mission. And there is a prediction of some snow this week… and you can kiss the sun goodbye also… overcast all this week."

Lt. Foley adds the enthusiastic comment, "Oh boy, snowball fights!"

Everyone immediately chimes in with sarcastic remarks to Foley. "Trevor, that's not funny… man I'm already freezing my ass off… now we're going to be wet also. Trevor, you're a sick puppy."

Rourke holds up his hands, "All right, everybody calm down." Rourke reminds Foley, "Trevor, I really appreciate you putting a positive spin on this… but this really does suck. So, everyone needs to check on your people and make sure your NCO's are checking on their people. Being wet and cold is the perfect formula for pneumonia or the flu or some sort of influenza crap. This is all preventable… keep everybody warm and dry. We don't need to lose a soldier because of stupidity."

Kiser raises the thermos, "Before I go… anybody else for soup?" He looks at Rourke, "Sir, I've got to check on a couple of things. I'll stop back later on… I think we'll be alright for the mission… all systems… men and equipment… this extra day really and I mean really helped."

Rourke nods, "OK, Number One, see you in a while."

Kiser turns to proceed to the company TOC tent.

Rourke turns his attention back to the group. For the next three hours Rourke goes over the possible courses of action they can expect during the mission the next day. There are a lot of, *'well if you do this, then I'll try and do that'*, kind of war gaming. There is a lot of advice and help offered to Lt. Heller on how to operate his Humvee platoon. That afternoon the TOW platoon leaders plan to show Heller's platoon how to move using different techniques based on the situation. They also plan to take Heller's platoon out on a little target practice with the mounted M-60 machine guns. This is a crash course in how to be a light Cav Platoon. Rourke hopes they can pick up at least a little knowledge. They are going to be asked to act quickly when the time comes to engage the OPFOR.

———————•——•——•———————

2/220 INF Battalion Assembly Area
TOC location
Thursday, 7 December 1989
16:00 Hours.

Josh backs into the same spot he used the day before. Rourke gets out, leans on the hood and tells him, "Josh, I really don't know how long I'll be. So, I want you to come with me... the TOC briefing tent won't have a lot of visitors and it will be a hell of a lot warmer than sitting in the vehicle... besides you could pick up some additional knowledge you could use at officer candidate school this summer."

Josh reaches in to grab his M-16, smiles and repeats, "Sir, you're like a dog with a bone... just give it up... It's not going to happen."

Rourke gives Josh a sly grin, "I know I'm breaking you down little by little. The idea is slowly growing on you."

Josh shakes his head, rolls his eyes, "Yea, growing like mold. Give it up, Sir, it isn't going to happen."

Rourke moves to the front of the vehicle, "Come on it's starting to get dark and... I am starting to break you down. I can feel it."

Josh falls in step to the left of Rourke. They work their way 60 meters through the trees and enter the TOC tent. Both stop at the table with the coffee and there are some assorted, brown packaged, MRE desserts lying in a tray. Rourke shuffles through the packages and picks two that say there's lemon pound cake inside. He hands one to Josh. Josh hands him a poured cup of coffee with cream and pours himself one. Rourke points to several empty folding chairs over by the S-2 map board. As they sit down, Rourke observes Captain Easton working on the map and asks, "Morgan, how are my guys doing?"

Without even looking back at Rourke, Easton replies, "OUR guys are doing quite well. Let me finish up with a couple more symbols and I'll give you a quick brief."

At that same time Francone steps into the tent from the opposite side, "Morgan, let me get a cup of joe and you can brief me too."

Francone sits down next to Josh, takes a sip of coffee, smiles at Josh and begins, "Josh, you're quite an impressive young man." He points with his coffee cup across Josh, to Rourke, "You know you have to be careful who you hang out with... you could pick up a reputation based on people seeing you with certain individuals."

Josh looks back at Francone, shrugs his shoulders, "Yes, Sir, but some situations are just unavoidable."

Francone reaches up and puts his hand on Josh's shoulder, "Josh, have you ever thought about OCS... Officer Candidate School? We have a couple of slots available for the battalion... I would be proud to highly recommend you."

Josh immediately swings his head around to Rourke. Rourke laughs, "Josh, I swear... I never mentioned anything about OCS to the Colonel... I swear!"

Josh turns back to Francone, "Sir, I really appreciate the offer but... right now I'm not planning on a big future in the Guard."

Francone advises, "OK, Josh... I only ask you to keep an open mind and if you ever want to talk about OCS... I'm a graduate of OCS by the way... if you ever need any information... my door is always open."

Josh shows a courteous smile, "Yes, Sir, I'll keep that in mind."

Francone raises his cup to Cpt. Easton, "Morgan, go on and give us what you've got so far."

Easton takes a deep breath, steps off to the left side of the map so he can use his pointer, "Let me start with what personnel the scouts have remaining and their current locations after," Easton glances at his watch, "ten hours of work." Easton points to the left edge of the battalion's boundary on the map overlay. "Let me move from left to right...or west to east. Lt. Fugate numbered the teams 1 thru 5 and his Headquarters team as number 6. Team 1, first on the west... They have all five team members... they have scouted the boundary and the west side of hill 32... they have gone all the way to Big Creek. They are going to try and cross using a one rope bridge at grid 144847." Morgan uses his pointer to indicate the location. He then points to the start point of team 2. "Team 2 is now down to... two guys. They ran into a bunch of OPFOR ... twice... right off the front of Hill 32. The two scouts have moved off to the east of the base of Hill 32 and set up an OP. They are at grid 149815."

Easton scrutinizes his audience of three to ensure they are following him, "Team 3... They have three... two just bought it as they got close to Big Creek. They mostly followed Beaver Creek on the west side from the LD all the way north till it runs into Big Creek. They probably won't be able to cross Big Creek... and I'll explain in a minute. They're working the area around grid 163824. Now Team 6, the headquarters team... The LT put his team in the middle of the zone... so he could better control his guys." Easton moved the pointer to the center of the map. "His team followed Beaver Creek on the east side all the way to the junction of Big and Beaver Creek. He has all five of his guys." Easton then moves the pointer to the start point for Team 4. "Team 4... They're down to two scouts and they are stuck at grid 170805... that's two and a half klicks north of the start point or the LD. They ran into a buzz saw on the west side of Hill 80... that's where they lost the three guys... the two remaining then came up on two BMPs with a platoon of dismounts in their way... so they went to ground and now have an OP keeping an eye on the BMPs with dismounts."

He moves the pointer to Team 5s start point, "Team 5 has all five guys... they reconned the east side of Hill 80 and walked all the way to the ravine at grid 188826. They are trying to find their way across the ravine now. They plan to get to Hill 40 tonight sometime." Easton takes a step forward, "Any questions on what we've got left and where they are?"

Francone, with a look of concentration, takes a sip of coffee and says, "I'm a little surprised our casualties aren't worse."

Easton nods and adds, "Sir, I think having five men on a scout team played to our advantage. What I mean is that the OPFOR typically uses three soldiers for their dismounted scouts. I believe the spacing of our scouts walking through the woods... allowed for some to get away when they came in contact. That the OPFOR never expected to encounter five guys... after killing three they believed they got them all... and I would guess that because of our use of all of CSCs Humvees and the Cav covering force operation during our defense... that they naturally expected to see Captain Rourke and the Dragon Slayers moving through the area mounted… conducting zone reconnaissance. It's just a guess, but I base it on some good Intel provided by our scouts, Sir."

Francone notices Rourke who is nodding in agreement. Rourke then adds, "I don't think they realized we have our whole scout platoon… They never go up against a whole scout platoon for the second battle.

Francone thinks that over for a minute then turns his attention to Easton, "Morgan, give us the picture you have of the enemy situation."

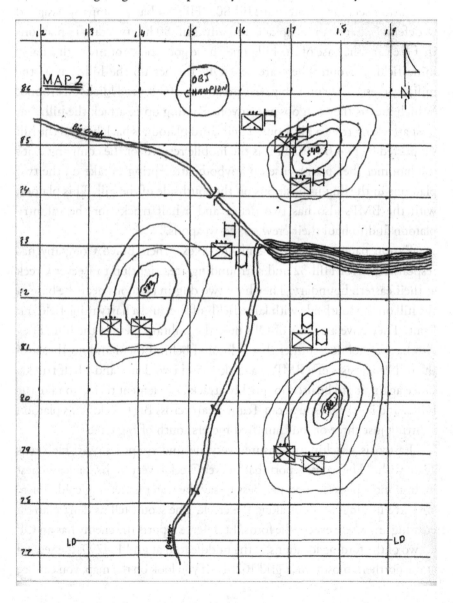

Easton answers, "Right, Sir... First, I'll tell what we know... a partial picture... then I'll give the best guess on what I believe will fill in the whole picture. This is based on the reports that the scouts have sent in. The enemy has two companies forward... both are south of Big Creek... in their own assigned area... which means each company has responsibility for an area that is bordered by Beaver Creek... and each has their own large hill as key terrain in their area."

Easton sets his pointer on Hill 80. "Hill 80 has a company assigned to defend it. Let's call it Alpha Company. Hill 80 has two dug-in platoons that are near the base of the hill. They have good fields of fire with a hasty mine field in front. There are two OPs further up the hill... near the military crest. They probably have great views for several klicks all around. Which means they can observe anyone coming up to attack the hill... at least attacking from a klick out. Their third platoon is back behind the hill supported by two BMPs. This is the mobile reserve for the company... it's the hammer they plan to use on anybody attempting to take on the two platoons in the dug-in positions on the southside of the hill. This platoon with the BMPs also has two deuce and a half trucks for the infantry platoon and to haul their crew served weapons."

Easton pauses for this to sink in, "Next, their Bravo Company has responsibility for Hill 32 and surrounding area right up to Beaver Creek as their eastern boundary. They have two dug-in platoons near the base of the hill on the southside with large fields of fire, and a hasty mine field out front. They have a couple of OPs near the military crest of the hill. They also have a mobile hammer that is located behind them and northeast of the hill. It consists of a BMP... a tank... and two deuce and a half trucks. Once again, it's to be used to quickly attack any element trying to take the hill... and it's the reason Scout Team 3 can't cross Big Creek. This platoon is sitting just three or four hundred meters south of Big Creek."

Easton is watching to ensure everyone understands so far. He starts again with, "The scouts report that Beaver Creek is very high... at least chest high in most places... and needless to say the water is freezing cold. There are three fording locations along the creek. The scouts tell us don't plan on crossing anywhere except the fords. Lt. Fugate reports the enemy has an OP at two of the fording locations... the middle ford at grid 154799, the second at the northern most ford at grid 162817. If you look on the map, you can see both of those mobile platoons are within a thousand meters of the northern ford. Bravo Company's hammer is on the west side and Alpha Company's mobile is on the east side. They could support each other if needed."

Easton takes a step forward, puts his hands on his hips, "OK, that's what we know... this is what I'm going to guess." He turns to step beside the map again, "Their Charlie Company is on or around Hill 40, north of Big Creek... along with probably a couple more armored vehicles... BMPs or tanks. I'm guessing they're overwatching the bridge, which we know is really the only way across Big Creek and the only way to our objective. So, to sum up what I think we've got. Three large hills... one north of Big Creek that controls the bridge. Two hills south of Big Creek one each on either side of Beaver Creek that runs right between the hills... that can only be crossed by fording... at only three fording locations... and a company occupying each hill. With a platoon sized armored vehicle support element... as a reserve or counter-attacking force."

Easton studies the map to see if he left anything out of his briefing, then continues, "Sir, that's all I've got for right now. My section will be doing a complete Intelligence Preparation of the Battlefield... the IPB... right after we get the scouts' last report. I'm figuring to brief the IPB around 22:00 hours."

Francone nods, "Sounds good, Morgan. I'll be back at 20:00. Just give me a quick update briefing then... basically let me know if this information is still good. I'm starting to formulate an operations order in my mind right now. I'll be ready to give the commanders an operations order by 22:00 hours... and speaking of right now... I'm going to catch a power nap... for a couple of hours. Captain Rourke, I recommend you do the same." Francone smiles, looks at Josh, "And Josh, I recommend you do the same, as much as I hear you talking on the radio... as Black 6... I suspect you actually run CSC yourself. I need the battalion leadership rested and ready to go."

Josh grins and nods, "Yes, Sir, you've finally figured it out... I'll make sure I get the necessary rest."

Francone stands up and walks to the tent entrance, "See you gentlemen later."

Rourke leans over against Josh, "That was pure bullshit flattery... He's working on you going to OCS. My money is on the Colonel by the way.

Josh holds his grin, "Yea, I know... but... my money is on me!"

CHAPTER 31

"A good plan implemented today, is better than a perfect plan implemented tomarrow." - General George S. Patton Jr.

Battalion TOC location
Thursday, 7 December 1989
19:55 Hours.

Rourke pushes the battalion TOC tent flap away and steps inside. It takes a moment to adjust his eyes to the white light. When he does, he sees LTC Francone, Maj. Dyer, Cpt. Morley, Cpt. Easton, CSM Morando and SFC McCallister sitting in front of the S-2's map. Off to the side, more or less in front of the operations map, he sees the company commanders: Dale Walker, Headquarters; Carson Young, Alpha; Andy Daugherty, Bravo; and John Bynum from Charlie. It appears everyone is sitting around drinking coffee, eating fruit or a candy bar, quietly talking, and waiting for the meeting to start. Rourke grabs a cup from the table in the back and then finds a chair beside Cpt. Bynum who nods at Rourke and asks, "You treating my platoon alright?"

Rourke smiles and replies, "I'm treating them so right... that they don't want to go back to your rag ass company. John… they say, no more humping rucks and rifles for them."

Bynum smiles back, "How long do you think that will last?"

"John, right up to the point they have to help change out an engine… or change some tires… or fix some headlights… or repair the exhaust or replace a windshield and its wipers… or grease all the fittings… oh, that one's a lot of fun. John, the bottom line is no one ever learns… the grass is always greener on the other side of the fence until you have to cut it."

Captain Easton stands and starts with, "OK, guys, I'm going to give you a complete IPB before the colonel gets his say."

For the next hour, Easton goes over everything the scouts were able to send the battalion Intel section. The updates that interest Rourke the most is that Scout Team 1 had crossed the Big Creek and are now at the objective and radioed back that it contained the OPFOR support and logistics assets. The other is that Team 5 has crossed the ravine and are working Hill 40. They had identified two BMPs, and a tank on the southwest side of the hill that provides complete cover of the bridge. And that the OPFOR has an infantry company divided up into three platoons that are not dug in but appear to be a Quick Reaction Force. The QRF is ready to react to anyone trying to cross Big Creek.

After the briefing, Francone stands up and tells everyone to take a fifteen-minute break in order to take a leak or refill their coffee cups. Rourke stands, grabs Francone's attention, and brings up his right hand to his ear as if he is making a phone call. Francone nods his understanding.

Rourke walks over to Easton and puts his hand on his shoulder, "Good briefing." Then asks, "Are you in contact with Team 5 right now?"

Easton nods, "Yea, we've got a 292-antenna set up and we're talking clear as a bell… you want to talk with them?"

Rourke replies, "Yea…that's Sergeant Callahan's Team. I asked him to check on something during the recon. It may impact what we decide here."

"Let's go over to the operations tent and give them a call."

After entering the tent, Rourke walks over to the radio set on the table and picks up the hand mic, "Green 5, this is Black 6, over." He waits a couple of seconds and then calls again, "Green 5, this is Black 6, over."

A couple of seconds later the speaker comes on with a hushed voice. "Black 6, send it." Rourke can tell by the muted level of the reply that

Callahan is close to the OPFOR and doesn't want to compromise his position by replying in his normal voice.

Rourke puts the mic to his mouth, "Green 5, did you get me some numbers, over?"

Callahan replies, "Roger, standby one."

Rourke pulls a pen from his shirt and a small notebook from his pocket ready to copy. A minute later Callahan comes back on the speaker, "Black 6, First is 60, second is 15, third is 50, break... both are marked... good approach and departure... from Romeo 43, right point 5, up point 4... how copy, over?"

Rourke's final reply, "Green 5, good copy, out."

Easton looks at Rourke and asks, "What's up with the coded message?"

Rourke waves Easton to follow him back to the briefing tent, "I'll explain to everybody in a second."

They enter the briefing tent and see Francone standing by the coffee table refilling his cup. Next to him is LTC Jeltsen, the battalion OC. Then Captain Chancy and two other OCs, including Captain Marcell, step into the tent. All have their field notebooks out ready to take notes. Rourke walks over to Francone and assures, "Sir, I've got the word from Sergeant Callahan. It's definitely doable with the info he sent us."

Francone turns to face the room, announces that everyone needs to take their seats, "Gentlemen, Captain Rourke is going to give us an option we should consider as we formulate an operations order. Captain Rourke, the floor is yours."

Rourke walks to the front of the tent and stands beside the operations map. Using his pen as a pointer Rourke begins his briefing, "All of us that have studied the map... have decided that the bridge over Big Creek is the key terrain feature and indeed the key to us successfully completing the mission. And observing the displacement of the OPFOR... they believe the bridge is the single key to preventing us from accomplishing our mission. They hold the bridge... we lose the battle. They want us to bleed ourselves fighting through their two forward companies so we won't have the strength to take the bridge... and be able to move on to the objective." Rourke turns, using his pen, taps on the map. "Everyone's focus is on the bridge." Rourke turns to face the room, "What if I told you there is another way across the Big Creek… that could change our chances… and give us the ability to… Win."

Everyone is curious, nodding and glimpsing around at each other with the, 'Oh Yea, let's see this other way' doubtful expressions. Maj. Dyer then speaks for everyone, "OK, Devlin… HOW?"

Rourke pauses for a second, "I've done this before… I was part of an Armored Cav Troop that moved all of its armored personnel carriers… that would be eighteen APCs… at thirteen tons per APC… across a big ass ravine similar to the one we face on the eastern portion of Big Creek." Rourke glances around to see he has everyone's attention. "It was at Camp Grayling, Michigan. It was in the dead of the night and it was pouring rain… in the middle of the woods. I don't remember whose idea it was but this was what we did. We called up two M-88 Recovery Vehicles… those great big track tank retrievers that belong to the maintenance guys. M-88's have these huge, powerful winches on the front of the vehicle… powerful enough to pull a tank… a 68-ton tank out of a ditch or mud hole up to the turret."

Rourke pauses, "We hooked the winch of the second 88 to the back of the first 88… we braced the second 88 against two big trees… the first 88 went over the edge and started down the near side of the ravine… actually being lowered down the slope with the winch. When the first one got to the bottom he un-hooked, drove across the creek to the bottom of the far slope, ran out its winch cable so the crew could take it up the hill and attach it to one hell of a big tree on the top of the ravine. With the combination of its tracks and the winch, it went up the slope. Once at the top it turned around, braced itself against a big tree and let out its winch cable to help pull up all the Troop's APCs… at the bottom of the ravine… Of course, after being winched down the first slope… We can do the same thing with our Humvees. Only using the winches of our deuce and a halves from support platoon. The winches are rated as 10,000 pounds capacity… however… they are recommended not to exceed 6,100 lbs. My XO, Lt Kiser, talked with Maintenance Chief Ronconi. Chief believes with the Humvee coming in at a little over 5,000 pounds and with the Humvee supplying braking on the first slope and its own traction by driving up the next slope with 4-wheel drive… that the load on the winch would be around 4,000 pounds… max. The Chief believes this is doable." Rourke looks around then asks, "Any questions?"

Captain Andy Daugherty of Bravo Company, raises his hand to get Rourke's attention and then asks, "Devlin, you know if the slopes of the ravine are… sheer cliffs… this isn't going to work… right?"

Rourke nods, "Andy you're right… conditions have to be within a curve of… what… let's call it… *do ability*." Rourke peers at Daugherty for confirmation then continues, "When I first saw the bridge… and realized that it is going to be the only way across to the objective… and saw the ravine… I remembered my experience with crossing that big ass ravine with the Cav. I then talked with the Scout Platoon Leader and Platoon Sergeant about reconning the ravine with this in mind. I just got off the radio with Platoon Sergeant Callahan. Callahan is also an old Cav Trooper… He's leading Team 5. His team went through the ravine and is the team on Hill 40 as Morgan stated in his IPB. Callahan sent me the following message."

Rourke pulls out the small notebook from his pocket, "The near side slope… the downhill slope is at 60 degrees… the depth of the water at this point is fifteen inches… the far slope… the hill side we have to drive up is at 50 degrees. This is steep but definitely doable with four-wheel drive. Both the entrance at the near side slope and the exit of the far side slope are solid and stable enough to work… He marked both sides of the ravine for us… the recon is done. He sent the location via TIRS. We just have to locate it on the ground… any questions?"

Everyone just sits there for a couple of minutes to soak in all the information and what that means for the battalion. Rourke walks over to his chair and sits down. Maj. Dyer gets up and walks over to the operations map. A minute later Francone gets up and walks over to join him at the map. For a couple of minutes, they have a quiet discussion on the feasibility of using Rourke's plan. Finally, they both agree. The battalion will cross the ravine to take Hill 40. Francone turns around to face the staff and his commanders. Dyer moves away to sit on the edge of a table off to the side of the map board. McCallister is already sitting there with a legal pad and pen waiting for any direction or guidance to take some notes. Francone checks with McCallister, "Gary, I see you're ready. Take some notes for the operations order."

Francone then gathers his thoughts, observes everyone in the tent, smiles and rubs his hands together. Not a little smile, a big smile. A smile that says, *'what the hell, we didn't come here to play it safe, we came here to win'.* "Gentlemen, listen up, here's the plan... the plan to win! It's going to take an effort on everybody's part... but I know we can do it. It's kind of complicated but if everyone does his part we'll be successful." Francone steps to the side of the map so he can use it to show his plan. "OK, let's take an accounting of the general picture. There are three major hills in our AO... the first hill... Hill 80 has an OPFOR company, two platoons on the southern slope and one platoon with two armored vehicles behind the hill. Now if you go about three or four klicks northwest... across Beaver Creek which runs south to north into Big Creek and is half way between Hill 80 and Hill 32, it can only be crossed at three fording places."

Francone pauses to point out the Beaver Creek fords then continues, "So, you have Hill 32 with another enemy company... two platoons dug in on the south slope... with another platoon with two armored vehicles behind it. Then looking Northeast by about two klicks... across Big Creek... which can only be crossed by the bridge that is half way to Hill 40... which has an infantry company and three armored vehicles around it... everybody got that?"

He grabs a pointer that hangs from the side of the map board, steps back a step and concentrates on the map. He's formulating the battalion's plan. He nods to himself, turns halfway to face the group to be able to use the pointer to direct attention to the map. Then he begins, "This will be a two-phase operation. First, I'm going to give you the maneuver concept... and then the timing... Carson, Alpha Company has Hill 32... your mission, Seize Hill 32. Andy, Bravo Company has responsibility for the three fords. Take them and hold them from the west side. No OPFOR are to cross to assist the enemy company under attack by our Alpha Company... Rourke, your guys have responsibility to take out... destroy the two armored vehicles and the platoon of the OPFOR behind Hill 32... And then secure the bridge on our side... the south side, to prevent those armored vehicles or the OPFOR grunts over at Hill 40, from coming across the bridge to help their guys... who by now are getting crushed by Carson... now as everyone can see... we're using Beaver Creek to separate the two enemy companies."

Francone uses the pointer, "I don't want to really engage the OPFOR company on Hill 80. John, I want you to use one of your two remaining platoons of Charlie Company to conduct a demonstration in front of Hill 80, to make them believe we're going to attack. I want the enemy focused on staying on Hill 80 to repel an attack that's never going to happen… and keeping their counter attack force in place… to support their guys from an attack… that's never going to happen. We're going to isolate that company east of Beaver Creek and bypass them in order to get Hill 32 and then Hill 40 across and north of Big Creek."

He surveys the group to ensure everyone understands his concept so far. "OK, let's talk about Hill 40. Rourke, Hill 40 is yours… with infantry support from John and his company. Obviously, you guys are going to be crossing the ravine and taking Hill 40 from behind and by surprise. According to the scouts the enemy vehicles and the platoons are oriented to the southwest covering the bridge." Francone assures, "It'll be like a walk in the park… a piece of cake." Everybody grins, Francone continues, "Alright let me go over the time line for everybody. Tomorrow, the 8th, probably around 09:00, you'll get the battalion operations order. Conduct your leader recon and formulate your company warning order, coordinate with fire support and logistics to put everything in place. Write your operations order on the morning of the 9th… brief it, do a rehearsal… make any last-minute changes… cross talk with your fellow company commanders on any issues. Make sure your fire support plan is squared away. Make sure any transportation to the LD is good to go; make sure you've got good comms with battalion."

Francone once again glances around, "We'll call this phase one. At 05:00 on Sunday the 10th I want us crossing the first LD. Alpha Company on the way to Hill 32… part of… or all of CSC on the way to the enemy counter attack platoon behind the hill. Bravo, on the way to capturing and holding the fords, and the one platoon of Charlie, on its way to Hill 80 for a demonstration." Francone nods to himself because he likes the way the plan is taking shape. He continues, "I'm hoping that by evening everyone will have accomplished their missions and report they are in firm control and holding their positions."

Rourke and Bynum are sitting beside each other. Francone addresses them, "Phase two. At 05:00 on Monday the 11th, I want Team Dragon

Slayer, CSC, and Charlie, to cross the second LD east of Hill 80...
bypassing the enemy on the hill... and get down to the ravine crossing
point. I want you guys to do a daytime crossing. This is our first attempt
at this kind of thing. I believe doing it in the daylight will add to our
success. Get the vehicles and the troops across by noon. Take the rest of
the day to recon Hill 40 and find some attack positions for early on the
12th. Make your attack and clear out all the enemy by noon on the 12th. I
want Alpha and Bravo to cross the bridge unopposed and moving to their
attack positions in front of our objective, Objective Champion. I want a
night time attack on the objective. I think by attacking their remaining
support troops at night... we should be able to clear and have the objective
by Wednesday the morning of the 13th. Any questions?" There are none.

Francone turns back to SFC McCallister sitting at the table, "Gary,
did you get all of that?"

McCallister finishes writing on his tablet, glances up at Francone
and asks, "Right, Sir, what comes after... I want Alpha Company to seize
Hill 32."

Everybody cracks up laughing. Francone breaks into a big grin. He's
learned to appreciate McCallister's sense of humor that always seems to
come at the right time, usually at a point that drains the tension and puts
everyone at ease. Francone turns back around to face the group, shakes
his head, "Such a wise ass." Francone then announces, "Gentlemen, with
no further questions at this time, I'm sure there will be many later on...
but for now you guys need to get back to your companies and prepare for
the mission."

Everyone stands and salutes. Francone returns the salute and walks
out of the briefing tent. Bynum turns to Rourke and asks, "What do you
think?"

Rourke thinks for a moment, "I love the concept and the timing.
I think by avoiding the fight on Hill 80... the battalion saves combat
strength for the important fights. Once we take Hill 32... the enemy can't
get at us... the enemy over at Hill 40 can't get across the bridge without
us killing them... and the enemy at Hill 80 can't get to us... unless they
try to cross at one of the fords. Bravo Company will have those well in
hand. Once we cross the ravine and secure the crossing on our side with
a squad, the by-passed enemy on Hill 80 won't be able to cross the Big

Creek to help their guys on Hill 40." Rourke breaks out in a thoughtful smile, "There are a lot of moving parts, but the timing allows us to make adjustments to provide any support to anyone that needs it… like I said… I love it. How about you, John?"

Bynum thinks for a second, "I'm just wondering if I'll have enough time to pick up my platoon conducting the demonstration at Hill 80 and take it with us to cross the ravine and attack Hill 40. We could use two infantry platoons, along with your guys, to take on all the enemy on Hill 40. Do you think we can make that work?"

Rourke nods, "Yea, talk with the Colonel. When we cross the LD for the ravine on the 11th… they won't be needed for the demonstration any longer. We could send three or four trucks to pick them up and have them with us at the LD. We really do need two platoons to clear Hill 40 of enemy infantry. I'll have my hands full trying to kill off the armor vehicles."

Bynum looks down, ponders Rourke's comments and glances back up at Rourke, "Yea, I'm going to talk with him right now… I'll make sure it gets in the operations order. We can do this."

CHAPTER 32

"Leadership is solving problems. The day soldiers stop bringing you their problems is the day you have stopped leading them." - General Colin Powell.

2/220 Infantry Assembly Area
Battalion TOC
23:00 Hours.

Bynum heads toward the exit to catch up to LTC Francone. Rourke glances around. The tent is emptying except for Cpt. Olivia Marcell standing by the back exit who appears to be waiting for Rourke. She smiles at Rourke. Rourke smiles and walks over with the intention of saying hi, exchanging pleasantries, and then getting out to Josh and the Humvee for a ride back to the company assembly area.

As Rourke approaches, Olivia's little smile turns into a look of concern. Rourke asks, "What's up, Olivia?"

"How would you like a cup of hot chocolate… and I'm a little curious about something?"

Rourke replies, "I never pass up hot chocolate on a night like tonight… and I'm an open book. Lead the way."

Rourke follows her out to her Humvee. Rourke opens the passenger side door and gets in just as Olivia gets in the driver's side. Rourke unclips his red lens flashlight, turns it on and sets it on the radio facing backward so they can have some light. Rourke starts the conversation with, "A cup of hot chocolate would be great about now."

Olivia replies, "Hold your horses... cavalry... let me get the lid off the thermos bottle." In a minute she passes over a small Styrofoam cup with steam coming off the top.

Rourke takes the cup, holds it up and asks, "Thanks for the shot of chocolate... you know I have a driver so you don't have to worry about me drinking and driving. I can get a second cup, right?"

"Sorry about the small cups. That's all they had at Walmart. And yes... you can get a refill."

Rourke looks back over at her, "What's up? You seem a little concerned?"

Olivia explains, "Part of my job as a support element OC is to check up on all aspects of the battalion's support elements. To cut to the chase... this evening I went by your battalion medic station. They are processing both real world injuries or sickness and the casualties from playing the game."

She intently observes Rourke to confirm his understanding. He shows concern, "OK, go ahead... I'm listening."

"Well, I talked with the battalion's Physician Assistant and I asked for the breakdown of real world injuries and any sick soldiers. There are always some during every rotation. I was just checking to see how your battalion compares with others. We put that data in with the final AAR package to let you know of any potential problems... you know... any health or safety concerns the data might be able to highlight."

Rourke nods, "OK, makes sense... what... what's this mean for me?"

"I asked the PA about sick call for the battalion. He says there are seventeen men he sent to the main post dispensary for possible pneumonia or, as the Army calls it, Upper Respiratory Infection or URI. There are three from Headquarters, four from Alpha, five from Bravo, and five from Charlie... that's an average of four per company." She stops, tilts her head and then asks, "How come Combat Support Company... your CSC Company doesn't have any. Not a one."

Rourke doesn't say a word. He is also wondering why his guys aren't sick. Finally, he expresses, "Olivia, I don't honestly know... maybe we take better care of ourselves."

"I called the dispensary and talked to the doctor on duty. I asked if seventeen men from an infantry battalion is an unusual amount or number of guys getting sick and ill with URI. He says it might be a little high for this time of year. But... because the weather was so warm the first couple of days, soldiers typically let their guard down and tend not to cover up or even wear a coat when working outside. He says all they need is a couple of days rest and they will be fine."

Rourke simply replies, "I honestly don't know, but I'll find out and let you know."

"Captain Rourke, I'm not implying anything troubling or alarming... I would just like to know why CSC hasn't anyone on sick call. It's unusual to say the least."

Rourke glances sideways at her and asks, "What's with the formal "Captain Rourke"... It used to be Devlin."

Olivia pauses, and then explains, "Captain Rourke, I'm trying to maintain a professional relationship with you."

Rourke watches her with suspicion, "Is there any reason we can't use first names and still be professional. I actually do this with every fellow company grade officer and haven't had a problem yet. Except one officer... in our battalion... let's just say we don't see eye to eye on... undeniably everything. He's a dick... pure and simple."

Olivia quickly sits upright, laughs and asks, "It wouldn't happen to be Captain Swoon would it?"

Rourke again looks at her suspiciously and asks, "How did you know?"

Olivia gives Rourke a knowing look and explains, "The good Captain Swoon occasionally comes back to the field trains to do some work. I've heard him interact with your XO and First Sergeant. He doesn't think much of Combat Support Company. I've noticed that they don't think much of him either."

Rourke takes a deep breath, "You're pretty perceptive. Anybody else in your OC world pick up on that?"

Olivia has fun with this knowledge. She teases, "No, I don't think so. Your little soap opera conflict with Captain Swoon is safe with me."

Rourke smiles sincerely at Olivia, "Good, as long as he does his job and stays out of CSC business... I guess I won't have to... knock his block off."

Olivia bursts out laughing, "Knock his block off! What are you... in a playground?"

"Well... kind of... I didn't want to come off being all hard ass and everything. So, I softened it up a little but I made my point... right?"

"Yea, I guess you could be a bad dude... going around knocking people's blocks off."

"So, what's with this maintaining a professional relationship? We can't be professionals as Olivia and Devlin?" Rourke brings up his right hand in a salute, "Both serving their country with honor and distinction."

Olivia pauses, explores Rourke's eyes with a sincere expression. "Devlin, you are proving to be a unique individual and one hell of a great soldier. I have to admit during our first meeting... I was not dazzled. I was actually unimpressed, but after observing you during this rotation... there is something about you that... attracts me to you. I don't... ever get this... feeling about someone that rotates through here. I've never had any thoughts or feelings about anyone I work with here on Fort Chaffee. You're really the first... remarkable soldier... I've considered noteworthy. I'm not sure how to process this. I know we have the second half of the rotation... so I want this to remain a professional relationship."

"Look, neither one of us really has the time to pursue anything other than a professional relationship. But I believe we have at least become friends. Two captains that are also friends can certainly call each other by their first names and still be professional. I appreciate the *excellent* soldier compliment and I'm flattered and... well... thrilled with your attraction to me... and the feeling is mutual on both counts. You're an impressive soldier that has certainly gained the respect of your peers, superiors, and the troops you help train. I like and respect that. And yes, I'm also attracted to you. But, we are both professional enough to get on with our jobs and finish this rotation... before we even consider pursuing anything else... right?"

"Maybe we could have lunch together after this."

Rourke nods and with a devious smile says, "Yea... we'll have lunch."

Olivia tilts her head, "Devlin, we'll start with lunch."

Rourke opens the door, slides out, turns around to tell Olivia before he shuts the door, "I'll get you that answer on why the men of CSC are so much healthier, and I know you're thinking handsomer... than the rest of the battalion."

Olivia laughs, "Thanks, looking forward to it."

Rourke works his way back to his Humvee where he finds Josh sleeping while sitting up in his sleeping bag behind the wheel. "Josh, wake up... time to go."

CSC Assembly Area
Friday, 8 December 1989
01:30 Hours.

Rourke has Josh pull up next to the company TOC; he lets Rourke jump out before finally parking in their assigned spot for the night. Rourke enters the TOC tent and sees Sgt. Matthew Sutherland, the company clerk, sitting behind a small field desk in the middle of the tent. "Matthew, first thing... don't have anybody wake me... or Josh until 09:00. We're going to try and catch up on some sleep. With the whole company in the assembly area we have enough leadership to handle any crisis that pops up. Got that? Besides the company practically runs itself now."

Sutherland grins and replies, "Yes, Sir, we run pretty smoothly... and I'll make sure you guys get up at 09:00 and not before then."

Rourke with a quizzical look asks, "Hey, Matthew, do you know why we don't have anyone going to sick call? Seems a little odd, right?"

Sutherland laughs, "Yes, Sir... Top's taken care of that."

"What do you mean? Top's taken care of that? Wait... do I want to know this?"

"Yea...we're good, Sir. When we pulled into the assembly area... I don't know how, but Top along with our Supply Sergeant, Joe Burke, got ahold of two GP medium tents, got some cots, blankets and a jury-rigged shower... with hot water... and set them up in the woods on the back side of the assembly area."

Rourke's expression changes to confusion, "What?"

"Before we even got here to Chaffee... at one of Top's NCO meetings they talked about the possibilities of our guys getting sick... being out in the weather with not much sleep. They knew, based on their experience

315

both as soldiers and as fathers with kids, that we are going to have sick soldiers. So, to make a long story short. If any soldier shows any signs of the sniffles or chills or looking like shit... the Platoon Sergeants send them over to Top's... 'get better tent'... they get a long hot shower and stuffed into a sleeping bag with a blanket in a dry warm tent. Most importantly, they get two or three healthy shots of the... Crud Killer Elixir... or better known as Vick's Nyquil. They get knocked out for twelve to fourteen hours of solid sleep. We've got two medics that monitor everybody in there. So, we're on top of the problems medically. Basically, because the NCOs are so vigilant, we catch this before it gets to the point we have to send them back to the battalion aid station. So instead of losing them for days. We get them back in one day."

Rourke is in a combination of surprise, amazement and awe. "How many guys have we... treated so far?"

Sutherland announces with pride, "Sir, we have successfully returned five back to duty and currently have six guys sleeping right now. They should be good to go and 100 percent by tomorrow afternoon."

Rourke shakes his head in disbelief, "I have never heard of such a thing... shit... I guess we can chalk one up for the company NCOs. Does battalion know about this? How long is Top going to run the... 'Get better tent'?"

Sutherland replies, "I'm not sure the battalion knows. I don't believe we ever offered them that information. Sergeant Burke will break it down and store it away right after we move out of... and clear the assembly area and start running the next mission, Sir."

Rourke chuckles to himself, "Damn, I don't know what to say. I guess... well... just make sure I'm up by 09:00 hours. Good night, Matthew." Rourke thinks, 'I can't wait to tell Olivia this one. She is going to love it'.

CHAPTER 33

"Leadership is unlocking people's potential to become better." - Bill Bradley

300 meters south of the western portion of the Line of Departure
Sunday, 10 December 1989
04:30 Hours.

Rourke puts his hands on his hips and inspects the faces of his five lieutenants. Rourke turns his attention to his 1st TOW Platoon Leader, Trevor Foley. "Trevor, you feeling good about this... feel good about the plan?"

Foley nods, "Yes, Sir, the plan is solid. I just hope Dan and I can execute it."

Rourke turns to Lt. Heller, "Dan, you have any questions?"

Heller shakes his head, "No, Sir, I'm also good with it. If I have any problems... I'll be screaming for help from Trevor."

The XO, Bob Kiser, speaks up, "I couldn't be at the back brief. I was just told our part of the operation is to provide two platoons to take out the enemy's counter-attack platoon behind Hill 32." He looks at Foley, "Are you guys going to need anything from the Logpac tonight?"

Rourke breaks in before Foley can answer, "Hey, Dan, how about you give Bob a quick... big picture of how your mission is to go."

All the lieutenants break out in grins. Heller glimpses around, "Pretty clever, Sir, getting me to give the XO a briefing. Because he's not read in on the plan, and not... because you're checking to see if I really know what I'm doing. Alright, I got this."

All the lieutenants start commenting on Heller's picking up the real reason for Rourke's request. "Good, Dan... you're not as dense as most grunts... good pick up... you're getting wise to his tricks. Maybe you could be a Dragon Slayer after all."

Rourke, showing a little red in the face from embarrassment, tries to recover with, "Dan... Dan I would never pull an amateur trick like that on you. Just because you're still kind of new to the Dragon Slayers. You and your men did a fantastic job back at the 'Battle of The Black Forest'. You've earned our deepest respect already." Rourke puts his arms across his chest and continues, "I'm really having you review the operation plan for the benefit of Trevor. He's the one... I know he doesn't appear to be slow... but he is a little bit... and he has been a little bit of a space cadet in the past."

A savvy Lt. Clegg chips in, "Oh... nice recovery, Sir. And it's true, Trevor is a little slow."

Foley shakes his head and glares at Clegg, "You're such a kiss ass, Chuck."

Rourke holds up his hands to bring order to the group, "Alright, alright... Dan, if you will, please continue with your briefing."

Heller looks around the group and continues, "We'll cross the LD here in a little bit... I have the lead platoon with 1st TOW behind. My call sign is Gold 1. We'll be traveling down a route using several trails that we reconned yesterday." He glances at Kiser to explain further, "Yesterday, we conducted a leader's recon. It was Trevor with three of his guys and me with six of my guys. We left three of mine with a radio up at our selected attack position overnight... And I just checked with them... no changes. We'll cross the LD, and using our route, we hope to skirt by slightly west of the two enemy platoons on the south side of Hill 32... without being picked up or noticed. We're hoping to get behind the hill and shut down the vehicles in our attack position. My Platoon Sergeant, PSG Walters, will lead a squad of dismounts up the north side of the hill to find out if there are any wandering enemy troops there. Yesterday there were none. There is a perfect location that we found on the recon that stages us over the top of the enemy counter-attack platoon. We can dismount four of the TOW launchers on tripods and set them up in the woods on the hillside and have great shots down into the enemy vehicles."

Heller looks around then continues, "Once I'm set with the four TOWs... I call Trevor... He has the mounted portion of the attack. There are a couple of trails that loop around the north side of the hill that actually come up on the rear of the enemy platoon. The down side is they also go past the bridge and the large open area in front of the bridge. Trevor's got to be fast and get past the bridge quickly or the armor on the other side could put a hurt on them... but also, my two remaining mounted TOWs will set up an overwatch position near the bridge to support Trevor's move across the bridge open area... with orders to shoot at any armor across Big Creek."

Heller pauses, gathers his thoughts, "We talked with Captain Young of Alpha Company. He's starting his attack on the two platoons at 12:00 hours. He would like us to be finished... meaning... destroy the counter-attack platoon before then. He doesn't care exactly when... just so when he starts his attack there are no enemy reinforcements available. Now our timing. We're pretty sure we can be ready to start our attack at 10:00 hours. If I can get two, clean, clear missile shots off and kill the two armored vehicles... that will start the fight. If I can't get the clear shots... I'll call for artillery and mortars hoping to get the armor vehicle to move in order to get a clear shot. When the artillery fire lifts... Trevor should be attacking the enemy infantry with his Humvees. We believe we can call for mission complete by 10:30 and then go on to our next mission of securing the south side of the bridge from any enemy trying to cross and help their company being attacked by Alpha Company. We also have a 'be prepared' mission to help Bravo Company at the northern ford... if needed." Heller checks around and asks, "That's it pretty much in a nut shell... any questions?"

Everyone in the group peers around at each other to see if anyone has a question. There are none. Rourke checks his watch and then puts out his hand to Heller, "Good brief...now good hunting." He then puts out his hand to Foley, "This is your mission. I trust you to get it done. Take care of Dan and his men… we might be needing them again in the future… good hunting."

The meeting breaks up with the three remaining lieutenants slapping Foley and Heller on the back and providing their fellow lieutenants encouragement with, "Go get 'em, killers… better you than me… unlucky bastards… don't fuck it up losers… try not to kill each other."

Rourke shakes his head, walks the 30 meters over to his Humvee to leave. His big day is tomorrow. He is thinking, *'Hopefully, I won't get anybody killed crossing that ravine'.*

CHAPTER 34

We call them leaders because they go first. We call them leaders because they take the risk before anybody else does. We call them leaders because they will choose to sacrifice so that their people may be safe and protected and so their people may gain, and when we do, the natural response is that our people will sacrifice for us. They will give us their blood and sweat and tears to see that their leader's vision comes to life, and when we ask them, 'Why would you do that? Why would you give your blood and sweat and tears for that person?' they all say the same thing: 'Because they would have done it for me.' And isn't that the organization we would all like to work in?" - Simon Sinek

300 meters south of the eastern portion of the Line of Departure
Monday, 11 December 1989
04:10 Hours.

Rourke is standing at the front of his Humvee, leaning against the hood drinking hot coffee and talking with Captain John Bynum, Commander of Charlie Company, along with Rourke's own XO, and two TOW platoon leaders, "John, what's the plan on picking up your platoon in front of the bad guys on Hill 80?"

Bynum replies, "That's my third platoon. We're picking them up right now as a matter of fact. They'll be the last four, two and a half ton trucks in the parade crossing the LD."

Everyone rubbernecks at a Humvee that pulls up next to Rourke's. It is the Battalion Commander's, LTC Francone. He hops out of the vehicle, walks over to the small group, smiles and asks no one in particular, "Any chance I could find a hot cup of coffee around here?"

Rourke peers over his shoulder to Josh sitting in the driver's seat. Josh gives a quick thumbs-up and reaches for the thermos and a Styrofoam cup. Rourke replies, "Josh has you covered, Sir."

Francone looks over to Josh, "Of course he does... the best OCS candidates always do."

Josh climbs out of the vehicle trying not to spill the coffee and walks over to Francone. As he hands it to him he says, "Damn, Sir... you are persistent, aren't you?"

As Francone accepts the cup and starts to turn to face the group he says, "Thank you, Josh... and yes, I am persistent, a trait you'll also pick up at OCS."

At that, Josh rolls his eyes, raises his hands in a gesture of, *'I give up'*, then gets back in the driver's side shaking his head.

Francone with his new, hot cup of coffee glances around the group and smiles, "I have a feeling this is going to be a great day for the 2nd of the 220th Fighting Infantry Battalion. I bet all of you feel exactly the same." Then he raises his cup and salutes, "To the fighting 220th Infantry... kicking OPFOR ass... again!"

All raise their cups and repeat with surprising enthusiasm, "To the fighting 220th kicking ass."

Bynum asks, "Sir, when you say, 'again'... I didn't have a chance to find out about Alpha and Bravo's mission... I guess they did well?"

"Gentlemen, they did very well. Alpha has the hill, Bravo has the fords and the Dragon Slayers have command of the south side of the bridge. There are casualties with all three elements but not as bad as I feared. They're all in good fighting shape. They are all talking to one another and coordinating any movement to support one another. As of 17:00 hours yesterday, all three have established a joint TOC on the northeast side of Hill 32. They have Maj. Dyer with them and are working on developing operations after we take Hill 40."

Rourke smiles. He knows that part of a leader's responsibility is to motivate his men. This is his commander doing that to him, getting him motivated for a difficult mission. It is working.

Francone then spots Lt. Jim Petrone, 3rd TOW Platoon Leader, and asks, "Lieutenant, give me a quick brief on the mission. How is it supposed to work?"

Lieutenants, Kiser, Petrone and Chuck Clegg stare at Rourke. Rourke asks, "How do you think I learned the, *'Hey LT, give me a quick back-brief... method'*?"

Petrone takes a small step into the circle toward Francone and begins, "Sir, this is an overall picture of the plan, based on completing a leaders' recon yesterday, and writing the final order late this afternoon. The recon consisted of Captains Rourke and Bynum, Lieutenants Clegg and Charlie Company's, Bill Miller, along with a five-man fire team for security. Yesterday we mostly walked the route we will be driving today. We took along two M-60 mounted Humvees for protection in case we had to run like rabbits. They mostly followed about 100 meters behind us and confirmed we can take vehicles from the LD to the ravine. We hooked up with Lt. Fugate, of the Scouts, about 200 meters south of the ravine crossing point. He guided us to the crossing point. We threw a rope down the ravine slope and the leaders all rappelled down. We waded across the creek and then got pulled up the other side with the help of PSG Callahan and his team on the north side of the ravine."

Petrone glances around, "Sir, when we cross the LD it will be... first, my platoon with six TOW Humvees and two additional cargo Humvees from Charlie Company, then Charlie Company 1st platoon riding in deuces with the two winch trucks... then Captain Bynum and Captain Rourke, and we have a place for your vehicle... then it's Lt. Clegg with the 2nd TOW platoon, and then Charlie Company's 3rd Platoon bringing up the rear."

Petrone again glances around, "When we get to the ravine Lt. Fugate will help us ground-guide my platoon into some defensive positions to provide security for the south side. Charlie 1st Platoon will move up and work to get the winch truck in place. Then get the first one down the slope… PSG Callahan will provide security on the north side and help with the winching up of the second truck and then putting it in place. Once everything is in place Lt. Clegg will move up and send his Humvees into the ravine one by one. As we're working to get the vehicles across, Charlie 1st Platoon will be using ropes to get down the slope and back up the other side. They have a plan to fan out and secure the north side… once they start getting their squads together."

He pauses for a couple of seconds and continues. "Once all of Lt. Clegg's guys are up on the north side it will be Captain Rourke, Captain Bynum and then yourself, Sir… In the mean time, we should have Charlie 3rd Platoon using the same ropes and crossing the ravine and assembling on the north side… Then it's my platoon with our six Humvees, and then finally it's Charlie Company's two cargo Humvees. These are pretty loaded and may surpass the weight limit of the winches… that's why we're taking them last. If the first one fails to get up the north slope because it breaks the winch… we pull off all the supplies and muscle them up the north side slope… secure the vehicle… leave it and call for vehicle recovery… our XO, Lt. Kiser."

Petrone gestures to Kiser standing on the other side of Clegg, "He is aware of the plan and has the battalion recovery guys getting ready with block and tackle equipment to pull the Humvee out of the ravine if need be. Hopefully we get both of Charlie's cargo Humvees across and never call Lt. Kiser. Once we get everyone across… we all move out to our assigned attack positions to start the next phase… killing the enemy." Petrone, checking with Francone asks, "Sir, do you have any questions or any comments?"

Francone survey's the group, "Good plan." Francone's expression turns serious. "But everyone here knows what happens to good plans when good plans first meet enemy contact. Those plans go out the window, then you have to rely on initiative, teamwork, and clear communication to get the mission accomplished." Francone pauses and lets that sink in. He then shows compassion, "Don't look so grim. If the plan goes to shit… I know all of you will pull together and get the mission done. It's what we do."

Rourke stares down at his watch, "Gentlemen, we need to load up and move out to hit the LD on time."

With that, everyone drains what is left of their coffee, turns and heads to their vehicles. Francone glances over at Rourke and gives him a small wave to have him move further forward of his Humvee. He wants a private conversation. "Devlin, we at the battalion TOC got a call three hours ago from the main post... via the Red Cross. Lt. Fugate needs to get home pretty fast. His wife is in her seventh month of pregnancy. I know you know that... she's having a hard time... According to the doctor everything is fine but there are a couple of complications and he thinks it best that Mark gets home soon." Francone pauses so Rourke can absorb the information then continues, "I called my wife. Cindy is a volunteer for the Red Cross. I asked her if she could find out anything more... she called me back and confirmed that Mark's wife, Karen, is having some trouble but everything is under control. The doctor and hospital are doing a great job of monitoring the situation. The doctor feels that having Mark there will relieve the stress on Karen."

Rourke, with a look of concern, asks, "Does that mean she's in the hospital now?"

Francone shakes his head, "That's the same thing I asked Cindy. Karen did go to the hospital yesterday morning. They got things stabilized and then sent her home. She's at home right now. I think the doctor doesn't want another... episode... and believes with Mark home... Karen will be much more relaxed and stress free. This is their first kid. Cindy will be going over there to check on her... probably every couple of days."

Rourke nods his understanding and checks the time on his watch again, "Sir, once we cross the LD we should be at the ravine within the hour. Mark and his guys are waiting there now. Once we get Charlie Company's first two trucks unloaded... which should take only a couple of minutes, we can throw Mark in one of them and get him back to the TOC in less than two hours."

Francone nods in agreement, "Your First Sergeant is getting all of Mark's personal gear together and will have it at the TOC within the hour. All the scouts turned their personal gear over to your supply sergeant for safe keeping before leaving for their mission. Captain Wright, the S-1, and Chief Halberstat are working out all the details for emergency leave. I'm assured by Connor that his S-1 shop will have everything in order by the time Mark gets to the TOC. Chief assured me he'll personally put Mark on a plane at Fort Smith airport no later than this afternoon… he's hoping sooner… but the airlines are the airlines."

Rourke nods, "I feel this enormous sense of urgency right now, Sir."

Francone wisely advises, "Devlin, that's the right feeling, but now you have to control it. All we need to do is run the mission as planned… the wheels are in motion… we'll get him home by this evening. By the way, I'm told that Captain Marcell is really helping with the coordination through JRTC Operations to make this happen." Rourke tilts his head and stares really hard at Francone trying to discern if there is a message in that last bit of information. Francone smiles, "OK, Captain Rourke, we need to mount up… let's get to the LD."

Eastern Line of Departure
04:55 Hours.

Josh pulls in behind Cpt. Bynum's Humvee and LTC Francone pulls in behind Josh. Josh turns on the wipers and then looks over at Rourke, "Five minutes till LD time."

Rourke jumps out, looks up at the sky and zips up his jacket even more. Bynum walks back to Rourke. Francone slides out and walks forward the couple of steps to Rourke and Bynum. Bynum searches the sky, "Snow… We're going to get snowed on… like right now. I don't know if this is good or bad."

Francone confesses, "John, I prayed for this snow. I've been wishing for this. This is the perfect time. I've been watching the weather like a hawk since yesterday morning. Right now, it's 30 degrees. We'll have snow showers for the next two hours. The winds are out of the northwest at fifteen miles per hours… this is going to be like a small blizzard. Visibility has been dropping since midnight, right now it's about 400 meters… in fifteen minutes it's going to be less than 100 meters." Francone can't hide his delight, "This blizzard is nothing our soldiers aren't used to back home. Hell, last month for deer season the first three days were a blizzard. That didn't stop our soldiers from going hunting. That includes you, John."

Bynum heartily agrees, "Yea I got a six point on the third day. It was about a 200-meter shot. I suppose you're right, Sir. With this cold snow blowing making visibility about 100 meters... we should be able to get the whole convoy down to the ravine without getting spotted by the OPFOR... who must be watching for us."

Francone adds, "I was really worried about the noise... those truck engines can be heard for a long way under normal circumstances. This blizzard will muffle that noise and all the noise we make at the crossing point. And with this weather... soldiers tend to want to hunker down to stay warm. All soldiers, to include the OPFOR. Yep, I believe this is going to help us." Francone peers at Rourke with a '*don't you agree look*'?

Rourke shakes his head, "I've got to tell you guys, I'm really... deep down inside... a warm weather fighter. Like, I'd do really well fighting in Tahiti or the Bahamas."

Francone laughs, "I always suspected that." He glances up and sees vehicles pulling out and moving forward. "Gentlemen, it's time to move or be left behind." Everyone jumps back into their vehicles and starts to move.

Ravine Crossing Site
05:45 Hours.

It takes them about 45 minutes to get to the ravine crossing site. It was a good thing that Fugate and his team met them 300 meters south of the crossing point. Rourke was getting concerned they might not find it in the blizzard.

Fugate's men position Petrone's Humvees out to 80 meters in a semi-circle or ark to provide security for the crossing. The two and a half ton trucks are guided to a position about 50 meters from the edge of the ravine. All the Charlie 1st Platoon soldiers dismount from the back and start moving to their multiple, rope rappel point under the control of their leaders. The rappel point is just 30 meters from the vehicle access point. It is the same on the other side. The infantry ascending point is just across the stream from the rappel point and 30 meters down from the vehicle extraction point. Rourke, Bynum, and Francone pull their vehicles to the side of the trucks out of the way. Francone and Rourke get out of their vehicles. Francone gets Rourke's attention, points to himself and then to the two trucks as if to say, '*I'll tell the drivers they're taking Lt. Fugate back*'.

Rourke jogs over to the vehicle access point hoping to find Lt. Fugate there. Fugate is talking with some of the soldiers that are going to be running the operation. Rourke walks over to him, puts his arm around his shoulders and quietly says, "I've got to have a talk with you." Rourke guides Fugate off to the side out of ear shot of everyone.

The talk is short. Fugate understands he is going home; that his wife needs him and it is essential that he gets there as soon as possible. The only thing he says is he is sorry he has to leave the company in the middle of an operation and that PSG Callahan should be made the temporary platoon leader. Rourke smacks him on the shoulder, "You've done a great job here... I'm proud of you. Yea, I'll make Callahan the platoon leader. Turn your weapon in to Top at the battalion TOC. Get your ass home as quick as you can and take care of Karen. The Colonel is over there getting the trucks ready for you. I know he wants to shake your hand. His wife, Cindy, is back home helping out with Karen... I'll see you in about a week. There'll be many, many beers at Pizza Hut after this." Rourke puts out his hand. Fugate nods, shakes his hand then turns and runs to the waiting trucks.

The first two trucks with the winches have already pulled forward to the ravine edge and are preparing to begin operations. The 3rd TOW Platoon Sergeant, Mike Stewart, has taken charge and is supervising everybody's efforts. They position the anchor truck against a large tree ten meters from the edge and block all the wheels. Rourke walks around to the driver's side of the truck that is going to attempt, what everybody hopes is, a controlled plunge to the bottom of the ravine. Rourke is really curious as to who the driver is. He knows he is a volunteer. Rourke just wants to know who is crazy enough to volunteer. He inspects the eyes of a young buck sergeant from the support platoon. Rourke asks, "Sergeant, are you OK with this?"

The reply makes Rourke smile, "Oh, yes, Sir, I've been driving these trucks for over ten years. I can handle it alright. It's steep... but I've got a great guy on the winch. If things start to go south... he'll be the one to pull it out... so to speak."

The driver turns, takes a couple of steps and reaches up for the door handle. Rourke asks, "I guess you put a lot of trust in the winch guy?"

As he opens the door and steps up into the cab he looks back grinning,

"Well, what makes me feel confident is… if he screws this up and I die in this ravine… our mother will kill him… he's my younger brother."

Rourke laughs and then realizes they are ready to go. He hurriedly moves off to the side and stands beside PSG Stewart. Stewart has a PRC-77 radio on his back and is talking to someone down in the ravine. Rourke asks, "Mike, who's down below that you're talking to?"

Stewart answers without looking away and without breaking his concentration from watching the first truck starting over the edge, "It's Callahan… he's got some of his guys down there." Rourke walks over to the edge keeping about 40 feet away from the truck operation. He wants to witness this feat for himself. This is his idea. He hopes like hell it works.

With the winch securely fastened to the back of the truck, the driver puts it in gear and slowly creeps to the edge and then over it in one smooth controlled move. As agreed to by the driver and his brother, after traveling twenty feet the driver pumps his breaks and his brother pulls tight on the winch cable, stopping the truck. The driver calls out the open window, "Bobby, we're good; it's going to work. Play out the cable just like we planned."

With a combination of braking and tightening up on the winch, the truck slowly crawls down the slope. At the bottom Callahan's men disconnect the winch, throw it clear and signal for it to be taken back up the slope. Rourke can see there is a conversation between the driver and Callahan who has jumped up on the driver side step. Rourke notices PSG Stewart who has joined Rourke standing on the edge just 30 feet up from the winch action. Stewart has the handset against his ear. He is listening to Callahan down in the ravine. He nods and speaks into the handset, "Green 5, go." After a minute of listening, "OK, sounds good to me… from up here the driver did a great job… if that's what he wants to do… it's OK with me. He obviously is the expert here… roger, out."

Stewart turns to Rourke, "The driver believes he can get enough traction to creep the truck all the way up to the top and then use the winch to get him over the edge. Callahan says he's got the perfect set up of trees to lock in the winch's hook and cable. Callahan is going to grab a couple of Charlie Company guys to work the bottom of the ravine. He's going back up the top to coordinate those efforts." Stewart breaks into a smile, "Shit, Sir, I think this scheme of yours is going to work."

Rourke, feigning hurt feelings, "Why Mike, I can't believe you even doubted it."

"Sir, the truth is… just about everybody in the battalion, and I mean everybody… thought this was bat shit crazy."

It takes them about twenty more minutes till the truck is up the slope, turned around and locked in place behind another big tree. Callahan radios over everything is set, that Charlie Company has provided some more guys for the operation, so we need to get the process started.

The first Humvee from 2nd TOW lines up, hooks up and is over the edge in about five minutes. Another minute down the slope, unhooks, crosses the stream, re-hooks, drives and is pulled up the north slope in about ten minutes, which leaves Rourke feeling relieved and happy. He knows the process will get smoother as they move along. Both Francone and Bynum come over by Rourke to watch a couple of the vehicles run through the process. Rourke looks over to both, "Sir, you and John need to get back to your vehicles; you're going to be up soon."

Francone nods and asks Rourke, "When are you going to take the plunge?"

"I'm going right before John's two loaded up cargo Humvees. I'll be last… behind Lt. Petrone.

Francone cracks, "Good deal! I'll see you on the other side… of the ravine that is."

Rourke and Bynum roll their eyes and shake their heads, "Good one, Sir… great sense of humor… while standing in a blizzard, Sir."

Francone gives a tilt of his head to Bynum signaling them to go. He puts his hand on Bynum's shoulder, "Sometimes it's good to be the commander. I don't recall telling any joke while commander that wasn't funny… everyone always laughs." Francone focuses on Rourke and winks.

Things are coming around. All of the 2nd TOW vehicles go over. LTC Francone and Cpt. Bynum both go down and up without any trouble. Right up until the third vehicle of the 3rd TOW platoon. On its way up the north slope, it blows its transmission. The engine starts racing like crazy but there is no forward movement. Everyone knows immediately it is the transmission. It also takes everyone by surprise. Everyone was so focused on the winches giving out, nobody thought about a transmission getting blown.

Lt. Petrone nudges Rourke, "Let's set it aside for last."

Rourke agrees and nods, "Sounds good… It's going to be nothing but pure winch… Yea, save it for last.

Petrone turns to PSG Stewart, "Mike, tell Callahan to tell them that they're going to be last."

The next Humvee, number four in the platoon, goes down and up without any problem. Number five is Stewart's vehicle. Stewart is not going to be on board. He is staying till last, by either getting in the last vehicle or using one of Charlie Company's rappel ropes if there is no room.

Stewart's vehicle is hooked up and then goes over the edge. About three quarters of the way down the winch makes a loud bang and the cable starts flying out of the coil housing. The Humvee is suddenly on its own. It takes the driver a second to realize that the winch is broken. He does a good job of keeping the vehicle pointed straight down and pumping the brakes to maintain control. Down at the bottom when it stops, both the driver and Stewart's gunner get out of the vehicle to catch their breath and get reoriented. Both look back up the slope, wave to show they are OK and yell up through the blowing snow storm that they are "good to go".

All three men walk over to the truck. The winch operator and his assistant driver are examining the winch. Stewart asks, "Bobby, what do you think?"

Bobby glances up and shakes his head, "It's shot! Besides the shear pin breaking, the actual winch is shot. It might need an overhaul… but my guess is it's done for good. We can't even wind it back up. We'll have to wrap the cable around the bumper."

Petrone crosses his arms, "Shit… we've got four more Humvees. Well, five, with the broke dick vehicle still down at the bottom."

Stewart walks to the edge and then points over to the rappel site, "Looks like it's dope on a rope for us. The drivers can take the Humvees back with the trucks."

Everybody turns when they hear Josh suggest, "Why not rappel the vehicles down?"

Rourke tilts his head down then examines Josh with skepticism and asks, "Josh, what are you talking about?"

Josh takes a couple of steps forward and then points to a row of three big trees right beside the truck. "What we do is interconnect eight or nine tow straps to make one big strap. Then we weave it around the tree trunks to provide resistance just like a rappel rope is wrapped around a carabineer or snap link, to slow down the guy on the rope. We can even choose the angle we want the truck to use to add or lessen the resistance... just like using your brake hand on a rappel rope. The trees are big enough and the straps are certainly strong enough... We just have the truck start out... I would guess 70 meters out that way, and using reverse gear, slowly back up and lower the Humvees down the slope. When the vehicle is down and unhooked we signal him to pull forward 70 meters and hook the next Humvee... Like I said, we rappel them down the slope."

Everybody gawks at each other and repeats, "Yea, we just rappel them down the hill."

Rourke steps in front of Josh, puts his hand on his shoulder and asks, "How'd you think of that so fast?"

Josh smiles, "That G. I. Bill money that sends me to Manchester to become an engineer isn't spent on only parties. I actually went to a couple of classes... before the parties."

Rourke steps aside, pointing his thumb at Josh standing next to him, and like a proud father says, "Hey, that's my driver. He's going to grow up and be a big engineer someday. Yes sir, a big engineer someday."

Stewart calls over to Callahan with, "Green 5, the winch is broke... we're going to rappel down the last... send seven tow straps, over."

There is a long delay, then, "Wilco... be advised... there are no volunteers to act as belay for your rappel, out."

Stewart turns to everybody, "OK, the straps are on the way. Let's use the rappel ropes to pull them up... and Callahan's belay comment... was kind of funny."

With everybody hustling, it takes them 30 minutes to get Lt. Petrone's Humvee ready for the first try. With the assistant driver acting as the ground-guide and Stewart at the edge to watch for and control the speed, the operation goes well. All four Humvees get safely down to the bottom. Petrone and Rourke's vehicles go up the north slope just like all the rest beforehand.

Callahan wants the two Charlie Company cargo vehicles to both be at the bottom. He wants to use the same tow straps on those two in addition to their own power and the winch to get them up and over the edge on the north slope. It works.

Now all that is left is the broke dick Humvee with the blown transmission. Callahan hooks up two Humvees in tandem to the tow straps along with the winch to get it up to the top. It also works. All the vehicles and all of Charlie Company are on the north side of Big Creek.

Two Kilometers Southeast of Hill 40
Monday, 11 December 1989
11:45 Hours.

All the 220th Infantry elements move 300 to 500 meters north from the ravine. The platoon leaders quickly work out a defensive plan for their large, hasty assembly area. Charlie Company assigns a squad with two machine guns to remain at the crossing site to provide rear security. This is a precaution just in case the OPFOR guys on Hill 80 find out what is happening to the other half of the 220th Infantry Battalion. Any OPFOR trying to cross the ravine are going to get annihilated by the two M-60 machine guns.

Francone calls for a leaders' meeting. The two company commanders and all the platoon leaders meet at Francone's Humvee that is approximately in the center of the assembly area. Francone points to a clump of trees twenty meters away. Everybody heads that way. No one is willing to sit in the snow so everybody stands in a large group.

Francone scans the sky, "Well it stopped snowing…we've got, what… three inches since 05:00 hours. The good news is that with these three inches it'll cover the noise of any movement through the woods. The bad news is we don't have any white camouflage for our men. Let's hope we don't get seen moving around. Our first task is to positively locate all of the enemy. Sergeant Callahan, can you give us what you've got? By the way I understand you'll be acting platoon leader for the rest of our time here… I'm sure you'll do a great job."

"Thank you, Sir. We'll miss Lt. Fugate… He's an outstanding platoon leader." Callahan walks across the circle of men to stand beside Francone. Callahan, like everybody, has his map in a protective, see-through, folding, plastic and canvas case. He has it out and is ready to point out various items of interest to Francone, and if need be, to hold it up for everyone to be able to see.

Francone asks, "Sergeant, I know you were at the crossing site early this morning... but what was the situation last night... before you came to the ravine?"

Callahan breaks into a big smile, "You guys aren't going to believe this... we've spent almost all of our time on top of Hill 40. Looking down and over the OPFOR like we own them." Callahan slowly surveys the group and waits a little bit to add some dramatic effect. Callahan's statement creates a stir amongst the group. Everyone feels a rise of anticipation and is now waiting for the explanation.

Captain Bynum gazing sideways at Callahan proclaims, "You're telling us that you occupied the absolute highest ground in the middle of the enemy for the last two days?"

"Yes, Sir." Callahan takes a deep breath, "OK, this is how it went. When we got across the ravine my original plan was to conduct a zone recon. I had a plan to move back and forth to identify the enemy locations, strength, weapons and equipment. But when I got across... I looked up at Hill 40 and thought... let's see what they have up there... and... if me and my guys can be seen walking around from up there. So, I left two of the men at the bottom... just in case we got caught or killed. They could still do the mission and report our situation." Callahan pauses and then continues. "The three of us slowly and I mean slowly... stopping many times just to watch... well, we work our way to about 100 meters from the top, and then we start to either low crawl or some high crawling to within 30 or 40 meters from the top of the hill. Then we wait and wait and wait some more. Finally, I signal to my other two scouts to continue on up the little bit that's left. We get to the top... and nobody is there and nobody has been there. We're crawling around and establish an OP... a really hidden OP... right on the very top is a small depression... obviously dug out many moons ago... but still... I can get all five of us in the depression and can't be seen by anyone... unless they walk up and look down.

So, I'm lying there resting and trying to figure out why there are no OPFOR on top of the hill?" Callahan can see that the group has the same question. "It's not an oversight on their part... they don't need to be up on top of the hill. First, they know we're going to pound the top with arty and mortar fire... we did it on Hill 80 and Hill 32. Why waste a couple of guys for no reason?" Callahan lets that sink in. "They know the only way to the objective is by crossing the bridge. They have that covered... in spades. They have two platoon's half way up Hill 40. One is on the southwest slope and the other is on the northwest slope... both have fantastic coverage of the bridge area."

Callahan shifts his weight and continues, "We did have a visitor. There's a trail that runs up to the top... it's on the north side. Yesterday morning this Humvee comes running up the trail. We kind of freaked out for a minute... everybody is grabbing weapons and rucks thinking we're going to be running down the hill in a few minutes. Then we notice it's an OC vehicle. As a matter of fact, it's Captain Chancy. He parks his vehicle on the west side showing everyone in the world that there's an OC on top of the hill. The OPFOR knows it's an OC... so there is no suspicion. No one will be coming up to investigate. Apparently, the OC's use this spot quite a bit. But we did surprise him. He plays it real cool. He gets out his bino's, leans on the hood of the Humvee and scans over the entire area. He's talking with us over his shoulder, but never turns around to look at us.

"He thought it was pretty wild that we were up there... and that the OPFOR had no clue. After about 25 minutes he got in his vehicle and drove back down the trail. We stayed up there until 04:30 this morning. Then we packed up and went down to the crossing point. Did a recon on our side... made sure it was clear, then set up some security and waited for you guys to show up."

Francone shows a bit of skepticism, "OK... that is pretty wild. What have you got for us after being in the middle of the lion's den for the past three days?"

Callahan scans his map, steps closer to Francone so he can point out the items of interest, "Sir, they have three platoons with either a tank or a BMP with each of them. The first platoon BMP is located at grid 163854. That grid is the vehicle location. The second is the tank location at 171852 and the third BMP is at 173844. The infantry are positioned around the vehicles to protect them from dismounts. They're in a wooded area a little over a klick from the bridge. They have the BMP... and just like the other two armor vehicles... they are all dug in.... and I mean dug in. They had two back hoes out here for two days. All the vehicles are dug down to turret level... which means the vehicle can't be seen. They're below ground... they constructed two levels. When the vehicle commander spots a target, he instructs the driver to pull forward onto the higher level to his front... a sort of platform which raises the vehicle with the gun turret up above the ground so he can shoot the target... the vehicle hull is still below ground. After killing the target, he has the vehicle back down into the lower level. It's just about impossible to kill one of these turret down vehicles while down in their holes."

Callahan uses his hands to illustrate the movement of the armor vehicles up and then back down. "Each vehicle has two of these positions dug... their primary and then their secondary... which is about 100 meters away. Probably the best time to kill them is when they're moving from one position to another. That's when they're the most vulnerable."

Lt. Petrone asks, "What if they don't want to move... like... they're doing some great killing from their primary."

Callahan shakes his head, "Then LT you've got yourselves an Arkansas tic. There ain't nothing harder than digging out an Arkansas tic... especially in Arkansas."

Petrone asks again, "We're all hoping we can get them from the rear?"

Rourke clears his throat and points out to the group, "None of our TOW Humvees can take on an armored vehicle in the woods when they are dug in turret down... from any position." Rourke looks at Petrone, "Jim, if the track commander realizes your behind him... he'll either traverse the turret or the .50 cal machine gun onto you. Granted the gun is actually below ground... so he'll best guess where to aim. He'll tell the driver to launch up to the shooting platform... as soon as the vehicle starts to rocket forward, he'll pull the trigger on the machine gun. Bullets will be flying in your direction before the vehicle gets up on the platform... and you'll be dead. The fact is his guns fire faster than our TOW missiles can lock onto the target. It's like having a cowboy gun fight... with him having a gun and you having a knife. You may be great at throwing a knife... but you'll never beat out a bullet."

Callahan raises his hand to get everyone's attention then adds, "And to compound our dilemma...those two backhoes dug in the grunts too. They've got at least two big bunkers with overhead cover and very low to the ground at each platoon location on both sides of the armored vehicle. I doubt if we'll get any kills with artillery and mortars. They'll just wait it out."

Francone has been leaning over and studying the markings on Callahan's map. He stands up straight, "Tell us what else you've got for us."

Callahan continues, "They put up one hell of a triple strand concertina wire obstacle. Actually, two rows about twenty meters apart. With a hasty mine field in between. It starts on the creek bank 200 meters upstream from the bridge. From the creek bank it goes northeast for 400 meters and then breaks to the east another 400 meters." Callahan holds up his map for everyone to get oriented on the wire. "If we have any plans on charging across the bridge making an immediate left turn and making for the objective... well you can forget that. That area is all open. While you are trying to clear the wire and mines, you would come under both direct and indirect fire."

Francone smiles, "I was really wishing this would be a piece of cake. I mean getting across the ravine and coming up on their rear. But, you would think by now I would have learned. There has never been a military operation go according to plan. One of Murphy's laws... no plan survives intact... on contact." Francone points to Rourke and Bynum, "Devlin, you and John walk with me back to my vehicle so I can get a cup of coffee. Sorry, gentlemen, I really don't have enough for everyone. Tell you what... let's all take a 30-minute break, get yourself some coffee, take a piss, stretch your legs, meet back here in 30." Francone raises his eye brows. "Then we come up with another 2nd battalion mind-blowing operation."

Thirty minutes later, Francone has his vehicle pull up to the clump of trees. The driver gets out, walks around the back, pops open the back hatch, lowers the tail gate, places a 2 X 4 across the open hatch and hooks a 3' X 3' plywood map board to it. Everyone is nodding their approval with a couple of 'pretty clever' statements thrown in. Francone points to his driver, "This is Vince's idea. Instead of getting the command group to gather around the hood and try to get a glimpse of a map... Vince came up with the portable, Humvee, map-presentation set up... and the best part is if I get tired of standing and listening to all the war gaming ideas, I can sit on the tail gate." Francone slaps Vince on the back. "Good job, Vince."

Francone steps to the side of the map so everyone can see. He pulls out a pen to use as a pointer. "First of all, great job to Sergeant Callahan. He did well for the battalion. I want him to look for a little something extra in his pay check... there won't be anything there... but he can still look." This brings a little laughter from the group. "But I want him to know we all recognize... he and his men did a super job."

Francone then begins his briefing for the next part of the mission. "That wire and mine obstacle is one hell of a monkey wrench into our original plan. We really can't spend the time or the manpower it would take to make a hole in the obstacle. Which means we need to take out at least two of the enemy platoon positions." Francone half turns and points to the enemy's first and second platoons, "The enemy third platoon... I feel that if we isolate it and keep their heads down... we can get the battalion past them without losing a whole lot of men."

Francone sweeps his hand across the group and asks, "Everybody on the same page?" He then continues, "The first priority is to kill all three armored vehicles. They pose the most threat. If we let one loose and cannot kill it... it could do a lot of damage to the battalion. We can leave the enemy's third infantry platoon intact on the south side of the hill and still move on the objective and complete the mission." Francone, using his pen again, continues, "We have to get around the wire obstacle. Which means taking out the 1st and 2nd platoons. Once they're gone and their 3rd platoon is contained... we can move the rest of the battalion. A and B Companies, with the rest of CSC... across the bridge... make a dash for the north end of the obstacle... turn northwest and attack Objective Champion." Francone stops and glances around, "Scout Team One is still at the objective and still reports very little enemy on the objective. They're calling it a 25-man platoon... with two machine guns... which they have identified by grid on the map." Francone turned to face Rourke, "Devlin, I believe you and John have come up with a good maneuver plan. Why don't you brief everyone?"

Both Lt. Clegg and Lt. Petrone look at each other and smile thinking the same thing. *'Francone is checking to see if his CSC commander has a full grasp on the plan by having him brief the group'.*

Rourke walks to the map, pulls out a pen and turns to talk to the group. "First thing, Sergeant Callahan... can you... or is it possible to kill the enemy's BMP... their 3rd platoon BMP on the southside of Hill 40...

from on top of the hill? Can you get a clear shot from the hill top to the BMP in their dug in position?"

Callahan tilts his head up to think for a couple of seconds. He starts to nod his head as he remembers peering down over the enemy's 3rd platoon. "Yes, Sir, from just a little back off the very top we could dismount a TOW on a tripod and shoot right down on top of the BMP. Yes, Sir, we can do it."

Rourke pivots around to search the map. "Alright, that's good… After talking with the Colonel and Captain Bynum… we came up with this… outstanding course of action." Rourke uses his pen to point out areas on the map. "Team Saber will be my 2nd TOW Platoon with four Humvees and Cpt. Bynum's 1st Platoon… will take on the enemy 1st Platoon with their BMP. Team Musket will be my 3rd TOW with four Humvees and Cpt. Bynum's 3rd Platoon… will take on the enemy 2nd Platoon with the tank." Rourke glances around to confirm that everyone understands so far. "Team Independence with Sergeant Callahan will take the three remaining TOW Humvees and his scout team and move up to the hill top. As everyone knows we only have two of Charlie Company's platoons… The priority is to take out the enemy 1st and 2nd platoons. I'll be with Saber and Captain Bynum will be with Musket. Sgt. Callahan… you're on your own."

Francone unexpectedly clears his throat. Everyone turns their attention to Francone. "Sgt. Callahan… If it's alright with you, I would like to accompany you up to Hill 40. I'll be there in case you need any help. I can still pull a trigger on an M-16 and it's probably a great venue to watch the battle. Am I right?"

Callahan grins from ear to ear, "Sir, it's perfectly alright for you to come on up to the hill top. It is a great view from up there… and yes, Sir, I bet you still can pull a trigger."

Rourke starts his briefing again. "The plan is pretty simple. We attack their 1st and 2nd platoons from the rear tomorrow morning at 09:00. Sergeant Callahan likewise will start his attack by killing the BMP from the hill top."

Rourke turns his attention to Callahan, "Doug, I would recommend that you set up two TOWs and fire them both… just to make sure you get your kill. After getting the BMP, start your indirect fires with smoke and HE mix. You also have three M-60 machine guns. Start firing down on the infantry with those... only... if you're identified by them. If they find out you're up there, they may want to return the indirect fire favor... and even start up the hill to take you off it. Disperse your guns so as to give the OPFOR a real dilemma if they choose to come up the hill. This isn't a die in place mission. You're Cav... give them a hard time then get out of there. But kill that BMP!"

Callahan nods his understanding. "Yes, Sir... we'll kill him."

Rourke continues, "Team Saber and Musket will move from here after the briefing to assembly areas about 1,000 meters behind our assigned enemy platoons. At 05:00 we start to slowly infiltrate into the rear of the enemy. Using darkness as a cover... and we checked... it should be snowing a little by then... that will help. Our hope is to get within 100 meters of the enemy platoon positions. The four TOW vehicles will be about 500 meters back. The LTs should have selected firing positions for their guys. When the attack starts, those Humvees should fly forward into their assigned firing positions and start firing either TOW missiles or machine guns. We want to overrun the positions."

Rourke puts up his index finger to signify one more thing, "Our guys across the Big Creek will start a demonstration at 08:30. They'll make it look like they're preparing to make a run at the bridge. They'll be moving a bunch of trucks and Humvees around as if they're loading up. There's a good bet the enemy has one or two scout teams in our area over there. This demonstration should distract the OPFOR on our side. We want their focus to be on what's to their front and not on us coming up from behind. Any questions?"

Rourke sets his eyes on Francone. "Sir, anything to add?"

Francone walks to the center of the group. "Surprise is the key to our success. Without it we'll come up short. We don't have the three to one force ratio normally used in an attack. So, ensure while you're moving up into your attack positions you maintain stealth. After we complete the mission... A and B Companies will come across the bridge and make for the objective. Maj. Dyer and those commanders already have a plan to take Objective Champion. They've reinforced Scout Team One with a 12-man squad... using a one rope bridge over the creek and have been in contact with them for the last two days. We just need to get our portion done. Good luck and good hunting."

CHAPTER 35

"Some succeed because they are destined to; most succeed because they are determined to." – Unknown

Team Musket
150meters behind the OPFORs 2nd platoon
Tuesday, 12 December 1989
08:45 Hours.

Lt. Jim Petrone, 3rd TOW Platoon Leader, has been lying on the freezing cold ground for about an hour. He is 50 meters behind the line of frozen Charlie Company soldiers, who have also been lying on the ground for an hour. In fifteen minutes, the attack will begin. He is hoping the enemy won't hear his teeth chattering before then. Thank God he is wearing polypropylene long underwear he bought at the local gun, archery and camping store back home. And thank God he bought the thickest pair available. The stuff the Army issues isn't bad, but once it gets wet, it is all over. You are never going to get warm the rest of the day.

Petrone has selected this spot to coordinate the movement of his TOW platoon with that of Charlie 3rd Platoon and what the enemy tank is doing. He has selected four firing locations for his four Humvees. Thankfully, they had all quietly moved into them this morning at 06:45 in the dark and in a small snowstorm. They are approximately 200 to 300 meters from the tank in a 400-meter arc around the back of the tank's dug-in position. The thick woods put some restriction on all line of sight shots into the tank. This results in the only available shot for the TOWs as down a bowling alley. Each vehicle has only one shot into the tank's position. Petrone is betting one of his guys will make the kill in the very beginning so everyone can switch to their M-60 machine guns and move forward to help Charlie 3rd take on the enemy infantry.

The attack is going to be what Captain Bynum calls, a creeping attack. They will all get up in a crouch and slowly start walking forward until the enemy sees them and starts firing. The plan is to get right on top of them before they realize it and kill them all. The closer they get the better the odds. Once the fight starts, it is going to be the old fashion grunt fire and maneuver by fire teams and squads working their way forward to take out the bunkers.

Petrone's hope is that the tank realizes they are being attacked from the rear so it will jump up to the firing platform, traverse the turret to fire on Charlie 3rd, just to have his guys light 'em up with shots down the bowling alleys.

Petrone, holding on to a PRC-77 radio secured in a ruck sack beside him, slowly slides over behind a large tree so he can raise up a little to see and still have some protection. Petrone is starting to feel settled when all hell breaks loose and Charlie 3rd is 40 meters away from the enemy bunkers. It starts with yelling and firing of M-16 rifles. They have been spotted.

The tank engine suddenly comes to life. Petrone tries to calmly speak into the radio handset. "Everybody get ready… if you've got a shot now… take it." Nobody can. The tank is still in its hole. Everyone is waiting for it to pop up onto its firing platform. Petrone can hear it running up its engine. Back on the radio, "Get ready!"

Petrone pushes himself up the tree another foot. The tank engine is revving up again. Petrone sees it jump out of the hole onto the platform. But it doesn't stop. Not even for an instant. It shoots over the forward berm and out through the tree line within seconds. It makes a sharp left turn and starts driving south down the front of the enemy's defense, all the time firing its tank commander's machine gun. The tank commander knows that the only men up and moving will not be his guys.

Petrone calls into the handset, "We got to move to get a shot... everybody move to get a shot." Petrone glances over his right shoulder and can see two of his Humvees crashing through the woods on the way to the tank. He looks over his left shoulder and sees those two vehicles quickly pulling out, breaking brush and moving to the left in the hope of getting ahead of the tank. Petrone turns back around to see what the tank is doing. What he sees makes him wince. The tank has traversed his turret over the left side and is using its coaxial machine gun, along with the commander's machine gun, to wreak havoc over Charlie 3rd.

With the turret and main gun still pointing over the left side, the tank lurches into reverse and starts quickly moving across the front of the battle position past its dug-in position and traveling another 100 meters. It stops so suddenly it actually rocks back and forth before it settles down. The commander traverses the turret a little more left, stops and fires its main gun. Petrone jumps up to stand and lean against the tree. His far TOW Humvee's strobe goes off 50 meters inside the tree line. The other Humvee slams on his brakes, throws it into reverse and starts backing up the trail it has just created. The tank jumps forward and starts racing back along the front of the tree line. Petrone raises the handset, "Blue 2, and Blue 4, the tank is now racing south heading your way." Petrone throws the ruck over his shoulder and sprints toward the left side of the enemy position in order to better ascertain the tank situation. As the tank again drives past the position it is firing its machine guns. Petrone jumps behind a tree. The tank slows. He is scanning for more targets. Unfortunately, he finds one. Sgt. Zach Lewis, Blue 4, is racing through the woods concentrating on getting around the many trees, but he fails to keep track of the tank.

Lewis is spotted. The tank once again jumps forward, races 50 meters and slams on the brakes. The tank commander slowly traverses the turret obviously tracking a Humvee. Petrone raises the handset and this time yells, "He's tracking one of you... change course!" The tank fires its main gun. Petrone, hearing the blast and seeing the smoke, follows the direction of the main gun and can see another strobe going off in the woods 100 meters to his immediate left. Petrone yells out. "Fuck... God damn it!" The tank once again lurches forward, picks up speed and starts up a little hill 50 meters further down the tree line. Captain Bynum runs up behind Petrone. "Hey, LT we got the bunkers... the position is ours... can you get the tank? If he comes back we're fucked." Petrone turns around and looks at Bynum with some despair. "Sir, we're trying... honest to God... we're trying."

Petrone turns back to find the tank. He raises the handset, "Blue 2... he went to the high ground... he's searching for you... what's your status, over." Petrone runs forward again and sees the tank sitting up on the little hill 100 meters away, sighting down, traversing his turret and having his gunner search for another Humvee. Petrone talks into the handset, "Blue 3... what's your location, over." Petrone glances up at the tank just in time to see its bright yellow strobe go off in a continuous pulse. He can't believe it. He lifts up the handset and with great relief asks, "Hey, which one of you got the tank, over." There is a long pause, then, "Hey, Blue 1, this is Red 1... you're welcome... and you owe me one, over." It takes a second for Petrone to realize that Foley's platoon across the creek, probably about two klicks away, took out the tank with a great TOW shot. Petrone shoots his right fist in the air and yells as loud as he can, "Damn, Trevor... I do owe you... you the man!"

Petrone is feeling pure joy. He is afraid his face will break with the huge smile spread from ear to ear. He lifts up the handset. But he's not going to let Trevor know how Trevor saved his ass. At least not now. "Red 1, thanks much... not a bad shot... pretty typical really, Blue 1, out." Petrone looks over toward Hill 32 and wonders if Trevor, using his TOW sights, can see him dancing around.

Petrone makes one more call, "Blue 2 and 3, meet me at the dug-in position, over." He gets immediate affirmative replies from both. It will take them several minutes to get there. Petrone starts walking. He gets to the dug-in position. It is also being used by Captain Bynum as his command post. Bynum peers up then points to a spot on the edge of the hole where he wants Petrone to sit.

Petrone plops down and slides the ruck off his shoulders and asks, "How goes the war, Sir?"

Bynum moves his attention off of his map and puts down his radio handset, "LT, it's all good... Team Saber took their objective with a few casualties... Callahan took out the BMP and is currently pounding the remaining enemy with arty and mortars. We of course took our objective… you lost two TOWs… I lost fourteen men… the Colonel just called across to Maj. Dyer… says we are secure, and for him to get the rest of the family together. Alpha Company will unload its troops over at Team Saber. Bravo will unload their guys here. Your guys are to drive by your commander… say hi… and then move out to your assigned forward positions. I don't know what the plan is… but it's to happen quick… and there's no stopping till the objective is taken sometime tonight. We are the battalion reserve. The colonel will meet up with Maj. Dyer over at Alpha Company. He's going on the mission to take the objective. You need to grab your guys and get up to Captain Rourke." Bynum puts out his hand, "It is a pleasure working with you LT."

Petrone takes a deep breath. Appearing kind of remorseful he says, "I'm sorry about losing fourteen of your guys, Sir."

Bynum, showing a sad smile, "LT, we are soooo lucky to only lose that many. Don't worry about it. Now go see your commander."

Petrone jumps in with his platoon sergeant, PSG Stewart, for the ride over to meet up with Captain Rourke. At Team Saber's position, they drive by eight trucks lined up with their tail gates down, dropping off all of Alpha Company. It is a typical, get organized drill after getting dropped out of the back of a truck. Squad leaders and platoon sergeants are yelling out to get the right men with the right unit. They are loosely forming up into platoons. Petrone figures after getting sorted out they will immediately move to their new attack positions over by Objective Champion.

Petrone finds Rourke at the enemy vehicle dug-in position. The BMP is still there. The strobe has been turned off. Rourke is talking with the vehicle commander. Petrone points to the BMP, asks Rourke, "I guess you got him right here?"

Rourke nods and points up to the guy sitting on top of the turret drinking a cup of coffee. "Yea, we got lucky. At 08:30 our BMP commander, Sgt. Rogan, got suspicious or curious about what was all the ruckus over across the bridge. So, he popped up here on the platform to take a gander. Well, he stayed up here until attack time at 09:00. At 06:30, while still dark and a little snow… we had quietly set up a dismounted TOW right down that row of trees… 200 meters away. At 09:00 we pulled the trigger.

Killed the BMP and initiated the attack from the rear. All four Humvees raced up here with M-60s blazing. We lost five grunts in the attack. It was over inside of ten minutes."

Petrone then asks, "What's up with us and the objective?"

"The Colonel was just here. He wants Charlie's two platoons to go over and help Sgt. Callahan finish up the enemy platoon on the other side of the hill. Callahan got the BMP while he was still in his hole and had been calling indirect on them off and on since 09:00. Trevor and Dan are going with Alpha and Bravo to the objective. They have screening missions while the rifle companies actually attack and take the objective. I'll be moving up to be with them." Rourke pauses for a second, gathers his thoughts then starts again. "The 2nd TOW and the 3rd TOW platoons are technically the battalion reserve. You and Chuck are actually assigned to cover the bridge and prevent any of the remaining OPFOR over there," Rourke points south to Hill 80, "from getting across and screwing with us. Any questions?"

"Yes, Sir. Who's in charge here?"

Rourke grins, "Since you asked... you are. I suspect Captain Bynum will release PSG Callahan once he gets to the hill and Callahan can give him the lay of the land. Callahan should bring his three Humvees down the hill and hook up with you. You pick your piece of land you're going to fight from. I would recommend right here. You've got some decent cover and have good fields of fire to the bridge." Rourke puts his hands on his hips then asks, "Jim, have you got any questions? If not... I've got to go. I want to hook up with Trevor on his screen line. I really don't believe this will go on much longer." With that said, Rourke turns to walk to his vehicle some 30 meters further in the woods.

CHAPTER 36

"Leadership is simply the ability of an individual to coalesce the efforts of other individuals toward achieving common goals. It boils down to looking after your people and ensuring that, from top to bottom, everyone feels part of the team." - Frederick W. Smith

Screen Line North of Objective Champion
Wednesday, 13 December 1989
16:45 Hours.

Rourke and Josh are sitting in their Humvee monitoring the battalion command freq. Both Captain Young from Alpha and Captain Daugherty from Bravo Company are providing updates on their movements and then attacks on the enemy at the objective. It comes as no surprise when Francone makes a net call telling everyone we have just taken the objective.

Josh looks over at Rourke, claps his gloved hands a couple of times and says, "Yeah… good for us… can we please go home now?"

Rourke shakes his head, "It isn't over till we get the End of Exercise call. As in… Endex… quit complaining. Besides the temperature must have gone up twenty degrees. Hell, I think I'm sweating just sitting here."

The radio comes on again. This time it is SFC McCallister telling each unit to move to their previous assembly area and to re-establish their assembly area and to remind us we are still tactical.

Rourke pulls out his map from underneath his left arm resting on a PRC-77 radio, then reaches over and picks up the handset to the radio already on his company freq. He knows his first priority is to get his whole company together. He picks out a location on the map then speaks into the mic. "All stations this net… from Romeo Tango 67… right 1 point 2… up point 8… execute now, over?" Three of the platoons immediately reply they will comply. Rourke speaks into the handset again. "Black 5, did you copy, over."

Ten seconds later the XO replies, "Roger 6… will comply, out."

Lt. Foley drives up, leans out the door of his Humvee and asks, "Sir, are you tagging along with me?"

Rourke thinks for a second, then replies, "Well, Josh and I will tag along behind your guys… but don't be surprised if we drop out of your little convoy. I suspect I might get a call from battalion wanting me to meet with the command group." Rourke thinks for a second, "If that does happen… when you get to the rendezvous point get a head count… get everybody organized. The XO should be there. I know he'll brief you on what's going to be expected of us for the next day… then do a tactical road march to the assembly area. Right now, I want CSC to get across that bridge before everybody else… that could be a traffic jam I want to avoid. You got all of that, Trevor?"

Foley looks over at Rourke and gives Rourke a thumbs-up, "OK, Sir… and you know Dan… Lt. Heller has picked up Scout Team One from the objective area. Callahan has been calling and directing all his scouts this afternoon… to call and hook up with the TOWs. So, I'm pretty sure we'll have everybody at the rendezvous."

Rourke nods, "OK… we'll fall in behind your last guy."

Rourke gets about one klick south of the bridge when he gets the call from battalion for a meeting. The location is 200 meters south of the bridge. This means Rourke has to turn around. When they get there, Josh pulls way off to the right of what seems like a parking lot of Humvees. There is even a lantern shining a dull white light sitting on the hood of the

Humvee in the center. Josh appears to be a little bewildered and mumbles, "I thought we're still tactical."

Rourke slides out and walks the thirty meters to the meeting. Halfway there he can hear laughter. This immediately puts a smile on his face. When he steps into the circle of light and can see everyone he recognizes all the company commanders, along with a bunch of OCs, Maj. Dyer, Cpt. Easton, CSM Morando and LTC Francone and his OC, LTC Jeltsen. Rourke knows the laughter is being used to release the buildup of the stress and tension of the last two weeks. Just about everyone is boisterously talking over each other.

Someone loudly proclaims, "Hey, the Cav finally arrived." Maj. Dyer with a beaming smile, along with a huge stogie sticking out of his mouth, promptly walks across the circle and offers Rourke a cigar, "Victory Cigar!" It seems like everyone is trying to recall some of the funniest, humorous events from the past two weeks. Rourke sticks the cigar in his mouth. John Bynum reaches over and lights it. As Rourke watches and takes it all in, it seems that most of the amusing remarks are coming from the OCs. After thinking about it for a second it makes sense. After all they are the observers. They watched everything the battalion did.

Captain Carson Young, Alpha Company, steps forward, removes the cigar from his mouth and asks, "How the hell did you guys get across that ravine? I would have bet... you would never have made it."

Andy Daugherty bursts out with, "Hell, the whole battalion was betting it would never work."

LTC Jeltsen chimes in with, "It is the craziest concept I've ever heard since I've been here at JRTC. There were four of us OCs about 300 meters east of your crossing point up on the north side watching with binos. It started off as one in ten odds you guys wouldn't get the first truck across."

Tim Chancy the OC for CSC chimes in, "When I first heard this back at the TOC tent, I thought for sure all of you were going to tell Devlin to sit down... that... that idea was way too crazy for them... but I got to tell you something... that it's pretty easy to see. You guys trust one another. You've been together so long. You don't know how rare that is. That's obviously a strength of the National Guard."

Jeltsen bursts out laughing, "An hour ago the OPFOR Commander asked me how you guys got to Hill 40. I told him you guys went through the ravine. He just shook his head in disbelief."

Rourke feels someone bump into him on his left. Someone trying to become part of the circle. Rourke takes a small step to his right. He gets another bump. He turns his head to the left and catches a glimpse of Olivia smiling at him. His first urge is to put his arm around her. He then realizes that would be ridiculous and really embarrassing for both of them. Anyhow, he isn't sure if it would be OK with Olivia. Is she just being sociable or is there more?

Rourke feels Olivia lean against him. It is hardly apparent and not even noticeable but she is indeed leaning on him. Rourke leans back just a little to try and tell if this is going to be reciprocal or just a chance encounter. She doesn't move. They are indeed leaning against each other. They are touching and remain so. Even through Rourke's winter gear and large parka, he knows this is on purpose. The most simple and basic form of showing attraction, probably since the beginning of the human race. Rourke feels thrilled and grateful she wants to be near him.

The jubilant conversations go on for another 30 minutes. It seems like everyone has a small, significant story about how they overcame a challenge or they experienced an event that at the time seemed crucial but now is really funny. Bynum tells everyone his driver was so nervous going over the edge of the ravine, he threw up halfway down the slope. His Humvee stunk like hell so they stopped in the middle of Big Creek at the bottom of the ravine so they could use the creek water to wash it out.

Finally, Francone steps forward which is the signal for everyone to listen up. He takes the cigar out of his mouth, searches around for everyone, nods and starts with, "First I want to thank Colonel Jeltsen for providing the cigars. I bought them… but he thought it's a great idea so he sent one of his guys onto main post to the PX and got us a large box. So, thanks Bob for the support. Well, I wanted to get the command group together along with our OCs… the folks that have been with us every single hour of every single day, to say thanks."

Francone sweeps his arm around the group. "You commanders have surpassed every test and challenge thrown at you… Of course, I always knew of your abilities and your leadership. But I think we surprised JRTC… I mean all of them… the Operations Group, the OPFOR and our Observer Controllers. You all had different adversities and difficulties within each of your companies… and you overcame them all."

Francone pauses for a second, "We're all going to be very busy for the next couple of days. We've got to get everybody home safe and sound. So, I just wanted to say thanks while I could still get you guys together. The Operations Group will call Endex when we have everyone back in the assembly area and we have a solid head count." Francone looks over at Jeltsen and asks, "AAR tomorrow at 09:00 hours, right?"

Jeltsen nods, "It will probably be a two-hour AAR. Then your battalion will get the order to go ahead and move out of the field and back to the cantonment area so you can prepare for your move back to Pennsylvania." Jeltsen holds up his hand, "I just want to say, you men from the 220th Infantry… very impressive. I'd be proud to fight alongside of you anytime and anywhere."

Maj. Dyer steps forward, "OK, guys, see you all at 09:00 tomorrow."

Everyone turns and heads for their vehicles. Someone grabs the lantern and turns it off. Rourke turns to face Olivia. They stand there till everyone is back in their vehicles, starts them up, and begins pulling out to get to their companies. Within a minute the place is empty.

Both Olivia and Rourke take off their helmets. Rourke instinctively rubs the top of his head to readjust what little hair he has.

Olivia reaches out and touches Rourke's arm, "Devlin… I've got to get going and you've got to get going. You've created quite a dilemma for me. I really am attracted to you. I don't know what to do. I don't want to get involved with a guy who lives and works all the way up in Pennsylvania… but… I guess I am."

Rourke reaches out and touches her face, "Yea, I understand. I told you I'm attracted to you… and I don't know what to do either."

Olivia leans forward and kisses Rourke on the cheek. She steps back and smiles, "You're killing me, Cavalry. I'll see you tomorrow at the AAR." She turns quickly, walks to her Humvee, starts it and drives off.

Rourke walks back to his Humvee, slides into the passenger seat. Josh doesn't immediately start the vehicle. He peers over at Rourke and asks, "It's pretty dark. I couldn't really tell… but did you just get a little kiss from Captain Bynum or was it the hot OC?… and please tell me it is the hot OC… Bynum's not even a little cute."

Rourke looks at Josh and throws his hands up, "Josh... man... I just don't know how to handle this."

Josh pivots in his seat and stares out the windshield. "Whatever you do, I'll never say anything to anybody. You know that... right, Sir."

"You've always been a good and loyal friend, Josh... I really appreciate your friendship."

Josh reaches over and turns the starter switch. "I bet the company is half way to the assembly area by now... lets head there."

Rourke nods, "Sounds good. Let's go."

CHAPTER 37

I hated every minute of training, but I said, Don't quit.
Suffer now and live the rest of your life as a champion. -
Muhammad Ali

AAR Building
Thursday, 14 December 1989
08:40 Hours.

Josh pulls into the parking lot, drives to the rear and backs the Humvee into the same space as the last time he was there. There are the same number of vehicles as the last time. Which means the OCs have already been there probably for a couple of hours getting ready for the AAR.

Josh checks with Rourke and asks, "Sir, do we need the radios on?"

"Nah, Top and the XO are coming to the AAR and the platoon sergeants can handle anything back at the assembly area."

The back door of the building opens and both immediately recognize Captain Marcell. She is headed directly to them.

Josh smiles and asks, "Hey, Sir, I'm going in to get a free coffee and donut... you want me to bring you back anything?"

Rourke, unable to take his eyes off of Olivia, stammers, "No thanks, Josh. We don't have any sensitive items in the vehicle, do we?"

Josh turns his head to do a sweep of the vehicle's interior then replies, "No, Sir, a little trash and the remains of some MREs. We're secure."

Rourke glances over at him, "This is going to be a long AAR. No sense you sitting out here and freezing your ass off. Get yourself some coffee and donuts and find a seat in the back... Pay attention... you may learn something that will help you in OCS."

Josh grimaces then asks, "Damn, you don't give up, do you, Sir?"

Rourke turns to look back through the windshield to see Olivia walking straight toward him, "Well I guess that will be answered in a couple of minutes."

As Josh slides out of his seat he quietly says, "Good luck, Sir."

Josh salutes and gives Captain Marcell the greeting of the day, "Morning, Ma'am." as he walks by her on the way to the front door of the AAR building.

She returns his salute, "Good morning, Josh."

Rourke smiles and asks, "How do you know Josh?"

Olivia smiles back, "Well, that's your driver. I really know quite a bit about you... actually. I spent time pumping information from your XO and your First Sergeant back in the Field Trains area. I don't think they got wise to it. I was pretty shrewd about it."

Rourke laughs, "You might have gotten by Bob without him noticing... but Top... no way! He knows you're more than a little interested."

Olivia looks down, pauses for a moment, "Well, that's what I want to talk to you about." She scans Rourke's face, "I spent a lot of time last night thinking about it." She hesitates, "Devlin, this isn't going to work. I would like to spend time with you... to really get to know you... you are a wonderful guy... that has the respect and admiration of your whole battalion. You have some wonderful personal traits; you're compassionate, caring and very smart. You are as close to the ideal man, as is maybe possible. But this can't go anywhere... I'm here... you're in Pennsylvania. Our only option is to become... or rather I hope... to remain friends."

Rourke looks despondently at her with understanding, nods then says, "Olivia, you're right... you're right... our only possible relationship is as friends and professional colleagues." Rourke smiles, "I'd like the opportunity to give you a call once in a while... to inquire about some of the new things and lessons learned here at JRTC. You could be my inside guy to the newest things happening in the Active Army."

Olivia brightens with a smile, "Absolutely, Devlin, I'm sure I could provide you with the newest trends and ideas developing here. I would enjoy providing you the scoop on the Army's newest tactics and techniques. It could make you shine in the eyes of your battalion and brigade commanders."

Rourke laughs, "Yes, there are some days I could use some public relations help with my bosses."

Olivia frowns, "I doubt that. I know for a fact that your battalion commander thinks the world of you. If your brigade commander has any common sense he feels the same way."

Rourke nods, "I am pretty lucky to have two great commanders. They've been really generous in my Officer Evaluation Reports."

Olivia smiles as she turns to walk back to the AAR building, "See you inside, Cavalry."

———————◆•◆•◆———————

As Rourke walks to the front door he notices the parking lot is now full. He is sure both his XO and 1SG are already inside. They are sitting about the fourth row from the front. Rourke gives them a little wave as he walks to his assigned seat in the front row.

LTC Jeltsen walks to the front, drops a welcome slide onto the projector. It also contains an agenda. Logistics is going to go first just like the last AAR. Jeltsen then gives a little welcome introduction, "Folks, this is the last formal AAR you'll get from the Observer Controller Team. Now we will always be available to anyone that has a question while you're still here on Fort Chaffee. After reviewing some of your Take Home Package, if you're confused or uncertain about anything, come on over to Building 27. That's where we're located. Be more than happy to answer your questions." Jeltsen glances around to ensure everyone understands. He points behind Rourke and says, "Captain Marcell will begin the logistics portion of the AAR. Captain Marcell, you're up."

Olivia, who had walked up from the back of the room and has been sitting behind Devlin, gets up and walks to the projector in the front.

She drops her first slide onto the projector. It is the same one she used to start her first AAR. It contains four headings: Arming, Fueling, Fixing, and Manning the Force. Once again, she proves to be an excellent AAR facilitator. She brings up issues and challenges the 220th logistic guys had to face. What has Rourke smiling through most of Olivia's AAR is a couple of guys will try not to own up to some of their mistakes. They still believe admitting to a mistake will result in public embarrassment or humiliation. Olivia expertly discourages their reluctance and brings out mistakes in order for them to learn.

Devlin always feels having some laughter mixed in with the lessons learned goes a long way in making those learned lessons permanent. Olivia has everyone chuckling more often than not. She ends her portion of the AAR with compliments to the whole logistics team. And she does it by speaking directly to the Battalion Commander, LTC Francone. This makes every logistics guy feel a tremendous amount of gratitude for Olivia publicly telling the Commander his logistic guys are GOOD! After her portion of the AAR, she walks back to her seat which is now the end chair three rows back of Devlin's. It is a subtle message. One that says to Devlin, I'm no longer interested. We're now just friends.

LTC Jeltsen stands up, faces the room and announces, "Let's all take twenty minutes to take care of any business. See you all back here in twenty."

Rourke gets up to walk to the back of the room to get a coffee. As he passes by Olivia he smiles, "Outstanding, Olivia, our guys really appreciate it."

Rourke gets to the back and has to stand in line. After getting his coffee with cream he peers around for his XO and 1SG. His 1SG is standing off by himself near the front door. 1SG Johnson stares right at Rourke and gives him a 'come on over here' signal with his head and a wave of his hand.

Rourke walks over and asks, "What's up, Top?"

With a solemn look, he then asks Rourke, "What's up with you and Olivia?"

Rourke gives him a quizzical look and asks, "You're calling her Olivia now?"

Johnson smiles, "Sure, she told me to... as she was pumping me for information about you. She was trying to be slick about it. I've been married for 24 years... and have two daughters. She might have gotten by the XO, who she was also pumping information from... but I'm hip to the feminine side of an interrogation. Just too many years."

Rourke asks, "What do you care?"

Johnson replies, "I've never gotten involved with a man's personal life... specifically his love life but this is different."

Rourke again has a bewildered glimpse, "Why is this different?"

Johnson reaches out and taps Rourke on the arm, "Because she'd be good for you. She's kind of special. She really helped us out a couple of times when she didn't have to. She could have let us fall on our faces... that's the whole point of this JRTC battle... and me and the XO were headed that way... more than once... but she quietly stepped in and provided a little guidance... saved our asses."

Rourke crosses his arms and considers Johnson's remarks.

Johnson continues, "I think she likes being around the Dragon Slayers... we work our asses off... and a big part of that is she wants you to be successful." Johnson pauses, "And I got to tell you... I really like her too. She's no dummy either. She'd be a great catch for you, Sir."

Rourke stands there and doesn't say a word for a long time. Finally, he says, "Well, Top... that's not going to happen. Captain Marcell and I have decided to be... just friends. She's not leaving active duty and as you know, we live and work in Pennsylvania. It's just not feasible to work out. Believe me... I agree... she would be an amazing woman to be with. It's just not going to happen."

Johnson shakes his head and sympathizes with Rourke, "Shit... Sir... kind of a raw deal... the perfect woman... and you can't have her." Johnson shakes his head in disappointment. "Man, this is a lousy situation."

Lt. Kiser, the XO, walks over, "Gentlemen, it's time to get back to our seats."

It is time. Everyone in the room starts to move. Most are throwing their cups into the trash cans provided on either side of the coffee table and making their way to their seats. Rourke goes by the table and refills his to take to his seat. It is probably going to be a long session. This is the maneuver portion of the battle. Rourke thinks there are going to be many lessons learned during this portion. He smiles to himself thinking, '*and many of those lessons learned will be by the vaunted, but now vanquished, OPFOR'.*

LTC Robert Jeltsen stands up, tosses a welcome and agenda slide on the projector, and then introduces LTC Charles Schulberg, the OPFOR Commander. Schulberg starts off the AAR with a briefing of his battalion's mission, how he organized his units and how they deployed throughout the sector. He congratulates the 220th on their performance. Francone speaks up and thanks Schulberg for providing his battalion such a great opportunity. The AAR then becomes a conversation between professional soldiers exchanging information in order to pass on lessons learned for the benefit of all. Jeltsen's role becomes that of a facilitator that keeps the conversation moving and selecting the individuals that raise their hands.

Schulberg says he was surprised several times during the mission. His first surprise was how the 220th turned the terrain into their advantage. Grabbing Hill 32 first and then isolating it by cutting off the three fords and the bridge. This prevented him from counter-attacking with his other two companies. The Charlie Company's single platoon demonstration in front of Hill 80 did actually freeze his company in place. They basically withered on the vine waiting for an attack that never came. His biggest surprise was the ravine crossing operation. This provided the 220th a way to come up behind his company on Hill 40. This was a move he and his staff never considered in all of their war gaming since the very beginning of JRTC.

Schulberg believes the key to the 220th success is the outstanding job the six scout teams did prior to the start of operations. They were able to precisely locate all of his units and to accurately provide strength and capabilities. Schulberg is blown away when he found out PSG Callahan had a team right on the top of Hill 40.

The rifle company OCs get up and each lead a small discussion and conversation on the operations the companies were involved in. They do a good job of also drawing out the lessons learned. All the commanders feel their companies did well. But everyone also agrees that if they had it to do over again they would do things a little differently. Lesson are indeed learned.

Rourke's OC, Captain Chancy, says he believes one of the reasons CSC was so successful is how they integrated Charlie 2nd platoon into the company. They had swapped out some of the infantrymen with some personnel with the three TOW Platoons and some with the Scout Platoon in order to give Lt. Heller a platoon with an appropriate amount of cavalry who had TOW gunner experience. This made his platoon just as capable as the rest of the company.

Finally, Jeltsen gets up and introduces the Chief of Operations, Col. Vance Harrison. Harrison strides to the front, faces the room and claps his hands together. Rourke is a little surprised at the enthusiasm that Harrison shows. He seemed rather restrained during the last AAR. His new opening statement is, "Outstanding rotation 220th infantry! You are one hell of a surprise. I was wondering if your first battle was an anomaly. It obviously was NOT. We're all about learning here at JRTC. Thanks for your efforts and accomplishments. I can honestly say that everyone involved with this rotation has learned something. Personally, I've learned that I can still be surprised by soldiers. That regardless of the component... either reserve or active... our soldiers... when well led will do amazing things."

Harrison glances around the room. "One of the most important affects you can have in life is to make an impact." Harrison beams, "Gentlemen, you have made an impact. You have proven to yourselves that your battalion can accept any challenge and do extremely well. You have proven to the JRTC that our training concepts are solid and that we are accomplishing our mission of developing better soldiers, units, and leaders. You've proven to the Army that the One Army Concept is working. No one better ever say again, *'Well they're just a National Guard Unit'*. You should be proud of yourselves... just as we're astounded by your performance here. You're a very good battalion and I would be proud to go and fight alongside you... anywhere... anytime. Truthfully, I've only said that to a few battalions that have rotated through here.

Now I impart upon you... your next responsibility. That is to pass on what you've learned to your fellow soldiers back home, to your sister battalions in your brigade. You've has this tremendous opportunity... now don't piss it away by keeping it to yourselves." Harrison shifts his stance and puts his hands on his hips, "Your last mission... is to pack up your vehicles, equipment and get everyone back to Pennsylvania safely. Once you do that... I think you guys deserve one hell of a party. Just remember to give us here at JRTC a toast before you finish off all those kegs of beer."

Harrison comes to attention. A signal for everyone in the room to stand up and come to attention. Harrison scrutinizes Francone then smiles, "Colonel Francone… Outstanding… simply outstanding."

Francone brings up his right hand in salute, "Thank you, Sir, we appreciate everything the JRTC has done for us." Francone smiles, "And to us! We are a much better battalion."

Harrison nods, drops his hand, turns to his left and walks out the front door.

Jeltsen quickly walks to the front of the room. "Ladies and Gentlemen, please stay on your feet… that concludes the formal portion of the AAR. Just like the colonel says, there's one more mission and that's to get you guys out of here. There's going to be a little meeting up front here with the 220th logistics guys and the Fort Chaffee main post guys to quickly work on a couple of issues to get you back on main post, prep for the load up and move back to home station. If that issue pertains to you, get up here… after I salute all of you." Jeltsen comes to attention, appears delighted and salutes, "I'm not ever… going to forget this one."

CHAPTER 38

"If you are going to achieve excellence in big things, you develop the habit in little matters." - General Colin Powell

Fort Chaffee Main Post
Dining Facility #2
Friday, 15 December 1989
08:45 Hours.

Dining Facility #2 is very much like every chow hall Rourke has ever been in. Some are newer than others with the latest interior layouts and fresher, brighter, painted walls but by and large they are still a huge room with approximately 40 to 60, four seating tables and chairs. At one end is the serving line. Usually staffed by three soldiers that are on their turn for KP duty. There are always four cooks that run the kitchen behind the serving line, with one of those operating as the Head Cook. He is usually a Staff Sergeant with fifteen years of service. Usually, with that much experience, he has seen all kinds of chow related calamities and emergencies. Everything from no food available, to spoiled food, to not enough food, to cooking out in the field for weeks with all of its challenges.

After three years in the battalion, Rourke is impressed with the good service always provided by the cook section.

Rourke never complains about the food. Yes, there are some days that it isn't up to par. But by and large the food prepared by Army cooks is pretty good. The 220th cooks are operating two dining facilities for the battalion. Alpha, Bravo and part of Headquarters Companies are eating in Dining Facility #1 which means that Charlie, CSC and the rest of Headquarters are eating in Facility #2.

Rourke is sitting at a table off to the side and about halfway into the dining hall. He finished his breakfast 30 minutes ago and is just sitting, drinking his second cup of coffee. He is joined by 1SG Johnson, the XO, Lt. Kiser and the Supply Sergeant, Joe Burke. They had all eaten together, cleared their trays, are relaxing and having coffee. They are joined by the five platoon sergeants. All grab a nearby chair and scoot in as close as possible. It is a meeting.

Rourke takes another sip of coffee, "OK, we all agree... today is equipment clean up, repair and maintenance... weapons... same thing... clean up, repair and maintain." Rourke surveys the table, everybody is nodding. "Then maintaining the soldier. I'm sure everyone got a hot shower last night... right?" Everyone again nods. "Also, soldier individual equipment, that's TA 50 web gear, chem suits, equipment, uniforms and boots... right?"

Rourke questions Staff Sgt. Burke, "Joe, are we good for cleaning supplies?"

Burke replies, "Sir, I've got a whole deuce and a half full of all kinds of stuff... been saving up for the last six months. Yes, Sir, we're good."

PSG Rob Donnelly chimes in, "Yes, Sir... we've got this. This isn't our first rodeo. Just like my platoon... we've all got this pretty much organized by squads and sections."

Rourke scans the group, "Yea, I know. Do you need anything from me or the XO right now?"

Everyone shakes their head and agrees that they can handle everything from here.

Rourke then continues, "OK, just like this morning... the cooks gave us an extended breakfast hour. They're extending lunch till 13:00 hours. Let's all meet back here at 12:45... after you've eaten... bring your coffee and we'll quickly go over our progress and any remaining challenges. Sound good?"

Everyone agrees, drains their cups, walks to the dirty tray turn-in and sets their cups down to be shoved into the dish washer.

As they are walking out the door, 1SG Johnson asks Rourke, "Sir, what's the schedule for the next couple of days?"

Rourke stops, puts on his soft cap and specifies, "Today is equipment and soldiers... let's give everybody some time off tomorrow. Tomorrow is a Training Holiday. I suspect most guys will stay on post. Top, see if the Service Club and bowling alley and gym will be open. I know the PX will be open. Some guys will want to go into Fort Smith." Rourke grins, "Drinking I suspect. So, we will need a curfew for tomorrow night. What do you gentlemen recommend?"

Lt. Kiser immediately chimes in with 22:00 hours. 1SG Johnson smiles, shakes his head, "Sir, let's make it 20:00 hours. They will have all afternoon to drink downtown. A head count at 20:00 will give us enough time to get out and police up the stragglers."

Kiser shaking his head at Rourke says, "I should know by now to wait for Top."

Rourke observes, "Yea, that's why I'm the commander and you're still the XO... but you are learning."

Johnson then asks, "What about the day after... Sunday the 17th, Sir?"

Rourke considers, "Vehicles... repair, replace and maintain. Because the 18th is load and leave."

Rourke begins to gaze at Kiser. Kiser anticipates the question, "Sir, maintenance is ready. We've got tires, belts, filters, oil, grease, and fiberglass body kits... I got with Chief Ronconi... battalion maintenance has a pretty solid plan. The only hiccup is the Humvee with the blown tranny... It's getting shipped back by commercial carrier next week."

Rourke fixes on the group, "Any questions? We have a pretty good plan with enough flexibility to provide you guys options on completing tasks... use your initiative to get things done. If you need any help... ask. And it really doesn't matter who... everyone in the company will pitch in and help... once again... any questions?"

There are none. Rourke says, "OK... go forth and kick ass."

As the Dragon Slayer Leadership stand, they all smile, look at each other, and repeat, "Let's kick ass!" as they stride off to their assignments.

———————————————————

Bachelor Officer Quarters (BOQ) Building 130
Saturday, 16 December 1989
11:30 Hours.

There is a knock at Rourke's BOQ door. Rourke gets up from the desk, takes three steps to the door and opens it. Standing there is his XO. Kiser asks, "You hungry?"

Rourke nods, "Yea, as a matter of fact I am. Let me put this stuff away then we'll go to the chow hall."

Kiser asks, "What are you working on?"

Rourke walks back to the desk and gathers up a stack of papers. "Actually, I was going over the plan that you and Chief put together for the vehicles. Seems like you guys put some thought into this. You've got a list of every vehicle and what's wrong with it."

Kiser goes on to explain, "Honestly, that is pretty easy... our crews are so trained on maintenance they all filled out their 2404s while still in the assembly area... while we were at the AAR. They're done correctly. So, chief went through them and did a vehicle triage... then listed them in order of priority of most work needed to least work needed. I talked with all the LTs here in the BOQ this morning. They and the platoon sergeants have the plan. They'll be ready to go to work at 08:00 hours tomorrow morning."

Rourke asks, "What do you want to do after chow? My work's pretty much done."

"How about we head over to the gym. Let's get a couple of the LTs and play a little two on two. I think me... and Trevor should be able to kick your ass... with any of the other LTs you pick."

Rourke laughs, "Shit... In your dreams. All you got is that lame fifteen-foot jumper and only when you're hot... and if you're cold... you have no game."

Kiser crosses his arms and nods, "How about we make it a little more interesting... maybe you would be up for a little wager?"

"What have you got in mind, Pistol Pete?"

Kiser concentrates then asks, "Well, you always pay for the first round of beer and pizza at the Pizza Hut for our Officer Development Program. How about the loser pays for all three rounds... for the next two ODPs back home?"

"How about for the next three ODPs?"

Kiser extends his hand, "Free beer and pizza for the next three drills... I'm going to love it."

Rourke reaches out and shakes hands, "Like taking candy from a baby... or more like taking beer from a lieutenant... way too easy."

Fort Chaffee Main Post
Gym #2
13:30 Hours

The walk from the BOQ to the gym is a little longer than Rourke likes. All five of them are wearing a combination of personal workout gear and their Army issued PT uniform. The original plan was for a couple of games of two on two but there is an extra lieutenant that wanted to come along. With just a sweat shirt and sweat pants the cold seems to cut through the outer layer and starts to make them really cold. All five are happy to get to the front door before they all freeze.

After walking through a little foyer, they open the double doors to the main gym floor. It is a full-size basketball court with the typical sections of pull out bleachers on both sides. Only one section on the right side at mid court is pulled out. This is the seating for all those using the gym today. On the left side there are two other backboards lowered from the ceiling for additional baskets to shoot at.

A quick glance around and they can see the gym is mostly bare. Rourke figures there is plenty of football on TV so nobody wants to venture through the cold to go to the gym. There are only six others on the floor. Four of those are already playing a game of two on two at the near basket. The other two are down at the far end shooting around with their own basketballs. Rourke fixes his eyes down the court to see if they can come up with a half decent ball player so they can play some three on three.

There she is. It's Olivia. She is one of the two at the far end shooting hoops. They stand there and watch for a minute. The first thing Rourke notices is she has a nice ten-foot jump shot. She squares up her hips and shoulders to the bucket, jumps a couple inches off the ground, raises up and releases the ball in one smooth motion. The next thing is her presence on the court. Her dribbling with both hands is with control. She has no problem with cross dribbling and breaking for the basket on a left-handed layup. Then finally, she looks damn good in shorts.

They walk to the right sideline in order to clear the near side hoop and stay out of the way of the two on two game. On the way down to the far hoop, Kiser asks Rourke if the bet is still on. Everyone stops at the bleachers at midcourt to listen.

Rourke thinks for a minute, "Yea, it's still on... how about this. You, Trevor and Chuck against... me, Jim, and if Olivia agrees... it'll be Olivia."

Kiser shows a sly smile, "Really... I understand you want to spend time with Olivia... and I think that's great... but you don't have to feel obligated to uphold the bet. We can just play for fun. We all understand why you would chicken out of the bet. I mean that's acceptable... she's a nice person." Kiser, still grinning, turns around in the circle of lieutenants and asks everyone to agree.

Rourke smiles at everyone and does a quick calculation in his head. This is all based on all the games they played on the gym floor back home in the armory, usually after the monthly Tuesday night training meeting. *I know I can beat Bob one on one, and Trevor is just a little bit better than Jim Petrone, but if Jim could have a good game, that could even those two out, the key here is Olivia against Chuck Clegg. Chuck is the weakest player here. Olivia, unbeknownst to any of these guys, is a small college All-American. Thank you very much Tim Chancy for that little bit of key information'.*

Rourke's smile gets bigger, "Bob, really, who do you think you are? Trying to prod or goad me into keeping the bet. I wasn't born yesterday... rookie. There is no prodding here... the bet stays the same... rookie!"

Kiser, looking like the cat that ate the canary, turns to face Olivia and calls out, "Hey, Olivia, can you come over here for a minute? We've got something to ask you."

Olivia trots and dribbles over to the Dragon Slayers. She gets right up to them and asks, "You need another player to make it three on three, right?"

Rourke asks, "Yes we do. How about it… you in?"

"Yea, I'm in. What are the teams? But we're not playing shirts and skins."

Everybody laughs. Rourke says, "Let me introduce you to the CSC Officer Corps. Rourke goes around and points to each of his lieutenants as he introduces them. "Olivia, you of course know Bob Kiser our XO… next is the 1st TOW Platoon Leader, Trevor Foley…then the 2nd TOW Platoon Leader, Chuck Clegg and then the 3rd TOW, Jim Petrone." Each man reaches out and offers his hand.

Olivia smiles, "Pleasure to meet you." as she shakes their hands.

Kiser announces to the group, "Olivia, it's me, Trevor and Chuck against you, Devlin and Jim. We'll play to fifteen… each bucket is one point… call your own fouls… meaning if you foul someone you call it on yourself. We exchange possession after each score. All new possessions have to start at the top of the key. A defensive rebound means it goes back out to the top of the key. Got it?"

Olivia nods, "Yea, pretty standard."

Trevor pipes in with, "And Olivia, this doesn't involve you… but you should be aware that there's some heavy wagering going on for this game. I'm talking about a lot of beer and pizza… but you needn't worry… or feel any pressure because of it."

Olivia returns the taunt, "Oh, I'm not going to worry about that… just like you shouldn't be worried about getting beat by a girl. I wouldn't want you to choke on your masculine ego while trying so hard to impress me."

Trevor, with a look of disbelief on his face, glances around the group who are nodding approvingly. Trevor says with a little surprise, "Nice… very nice… I think we're going to have a game here."

Rourke asks Kiser, "Bob, pick a number from one to five?"

Kiser shakes his head. He's been through this pick a number game before. "How about… four?"

Rourke reaches over to take the ball out of Olivia's hands, "Nope… sorry it is two… our ball first. We'll take it out at the top of the key."

The match ups are just how Rourke hoped they'd be. He is guarding Bob, Jim on Trevor, and Olivia against Chuck.

Rourke goes to the top of the key to start play. Jim sets up off to the right of the foul line and Olivia sets up deep in the left corner covered by Chuck who is cheating towards Rourke.

Rourke says, "All right, it's on!" as he starts to dribble to his right. Jim comes racing up to set up a block on Bob to free Rourke for a possible drive. Trevor calls switch and slides out to block Rourke's path. Rourke sees Olivia take a stab step toward the top of the key faking Chuck into believing she is headed that way. She then darts to her left to run the baseline. She is quick. She easily gets a full step on Chuck. She is fast. Chuck is never going to catch her. Rourke fires a pass off his dribble to Olivia who easily catches it in full stride, takes one dribble and goes up for a reverse layup.

Rourke smiles and says to himself, *'Man! That looked good. Let's see how she plays defense.'*

Rourke and Kiser change places. Jim is covering Trevor on the left of the foul line and Olivia is guarding Chuck on the outside over on the right. Bob puts the ball on the floor for one dribble and then passes to Trevor. Bob reverses course to try and get behind Rourke and races down the lane for a return pass from Trevor. The standard give and go. Rourke easily and quickly drops back to cover the lane making Bob harmlessly continue running through the lane and off to the left along the baseline.

Trevor tries to drive to his right but is cut off by Jim. Chuck fakes like he is going to the hoop then posts up on the foul line to receive a pass from Trevor. Chuck then spins around to square up on Olivia. He tries to drive right. Olivia's great anticipation cuts him off. He tries to drive left and again Olivia cuts him off. Chuck then backs off still dribbling now waiting for one of his partners to make a move.

Bob makes a dash from the left corner to the hoop trying to get a step on Rourke. Chuck stops his dribble, brings up the ball to pass and tries to fire it over Olivia. She is reading his eyes. Her right hand shoots up and tips the ball into a slow high arc toward Bob and Rourke. Rourke knows he has this. He is already planning to grab it and fire it off to Jim who is headed out to get beyond the top of the key. Bob and Rourke collide on the way up for the ball. Rourke has both three inches of height and better jumping ability than Bob. Rourke grabs the ball, while still in the air, brings it down and fires a perfect behind the back pass to Jim now at the top of the key.

Olivia spins around to block Chuck out of the lane for a couple of seconds then raises her hand to signal for Jim to lead her down the lane with a floating pass. It is right on target. With Chuck behind her she catches the pass, takes another step and lays it in over the front of the rim.

The rest of the game is pretty lopsided. The final score is 15 to 7. Olivia is high scorer with 8, Rourke has 4 and Jim has 3. Chuck never could keep up with Olivia. Whenever Rourke or Jim got backed into a corner or got in trouble, Olivia was always the outlet pass. She did shoot and make one twelve-foot jumper. That was to keep Chuck honest. He was playing off her too far. She just pulled up and let one fly. All the rest were layups.

Rourke made the last shot. It was off an offensive rebound. Rourke went up through three others, grabbed the ball, took two steps in a short powerful drive and slammed it in on a layup over the rim. He came down, turned and yelled, "That's Game... Rookies!"

Jim and Olivia both run over to give Rourke the obligatory high fives. They also start the required ridicule and teasing the losers. Jim lets them know he is sure those pizzas are going to be the best tasting he ever had.

After everybody finishes taking a break and getting some water, they decide to mix up the teams and play again. This time Rourke plays against Olivia. This time it is just for fun. Rourke can't remember the last time he had such a great time playing ball.

Occasionally during a switch or a move to cover an open man, Rourke is one on one with Olivia. And that is fantastic. They get into a little bit of trash talking. They challenge each other during attempts to drive to the hoop. Rourke is sure she enjoys doing a little bumping and pushing under the boards with him. He enjoys leaning against her to block her out from getting position for a rebound. The score goes back and forth. Finally, it is over at 15 to 13, with Rourke's team as the victors. Everyone heads to the bleachers. Along the way there is a lot of laughter in reviewing some of the more unique plays. They sit at the bleachers talking and just bullshitting for quite a while. Finally, Trevor asks Olivia where she learned to play ball.

"Well Trevor, I last played organized ball in college four years ago."

Trevor gets this look of suspicion and asks, "You played in college... shit, none of us played in college. What college?"

Olivia declares with a matter of fact manner, "It's a Division II school south of Indianapolis... Franklin College. I was a small college All-American my senior year."

Kiser jumps up off the third row of bleachers he is leaning on and yells, "I knew it... I knew there was something fishy going on!" He glares at Olivia. "When you blew Chuck away with that first reverse layup, I knew then... you were no neighborhood playground pickup player." He stabs his finger at Rourke, "I know you knew that! That's why you were so anxious to pick her for your team... yea... hey guys, the fix was in."

Olivia bursts out laughing, raises her arm to signal a stop, "No, no, no... in the few conversations I've had with Devlin, I never mentioned I played basketball... let alone that I was an All-American."

Kiser shifts his attention back to Rourke. This prompts everyone to look at Rourke. Rourke sits there and is showing no emotion.

Kiser eagerly exclaims, "Captain Rourke... I know that... *'please don't ask me a question look'*. I've seen it when you're with the Colonel. And we've done something that he really shouldn't know and you're praying he doesn't ask... 'cause if he asks... as an officer you would have to truthfully tell him."

Rourke with all the indignation he can muster blurts, "Bob, I really don't know what you're driving at."

Kiser jumps down off the bleachers, stands in front of Rourke and asks, "Did you know that Olivia was an All-American basketball player... before today?"

Rourke shifts his weight uncomfortably, slightly shakes his head with an, *'I give up expression'*, winces and admits, "Yea, I knew... damn. This doesn't change anything." He scrutinizes Kiser, "I didn't know she would be here at the gym. That was a complete surprise. But, since she was...why not ask her to play some hoops?"

Kiser, smiling like a prosecutor who just caught the guilty person on the stand, declares, "So you thought... since this involves a little wager, why not have the All-American play on my team?"

Rourke throws up his hands and laughs, "Yes... that is exactly what I thought." Rourke stands, shrugs and holds his hands up, "Did you really think with three months of beer and pizza on the line... I was going to ask you guys if we could ask the All-American basketball player if she would like to play on one of our teams." Rourke stares at all of them and asks, "Really... think about that. What would you do in my... sneakers?"

Olivia, with a puzzled look, asks, "When and how did you know I was a ball player?"

Rourke puts his hands on his hips, glances up for a moment and then down at Olivia to explain, "Tim Chancy told me at the first AAR after you stopped by in the parking lot and said hi." Rourke then gets a, *'caught with my hand in the cookie jar look'*, and continues, "I kind of asked about you... he gave me a quick Bio." Rourke gives Olivia a sincere look, "It is all good stuff. He thinks highly of you... very highly."

Showing a big smile, Chuck Clegg speaks up, "Man, this changes my whole morale. I was feeling pretty bad about my performance... now... shit... I just held an All-American to 8 points!"

Everybody laughs and agrees with some additional comments, "That's right Chuck... you took on an All-American... you the man, Chuck. And don't forget... you scored twice on her. We could tell... you had her all confused with some of those moves of yours. Like putting up what was supposed to be a left-handed layup... with your right hand!"

Kiser puts up both his hands to get everybody's attention. He scans around, "Alright... let's take a vote." He observes Rourke while still talking to the group, "I think it only fair... now that we know about Olivia. We either agree with the final score on the first game... as the fair and correct score or we throw it out and say the bet's off... think about it for a minute."

Everyone glances around seeking confirmation and agreement. Everyone agrees. The consensus is that it was fairly played and the bet still stands.

Jim Petrone stands and announces, "Hey, Sir, I really need to get going. I want to get cleaned up... go eat some chow... and then get ready for tomorrow."

Rourke nods, "Yea, Jim... good plan. Maybe we all should get going. It's going to be a long day tomorrow."

Except for Rourke and Olivia, everyone gets up and starts moving to the front door. Kiser stops near the door, turns and looks at Rourke with a, *'you coming expression'*. Rourke shakes his head, waves to Kiser to go ahead. He'll be along later. Kiser raises his arm as if he's putting a spoon in his mouth, signaling the question, *'Do you want to eat chow together, later on'*?

Rourke gives a thumbs-up sign. Kiser responds with his own thumbs up, then turns and heads out the door.

Rourke turns to his right where Olivia is sitting three feet away and smiles, "I can see why you're an All-American. Good game."

Olivia lowers her gaze and discloses, "Devlin, I had a good time. Your guys are a special group."

Rourke replies, "They are some very good soldiers and leaders. They've earned the respect of all our soldiers and especially the NCOs."

Olivia pauses then says, "They reflect on you, Devlin. You should get a lot of credit for their development."

Rourke unconsciously sits up a little straighter, "I am very proud of them... especially after this."

Neither one says anything for a long couple of minutes.

Rourke wonders aloud, "I can't believe we ran into each other here at the gym. Bob asked me to come to the gym with him because... well... we were bored. Why are you here?"

Olivia slides closer and sincerely replies, "I love basketball. Playing lets me get away from things for a while. It's an outlet for me. Here in the gym it's simple, just shoot the ball in the hoop. I can dribble around and take shots and just forget about the world for a while. Just concentrate on basketball fundamentals... simple... right?"

With a quizzical look, Rourke asks, "What are you doing here today? The rotation's over. Your work is done... and you did great work by the way."

Olivia slowly shakes her head, "I came here to try and put YOU out of my mind." She smiles, "I was hoping a good basketball workout would drive the thought of you out of my head."

Rourke laughs, "And then I come walking through the door."

Olivia concedes, "It's not funny, Devlin."

Rourke sympathizes, "Well... maybe a little. In all honesty I've been spending a lot of time thinking about you."

Olivia perks up, "What have you been thinking about?"

Rourke lets out a sigh and begins to slowly explain, "I don't know how, but I'm not giving up on what this is... this possible... serious... budding relationship. There's an answer for this. I haven't figured it out yet. But I know there's an answer and I'm going to figure it out."

Olivia reaches out and puts her hand on Rourke's, "Devlin, that would be wonderful. I would like a serious relationship with you. But I don't see how."

She stands up and sadly looks down at Rourke, "Devlin, be safe getting home." She then turns and walks out the back door.

Rourke plops back to lean against the second row of bleachers. He feels like he was just punched in the chest and lost his breath. He settles there for twenty minutes trying to regain his composure. He can't remember when he ever felt so utterly dejected.

CHAPTER 39

"When your values are clear to you, making decisions becomes easier." - Roy E. Disney

Fort Chaffee Main Post
Dining Facility #2
Sunday, 17 December 1989
12:45 Hours.

After putting his tray on the stack of dirty trays at the turn-in point, and after getting a coffee refill, Rourke walks back to his table. Lunch is over. 1SG Johnson is in the process of getting everyone to put three of the tables together. This is going to be the after-lunch vehicle status meeting that Rourke called for at the morning formation. This will give the CSC leadership a last time to change the vehicle repair and maintenance plan. Rourke figures they have about six hours left to get all the vehicles on deadline, back up and in service.

Everyone is there. The five platoon leaders and their platoon sergeants, the XO, Battalion Maintenance Chief Ronconi, CSC Mechanic, SSG Ron Mason, and the First Sergeant. Rourke sits down at the head of the makeshift conference table with everyone else grabbing chairs and placing them in no particular order. Everyone seems to find a piece of table and have their open notebooks out ready to either take a note or read some of their data to the group.

Rourke glances around, "OK, let's start with the XO and get a general view of how we're doing."

Kiser looks down at his own notebook and then starts his briefing, "Chief here can provide you with any specifics if you need them. So, first the bad news. We have four on deadline that are NOT going to get fixed here at Fort Chaffee. We don't have access to the facilities here to make the major repairs that are required."

Kiser glimpses at Chief Ronconi for agreement. The Chief nods and explains, "The one with the blown transmission... needs a new one. We have one that has no engine compression. The gaskets and seals are shot. One with ball joints that are gone and one with brakes that are shot. I've made arrangements with our log guys to have all four of them commercially shipped to State Maintenance at the Gap... by the end of the week." The Chief looks around to ensure there are no questions, then looks over to Kiser for him to continue the briefing.

Kiser studies his notes, "Everybody got through the wash rack by 10:00 hours." Still looking at his notes, "Our TOW Humvees are in pretty good shape... except the blown tranny... the other seventeen had minor repairs and maintenance problems that will all be fixed by this evening. All will have an oil change, greased, many with new lights... front and back... a couple of new wind shields and wipers, fiberglass fenders fixed, a couple of exhaust systems repaired... two radiators repaired." Kiser observes Rourke to confirm he understands then continues, "The biggest problems are with the Scouts and the Mortar Humvees. Probably because number one... we got these from other units and we certainly didn't get their newest vehicles... and then there's the fact the Scouts and Mortars never had Humvees before."

Chief Ronconi raises his hand to interject, "Yea, the XO is right. They got a lot of miles on them. The minor stuff the soldiers are taking care of... the regular repairs and stuff like that. Battalion mechanics are doing quick engine tune ups... plugs, belts and engine timing. Some of these vehicles need major engine overhaul or replacement. But we'll have you serviceable by tomorrow morning... except for those four on deadline."

Kiser jumps in again, "Of special note is that Lt. Heller... Old Dan... sent over eight guys from his platoon to help with vehicle maintenance. Three of them are actual mechanics back home. I sent all of them over to help the battalion mechanics."

Chief Ronconi agrees, "Yea, they're doing a pretty good job for us. They don't know the Humvee... but they are mechanics and know how to turn a wrench. We just give them a little guidance. They can take anything off or put anything back on properly. The other five guys are really a help... just by running for parts or holding on to something, lifting up stuff... you know... kind of a gopher for the mechanics."

Rourke glances around the table and asks, "How about from the platoons? Any of you guys have any questions or comments? It appears everything is going well, right?"

Lt. Foley speaks up, "Sergeant Mason has been doing a great job of occasionally walking down the line of vehicles and spot checking and asking the crews if they need any help and of course offering advice and guidance. I know the guys appreciate it." Foley points over to Mason and gives a thumbs-up. Everyone again chips in and provides positive remarks and thanking Mason for his work.

Rourke looks at the XO, "OK, Bob, keep doing what you're doing. Everybody the same with you, keep doing what you're doing. How about a final meeting at 17:45 hours after chow? We meet right here again?" Everyone agrees on the plan. Rourke tells them, "I'll be down at the south end of the motor pool. Josh and I have a couple of things to do on our wheels. If you need me... that's where I'll be... any questions?" There are none. Rourke says, "OK let's get our 'Mounts' ready for the next operation... whenever and whatever that will be."

———————

Fort Chaffee Main Post
South End of Motor Pool
14:10 Hours.

Rourke, holding a screwdriver, is standing behind his Humvee directing Josh to flip the turn signal switch up or down to test the new lights they had just repaired when a Humvee pulls up. Josh slides out of the driver's seat, gets a glimpse of the driver, nods acknowledgment then asks the battalion commander's driver, "What's up, Vince?"

Vince raises his hand and points to Rourke, "Hey, Sir, the Colonel sent me to fetch you... he wants to see you."

Rourke walks to the front of his Humvee. With an inquiring look he asks, "Vince, did he want me to jump in with you... or... that I was to get there as soon as possible?"

Vince replies, "Sir, I am to get you and take you back to the JRTC Operations building where the Colonel is."

Rourke asks with curiosity, "Vince, do you know what this is all about?"

Vince shakes his head, "No, Sir... I was told to come get you and not to waste any time, Sir."

Rourke reaches in his Humvee to grab his coat and his field notebook. He looks at Josh searching for a clue as to what this might be about then asks Josh, "We had everybody at the head count formation last night at 20:00 hours... right?"

Josh appears just as confused, shrugs his shoulders and recounts, "Yes, Sir, we have everybody... a couple had a little too much to drink... but they were good to go this morning. Nothing in the rumor mill about anybody fuckin' up in town." Josh then brightens up with a big smile, "Maybe you made Major!"

Rourke amusingly says, "Yes, Josh, I'm sure I made major... and tonight while wearing my new major leaf's... I'm going to put you in for First Sergeant. Unless you would rather go to OCS?"

Josh rolls his eyes, shakes his head, "It'll never happen."

Rourke jumps into the passenger seat and asks Vince, "Where are you taking me?"

Vince puts the Humvee in drive while still staring out the windshield, "The Colonel is with the JRTC Operations Colonel in building 27. That's where we're going, Sir."

Vince pulls the vehicle into the parking lot behind the building. Finds a parking space near the back door, backs in, shuts the engine off, points to the rear door then says, "Sir, through that door, down the hall to the reception area, tell the lady you're there for the colonel. She'll take you to his office... Colonel Francone is with him." Vince shrugs his shoulders, "And I guess... good luck... whatever it is."

Rourke finds a young attractive blonde woman, Rourke guesses about 30ish, sitting behind a desk that is behind a reception counter. On the counter is an open visitor's log. Rourke smiles and asks, "Do I sign in, Ma'am?"

She looks up, smiles back and asks, "Are you Captain Rourke?"

"Yes, I am."

"There's no need. Just follow me please."

She gets up and starts down the hallway behind her desk. She stops at the door at the end of the hallway, steps in and announces, "Colonel, Captain Rourke."

Colonel Vance Harrison, Infantry, Chief of Operations, JRTC, turns and says, "Thank you, Judith. Will you show the captain in and please shut the door."

Judith turns her attention to Rourke, gestures with her hand for him to step into the office and politely says, "Captain, the Colonel will see you now."

It is a big office. The left wall is all shelving. Most are filled with books. Some shelves have the usual military paraphernalia, coffee cups, several beer steins, a saber, some plaques, and a couple of trophies. The right wall has pictures. They document the colonel's exploits from a young lieutenant to his years as a colonel. Centered in the middle is a large painting of a civil war battle scene with a small brass plate describing it as a presentation to Major Harrison. The Colonel is sitting behind a large oak desk. LTC Francone is sitting in front of the desk on the chair to the right. It is one of a pair of overstuffed chairs in front of the desk. Harrison points to the chair on the left and invites Rourke to have a seat.

As Rourke hits the seat, and opens his notebook, Harrison leans forward and begins explaining. "Captain Rourke, I'm about to ask you the most important question you will have to answer up to this point in your life." Harrison pauses. Rourke turns his head, stares over at Francone. LTC Francone looks back with the most serious expression Rourke has ever seen on his Commander's face.

Rourke looks back at Harrison, "Yes, Sir."

Harrison takes a deep breath, sits back a little, puts both arms on his desk, "Devlin, the United States Government is about to invade the country of Panama. This will be a large-scale military operation to take down the Panamanian Government... and the Dictator, Manuel Noriega. I can't go into great details simply because I am not privy to them. But I can tell you there will be units from the 7th ID, the 5th ID the 82nd Airborne, Army Rangers, and Marines... and probably others that I don't know about." Harrison pauses to allow Rourke to take it all in then continues. "I'm not going to go into the political reasons for this... just suffice it to say... our leaders in Washington believe it to be in the best interest of our country to do this. We've been given the job to carry it out. We will carry it out. This is all going to happen sometime on the 19th or 20th... 24 to 48 hours from now. There have been some units already prepositioned in country." Harrison pauses again.

During that pause Rourke asks, "Sir, what has this got to do with me?"

Harrison takes another deep breath and continues, "Colonel Thomas Padgett is the commander of the 1st Brigade of the 82nd that is jumping into Panama. Tom and I go way back. As a matter of fact, if you look over at the wall, that third picture from the left... that's me and Tom back in Vietnam... when we both led infantry platoons. Tom called me, with permission from the Operations Commander, to ask me about finding a Delta Company to help him out. His anti-armor company isn't going to jump... they might, be coming later... way later... when the airfields are open. He needs some immediate mobile anti-armor capability. His Intel folks say there might be light armor vehicles belonging to the Panamanian Defense Force, the PDF, within his assigned AO." Harrison lets that sink in. He sees Rourke isn't going to ask anything, so he continues. "I told Tom that I have the perfect company right here at Chaffee... that just completed our training... and is one of the finest companies we've seen. That this is a Combat Support Company with anti-armor, scout and heavy mortars... that this company operates as a light cavalry troop. That they had pretty much beat up on the OPFOR." Harrison stops.

Rourke looks at Harrison with a sideways glance then asks the big question. "Sir, is that about the time you told him we are a National Guard Unit?"

Harrison smiles and nods, "Yes, I told him. It gave him pause for a second. Then he asks me why I brought it up. That if this CSC is good enough to beat up on the OPFOR, he didn't much care what or who their parent unit is. And I agreed." Harrison leans forward. "Devlin, you've developed a very good and what I would call... as close to a combat ready unit that there is. Keeping in mind from my personal experience... nobody is ever ready for actual combat. Devlin, your men are the best we've seen here in a while... and that's from all of the JRTC Operations Staff and I might add, the OPFOR." Harrison gazes over at Francone.

Francone moves his chair so that it faces more towards Rourke. "Devlin, this is something new... that nobody could foretell... it is always assumed that the Guard would be called up from their hometowns. Here we are at Fort Chaffee, just completed the best training the Army has. Proved we, at least the 2nd 220th Infantry... proved we're pretty good. Now we have an active duty brigade asking for the Guard to provide them an additional combat arms company." Francone pauses, "The brigade wants your company. Now we have a little challenge... since this has never been done before. We've been on the phone to our State Headquarters back at the Gap, and with the National Guard Bureau in Washington, and the Pentagon. To make a very long story short. We can do this... with one caveat... and I'm not sure who wants this." Francone looks back at Harrison.

Harrison leans forward and clasps his hands together on the desk, "Devlin, they want the commander of the unit... YOU... to accept the offer to go on active duty and participate in this operation. They want you to volunteer your company for combat in Panama. I'm not sure... but I would bet someone or a bunch of someone's... want to cover their asses. If things don't go right... they can come back and say the commander wanted to commit to combat." Harrison pauses for Rourke to take it in, "So the question to you is... Do you want to take your company to Panama?"

Rourke slides back in his chair, crosses his arms, gazes down and has a hundred thoughts racing through his mind. He looks up at Harrison and asks, "Could I get a cup of coffee?"

Harrison nods, "So, you want me to have Judith bring you a cup?"

"No, Sir, I would rather just get it myself. I need a minute to think."

Harrison spins around in his chair, picks up a cup off the credenza and spins back around to hand it to Rourke. "Here's a clean cup; the break room is back down the hallway past Judith... and you'll see it on the left... there's a coffee maker in there. If there's no coffee in the pot just tell Judith... she'll make you some."

Rourke takes the cup and gets up. Harrison gives him a sympathetic look, "I'm sorry, Devlin, but we need an answer in fifteen minutes. For this to work... if you're going... the planners need to know immediately."

Rourke nods, "Yes, Sir, fifteen minutes." He turns and walks out the room. He finds the break room and the coffee pot. There is plenty of coffee and creamer. Rourke makes himself a cup, turns and leans against the counter, begins taking slow sips of hot coffee and thinking. *'Do I commit my guys to combat... combat... possible death or dismemberment? I never, ever thought I would be making this decision... I had always assumed we would be ordered to deploy to a hot area... a possible battle... after all the talking and diplomacy failed... that we would have at least a little time to mentally get ready. That the decision was already made... we would be following activation orders... that we could all justify it by saying orders are orders... and this is what we signed up for... we all knew it was a possibility. Everyone would have a chance to say good bye to their families and make promises that their families shouldn't worry because they would safely return'.*

'But this... Holy Shit... If I say no... we don't go... the active guys may use this as leverage to say... see we told you... the reserve components really don't want to get in and mix it up with real bad guys. They are truly only weekend warriors. Don't expect the same level of dedication as the Regular Army'.

'Then there's the guys within the National Guard. The whole Guard will be pretty disappointed. This is a chance to show our country that when called upon, we are ready and able to fight alongside our active brothers. Damn... I just never thought being called upon was going to be within fifteen minutes'!

'If I say yes... we'll be leaving within 24 hours for... possible combat. Really no time to tell the families and really no time to prepare the men for leaving their families. How strong are my soldiers... how mentally strong are they? There is no doubt in my mind we are just as capable as any company in the whole Army. Skill wise, soldier craft, and field knowledge... we have it all. What about their will to fight... If I explain we are called up to go fight... because our country says we need to... There is no doubt they will fight. The Dragon Slayers' primary strength is our esprit de corps... we believe in one another... we trust one another... we'll fight for one another'.

Rourke raises his cup for another drink. He reads the cup. It is stenciled, U.S. Army Infantry School and Center, Fort Benning, Georgia, and decorated with the school patch and the back is stenciled with the infantry motto; Follow Me. The motto is only two words. But Rourke knows they are the two most powerful words for any military leader to ever say. Follow Me! Two words that say; I am your leader, trust me, believe me, we will accomplish all our missions… no matter how difficult or dangerous. I will show you the way; all you need to do is 'Follow Me'.

Rourke finishes his coffee, walks to the sink, rinses out the cup, dries it with a paper towel and walks out of the break room. As he begins to walk past Judith, she glances up. Rourke looks down to meet her eyes. With a knowing and understanding look, she quietly says, "Good luck and be careful Captain Rourke."

Rourke stops, turns to face her, studies her for a couple of seconds, wondering how she was so sure of his decision and asks her, "How did you know I decided to go?"

She looks him squarely in the eyes, "Captain Rourke, you are a soldier. I've been around soldiers all my life. I'm a daughter of a retired armor officer." She pauses, "You have it… Just looking at you. You're a soldier down to your core." Her eyes brighten as she hints of a slight smile, "I'll be cheering for you and your men."

Rourke returns the smile and sincerely says, "Thanks Judith, I appreciate your thoughtfulness. That is very kind of you."

He then does a left face, continues down the hall and enters the Colonel's office. Rourke walks up to the desk, as he sits down in his chair, he leans forward to hand the cup back to Harrison. As Harrison reaches for it, Rourke asks, "How many times have you been to Benning, Sir?"

Harrison leans over the desk, clasps his hands together, "Well, there was infantry officer basic… then the officer advance course and then not too long ago I taught at the advance course. I know you're a cavalry officer by trade. You ever been to Benning?"

Rourke nods, "Yes, Sir." Rourke smiles and points his thumb at LTC Francone. "My battalion commander sent me to the advance course about three years ago… great school… they don't screw around. It seemed like getting a two-year master's degree in tactics and leadership in only six months."

Harrison smiles, "Yea, the Infantry School likes to get its money's worth. They don't waste time."

There comes a look of seriousness over Rourke. He stares directly at Harrison, "Combat Support Company, 2nd of the 220th Infantry is going to Panama, Sir."

Harrison nods, "I know you didn't make this decision lightly, Captain Rourke. I've got to make a lot of phone calls now. You have to get back to your men and prepare for your operation." Harrison stands and offers his hand, "Good luck, Devlin. I believe you made the right decision."

Rourke stands up and reaches for Harrison's hand, "Thank you, Sir, and thanks for the support. When I'm knee deep in alligators… I can always say, well the colonel thought this was a good idea."

Harrison laughs, "By then I'll deny it." He glances down at his desk then shifting his eyes to Rourke, counsels, "Plan on flying out your whole company at Fort Smith Airport sometime tomorrow. As far as an operations order… I'll see what I can do but this has been thrown together so fast… If I were you, I'd plan on getting a copy handed to you on the plane, on the way down. Just get your men and equipment ready to move."

Rourke and Francone both come to attention and salute. They turn and go out the office, down the hall and out the back door. They see Francone's Humvee with Vince sitting in the driver's seat reading a paperback book. Both start walking over to the passenger side. Rourke stops about half way there and asks, "Colonel, did I make the right decision?"

Francone stops, turns to face Rourke. He has a concerned look. He lowers his voice to ensure only Rourke can hear, "Captain Rourke, I am not going to second guess your decision. And now is not the time for you to second guess your decision. You made the decision based on all the available information you have. I've known you for three years now… in all that time I've never seen you make a bad important decision. You've weighed the pluses and minuses; you analyzed the situation on how it would impact your men and your mission. Don't start second guessing now… now is not the right time. When you tell your men that they are going to war… you better sound confident, no second guessing or hesitation in your voice. Do you understand?"

Rourke takes it in and with renewed conviction, "Yes, Sir… CSC is going to war."

Francone nods his acknowledgement, "Devlin, I'll have a meeting with the staff. We'll do everything we can to help you get ready for tomorrow. This will include getting you four replacements for your deadline Humvees and anything else we can think of. Our support platoon and the S-4 will get you the live ammo from the Chaffee ammo point... all that you'll need." With a hint of amusement, Francone says, "At least you'll be able to fight your way off the planes in Panama."

Rourke laughs, "Not a good thought, Sir."

Francone puts his hand on Rourke's shoulder, "Devlin, tell your men that the battalion family support group will do everything they can to help their families. I know and you know everyone in all the companies will pitch in and help no matter what it takes, got that?" Francone turns, walks to the Humvee passenger door, "Come on... we've got a lot to accomplish before tomorrow."

CHAPTER 40

"I don't know whether this is the best of times or the worst of times, but I assure you it's the only time you've got." – Art Buchwald

Fort Smith Air National Guard Base
Air National Guard aircraft loading ramp
Monday, 18 December 1989
09:45 Hours.

The Air National Guard Base at Fort Smith Regional Airport isn't very big but Rourke is glad it is there. First, it is secure. Nobody, meaning civilians, are going to walk up to the rows of parked Army Humvees out of curiosity. Next, they have a large ramp that is fed by two taxiways. One on either side of the ramp. It will be easy for the Air Force C-141 cargo planes to come in on the south taxiway after landing, load up the vehicles and their crews, and then move out by way of the north taxiway. All the vehicles are staged on the southwest corner of the ramp. They are lined up per the instructions provided to Rourke last night by the Air Force liaison at Fort Chaffee. Rourke guesses they can easily park and load four C-141s at a time. He is told CSC will require ten aircraft to get his company to Panama. They will be arriving one at a time every twenty minutes. Rourke is confident that the Air Force knows how to schedule and load his company. Hell, they move the whole 82nd Airborne Division like moving a family across town.

Rourke will put himself and Josh on the first C-141 to land. It is imperative he arrives at Panama in the lead. Colonel Harrison stopped by early this morning and informed Rourke he would get his Operations Order and meet with someone from SouthCom Headquarters when he gets off the plane. Harrison has also talked to the 82nd, 1st Brigade Commander, Tom Padgett, who stated he is looking forward to working with Rourke and his company. Rourke appreciates the Colonel stopping by to check up on the company in order to boost everyone's morale. He said a lot of encouraging words to all the men.

Rourke appreciates the Battalion Commander, LTC Francone, talking with the company. After he left 30 minutes ago, Rourke heard a couple of his guys remark that they are glad Mrs. Francone is in charge of the Family Support Group.

Rourke is leaning up against the front left fender of his Humvee that is parked some 100 meters up from the rest of the company. If he has to do any more company business he wants some privacy. He sees a cargo Humvee pull out onto the ramp from the side driveway on the northwest corner of the ramp about 300 meters away. It drives right to him and stops. Rourke recognizes the Air Force liaison officer, Major Bookner, who slides out the passenger door. Rourke salutes and Bookner returns the salute. "Captain Rourke, sorry about this… but your aircraft are not going to start arriving for six more hours. The Air Tasking Schedule for this operation was revised about 40 minutes ago. Your C-141s don't start arriving till 16:00 hours."

Rourke can't help appearing rather disappointed but not surprised, "Yes, Sir, no explanation needed. It's a typical military operation."

"You got it… hurry up and wait."

Rourke asks, "Any chance they might come earlier?"

Bookner looks at Rourke with skepticism, "Any chance the Dallas Cowboy Cheerleaders show up to give you guys a sendoff?"

Rourke grins, "Thanks for bringing us the word, Sir. I should have bought a paperback at the PX last night. Does my battalion know?"

"Yes, they do, and so does everybody in the JRTC Operations Group.

They really want you guys to do well. They're rooting for you." Bookner pauses then continues, "I'll be back out here at 15:30 hours to see if you need any help. Otherwise, get some sleep… you're going to need it where you're going." With that Bookner climbs back in the Humvee and drives back out the same drive.

Rourke glimpses over at Josh sitting in the driver's seat holding up and reading a school text book. Josh leans out the door, "I knew this was going to happen. It always does."

Rourke gives Josh a helpless look, "How about you jumping out and jogging down to tell the company we got delayed for six hours."

Josh tosses his book aside and gets out, "Are you sure you don't want to do it?"

Rourke grins, "I'm the one that told them we're going to war. I'm afraid if I give them any more bad news, they'll all beat my ass… and I wouldn't blame them."

Josh laughs, turns and starts to run the 100 meters down to the staging area. On the way he stops and talks with the First Sergeant and the XO who are walking to Rourke's Humvee. Rourke can see them acknowledge Josh's message. Especially when he sees Kiser throw up his hands in a 'what the hell' gesture.

Rourke wipes a slight smile from his face when the First Sergeant and the XO walk up to his vehicle. He is waiting for the typical remark from Kiser.

Kiser shakes his head in disbelief, "Can you believe this… six hours… six, not a damn thing to do, hours. This really pisses me off."

1SG Johnson chuckles, "I got to tell you XO… you don't disappoint… does he, Sir?"

"No, Top… we knew this was going to somehow piss him off. I bet the Air Force did this on purpose. Just to piss Bob off."

Kiser fakes being pissed with his retort, "Both of you can kiss my ass."

Rourke changes the subject, "Top, I keep racking my brain trying to think of anything we've missed or forgotten."

Johnson glances down, crosses his arms and thinks for a couple of seconds, "Don't waste your energy. We got everything we need and if we don't have it, we'll get it somehow. Most importantly we've got the best

125 soldiers in the Army. We'll do just fine; stop worrying... by the way... did you call Lieutenant Fugate last night?"

Rourke nods, "Yea that was kind of a tough call. You could tell his wife was in the room with him. I sensed he wants to get back here to deploy with us. But there is no way he is going to say that out loud. I tried to reassure him he wouldn't be missing anything. That the best thing for him is to stay home and help his wife... and future kid. That after we kick ass... there would be other deployments down the road." Rourke readjusts his leaning against the vehicle, "But I can tell you he really wanted to get back here and we could use Mark... not that Callahan isn't doing a damn fine job."

Just then all three look up at the driveway that enters onto the north end of the ramp. The same one the Air Force liaison used. They hear the sound of a high-powered, muscle car, the low rumble that automatically puts a small smile on every guy's face. When they see the car, their faces light up. Kiser lets out a whistle followed by a, "Holy shit, that's a 1969, Boss 429, Mustang Fastback... painted in a gloss black pearl... shit that's nice... real nice."

Johnson, while still staring at the Mustang that has slowly turned and is headed right at them, says with the utmost admiration, "These Air Force pukes always seem to have the best toys."

All three slowly move to the front of the Humvee, drawn by everyman's respect for rumbling high horsepower and the car body contours shaped by Detroit's finest design engineers.

The car picks up a little speed with the corresponding increase in engine rumble. The driver swings the car so it will pull up with the driver's side right next to the three standing in line. It abruptly stops four feet right in front of them. The window quickly comes down. All three immediately recognize the driver and all three involuntary holding their breath as they take a small step back in surprise.

1SG Johnson is the first to recover, "Good morning, Olivia... nice day for a drive."

Olivia, wearing a worn jean jacket, her shining brown hair let down to below her shoulders, gives them a warm smile, "Good morning, Gentlemen. I understand you have a delay?"

Kiser, smiling in awe, says, "Yes, we're stuck here for another six hours."

Olivia looks down as she is contemplating her next words. She takes a deep breath, gazes up at Rourke and announces, "Devlin, my apartment is ten minutes from here."

Both 1SG Johnson and Kiser turn their heads to the left to look at Rourke. Rourke who can feel his heart pounding, glances to the right, sees both of them gawking at him, but can't say a word. Finally, what seems like minutes later, Johnson, with a look of wonder says under his breath, "Go! Sir... Go!"

Kiser now with the same look of *'I can't believe you're not running to the car door'*, says, "Yea, Go. We've got this, Devlin... Go!"

Rourke recovers, knows he's going. He immediately walks around the front of the car to get to the passenger side. As he starts around the car, he calls out, "I'll be back in two hours. Hold down the fort."

Kiser looks down at Olivia. She reaches over on the passenger seat and picks up a Day Planner. She opens it up to the note pages, pulls out a pen from the front cover and quickly scribbles a note. She then rips it out, folds it in half and hands it out the car window to Kiser. She then tosses the Day Planner up on the dash. Rourke slides into the passenger seat. She reaches over, takes his hand in hers and asks him, "Are you ready?"

Rourke looks at her, takes a breath then confidently says, "Yes, let's go."

The rumble slightly increases as she pulls out from in front of Johnson and Kiser, turns right, increases speed and heads to the driveway.

Johnson asks, "What's the note say?"

Kiser unfolds the small piece of paper, reads it and smiles, "Well it's pretty simple and to the point. *"Four Hours. Then her phone number, and then... Emergency Only!"*

Kiser turns and looks at Johnson. "Damn, Top... that's a big smile across your face. Why so happy?"

The First Sergeant leans back against the brush guard, "Yea, I'm happy... 'cause this is perfect... with a kind of poetry. This is like one of those Greek tales. Where the Warrior Man meets and falls in love with the Warrior Woman. I'm happy for Captain Rourke... Olivia's a good woman. He deserves this."

Kiser leans back on the brush guard behind him and asks, "What's the poetic part?"

Johnson thrusts out his hand and points to the car now halfway down the driveway. "They ride away in what else... a Mustang!"

Get ready to follow the Dragon Slayers exploits in Operation Just Cause, the invasion of Panama, in book II, **Valiant Challenge,** of the "Decisive Duty" Trilogy.

GLOSSARY

1SG – Abbreviation for First Sergeant. The senior Non-Commissioned Officer in a company.

AAR – After Action Review. A process used after an event to find out how the actions of the personnel resulted in the outcome. A facilitator uses open ended questions to encourage the participants to find out for themselves why, how and what happened during the battle in order to learn and improve future performance.

Abrams – US Army main battle tank. Named for Gen. Creighton Abrams.

AIT – Advanced Individual Training. After Basic training all soldiers are required to attend a training school that provides them with their specific military occupation or MOS.

AO – Area of Operation. Areas of operations are geographical areas assigned to commanders for which they have responsibility and in which they have authority to conduct operations.

APC – Armored Personnel Carrier. An armored vehicle (either tracked or wheeled) used to move infantry units around the battlefield while under armor protection.

ARTEP – Army Training and Evaluation Program. A program that requires units from squad thru battalion to train and to be evaluated by published tasks meeting certain standards under realistic conditions.

ATWESS – Back blast and smoke simulator for the TOW missile. Used to replicate the firing of a real missile.

AWOL – Absent Without Leave. Leaving and staying absent from your duty station without proper authorization.

Blue Force – Term used to describe US Army units that are engaged in simulated battle with opposing forces, typically designated as the Red Force.

BMNT – Beginning Morning Nautical Twilight. Begins when the sun is twelve degrees below the horizon. Enough light is available to identify the general outlines of ground objects.

BMP – An armored tracked personnel carrier, developed in the 1960s, manufactured by the Soviet Union. It has three crewmen, can carry eight infantry soldiers inside and has a 30 mm gun mounted in a small turret on top.

BOQ – Bachelor Officer Quarters. On post transit quarters used by personnel assigned to that post for temporary duty. Similar accommodations to a motel.

Bradley – US Army armored tracked fighting vehicle. Has a crew of three: Driver, loader and commander. It is designed to transport nine infantrymen or scouts under armor protection, while providing covering fire with a 25 mm gun and two TOW missiles mounted in the turret. Named after Gen. Omar Bradley.

CSC – Combat Support Company. A company assigned to an Infantry Battalion that contains three anti-armor platoons, the scout platoon and the heavy mortar platoon.

CSM – Abbreviation for Command Sergeant Major. A battalion has only one CSM.

EA – Engagement Area. An area in which the commander intends to trap and destroy an enemy with massed fires of all available weapons.

FDC – Fire Direction Center. Receives target intelligence and requests for fire and translates them into appropriate fire direction data for artillery guns. They provide timely and effective tactical and technical indirect fire control in support of current operations.

FM – Field Manual. US Army field manuals contain detailed information and how-tos for procedures, tactics, and techniques fundamental to soldiers serving in the field.

FO – Forward Observer. An artillery observer with forward operating troops specially trained to call for and adjust supporting indirect artillery and mortar fires and pass on battlefield information.

FRAGO – Fragmentary Order. An abbreviated form of an Operations Order used to make changes in missions and to inform units of changes in the tactical situation.

HE – High Explosive.

Heavy Mortars – The largest caliber mortars within a battalion. Normally 4.2 inch (107mm) or the newer 120mm size mortar tubes. Control and responsibility of heavy mortars is normally held at the battalion level. Infantry companies have 81 mm size mortars and control their use.

IPB – Intelligence Preparation of the Battlefield. A process used by the intelligence section to help the commander by best guessing and speculating who the enemy is, what their strengths are, and what the enemy's best course of action could be.

JRTC – Joint Readiness Training Center. An army training center located in Ft. Chaffee, Arkansas which is dedicated to training troops for real world tactical encounters with the enemy.

Klicks – Soldier jargon or slang substituted for the word Kilometers.

KPUP – Key Personnel and Unit Program. A program used to place reserve component soldiers in with active duty units in order to broaden the experience and add knowledge of current procedures used by active units.

LTC – The rank of Lieutenant Colonel. Pay grade of O-5. The position of battalion commander is typically a lieutenant colonel. Normally, lieutenant colonels are referred to as Colonel.

LT – Pronounced: (el tee) Short for lieutenant. As in; "Hey LT the vehicles are all fueled up."

LD – Line of Departure. A line designated to coordinate the commitment of attacking units or scouting elements at a specified place and time.

Logpac – Logistic Package. The process of gathering up all the supplies, fuel and ammunition the forward units require and request, then sending them forward by protected convoy to the fighting positions so units can maintain their current positions and situations on the battlefield.

Mikes – Used as a substitute for "minutes" while transmitting over the radio.

MILES – Multiple Integrated Laser Engagement System. MILES provides tactical engagement simulation for direct fire force-on-force training using eye safe lasers. Each individual and vehicle has a detection system to sense hits and perform casualty assessment. Laser transmitters are attached to each individual and vehicle weapon and accurately replicate actual ranges and lethality of the specific weapon systems.

MILES God Gun – A small hand-held laser gun that can be set to emit a laser that can "kill" everything and everybody on the MILES battlefield. God guns are carried by Observer Controls who may need to provide a kill due to unforeseen circumstances on the battlefield.

MOS – Military Occupation Specialty. A soldier's job. The duty or related group of duties that a soldier by training, skill, and experience is best qualified to perform, and that is a basis for the classification, assignment, and advancement of enlisted personnel.

MTOE – Modified Table of Organization and Equipment. A table of organization and equipment (TOE) is the document that specifies the organization, personnel, equipment and weapons for different categories of Army units. A modification table of organization and equipment (MTOE) is an authorization document that prescribes the modification of the basic TOE necessary to adapt it to the needs of a specific unit.

MUTA – Multiple Unit Training Assembly. Reserve Component soldiers are paid in four-hour blocks. One four-hour block is a Unit Training Assembly (UTA). When a soldier works during a weekend drill, both Saturday and Sunday that is equivalent to four, four-hour blocks or referred to as a MUTA 4. Therefore, a MUTA 6 would be two, four-hour blocks on Friday; two, four-hour blocks on Saturday; and two, four-hour blocks on Sunday.

NBC – Nuclear Biological Chemical. Unconventional weapons of mass destruction.

NCO – Abbreviation for Non-Commissioned Officer. A soldier that holds the rank of Sergeant. From pay grade E-5 to E-9. The ranks are; Sergeant, Staff Sergeant, Sergeant First Class, Master Sergeant, Sergeant Major. Regardless of rank, all NCOs are typically called Sergeant. The First Sergeant is actually a single position held within a company and is the same pay grade as a Master Sergeant, E-8.

NTC – National Training Center located at Fort Irwin California, is an Army base nearly the size of Rhode Island, located in the Mojave Desert about an hour's drive northeast of Barstow. A training center akin to JRTC.

OC – Observer Controller (OC). Army Soldiers selected to provide feedback to JRTC and NTC rotational units who have a duty to the training unit and the Army to observe unit performance, control engagements and operations, teach doctrine, coach to improve unit performance, monitor safety and conduct professional AARs. OCs are required to have successfully performed their counterparts' duties. They constantly strive for personal and professional development and are well versed in current doctrine and tactics, techniques, and procedures.

OCS – Officer Candidate School. A 90-day school that, when completed, trains and prepares officer candidates to be eligible for a commission as a 2nd Lieutenant.

ODP – Officer Development Program. A formal or informal program established by a commander to promote the professional and personal growth and advancement of junior officers.

OIC – Officer In Charge. A temporary position requiring an officer to be responsible for the completion of the assignment or task. An officer held to be responsible for the success of a specific mission.

OPFOR – Opposing Force. A unit designated to act as the aggressors to challenge the Blue Force. Army organizational unit which conducts combat training operations as an opposing force to provide realistic, stressful, and challenging combat conditions for Army units. The OPFOR is an uncompromising threat unit that provides the challenge of a real-world conflict by using doctrinally generic tactics and provides a level of realistic collective training, which cannot be duplicated at a unit's home-station. The OPFOR is a dedicated US Army unit that is highly skilled, both individually and collectively, at executing threat force doctrine and TTPs.

PSG – Abbreviation for the position of Platoon Sergeant. Typically, the platoon sergeant holds the rank of Sergeant First Class, pay grade of E-7.

PT – Physical Training.

QRF – Quick Reaction Force. A unit that has been designated as the first unit to respond to any emergency involving units in contact with enemy elements.

S-1 – The Battalion staff section responsible for personnel and human resource actions for all the battalion members.

S-2 – The Battalion staff section responsible for gathering and disseminating enemy intelligence.

S-3 – The Battalion staff section responsible for supporting current operations, training and conducting future operations planning.

S-4 – The Battalion staff section responsible for providing all the logistical support for the battalion.

SFC – Sergeant First Class. Pay grade of E-7. Platoon Sergeant positions are usually held by an SFC.

SOI – Signal Operating Instructions. A small booklet published by the Division Communication and Signal section that provides a listing of all radio frequencies and the units that are assigned them during a 30-day period. This is in combination with a section that provides the user with the ability to encode and decode radio messages. SOI's are a classified document and must be immediately reported if lost or misplaced.

STRAC – Standards in Training Commission. DA PAM 350-38. A manual used to forecast the required ammunition for the upcoming training year based on the type of unit and training events scheduled.

TIRS – Terrain Index Reference System. A quick, secure method of sending the locations of friendly units. Randomly selected tic marks on a map that are only shared and known to local units. Each new mission uses a new set of TIRS marks to ensure operations security. Used as a known location in which to orient or direct another friendly unit to.

TOC – Tactical Operations Center. The element consisting of staff activities involved in sustaining current operations and in planning future operations. It is located well forward on the battlefield so the commander is in proximity to subordinate commanders and can directly influence operations. A communication hub and nerve center for field operations.

Top – Army slang used to describe the First Sergeant of the company. From the term: Top Sergeant. Pay grade of E-8. There is only one First Sergeant per company. The senior NCO in a company.

TOW – Tube-launched, Optically-tracked, Wire-guided missile. Used worldwide as an anti-armor guided missile with a range out to 3,750 meters.

TTP – an acronym for; Tactics, Techniques, and Procedures.

XO – Term used for the Executive Officer in the command. The XO is second in command and reports to the commander. The commander has the liberty to assign any tasks or duty responsibilities to the XO. Since the XO is the second in command, it is inherent and customary for the commander to act as mentor and coach to the XO in order to prepare him for command.

Printed in the United States
By Bookmasters